A HOLLOW IN THE HILLS

D1428034

RUTH FRANCES LONG is a lifelong fan of fantasy and romance. She studied English Literature, History of Religions, and Celtic Civilisation in college and now works in a specialised library of rare and unusual books. But they don't talk to her that often.

Ruth's first book about Izzy, Jinx and Dubh Linn, *A Crack in Everything*, is published by The O'Brien Press. Ruth is also the author of *The Treachery of Beautiful Things*.

A HOLLOW IN THE HILLS

Try to outrun ...

the fear

RUTH FRANCES LONG

THE O'BRIEN PRESS
DUBLIN

First published 2015 by The O'Brien Press Ltd,
12 Terenure Road East, Rathgar, Dublin 6, D06 HD27, Ireland.
Tel: +353 1 4923333; Fax: +353 1 4922777
E-mail: books@obrien.ie
Website: www.obrien.ie

ISBN: 978-1-84717-636-3

10 9 8 7 6 5 4 3 2 1
19 18 17 16 15

Cover image courtesy of iStockphoto
Printed and bound by CPI Group (UK) Ltd, Croydon, CR0 4YY
The paper in this book is produced using pulp from managed forests.

To Pat, Diarmuid and Emily

Blasphemous Work

The angel stumbled and fell, unable to save himself with bound arms in front of him and pinioned wings behind. He hit the stony ground hard, unaccustomed pain biting through his skin. For a moment he could only lie there, breathing hard. It shouldn't be like this. He was one of the Host of Heaven, an angel, the Joy of the Lord.

No joy remained. She had beaten every last scrap of it out of him. And now she brought him here, to this place of wind and dark clouds, to a gorse-covered hilltop where the earth itself writhed and screamed as if fighting against what lay beneath. The sea crawled and crashed against rocks, squirming away from the headland. Even the water couldn't bear to touch these stones. He could feel it deep inside his broken body.

There had once been a cairn raised here, an ancient seal to guard against what had been buried long ago. Not anymore. Mankind had razed it to the ground. They named it and renamed it, making up stories about kings buried beneath piles of stones and then forgot even those tales. They used this place to walk their dogs, or exercise away the excesses in which they indulged. Sometimes they climbed here just to look at the view or to instinctively add another rock to the piles scattered around. They couldn't say why, just an urge. They knew nothing, let alone what they had done by destroying it in the first place. The arrogance of mankind.

The kick took him in the ribs, lifted him from the ground and drove his breath out of him. With a burst of red agony, he crashed into a heap of stones behind him. Something made a dreadful breaking sound. Ribs cracked, fractured ends stabbing into him. He slid down into the depression below it, amid crushed beer cans and ashes.

'Did I say you could rest?' his captor asked, her voice as smooth as a hot blade. 'We have mighty work to do, angel. Mighty work indeed.'

'Why do this? You were one of us.'

She smiled, an expression with no warmth, no joy. 'And I was cast out. For doing nothing.'

He couldn't argue with that. She was one of those who had indeed done nothing. While other angels had fought and died and fallen in flames.

'Please,' he whispered. 'You were one of the Didanum. You stood in the ranks of light.'

'Nothing is forgotten. Only we call ourselves Dé Dannan now. And it doesn't mean what you think it means.'

'You were chosen.'

'We were accursed. We questioned Heaven's actions. Imagine, being cast out for asking questions. Does that seem fair to you, angel? Does that seem just? We took no side. We merely asked why conflict was necessary.'

'Cuileann.' He had to try, one last attempt to reach her, using her now forbidden name. The one she had borne so long ago. She had to answer to that. She had to recognise their kindred spirit.

Instead she seized him by the back of his neck and slammed him back down against the stones. He slumped across them, broken.

'Cuileann is gone,' she said in a voice as cold as the void itself. 'I'm Holly. Now, we ought to begin – Heaven forbid we should drag this out.'

Sunlight glinted off the razor-sharp edge of her knife.

'You know why knives are so dear to my kind?' She cocked her head to one side as if waiting for an answer. 'They're personal. You have to get up close. Or have a spectacular aim.'

'What are you doing?' he asked, wishing he hadn't. He didn't want the answer.

'You know what I'm doing. You know this place and what lies hidden beneath it. Locked away for so long. You can thank Sorath. She gave me the idea, cunning little bitch that she was.'

'Sorath?' He stared at her. 'Sorath fell. Sorath's gone. That girl …'

'Oh yes,' Holly's smile widened like the maw of a beast. 'That girl. I'm going to deal with her as well. But first you.'

Emptiness opened up under him, another place of nothingness and loss. A thousand voices called out, voices lost and damned.

A burst of agony engulfed him as she drove the knife into his stomach, deep, hard. The angel screamed, his body twisting as he tried to escape. Holly drew out the knife and watched his blood spill onto the dirt and stones.

Then she stabbed again.

Darkness rose like a wave, winnowing its way through his veins, thrusting tiny barbs through his body. His spark burst from his chest, blinding him, wrenched out of him. He wept hot tears, cried out for his Lord, but no one answered. He was lost, he was falling. Holly pulled the spark from him and threaded it through her fingers, crushing it in her fist. She pulled at it, refining it to a long line that shone like silver.

The last thing he saw before the light burned out inside him, was her smile.

The smile of a predator. The smile of a killer.

CHAPTER ONE

A Tell-tale Strangeness

The ground shuddered, sending books and trinkets tumbling off the shelves. Izzy rolled out of bed onto the floor before she was even fully awake, her body trying to get itself into the best position for defence before her mind even knew what was happening. Just as abruptly as it started, everything went still.

She crouched on all fours, the sheet still half twisted around her, breathing hard, looking for something – anything – to explain what had just happened.

The tattoo on the back of her neck felt so cold she could sense each line in all its intricacy, like someone had sketched the design on her skin in acid. The door crashed open and Dad stood there, looking like he'd tear something limb from limb if he could just find something to tear.

'Are you okay?'

'I think so. Dad? Was that an earthquake?'

'I don't know.' Izzy checked the clock – three in the morning. Great. Shaken awake at three am. That was no way to start any day, not even the last day of school before half term. Izzy scrambled to her feet.

'If it wasn't an earthquake, what was it?'

'An explosion? Maybe. Gas or something.' He sagged a little, looking more like her dad again and less like some sort of mortifying superhero rushing to her defence. 'An earthquake's more likely.'

He rubbed the back of his neck as if it hurt. She often wondered if his tattoo warned her in the same way hers did. She'd asked him, once or twice, but never got a straight answer. He wouldn't admit it, or didn't really understand it and wouldn't admit *that*. She wasn't sure. They didn't talk like they used to, even though she knew many of the secrets he had kept from her. Somehow it changed everything. Not knowing had been easier than knowing.

'An earthquake here? In Dublin?'

He shrugged. 'We get them. Usually off the coast and never as strong as that before. And sometimes "earthquake" is a good explanation for something else. Maybe you should go back to bed.'

As if she could sleep after that; she felt energised, wide awake, but she knew it wouldn't last. It was just a case of her other nature kicking in, expecting danger and preparing to fight it. Being a Grigori, she had discovered since the summer,

12

was more than just a surname and a funky tattoo. It was a hell of a lot of work without any recognition or gratitude. She didn't even get a fancy hat.

Dad looked tired, like he had when he woke up from the coma three months ago. She'd healed him then, but the ability to do anything spectacular like that had faded. The last vestiges of the angel's spark for which she'd been a vessel had let her do that one thing, the thing she needed most.

Strange, the hole that had left within her. Unexpected, and unwelcome. As a fallen angel, Sorath had slipped under Izzy's skin and changed her, making her capable of a magic she would never have believed possible. Brí called her a grail, her birth mother never one to speak plainly, but Izzy hadn't appreciated what that meant until she had the power to save lives. She had used it, even in the most desperate straits, and she'd won. She'd saved Jinx, and Dad. And now? Without the powers Sorath had given her, what was she? A Grigori? But one too young to be of any use, to be trusted with the responsibilities it entailed. She hated the angel. She missed her as well. The psychotic, dangerous, glorious fires that Sorath, the angel of the dawn, had brought with her, which had almost consumed Izzy without any resistance, were gone now. She was bereft, like a ship without wind for its sail. And her life was her own once more.

Well, apart from all the extra studying that Dad and Gran felt she needed to put in, self-defence classes and dusty old tomes she couldn't even get digitally. She'd suggested scanning them. Gran had told her to go home. Her anger was more painful than a fencing lesson from Dad.

A knack with fire had joined her knack of destroying electronics. If she concentrated really hard she could still conjure up a little flame. No more than the flare of a match-strike, really. It wasn't much use for anything. Plus, it drove Dad up the wall. Another reminder.

'Should we check with Brí? Make sure everything is okay on that side?'

Dad winced. Mention of Izzy's birth mother, the Matriarch of the South Dublin Sídhe, usually caused that expression. He didn't have good memories of her. And even the vaguest reference to Dubh Linn, the shadowy Sídhe world that coexisted beside the human one, tended to close him down these days. He only told Izzy what he needed to, she realised that. He still didn't want to put her in danger perhaps, or didn't want her learning too much about it too quickly. But it was driving her crazy.

'I'll see to it. You go back to bed. School's in a few hours.'

'But we'll be doing next to nothing. Halloween break's starting. It isn't even a full day.'

Dad had already closed the door. Izzy dug out her phone and put in her earbuds, flicking through the tracks she had on it. The phone had been a present from Mum to replace the one that she'd lost to the creepy Sídhe tramp, Mistle. When she'd first met Jinx. She remembered his long, elegant hands helping her pick up the broken pieces in the alley that led her into Dubh Linn. That first day. Before she knew anything about the Grigori and the fae, the supernatural world that lay alongside her own. Before angels and demons had become a part of her everyday life.

Izzy lay back on her bed and closed her eyes, listening to the soft, lyrical strains of a song she shouldn't play, a song that always made her think of him. Jinx had been heartless and cruel, flippant and obnoxious. He moved like a hunting animal, his silver eyes seeing everything, especially her mistakes. Tattoos and piercings covered his lean, pale body, contrasting with his long, jet-black hair. He thought he knew everything!

But … he'd helped her time and again. She'd never meant to fall for him. She'd never dreamed he could feel the same, but he had. She knew he had. He'd kissed her, shed tears of grief when he thought he'd lost her, begged her forgiveness – impossible for one of the fae – and saved her life.

And then he'd completely vanished from it.

Izzy wasn't sure if she slept or not. Her thoughts kept turning back to Jinx and that whole tangle of misery no matter what she tried. She kept telling herself that she should forget him, that she shouldn't dwell on it, that he wasn't worth it. But sometimes, late at night, she couldn't help it.

The sun glowed red and gold around the corners of the blinds, but she didn't welcome the sunrise anymore.

Besides, morning meant getting up and plastering on a brave face, getting on with things. Morning meant school, even if it was just one more half day before the half-term break. It wasn't like there was going to be much to do. But still, she wished she didn't have to go.

Mum called her from downstairs. Already up and making coffee, no doubt, the early bird, always brightest in the morning. Infuriatingly chirpy. Not like Izzy and Dad, who were better off not talking to anyone for at least two hours after waking up. But of course, Izzy now knew her mum wasn't her real mum, not her birth mother. She wondered what Sídhe matriarchs like Brí did in the early morning; she'd bet they didn't make coffee and sing along with the radio.

Murder, torture, general sadism – or did that wait until after brunch?

Dad drove her to school, blissfully silent the whole way. A stream of uniformed girls flowed towards the gates, a strangely hypnotic sight. She saw Clodagh, surrounded as usual by a host of friends. She turned and waved at Izzy, hanging back waiting for her while the others went on.

'Don't be late back tonight,' said Dad. 'We have training.'

They were the first words he'd said to her since the earthquake. The radio had been filled with chatter about it. They couldn't pinpoint the epicentre, which was unusual, but it had been one of the strongest ever felt on the island. Dad had huffed, clearly finding that dubious. She didn't want to ask why.

'Training?' She sighed. 'Again?'

'You know why. It has to be done, Izzy.'

And here she thought being the latest descendent of the line of Grigori would be glamorous and exciting once the turmoil of last summer had passed. With Dad recovered from the accident that had sent him into a coma, she'd also thought her life might at least return to some semblance of normality, but she was wrong on both counts. Dad, and Gran, had decided on extracurricular activities – fitness training, fencing, martial arts, endless myths and legends, secret histories – to prepare her for the inheritance they'd so far hidden from her. Mum agreed with them. There was no escape.

'It's half term, Dad. I was going to meet Clodagh and—'

'Straight home. We have to go through the annals and you need to—'

'I know, I know. Fine. I'll be back home straight after school. It's not like I need a life or anything.'

'Izzy.' He sighed as he said her name and looked out of the window. Was this how he had spent his teenage years, she wondered? He never spoke of it. 'It's important. Besides, there are those who would use you against us. Think about it.'

She could think of any number who would try. For a while. And then they'd learn. She'd make sure of it. She wouldn't let herself be used again. Dad ought to know that, but he didn't believe it. Not really.

'Fine.'

It wasn't, but what else could she say? She got out of the car and slammed the door behind her.

'You okay?' asked Clodagh as Izzy joined her.

'No.' It wasn't worth more than a one-word answer. Clodagh got it immediately.

'Parentals?'

'Fun times.'

Another girl was standing by the entrance to the school, watching them with overly curious eyes. There was something about her that caught Izzy's attention, held it in an unnerving way that was seldom good news. Izzy frowned, trying to make out the tell-tale strangeness that marked the Sídhe when they walked among humankind. But there was nothing. No metallic glint to the eye, no instant attraction and desire to please. She was just a girl, very pretty, with jet black hair and olive skin. And the most startling hazel eyes Izzy had ever seen.

'Who's that?'

'The Newbie,' said Clodagh. 'She's been in our class since September. Her name's Ash. Haven't you been paying attention?'

Not much. Not really. Now that she thought about it, there had been a new student in the class since the start of term. Izzy just hadn't taken any notice.

'Um … maybe. I don't know. How do you even know these things?'

Clodagh shook back her long golden locks and tapped her nose with a perfectly manicured finger. 'I have my sources. They include talking to people and being sociable. You should try it. Did you do the maths homework? I completely fecked it up. Can I cog yours?'

CHAPTER TWO

Emissary

Jinx came up snarling, the taste of blood in his mouth and a white fire blazing in his head. The bodach reared over him, arms thick as tree trunks, a body like rock. Another blow like that would crush him. His head still ringing, he rolled and the giant creature slammed a foot down where his chest had been a second earlier. It laughed at him, stupid and conceited, but Jinx kept rolling and came up onto his feet, crouching low, ready. The bodach lunged again but Jinx twisted aside, just in time, and brought both fists down on the back of its thick red neck, ramming it face first into the floor. It went down in a heap, with little more than a grunt and a crash of flesh on flagstones. Jinx leaped on its back and slammed its head down again and again until it wasn't fighting any more. It slumped there, its chest heaving up and down.

Jinx straightened, wiping his face with his hand, and glared at the crowd surrounding him. Some grinned, others muttered curses, but they still waited, mostly in silence. The bodach didn't move.

'A winner!' The voice bounced off the copper dome of the Market's ceiling and money slapped from hand to hand.

In most hollows, the homes of the Sídhe, there were strict rules to be obeyed, and a matriarch to follow. Once they had been places of hiding, of safety, of absolute Sídhe power, places closed to all who did not belong there. Not here in the Market. Accessed from the gate in Smithfield, the Market was open to all, and money talked. All kinds of currency really, from euros to … well, anything … And anything could be bought. That was how Holly had liked it and even with her gone, the Market continued on its well-worn path unchecked.

'Too quick, Jinxy-boy,' said a drawling voice behind him. The Magpies stood there, pristine in their black and white, beady eyes fixed on him. 'Not exactly entertaining when you finish them in a couple of heartbeats, is it?'

Jinx lifted his head and fixed them with his most intimidating stare. Mags looked away, but Pie held out.

'What do you want?' Jinx asked.

'Just watching the fight. You're making quite a name for yourself. Or don't you care?'

'Silver isn't going to like it, is she?' Mags said, his tone darker. 'She's not going to like it at all.'

'So?' Silver was going to flip. He knew that. Because she already had several times. Silver didn't like this and made her feelings abundantly clear on the subject. And now more than ever she was someone whose word he ought to heed; she had bested Holly and driven her from the Market. There were rules about that sort of thing, old laws, older than anything. It meant Silver should take charge and be matriarch. No one had the power she had. No one had imagined Holly could be beaten, and yet Silver had done the impossible. He was her emissary now and that ought to mean he didn't go around fighting for money. An emissary was a peace-bringer, she had told him in those measured, musical tones. The role protected him, and he could walk in the shadows, in the light, in the halls of her enemies. He really should take it more seriously.

He didn't like to fight, but he needed to. Little else made him feel alive. Silver couldn't, and wouldn't, stop him; she knew it wouldn't do much good to try. Jinx just didn't care anymore.

Broken inside. That's what he was. Completely and totally broken inside.

He only had to look at those around him to see what they thought – that long-ingrained suspicion. He'd been Holly's to the core, once. Not through choice, but who understood that? He was Cú Sídhe. They all looked down on him, despising him. By-blow, son of a traitor and an assassin, Holly's dog.

Holly was gone, slunk away from the Market in the chaos that followed Silver's victory, and her people were only just beginning to actually believe they were free. Which meant their need for revenge where they could get it was beginning to bubble up from wherever they had hidden it long ago. They couldn't get Holly, not now, but Jinx was still there. As good as having a target painted on his back, that was. He couldn't afford to be complacent. Fights like this just showed them it wasn't worth the risk. Not yet.

The Magpies were looking at him like he was the next course in their dinner. 'What do you want?' he asked.

'The boss asked us to fetch you to see him. To extend his invitation, as it were. As an emissary, naturally.' Pie sketched an overly formal bow and grinned his filthiest grin. 'He'd like a word.'

'I'll give him a word.' Jinx grabbed a towel from the pile by the edge of the makeshift ring and looked around for Art. The lep owed him his cut. You couldn't trust the little bastards.

'The boss doesn't like words like that, Jinx.'

Another Suibhne Sídhe, a bird man like the Magpies, shouldered his way through the milling crowd. Smaller and slighter by far, he cast furtive glances at them and at Jinx before thrusting a grubby pile of banknotes at Mags and fleeing.

Mags grinned broadly and began to sort them, flattening each one out and forming a fan worth several hundred euro, which he waved at his brother.

'Who said we didn't have a dog in this fight?' He laughed.

Jinx stalked away from them, aware that they were following, silent and malignant as ever. It didn't matter. They wouldn't dare to do anything here in the Market. They were irritating, that was all.

Art sat on top of a barrel, his legs crossed, counting out his own pile of notes. 'Ah there you are, Jinx, my boy. Come for your share, eh? You did well out there. You did—' The words dried up as he saw the Magpies behind Jinx. Very little could silence the leprechaun, but the Magpies had a fearsome reputation.

'Here,' said Art, shoving all the cash towards Jinx. 'Here, take whatever you want.'

Jinx rolled his eyes, and stepped up to the trembling leprechaun. He didn't speak – might as well make use of the intimidation, even if it wasn't his doing – but carefully counted out what he was due and no more. No doubt Art would have tried to fiddle him. That was in his nature. Leps couldn't be trusted, especially when it came to money. Lucky for him most Cú Sídhe were inherently trustworthy so Jinx only took as much as he should have earned in that fight.

And he *had* earned it. He could already feel the aches and bruises working their way through him. He was going to suffer tomorrow. But what else was new? He always suffered. It was his lot in life.

'So you'll come with us now?' Pie sounded bored.

'Why on earth would I do that?' Jinx asked.

'Because we asked nice-like. The Old Man said to ask nice. And to tell you something. What were we to tell him, Mags?'

Mags grinned, showing all his teeth. 'That if you don't want to come, we'll have to ask the girl.'

Izzy? Hell no, he didn't want them even thinking about Izzy.

'I don't have anything to do with her. Not anymore.'

'Aww,' Pie said. 'Lovers' tiff?'

Jinx curled his lip in a snarl that would terrify more than half the Market, but only made the Magpies grin even more.

'But you did,' said Mags. 'We all know you did. And still would. Isn't that true? Don't lie now. It's you the Old Man wants to talk to though, not her really. She's tricky, that one.'

'I'll need to talk to Silver first.'

'Sure. Get her permission.' Mags sneered at him. 'Wouldn't want to annoy her any more, would you?'

Silver was surrounded, as always. With her head bent over her work, her long white-blonde hair fell forward to shield her face. Slender and delicate, she didn't look strong enough to rule the whole Market, but she did. Or at least, she should. Silver was more than just fae. She was Leanán Sídhe, muse and inspiration and one of the most powerful Aes Sídhe alive. She sifted through a pile of petitions while those filing them with her gathered around, waiting. As Jinx approached, she looked up, aware that the murmuring fell silent, that they were all staring at his dishevelled form, at the cuts and bruises, at the evidence of his fight. Then they saw the Magpies behind him, which just made it worse. He could almost sense them thinking out loud.

He can't be trusted. He's still Holly's. She's marked and bound him. Just look at him.

Silver's eyes fell on him and narrowed. 'Where have you been?' she asked quietly.

'Um ...' What could he tell her? She already knew anyway.

'I hope it was worth it.'

He thought of the money in the pocket of his jeans. 'Yeah. Kind of. The Magpies request that I go with them on your behalf. They say Amadán wants to talk to me.' He stepped closer, close enough to hear her breathe, and continued in a whisper. 'Or he'll go and talk to Izzy.'

Silver winced, though only he would have seen it. 'Are you okay with this?'

'What choice do I have? You made me your emissary. I've got to do your running around, don't I?'

Just as she used to do it for Holly. The echoes of their former matriarch still surrounded them. They'd never shake them off.

But Holly had been defeated. Silver had shattered her touchstone and driven her out. They really didn't need to worry about her anymore, did they?

She frowned, but then nodded. 'Very well then. Come back right away. Don't let him get you to agree to anything until you check with me first. Understand?'

Jinx glared at her. Check with her? 'Emissary' must mean different things to them. She didn't have to treat him like some kind of child. But Silver could do that without even think-ing about it. She probably still saw the little feral boy she'd collected from Brí's hollow a lifetime ago. And now, though she didn't have to check her every action with Holly, she just treated him like she always had. It grated against his senses, but he didn't know what to say. What she told him wasn't wrong, that was the problem. But he already knew it.

Instead of arguing, he quelled rebellious thoughts and nodded to her. 'Yes, Matriarch.'

Silver narrowed her eyes. '*Don't* do that.'

'You're going to have to accept it sooner or later. You're the matriarch here now.'

And without a matriarch, the Market was spiralling into chaos. He knew it better than anyone. Thinking of the money he'd just won blatantly disregarding her instructions, Jinx's stomach tightened unexpectedly. The Market out of control was becoming a dangerous place. And Silver did nothing to rein it in. Not yet. He wasn't sure she would. And then what?

'So,' he turned to the Magpies. 'Where are we going?'

'Underground,' said Pie with a smirk. 'We're going underground.'

CHAPTER THREE

Music and Memory

Dylan woke with a cry on his lips, though he hadn't been aware that he'd been dreaming. He struggled out of the tangle of sheets and tried to force himself to breathe evenly. His pounding heart made his chest ache, but he couldn't remember a nightmare. He couldn't remember anything at all. Only falling into bed the night before, exhausted and longing for the oblivion of sleep. The moment his head hit the pillow, everything was blank.

Except for the music. Oh yes, he could remember the music. So clear it drowned out everything else. Every single thing.

But something had happened. He knew that. Paper littered the floor, notes scrawled on lines, pages and pages of sheet music. The recording equipment was all on, the computer showing .wav files from the middle of the night.

Again.

Dylan shook his head and gathered the papers up into a pile, putting them together as he did so, scanning the music with a practised eye.

It was beautiful. It always was. So very beautiful, this music that came from somewhere else, somewhere far beyond him. But it came through him, igniting the magic that welled up inside him. He couldn't help himself.

It just scared the hell out of everyone else.

Mum looked up bleary-eyed from her coffee when he entered the kitchen. Dad had already gone.

'Sorry,' Dylan mumbled.

She shrugged. 'It's okay, love. Remember what the psychiatrist said.'

So he *had* done it again. It didn't happen all the time. There was that, at least. But every so often it just spilled out of him, all at once. And he couldn't help it. Couldn't remember it. The music just rose up and swallowed him whole. The psychiatrist said he had to get it out, that it was a way of coping with Marianne's death. And what could he say? *No, actually, I was kissed by Silver, who's a Leanán Sídhe, and accidentally became a touchstone. I'm now the source of her magic and its main conduit. Eventually it's going to kill me, but if I'm lucky it won't turn me into a raving madman first.* Yes, psychiatrists loved that sort of thing. So it was easier to nod and agree and promise to work with headphones as much as possible.

Which was kind of an impossible promise to keep when you were sleep-composing and had no memory of what you were doing. His subconscious didn't seem to be particularly mindful of others.

He hadn't wanted to go to see Dr Patterson, but Mum had insisted. It was family therapy and Dylan had to make sure he watched every single word. What was normal to him – the Sídhe, Grigori, angels and demons – might see him committed if he described his experiences to the wrong person. He was still coming to terms with them himself.

It had to be hidden. But the magic wouldn't be contained. It was bleeding out in his dreams, making him compose in his sleep.

But the music was incredible. More than incredible.

Transcendent.

'Are you going to college today?' his mother asked.

'Sure.' He hadn't explained how he'd managed to get himself transferred to a pure music degree course. It wasn't law, which was what they'd wanted. They knew that much and he felt their displeasure keenly. They didn't know what he did in college and didn't ask. Sometimes he wondered if they even cared now. The summer had changed everything.

The first month of his first year in Trinity College had saved his sanity. He slotted into the department of music from the moment he had that late interview.

A gift from Silver. Someone owed her a favour, she'd said. And the three staff members assessing him sat open-mouthed as he played.

That, at least, had made him feel real.

'Good,' said Mum, and went back to bed, leaving him feeling more guilty than ever before.

As he packed up all the musical creations of the night before and headed for the train, he couldn't shake the feeling that he was missing something, that he was overlooking a crucial fact – something dangerous and desperately important. Checking online he glanced over the reports of a mysterious earthquake, without taking it in, and wondered about ringing Izzy. But she'd be in school and answering the phone would only get her into trouble. Fifth year offered more freedom to go with the pressures of the senior exam cycle, but that only went so far. She still had to obey some of the rules. Not that she bothered much about that these days. She didn't seem to care anymore.

He wasn't the only one to have changed.

When he got off the train, making his way down the slope to the street level amid a horde of students and other travellers, heading for the gates into the academic island of Trinity in the heart of Dublin, he saw a familiar figure waiting for him.

Because she had to be waiting for him. What else could she possibly be doing there, standing by the gate, looking right at him, smiling that infuriating, knowing smile?

Mari.

But Mari was dead.

CHAPTER FOUR

In The Mist

Since the summer, the notice board outside the Maths room had turned into the most uncomfortable place in the entire school. They meant well. Izzy knew that.

The photograph of Mari dominated it. One of those perfectly posed school photos that Mari had excelled at sitting for. She looked like a model. Once, she'd said that was what she wanted to do for a living. Dylan had laughed at her and she hadn't spoken to him for days.

But she had been so very beautiful.

Smiling, her eyes bright, eternally alive, eternally beautiful and unchanged.

There were notes pinned to the board, fluttering coloured pieces of paper, upon which most of the girls in the school had written some lines of farewell. Or good wishes. Or something anyway. Izzy hadn't. Neither had Clodagh. Neither of them knew what to say.

Marianne had been their friend and now she was gone. There were no two ways about it. She'd died because of Izzy.

No, she had been killed, had been *murdered*, to send a message to Izzy. But it amounted to the same thing.

Holly had a lot to answer for.

Izzy frowned at the picture and the notes. A breeze made them flutter like pastel petals, drawing her attention from the photo. Irritated, she forced her gaze back to Mari's perfect smile. She was glad she hadn't seen Mari's corpse. She could still remember her like this.

Vain, shallow, callous, laughing, *human* Mari.

'Did you know her?' asked an unknown voice. Izzy turned to see the new girl, Ash, standing beside her.

Izzy scowled. 'Of course I did. We all did.'

'Izzy and Mari were friends,' said Clodagh, coming up on the other side of her. 'Izzy, you remember Aisling?'

'Ash,' the girl said in a flat tone, as if she had to do it all the time. 'Not Aisling. I'm not actually Irish at all.'

'Where are you from then?' asked Clodagh.

The girl waved her hand dismissively. 'All over. My family moves around.' She had that look – London or New York, more than sleek and polished, slightly unreal, and her accent carried whispers of other places. Lots of them. Her dark skin tone didn't come from a bottle or a sunbed. It was all natural. Izzy had just assumed her name was 'Aisling', like everyone else, and hadn't noticed her cosmopolitan looks. She could come from anywhere. She studied Izzy with hazel eyes framed by thick lashes, so dark she'd never need mascara. The heavy plait reached the small of her back and little butterfly clips held back any strands from her face.

Some of the transition year students went by, talking loudly about a party or something for Halloween – who was dressing up as what, who was going to be there, how late they'd be and how they'd get the alcohol inside – and one peeled off, heading for the loo.

As the girl opened the door, Izzy felt a chill between her shoulder blades, a shiver from the tattoo at the top of her spine that snaked all the way down. It appeared the moment the door opened and vanished the moment it closed. But it was there. Distinctly there.

Bad sign. Really bad sign.

But here in school? They wouldn't. They couldn't!

She sucked in a breath and caught Clodagh's eye. 'I'll just be a second.'

Clodagh's face turned pale, her eyes hardening. Izzy wasn't entirely sure what Clo knew and didn't know and she didn't dare ask. Especially since Clo and Dylan were the only close friends she had left. Clodagh, however, was no fool, despite the outward façade she sometimes projected. She gave a brief nod and stepped closer to Ash, starting a long and detailed story about Marianne and that time in Dundrum when she'd argued with the security guard and ended up getting complimentary shopping vouchers for all of them, while Izzy stepped away. She laid the flat of her hand on the bathroom door and the shiver came back.

Definitely something going on. And she didn't like it.

She stepped inside, letting the door swing closed behind her.

Mist filled the room, mist so thick and heavy she could barely see anything. The utilitarian green and white tiles looked washed out and the fluorescent bulbs overhead hummed, feebly illuminating the room. Not enough to see further than a couple of feet though. Her breath misted in front of her face as the temperature around her plummeted, joining the mist, becoming part of it, enforcing and empowering it.

'Hello?'

The air crackled, charged, the smell of ozone hanging heavy.

There was no answer. The world was curiously still and quiet, as if something beyond the door muffled or smothered all sound. Izzy swallowed hard, aware that her heart was suddenly the loudest thing in the room. A hum like electricity, bright and sharp, trembled through the air. The mist swirled around her, curling where she moved, folding back from her as if to avoid her touch. Or maybe it was playing with her. It seemed too aware, almost alive.

Something shifted inside her. She had the uncomfortable feeling of being a target. It wasn't avoiding her, but circling her. This was a game and she didn't want to play.

'Hello? Anyone in here?' The other girl had to be in here. She hadn't left. There hadn't been time. Izzy could see only whiteness, mist everywhere, like someone had left a shower on with the boiler overheating. But there were no showers here. Not to mention the arctic temperature. And in the mist ... movement, shapes, forms half made.

A small whimper came from the left, in one of the cubicles. Izzy turned towards it, but she still couldn't see anything. This was impossible.

She conjured a small flame, a flicker no larger than her fingernail – about all she could manage – even though Dad and Gran had been absolutely specific on the restrictions about doing so. Not in school, not in public – never, if she could avoid it. But magic drew on magic. It needed something to feed on and she had no doubt that what was happening here was magic. It had to be. Might as well take advantage of it.

Though all she could manage was a tiny flame, golden light filled the room, tempering the whiteness, and with a violent hiss, shadows moved, shadows made of mist instead of darkness. Figures stretched too far, too long, wisps of smoke and tangles of fog.

Izzy swallowed down a cry of alarm. They peeled away from her, writhing back like ghostly vines from the flames, like living things, revealing the girl. She slumped against the cubicle wall opposite, her eyes vacant, staring at the ceiling, and her mouth stretched wide in fear. She'd scratched her face, blood dark under her broken fingernails, gashes on her cheeks, but all the fight was gone from her now. Mist trailed over her skin, curling from her mouth and nostrils like cigarette smoke. Her skin looked pale and puffy, her lips blue as if she was suffering from hypothermia. For a moment, Izzy couldn't breathe. Was she dead? Jesus Christ, had she left it too long?

The girl whimpered again, a sad mewling sound, but she didn't blink or otherwise move. She just slumped there, eyes too wide, her arms and legs twisted at odd angles. Her breath sawed in and out of her chest, too fast, too desperate.

Izzy edged towards her, trying to keep an eye on those misty shadows. The cold was growing again and her heart was beating louder and louder, as if it was calling them. She'd thought to use their magic to strengthen hers, but that wasn't the case anymore. Who was taking advantage of whom here? She cursed silently, words she couldn't quite force out. She hadn't thought that her magic might make them stronger too. And there were more of them …

They whispered now, following her every move. The humming in the lights overhead was becoming painful, like a wasp loose inside her skull. The fire in Izzy's palm was dwindling as her own fear paralysed her. She reached out, touched the girl on the floor. Her skin felt like ice and she breathed shallowly. She needed help and fast.

The creatures laughed and whispered and pressed closer. Tendrils of icy mist drifted towards her, floating on the chill air. Only a foot away from her. And Izzy couldn't quite catch her own breath. She couldn't force words from her mouth, couldn't stop her heart from racing, thundering against the inside of her ribs. The mist swirled, drifted together, apart, together again. A hand formed – too smooth and lacking in any actual features, just a hand formed of mist. It reached out to brush icy fingers down Izzy's cheek. Like a lover. An unwanted, terrifying lover. Energy crackled on her skin. Static lifted her hair, sent shivers down her spine.

'Daughter of Míl,' whispered a sibilant voice. *'How long I have waited to see you? How long I have waited … Will you come to me, Grigori? Will you come?'*

Then a face – an impression of a face – born out of nightmares, thin, too thin, blue-grey and lined like old sea-washed oak. His eyes gleamed like stars in the night's sky of his sockets. His mouth drew up into a cruel smile.

The voice echoed on and on, repeating the phrases like they were malformed or mangled poetry. Others joined it, over and over, and in her mind's eye Izzy saw something, an image that shouldn't be there. A cross on a headland above the sea, stark against the sky. She knew it, but couldn't quite grasp it, not now. She choked on the next breath and the image blurred and twisted, changing to become a bleak grey ruin on a hilltop, lit by a bonfire, with stars exploding in the air overhead. Just for a moment, as if the creatures from the mist had pushed it into her head with their clammy insubstantial fingers.

She couldn't help it; she screamed, the noise loud and shattering, breaking off the ceiling and the mirrors, thundering around the cubicles to fill the room with echo on echo. The guttering fire in her hand flared up in a column of incandescent light and the mist shadows flung themselves away from her, sliding through the cracks in the tiles, under the skirting boards and away. Light drained from the room with them, and the cracks all glowed for another moment and went dark.

An alarm screamed, louder than anything she'd ever heard, a long wail that went on and on.

The flames she had called snuffed themselves out, burnt away in panic. But the fire alarm went on and on.

The door behind her was flung open; Ash entered first, closely followed by Clodagh and half a dozen girls who had been in the hall when Izzy came in. And then all the noise of the world burst upon her. Voices babbling, calling for help, someone shouting that they had to get a teacher, someone else yelling the name of the girl on the floor.

Ash caught Izzy's shoulders and pulled her back gently. 'Are you okay? What happened?'

'I just ... I just found her like this.' It was sort of true. She had to keep her head now. No one would believe in shadows from the mist and blinding fear.

'We have to get out of here,' said Clodagh. 'The fire alarm—'

But Ash wasn't listening. 'Izzy, are you sure she—?'

'Of course she's sure,' Clodagh interrupted, her voice uncharacteristically harsh. She linked her arm with Izzy's, pulling her away. Ash let them go, watching like a hawk. 'C'mon, evacuation time. You look like you'll either puke or pass out.

Hell of a time for a fire drill.'

Grateful that Clodagh had come to her rescue, Izzy didn't argue. Her stomach knotted in on itself and she couldn't stop shivering. The thought of that thing touching her, of the image in her mind ... 'Thanks, Clo.'

The alarm went on and on, everyone heading for the exits in a stream.

'Just keep walking. They're going to be all over you when the panic's died down. What happened in there?' said Clodagh.

'I just found her. Passed out.'

'Do you think she was on something? Do you think she took something?'

'I don't know. Maybe?'

The poor kid was going to be grilled. Izzy didn't envy her. But while she saw supernatural activity, probably fae in nature, she knew the human world would see drug abuse or psychiatric disorders. She only hoped someone would help the girl – indeed, that she could be helped.

At least she was alive. Or at least, Izzy hoped she was still alive. Oh God, what if she wasn't alive, if Izzy had been too late?

'Did you set off the fire alarm?' asked Clodagh.

'Er ...' There wasn't an alarm in the bathroom, was there? Or maybe there was. A sensor. There'd been that time one of the fifth years was smoking and the fire brigade turned up. At least once. A sensor then, but not a way to trigger it. So how could she explain setting it off? 'Um ... maybe?'

Clodagh sighed, the heaviest world-weary sigh she could manage.

'Only you! All that shit during the summer ... ' Clodagh said cautiously, glancing around to make sure no one was near enough to overhear. 'That crazy club and Mari ... '

To be honest, Izzy was surprised Clodagh even remembered it. She'd missed most of it and she'd got pretty much wasted on her one trip to Silver's hollow. They reached the hockey pitch, standing a little bit away from the main huddle of their class who were all talking animatedly, like birds after worms.

Clodagh's tone was unusually firm. 'She told me everything, Mari did.'

But Mari knew bugger all as well. Right up until it cost her life. Izzy took a deep breath. 'Clodagh, I know you think you've got some sort of handle on this, but really—'

'I'm not an idiot, Izzy. I've been watching you ever since the summer. It's all different. And I've talked to Dylan. You don't have a monopoly on him.'

No, she had to be bluffing. Dylan wouldn't tell her anything. He wouldn't! A surge of jealousy rushed through Izzy. Which was unfair because Clodagh was right – she didn't have a monopoly on Dylan.

'Dylan doesn't—'

But Clodagh interrupted her impatiently. 'I just need to know if it's starting again. Because if it is, if you've brought it here, to *school*, of all places, I'm getting the hell out of Dodge.'

Izzy wanted to say it wasn't fair, that she hadn't *asked* for any of this, but that wasn't entirely true, was it? She hadn't asked for it, sure. Nevertheless it *was* her fault. It followed her. There was no denying it. She let the moment of silence drag on too long and Clo's eyes narrowed, her gaze hardening.

'Isabel Gregory!' It was Miss Collins' voice, their maths teacher marching on to the pitch in pursuit of them. 'I'd like a word with you.' But then she took one look at Izzy's face and her expression softened. 'You look like you've seen a ghost. Are you all right? We need to know what happened in the toilets. Charlotte's barely conscious. Did you see or hear anything that can help?'

Izzy shook her head. 'I just found her like that. I went in and she was lying there. Then the alarm went off. I don't know what happened.'

And anything else ... they wouldn't believe. There hadn't been time for anything else anyway. Miss Collins gazed at her for a long moment and then sighed, rubbing her head absent-mindedly.

'Very well. We've called an ambulance and I'll need you to come with me to the headmistress' office to make a statement. This looks very bad, Isabel, and if you know anything, if you saw her with anything or anyone, we need to know now.'

'She collapsed, Miss,' said Clodagh, out of the blue, her eyes wide and her voice ringing with innocence. 'She wasn't looking well earlier.'

'When? When did you see her, Clodagh?'

'When she went in there. In the corridor by Mari's … Mari's …' She choked artfully and made a show of composing herself, holding back tears. Damn, she was good. 'I thought she was going to throw up. And poor Izzy's had a dreadful fright, Miss. She found her in there and thought she was … was … *dead*. And then the fire alarm … Now everyone's acting like Izzy did something when she didn't. I mean, she couldn't. She was only a minute or two ahead of us in there. She really ought to call her Mum … if this carries on.'

Miss Collins stiffened, her eyes sharpening on Clodagh. 'Yes, well I'm sure there's no need for that. Stay here and get some fresh air, Isabel. Come to the office when you're feeling better, but before you go home, understand? For Charlotte's sake, we have to find out what happened to her.' She turned away, raising her voice. 'All right, girls. Back inside now. False alarm. Come along. Sarah Lowell, stop that at once!'

She bustled off and Clodagh rolled her eyes to heaven. Maybe she was a better actress than Izzy had given her credit for. 'You can thank me later.'

'What did you just do?'

'Do you miss everything? I just threatened them with your kickass lawyered-up mother, that's what. Come with me. I still want some answers.'

'No you don't. I wanted answers once and all it got me was trouble. You have to stay out of this business, Clodagh. Please.'

'Or what?'

Izzy pulled away. 'Or you could end up like Mari.'

In stunned silence, Clodagh opened her mouth and closed it again like a goldfish, her eyes wide.

No matter what, Izzy *had* to get Clodagh to lay off. She couldn't afford to get anyone else involved in the world of the fae. It was far too dangerous. And if something had followed her to the school, she needed to deal with it. And fast.

The stunned silence went on and on. 'Please,' Izzy whispered, instantly regretting saying it.

'What-*ever*,' Clodagh replied, with an attitude that said this was far from settled. 'But eventually you'll have to stop pushing everyone away from you. What happened to Mari wasn't your fault. You weren't even there. It wasn't you and it wasn't Dylan. It just happened and it was shit.'

If only she knew. But Izzy wasn't going to tell her that. Everything was connected and Mari had been killed instead of her. If the banshee hadn't come looking for her, Mari would still be around as Queen Bee of this school and they wouldn't be having this conversation. Charlotte wouldn't be carted off to hospital. And Clodagh wouldn't be asking all these questions that were only going to get her in trouble.

'Leave it, Clo. Please.'

With a snort of frustration, Clodagh turned heel and stalked away, leaving Izzy standing alone.

She dug out her phone. She needed to talk to Dad about

this. But she really didn't want to.

But what choice did she have? The only other person she could have asked was Jinx.

And he was gone.

CHAPTER FIVE

Amadán

Jinx hated travelling with the Magpies. Their snide remarks and constant chatter grated on his nerves and made him want to smash their heads together. The problem was, they knew it, which only made them worse. They pushed to see how far he'd let them go. But the worst thing was their handling of the Sídheways. They never got it right.

They followed the paths across the city, in and out of Dublin and Dubh Linn, past the traffic and the shoppers, in front of the offices and along the rail line, over the motorway and up into the foothills of the mountains, further out than Jinx had ever gone. It made his city-bred skin crawl — all this green hanging over him, a world half-civilized, with the pavement on only one side of the road and intermittent lampposts. It was easier in daylight at least.

They passed a pub that had taken 'Oirish' to the extreme,

no doubt for the benefit of the tourists, and then made their way through a gate, into a landscape of green and grey only – just scrubby fields and dry stone walls.

The next gate jumped them by several miles and about an hour ahead in time. They were sloppy that way, the Magpies. It set his teeth on edge.

'You're really crap at this,' Mags told Pie, who muttered an obscenity and pointed to the summit of the hill on which they were now standing. Wind snatched his actual words away, but Jinx caught the gist. How could he not?

The entrance to the Amadán's hollow stood at the top. It figured – they all preferred high places, vantage points. When the whole island had been covered in forests, the hills and mountaintops offered the only clear spaces, the only way to see those approaching, the best point from which to attack if necessary. Forests invited ambushes. Everyone knew that, even a city-born fae like Jinx.

Only a few chose low-lying locations – Holly and Silver preferred the city centre and the advantages it gave them. Jinx suspected that it was a kind of smug superiority on Holly's part, a snub to all the others – 'Come and take me if you can.' Silver just couldn't stand anything rural or quiet. She thrived on sound, on noise, on the music of the city.

'How far up?' he asked.

'All the way. See those big rocks?'

There was always a marker of some kind. Often humans did it as a way of warning others of what lay beneath; sometimes his own kind did it for much the same reason. 'Stay away or else,' with a slightly different subtle and not-so-subtle inflection. Who wanted a shower of humans hanging around with their iron and their fire and their bad attitudes?

'We don't mix,' Silver had told him while he'd been trying to chase thoughts of Izzy Gregory out of his head with an industrial amount of loud music and alcohol. 'We never have. It always ends badly, usually for both parties. They fear us, and they hate anything that reminds them that they can fear. You, of all people, know how that goes.'

Of course he knew. The fae barely tolerated relationships with fae from different castes. His own parentage – Cú Sídhe and Aes Sídhe, the lowest and the highest of the Sídhe hierarchy – was proof of that. Human and Sídhe? They didn't mix at all. Not unless they had to. Like Brí and David Gregory, a union that had produced Izzy and nothing else of any good. The fae hierarchy was strict and unyielding. Those who flouted it were punished and so were their children and their children's children. Human and fae … it never ended well. And he knew it more than anyone.

Stay away or else.

Jinx looked up at the huge stones jutting from the barren landscape. He wasn't even sure where he was anymore – if he was still in Dublin, or in Dubh Linn or somewhere else altogether. They might have been the gates to the hollow, or portal stones to take them there, or simply a warning to others to stay away. The stones were a matt black, unnaturally smooth.

They made his stomach twist unpleasantly.

'Come on then,' said Mags. 'He doesn't like to be kept waiting.'

Beyond the black stones, a cairn of white stones rose, gleaming in the afternoon light. In the front there was a gap, like a mouth waiting to swallow him, darkness beyond. Pie went first, stepping through the half-seen shimmer and vanishing. Mags waited, watching Jinx. Taking a resigned breath, Jinx followed. What choice did he have?

He didn't have to like it, but Silver had named him her emissary and this was his job now. Running around, a representative, guarded by the Council's word and available to all who wanted Silver on their side. He was safe enough while Amadán and the others wanted to play nice. While the Council, such as it was, still remained intact. An illusion of safety perhaps, but it was all he had. So long as everyone played nice. It was a crappy job.

The darkness of the hollow closed over him and the world changed.

He'd expected something dark and primal, like Brí's hollow on Killiney Hill or perhaps the barely governable chaos of the Market. He'd expected grim customs of the past, the blood of enemies painting the walls, enslaved humans or a throne made of bones.

But while the walls wore the traditional lining of bronze, there was a thick, emerald-green carpet underfoot instead of packed dirt or cold stone. Mahogany dressers, occasional tables and bookshelves lined the corridor, interspersed every so often with a comfortable-looking leather chair. It felt like stepping into some kind of mothy old gentleman's club out of the nineteenth century. It looked like the set of a Sherlock Holmes movie.

From the distance Jinx could hear music, a harp being played with skill and ingenuity, a lively tune that echoed down the halls.

Be careful, he warned himself. It was too easy to fall for the Amadán's friendly façade. Nothing could charm like the trickster, and nothing was as dangerous. Wolfish teeth lurked behind every single smile.

The Magpies stopped at a wooden door, the surface so highly polished that they were reflected in it. They knocked, waited, fidgeting. Mags lifted one foot to rub his shoe on the back of his trousers, a perfunctory attempt to shine it. The door opened slowly, and a butler stood there, with a Jeeves-like look of efficiency, everything about him trim and elegant.

Pie sniffed loudly and then wiped his nose along the length of his sleeve. The aura of disgust rolled off the man, though his face betrayed nothing at all.

'The gentlemen are here, sir,' he said in a voice that carried with stiff formality. 'Along with your guest.'

'Send them in, Rothman. Send them right in. This can't wait.'

The Magpies preened as they swept by the butler. Rothman looked as if he'd willingly snap both their necks given half a chance, though once more he said nothing.

Human, Jinx realised. The man was human, but he clearly knew what his employer was, and all about those who served him. Rothman wasn't in the least bit surprised, nor was he enthralled. No trace of magic lingered around him, neither to compel him nor bind him. He was here willingly.

The Amadán sat in another of those leather chairs with a high back and wings, though this one, Jinx thought, was bigger than the others. It had been placed in front of a period fireplace with a roaring fire, though where the smoke was going to, Jinx didn't like to imagine. He had a large glass of brandy in one hand and an unlit, fat cigar in the other. With an expansive gesture, which made Jinx wonder how much alcohol he'd already consumed, he motioned towards the other chair and it took a moment for Jinx to figure out it was here for him. He sat down, trying to appear more relaxed and at ease than he really was.

'Have a drink, Jinx by Jasper. Rothman will get you whatever you want.' Jinx, however, shook his head. He didn't want a drink, nor did he need anything that might addle his brain right now. The Amadán might like to play at being the gentleman of leisure, but he was a skilled player of the Council's games. Though Holly might be gone, those games were far from over. Only an idiot would think that and Jinx, while not the brightest star in the Sídhe galaxy, was not an idiot.

'How can Silver help you?'

'Ah, that's the question, isn't it? That's what she wanted you to ask. And there'll be a way I can help her, no doubt.' He waved the unlit cigar at Rothman and the Magpies. 'Off you go, all of you. This is just for young Jinx and myself.'

They all obeyed at once. Jinx had never imagined that the Magpies even knew how to be obedient, let alone were willing to do it, but they went without a murmur, without a word of complaint or even a snide look. Rothman closed the door behind him with a discreet click.

'A butler?'

'Palace-trained, I'll have you know. I picked him up about a hundred years ago. So long as he doesn't leave the hollow, he's fine. And he wouldn't. Devoted to me, is Rothman. And I for one wouldn't be without him. Now, that drink? Would you prefer whiskey?'

'No, thank you.' Even for one of the Sídhe, taking food or drink in someone else's hollow was fraught with danger. Poison was the least of the threats. 'Can I cut to the chase and ask why you invited me here?'

'They were meant to ask politely. I hope they did. That's the trouble with Suibhne Sídhe – bird brains. But no harm done.' Jinx wasn't so sure, but decided to let the matter lie. He waited while Amadán drained his glass and refilled it from the crystal decanter on the table beside his chair.

'You felt the disturbance last night, I presume? Indeed, who among us could have missed it? That much power, rolling over the city. Even the humans picked it up. They might make the wrong interpretations but their scientific instruments don't lie. An earthquake, they said. Did you ever hear such a thing? Do you know what that means?'

'Shaking earth.'

'Yes. And I fear it shook with reason. Very good reason. Come with me.'

He rose from his chair so swiftly that Jinx had to scramble to his feet and follow. Amadán stopped at a small and unobtrusive door on the far side of the room, rather than the one by which he had entered. Jinx's eye had glanced over it for a cupboard, but as Amadán undid a series of locks, he grew doubtful.

The room beyond was carved from solid granite, cold as a freezer and very dark. Amadán entered first but stepped back to usher Jinx inside. It was more than a store room, but less than a room. At first Jinx wasn't sure what he was looking at. In the centre was a large block of stone. It was only when he recognised the swollen shape lying on it that he realised. It was a morgue. Although what Amadán was doing with a morgue adjoining his study was a question he knew instinctively not to ask.

Her skin looked pale and grey as if colour had been leeched from it by an extreme drop in temperature. It had left her puffy and bloated where she should have been bird-like, delicate. But that wasn't the worst thing. Her face had been clawed away, bleeding holes where her eyes should have been. Blood covered her hands and stained her blue and brown striped hair. She'd done this to herself. The way her muscles had stretched, ratcheted with terror and agony, the way her jaw stretched far too wide and wouldn't close … She'd been terrified. So terrified she'd scratched her eyes out before she had frozen to death.

'Who is it?' he asked.

Amadán circled the slab, his hand stretched out as if he wanted to touch it, but couldn't quite bring himself to do so. 'Her name was Jay. She worked for me. A beautiful singing voice, like a songbird. And she could dance. She'd hypnotise you when she danced. So understand, I am *most* put out.'

It was stomach-churning. No one sane could do this. Jinx could think of a few possibilities who might think it was the most hilarious thing ever, but most of them were thankfully dead. Or Holly.

But someone – or something – clearly had been amused, because why else would one of the fae terrify someone like that to death?

'I don't—' Jinx's voice caught unexpectedly in his throat and he had to cough. For one desperate moment he thought he might throw up, but he pressed down the nausea. Because that would go down brilliantly, wouldn't it? So professional. 'I don't understand, Lord Amadán. You can't believe *I* did this?'

Amadán's eyes widened in utter surprise. There was no guile there. 'You?'

Jinx felt instantly foolish. If Amadán had thought that, he'd probably be dead already, or, if he was really unlucky, wishing for death.

'No,' said Amadán and his voice grew bleak again. 'You couldn't do this. No Cú Sídhe would, not even if he was rabid.' He looked back at the corpse. 'I know what did this. The trouble is, it's impossible. They're gone. Thousands of years gone.'

'What are?'

'We called them the 'Firshee'. Like the banshee in a lot of ways. Sometimes they were known as the Fir Bolg. They target girls for preference, the younger the better. They feed on terror. You can see the result.'

He'd often wondered about the banshee. Bean Sídhe in the old language. It meant 'woman of the Sídhe'. Always women. Their voices could kill. Hell, everything about them could kill but it was the voices they were known for, their weapon of choice. One of them had killed Dylan's sister – just to get at Izzy, or because Izzy wasn't there – out of pure spite. Holly had always kept a few on as assassins, but mostly the rest of the Sídhe avoided them. He had always wondered, if they were the women, where were their men? He had only asked once, when he was very young, and Holly had ordered them all to beat him, all the banshee in her service. They'd done a thorough job. They'd enjoyed it. But he had never found out. Now perhaps he had an answer. Albeit a cryptic one.

'Jay sings in town,' Amadán went on. 'In the pubs, on street corners, for her own amusement as much as anything. A busker half the time, a travelling performer. Distinctive looks, colouring ... the tourists think it's face-paint and hair dye.

They can't get enough of her. Her voice would put angels to shame, I swear it. She's much sought after. She was ... We found her this morning, out by the docks. Right out of town as we know it. Further than she'd willingly go. She was beautiful, Jinx by Jasper. I am not amused.'

Who would be? But again, Jinx's mind supplied some answers. Holly for one. Why couldn't he get his mind off his sadistic former mistress? She haunted him, lingering on the edges of his nightmare. Yes, Holly would have been highly amused. And maybe, if Jay hadn't worked for him, Amadán would have been as well. What did he use this room for? There was a smell of blood to it that was ancient and deeply ingrained. Not just Jay's blood. So much more than that, so much older.

Jinx's mind lurched away from that prospect and back to the question at hand.

'Firshee. I've never heard of them.'

'Haven't you? Think back to your earliest childhood. When Brí's people had you rather than Holly. Holly knew all this but she didn't allow talk of it. No time for old lore. She wanted to think ahead, or so she said. Although I suspect she didn't want anyone else knowing the things she knew. But that's beside the point. Think back to the nursery rhymes and ghost stories your pack told. I know they do. Cú Sídhe love their bogeymen and their songs. They love howling away together.'

Nursery rhymes. Every race had them, songs and ditties which carried warnings and made sure every child knew the real dangers from the moment they could sing. Warnings of monsters in the dark, hiding in the shadows beneath the bed or behind the door, bogeymen … Fir bolg.

'Fir' meant 'men', but it sounded like the English word 'fear' and given what they did, given that they could drive their victims insane with terror, it had stuck and become their name for good. The Sídhe loved to play with words, break them, abuse them, put them to other uses. They liked to do that with many things.

'Bolg' meant 'bag' because of the lives they stole away, as if they packed them into bags and carried them off. 'Bolg' meant 'belly' because of their ferocious appetites. He wasn't sure which meaning applied here. Maybe both. Something about the shadows in a nursery …

The rhyme came to him, echoing through his head like a mocking echo.

Whenever the fog is dense and thick
When the whispers are all you hear
They'll feed on your terror, freeze all your hope
Try to outrun—

'The Fear,' Jinx whispered. He sucked in a breath and looked at the Old Man, no longer doubting. And yet still needing to ask questions. 'But the Fear are a nursery rhyme, a made-up monster.'

'Not made-up. Defeated. Long ago. When we first came here we defeated them and locked them away. Someone has let them out.'

'Where did you lock them away?'

'In a prison that was already here, in the earth itself. Like that thing on the hill Brí guards that you found out far too much about last summer. We made use of what we could find and tossed them all inside. We sealed it. Now someone has released them.'

'And what do you want me to do?'

'Stop them, of course.'

'But why me?'

'Well, you see Jinx by Jasper, you have a certain in with the only people who can hope to do it. David and Isabel Gregory.'

'You're wrong. Not anymore.'

'A lovers' tiff, lad?' The mocking tone faded to sharpness. 'Go and buy her some flowers or something. This is more important than your adolescent emotions. If the Fear are loose, who knows what else may be set free. There are things imprisoned on this island we cannot afford to have running around, if you know what I mean. The Fear are only the first step to something much worse. And they can do damage enough. They know nothing of temperance. They have no self-control. They'll fall on the human world when Samhain lets them take physical form, and then what? Eh? What will humanity make of that?' Jinx made to answer, but Amadán raised a hand to silence him. 'Don't say anything. I know what you know.' He pointed upwards. 'Our celestial cousins wouldn't take kindly to us using their toys, if you know what I mean. It never ends well for us. They can't be allowed to find out about this. Or they'll destroy us all.'

Amadán beckoned Jinx to him, wrapped an arm around his shoulder, the hand that was still holding the unlit cigar gesturing expansively as he turned them both around and headed back towards the door. 'If they find out about this they could decide to eradicate us all, just to be sure.'

CHAPTER SIX

Visitation

Dad strode out of the principal's office as if he was looking for something to dismember and had to remember he didn't have the right to do that here. Izzy waited in the hall, Clodagh beside her.

'Ouch,' said Clo, seeing his expression. 'See you later.' She faded into a group coming down the corridor before he reached them.

'Would you like to explain how the fire alarm went off?' Dad asked.

'Some sort of malfunction?' It was worth a try. That was what she'd said to everyone else.

Dad looked far from convinced. 'Sure. And the girl just collapsed.'

Izzy lowered her voice to a whisper. 'That wasn't me. There were things in the mist. I couldn't breathe. I only managed to drive them off with—'

He held up a hand in a combat gesture calling for silence. Training made her comply at once and she hated him a bit for that. But his voice softened. 'Not here, love. Appearances and all that.' And he gave her that quirk of his lips just for moment. He believed her. She had that much at least. Relief made her sag on her feet. 'I've spoken to your headmistress and she's checking with the fire brigade but it does appear that the sensors malfunctioned, picked up heat where there couldn't possibly have been fire, if you see what I mean. Okay?'

She nodded solemnly. 'So are we going home?'

'Sure. We have to pick up your mum first though. She was at a meeting in town so she wasn't too thrilled when the school rang her, especially as they're only meant to ring me these days. But someone thought of your mum first and so that happened. She had a good rant to me about casual sexism. She probably enjoyed that anyway. Train is in ten minutes. Come on.'

Mum was coming up the steps from the platform as they pulled up outside the little redbrick station. She glared at Izzy and got into the car beside Dad.

'What happened?'

'I believe Izzy encountered something impossible.'

'Impossible.' Mum looked at Izzy through the vanity mirror in the sun visor. She raised an eyebrow. 'Must be a day ending in a "y" then.'

'I didn't do anything wrong,' Izzy grumbled.

'You weren't careful enough.'

'Those … those things would have killed Charlotte.'

'The Fear,' her Dad said, his voice taking on that tone of preachiness she was beginning to dread. It was his teaching voice. He could go on for hours and hours when he started. 'A fae fairytale. A myth and a monster, the male version of the banshees. What do they say? *When the fog is dense and thick, When the whispers are all you hear* … something like that. And yes, they would have killed you both.' He sighed heavily and rolled his shoulders as if trying to loosen up taut muscles, uncurling his fingers from the steering wheel and stretching them out. Trying to calm himself down. The idea that Dad was shaken by the thought of what she'd seen wasn't comforting. 'You actually did a remarkably good job considering.'

'High praise,' Izzy muttered, squirming in her seat.

'You did,' said Mum, in tones far more gentle than Dad's. 'You're still here, that's what matters. David, you're not angry at Izzy. She's safe. She drove them off. And someone else's daughter is going home to them as well.'

'Any number of daughters, if the Fear had gone on a killing spree. The Sídhe used to be terrified of them and that's saying something. Whoever has let them out has a hell of a lot to answer for. They won't stop here. I'll have to—' Dad turned the corner into their road, rounded the bend to approach the house and swore loudly. For the second time that day, Izzy's tattoo flared with an icy cold warning and she gasped in alarm as she saw what he saw.

Five angels were waiting in the front garden. The car shuddered to a halt as it stalled in the drive, the engine coughing and spluttering. Dad growled under his breath.

'What are they doing here? Those—'

'David!' Mum cut in, silencing his litany of curses before they even began.

Izzy swallowed hard on a suddenly dry throat and tried to grin. The flood of adrenaline brought out her reckless sense of humour. 'Why not go with "morons", Dad?' she offered.

'*Isabel!*'

Her parents did that one in harmony.

An uncomfortable silence settled over the interior of the car. The angels watched them, keen as cats on a mouse that had unwisely wandered into their domain.

'We'd better see what they want,' said Dad and opened the door.

As Dad approached them the angels' wary attention sharpened to a knife point. They watched his every move. Izzy followed him out of the car, painfully aware of the way their eyes flicked over to her and away.

They dismissed her so very quickly. Or couldn't bear to look at her for too long. They saw Dad as a challenge though and respected him for it. She'd already encountered the deep seated loathing the angels seemed to have acquired for her. Luckily they hadn't shown their faces much since August. Very few supernatural things had until today, in spite of all her extracurricular training and study. She should have been relieved. But seeing them now, after almost three months of almost nothing, this was much worse.

The angels wore white from head to toe. Tailored clothes, expensive, perfectly fitted to their perfect frames. They were so beautiful, so painfully beautiful, that they didn't seem quite real. Their shoes didn't even carry a mark from the grass.

They reminded her of a nineties boy band. They probably sang in close harmony too.

Izzy clenched her teeth as one of them stepped forward, the others falling into formation behind him. Had there been a key-change? She hadn't heard one.

'Zadkiel,' said Dad. 'To what do we owe this honour?'

He didn't make it sound like an honour. Izzy had never known her father to sound so passive-aggressive in her life. But then again, she was learning all sorts of new things about him.

He was a Grigori, a Watcher, keeper of the balance between the worlds of humankind, fae, angel and demon. His blood was the blood of all races carefully blended over millennia of interference from creatures just like the angels who faced him now. Her father was special.

And so, apparently, was she. Worst luck.

Not that this lot were inclined to treat her as such. No, she was just a child to them, one with questionable loyalties.

'You are too kind.' The angel's voice slid like warmed honey through the air, weaving a spell of trust and reliability all around him. With his golden looks and hazel eyes, how could he be anything else? Izzy shuddered, her skin crawling in response. Mum's features softened and her eyes took on a dreamy look; Izzy took her hand, holding it tightly just in case. 'David Grigori—'

'Gregory,' Dad interrupted. 'And your charms don't work on me. Or on Izzy, it would appear. Our blood, no doubt.'

Zadkiel raised his eyebrows. 'Indeed. Remarkable blood it is too. Even if it is easily … what is the word? Corrupted.'

Venom infected the angel's voice on that final word, but Dad didn't flinch.

'No. Balanced, perhaps, in perfect harmony, even. You should try it some time. Being balanced, I mean. Well, maybe we should go inside. I don't think the neighbours will under-stand, do you?'

He hooked his arm around Mum and swept past Zadkiel who stared at him, his mouth hanging slightly open in shock as Dad seized all the power of the moment out of his hands.

'Izzy?' Dad called. 'Be a love and open the door, will you? I don't have my keys.'

What could she do? No snotty angel was going to make her look like a coward, especially when Dad had already faced him down. Of course Dad had his keys. What was he up to?

As she passed the angels, their eyes focused on her in unison, and a shadow passed over her, chilling her to the bone. But she didn't hesitate, smothering the fear down deep inside her and recognising it for what it was – not her own, but something foisted on her by their very presence. They wanted her to be afraid.

So she wouldn't. That would show them. Somehow.

The key skittered against the lock, but eventually went into the keyhole and turned. She darted inside and disarmed the burglar alarm with trembling fingers. She took a moment, forcing her breath to be calm, and then turned around.

The garden stood empty. They were already inside the house, all five of them. Zadkiel gazed at her with his searching eyes, while the others inspected the framed photos in the hall and the collection of little china fairies Mum had arranged on the occasional table.

'Don't touch those,' Izzy said. 'They're fragile.'

The angel looming over them glanced back at her, smiled a slow, sinister smile, and tipped one with the end of his fingertip. There was a rumble in the air, like distant thunder, and the figurine shattered, crumbling into tiny fragments.

Izzy sucked in a cry, but Zadkiel got there before her.

'Suriel, enough! We are guests.'

The angel stepped back and bowed his head, eyes fixed on his shoes. If he was chastened or simply acting, Izzy couldn't tell.

Suriel. She studied him closely. And Zadkiel. She'd look them up later, try and find out what the internet had to say about them. She was making a list. It seemed like a good plan.

Know your enemy.

Of course they weren't meant to be the enemy, and Dad would tell her that they weren't. But she knew for a fact, they didn't like her, and she didn't like them.

Dad knew it too. It didn't make for a good starting point, really.

Mum on the other hand was staring at the little pile of porcelain shards with a new and rather impressive look of murder in her eyes. She glared at Dad, who lifted his eyes to the ceiling. Whatever spell they'd used on her had worn off. Now she looked fit to spit nails.

'Right,' Mum snapped, and the word dripped loathing. 'Right. I'll make some tea then.'

She stalked out of the room. Mum, it seemed, was not a fan of angels either.

'You're going to replace that,' Dad told Zadkiel.

The angel bowed his head. 'As you say, Grigori. And now we must talk. In private.'

'Anything you have to say to me you can say in front of my daughter. She is a Grigori too now, thanks to your sister, Sorath.'

Zadkiel's expression suggested he had sucked the largest lemon in the world. 'My sister was … misguided. She is fallen and lost to us forever, thanks to your daughter.'

Izzy took a step towards Dad. Sorath may have been an angel, but she was also a psychopath obsessed with freeing her beloved Lucifer from his prison, and she had manipulated, coerced and possessed Izzy in order to try to achieve her ends. Zadkiel made her sound like a victim and that didn't bode well.

'What am I supposed to have done now?' she asked, painfully aware of the edge in her voice.

'You gave the spark to Azazel. All that was left of Sorath is in the hands of a demon.'

'Well, given what that angel had just tried to do to me it seemed like the best plan. Anyway, isn't that old news? That was months ago.'

Fire flared in his eyes again. 'You are a fool, girl. You put your trust in the wrong places. It will see you damned.'

From him that really meant something. She ought to be afraid, she knew that. But she wasn't.

Her anger was too strong for that. Balling her hands into fists she jerked forward a step, but Dad's arm blocked her way.

'Enough,' he said, before Izzy could explode and tell the sanctimonious cretin exactly what she thought of him and all his kind. 'This isn't helping anyone. Sorath manipulated us, every one of us, my daughter most of all.'

Zadkiel glared at her. 'And yet she walked away.'

'Which is just what I'm going to do now.' Izzy twisted away, rage simmering through her, ready to reach boiling point and overflow.

'You are going nowhere. If we must include you, so be it. You will stay. There is more we need to know from you.'

'I've told you all there is. All I'm going to tell you.'

'One of our brethren is missing. An explanation is needed from you.'

'From me? Am I responsible for every lost angel around

here now?'

But Dad interrupted before Zadkiel could say anything. And probably before Izzy could make it into a complete unmitigated disaster. He even managed to smile although it went no further than the corners of his mouth. 'Who is missing?'

Zadkiel visibly calmed himself, turning his attention back to her father. At least he was willing to be polite there. She wondered what Dad would do if he wasn't. She'd never thought of her father as in any way, remotely kick-ass, but the supernatural world seemed to regard him with respect, and not a little awe. It was a shame she couldn't get the same treatment.

What had he done for them, over the years? What had he done to them?

She'd have to ask him. One day. Whenever there was a moment. It certainly wasn't going to be now.

'Haniel,' said Zadkiel. 'The joy and grace of God.'

Dad frowned and glanced in Izzy's direction, just for a moment, but she could see his genuine concern. 'Haniel is powerful. It would take something very great indeed to overcome him. And you can't find him anywhere?'

Haniel was also one of the angels who had come after her and Jinx. She remembered his icy glare and complete lack of empathy. Not someone she was going to regret never seeing again.

'Nowhere,' Zadkiel replied. 'Not since the hilltop last summer. Not since your daughter gave away Sorath's spark.'

Back to that again. Joy. Izzy bristled. 'Well, I haven't seen him.'

'No,' the angel gave her a withering glance. 'And yet you were among the last who did.'

'So were a whole load of other angels who did sod all to help Jinx, Dylan and me.'

Zadkiel turned to her father, ignoring her completely. 'Perhaps, without your daughter present we might discuss this rationally?'

'Go right ahead,' Izzy said, heading for the door as fast as she could.

'Izzy.' Dad's voice was low, soft and apparently unconcerned, but somehow she caught the barb hidden deep within her name and looked back at him. He stood there, very still, very calm, but he looked unexpectedly … tired. There was a wariness in his eyes that wasn't there before. A chill ran over her, a ripple of apprehension in her stomach that gave her pause. 'Don't do anything rash. Wait and we'll talk later. Just you and me.'

'When?'

He tried to smile, but it didn't seem to work. 'As soon as we can.'

That was it then. She glared at Zadkiel again, knowing that she was treading on dangerous ground, that she ought to be terrified of him. He met her gaze with disdain and the chill inside her turned to a block of jagged ice. The cold mark on the back of her neck would have made ice evaporate in an instant. But she wouldn't show him that she was afraid of him.

She couldn't. Not now. She schooled her face to return the disdain with disgust and then turned from the room, slamming the door behind her. In other times that would have brought a shout of outrage from Mum, but not this time.

Up in her room, Izzy threw her rucksack on the bed and stuffed her belongings into it. Her book, her purse, makeup, the new phone Mum had bought ...

Then she emptied it all out again because she had no idea where she would go and leaving the house right now was not an option. Even if the angels would let her, which she sincerely doubted.

The knife nestled in the middle of the jumble of lip balms, bracelets, hair clips, small change and the other bits of detritus that made up her normal life. What she could remember of normal.

But the knife was nothing to do with normal life. It was cold iron, with a handle made of human bone. She'd used it to stab Jinx, although she had been trying to kill Holly at the time and her actions had not been entirely her own thanks to the presence of the angel Sorath inside her. She'd used it to stab herself to drive the angel from her.

That hated, hated knife.

A wave of cold came off it, sweeping up her outstretched arm and making the hair stand on end, the skin turning to goose bumps. Only then she realised that she was reaching out to it, about to grasp it and pick it up again.

And she didn't want to do that.

Wrapping it carefully in the hand towel from her bathroom, she buried it in the bottom of the bag again and scooped everything back in on top of it. She might not want to touch it, but she couldn't afford to be without it. Not anymore.

That knife had kept her alive.

The worst part of it was that the thing served as a constant reminder of Jinx. And Izzy wasn't sure she wanted to remember him. Not as clearly or as keenly as she did. He was etched into her mind's eye.

Which was just as bloody well because she hadn't seen him for months. Three long months.

Jinx was all about broken promises. She understood that now. Perhaps she always should have known it. He was Sídhe. They weren't exactly known for reliability.

And yet every time her shiny new phone rang, she jumped, grabbing it with eager hands. Stupid, because Jinx didn't have a number for her. She hadn't even had a phone when she last saw him. Mum had bought it for her when she went back to school in September.

But it didn't stop her rushing to answer every time. Even now.

The jangling tune rang out as the phone buzzed and hopped on the bed. She seized it and saw Dylan's name come up. Maybe he had news. Maybe he'd heard something – anything – from Silver.

She answered breathlessly. 'Dylan?'

'Yes.' He hesitated, ready to say something, then paused in

concern. 'Are you okay?'

'I'm ... crappy, to tell the truth. There are angels swarming all over the house. Pissed-off angels who seem to blame me for everything. One of them's missing and apparently that's my fault too. You?'

'I'm ... okay. I think. Or maybe not. Izzy, I thought I saw her today. I thought I saw Mari.'

Mari? Izzy thought about what she'd seen today, what she'd done. Why was Dylan seeing a ghost surprising?

'Where?'

He breathed a sigh that was riddled with relief. Had he expected her to doubt him? To call him crazy? 'In town.'

'Did you tell anyone?'

'God, no. Could you imagine what they'd say?'

His parents were not dealing with Mari's death well. She was sure they didn't really blame him, but he'd been there and then he'd vanished and he'd never talked about it. Because he couldn't say anything. Nothing rational. And the magic stored up inside him just made everything all the more difficult. Human touchstone was not a good job description. There were side effects.

At least her mum and dad were here for her. At least she hadn't lost a sister like Dylan had. Or a daughter ...

'How are your parents?'

'Grieving. Lost. Getting through it slowly. Very slowly. Dad's away a lot. Business trips and stuff. Mum's ... They don't understand, but how could they?'

There was no way. And right from the start, she and Dylan made the decision not to tell anyone who didn't already know, not to do another Marianne on some other unsuspecting soul and let them fall prey to the supernatural world into which they had stumbled.

But Clodagh had guessed anyway. That was something she was going to have to break to Dylan, if he didn't already know. Clodagh had been getting information from him as well. He needed to be more careful what he said.

And that was the problem.

Dylan had no one else to talk to. Neither did Izzy. So they checked in with each other every day and every night, when nightmares marauded through their minds, sleeping and waking, when the magic ignited in him or when weird shit exploded all over her life like today. If he hadn't rung her, she'd already be dialling his number.

A knock on the door made her jump. She almost dropped the phone, but scrabbled to keep hold of it. She was too nervous. The memories were too frightening, the darkness sweeping over her today, too close to the feeling of Sorath taking control of her and leaving her lost in the back of her own mind, a helpless observer. Time didn't have any sort of mitigating effect. Nothing did.

The door opened a little and Dad peered in.

'Dad's here,' she said to Dylan. 'Ring you back?' They couldn't talk in front of her dad. He didn't know everything – not every detail about what had happened to Dylan anyway –

and they both wanted it kept that way. So it was understood.

'Sure. Stay safe.' He hung up and Izzy locked the phone.

'Are they gone?' she asked. Dad nodded.

The oppressive atmosphere that enshrouded the house hadn't gone with them, more was the pity. Dad sat at the other end of the bed looking distinctly uncomfortable.

'Izzy…' he began and fell silent again. Awkward, worrying his fingers together. Not a good sign.

'Dad?'

'I'm sorry about earlier. Like your mum said, I know you did the best you could.'

Damned with faint praise. A sarcastic thanks was probably in order, but the word didn't want to come out. It was an apology and their relationship was so confused right now, since Dad had become teacher and boss and everything in between … She didn't know how to say thanks even when she didn't mean it.

'What did they want?'

'They aren't happy. Their missing brother … well, he's family to them. As well as a comrade in arms and an important piece in their plan.'

'I don't know where he is, Dad. I swear. Most of them left us at Smithfield, when Sorath was in control. It's been months. I don't … I don't remember.'

'I know, love. I believe you. They, on the other hand …' He sighed and hung his head. 'They don't forget. They want us to find him.'

'How are we supposed to do that when they can't?'

'There's a magic book,' he said, as if it was the most normal thing in the world to say. Use a magic book to find a missing angel.

'A magic book?' Izzy wondered for a moment if he was winding her up. But he didn't have that Dad–pulling–her–leg look. He rarely did these days. Still, she had to try. 'Am I off to Hogwarts library now?'

'Yes,' he said, the word like a deadweight. 'I mean, no, not Hogwarts. But it *is* a magic book. And *you* aren't going to be doing anything, no matter what they say. I am. But you can come with me. It's time you learned more on the ground. We have to fly under the radar a bit, that's all. The angels are angry and they don't think straight when they're angry. They really won't like this.'

'This? They won't like that you're doing what they asked?' Angel logic sucked.

'No, the book. They won't like that it even exists, let alone where it is. The book is special, a creation of the Aes Sídhe and one of their most powerful treasures. If the angels found out what it could do, they would try to seize it and then … well, we don't want that to happen. It's a delicate balance, the work of a Grigori, and none of them trust us entirely. No more than we can trust any of them. Perhaps the angels least of all. They always think they know better. They'll try to follow us. Micromanagers to the core, that lot.'

'The angels.' She didn't like the thought of annoying them

any more than she had already done. But this was Dad asking her. It had to be okay. Didn't it?

'Yes. Although … any of them actually. The people of the other races. And some humans would be pretty negative about it too, your mum included. We'll go now, okay?'

CHAPTER SEVEN

Touchstone

Dylan had promised so many times that he wouldn't go back to the Market. He always failed to keep his promise. He'd promised himself, Izzy, her father, Silver, even the ghost of his sister. It didn't seem to matter. The Market always drew him back.

No, another lie. *Silver* drew him back. Even if she wished it otherwise. Even if he didn't want to see her.

Silver was surrounded. He knew, even as he walked towards the centre of the Market ignoring everything else around him, he'd find it difficult to get time to talk to her alone. Perhaps it was for the best. She had secured a small private chamber off the main hall that reminded Dylan of her own hollow, now desecrated and destroyed. But any moment she put her nose so much as an inch outside her sanctuary, the hordes descended. Petitions, offerings, promises of service, pleas for intervention or clemency … all the things she never wanted. And though she denied all trappings of matriarchy, she couldn't turn them away.

Not Silver. Not when she was needed.

Dylan alone seemed to realise that. He saw through her now. A surprise to him, but even more so to her. She didn't like it either.

He watched her in the heart of the Market, with a host of suitors moving like waves around her. She had become the fixed point, the thing around which all else revolved.

'Well now, whatever are you doing out here?' asked a fluid, female voice, ripe with amusement and seduction.

A woman stood behind him, hair as golden as a summer cornfield trailing down her back. Threads of gold were woven through it, as thin and delicate as the shining strands of hair they touched. She had overly large violet eyes and skin like burnished copper. Her ears were long and elaborately pointed, like a fairytale version of an elf rather than the high Aes Sídhe he'd seen before, who liked to model themselves on the humans they despised. But this one, she didn't even attempt to look human. But then again, why would she bother here, in the heart of the Market?

'Can I help you?' Dylan asked. It was long since he had been allowed the luxury of staring at one of the Aes Sídhe, beneath their notice. It was too dangerous. They saw him now – as a way to reach Silver, as a fascinating oddity in their midst, or maybe only as a source of magic. The magic that seethed through his body, writhed along his veins and knotted around his heart. The magic that was all Silver, through and through. Beneath his skin. Deep inside him.

No matter what it was, they could no longer ignore him.

And neither could Silver, no matter how she might pretend. Or wish to. He wasn't prepared to be ignored any more.

'Are you lost?' Her voice was sleek and fluid, like silk between the fingertips, with an accent he couldn't place – not Irish, not quite. And yet there was music there, hidden between her words, lurking in the lilt and cadence of even so mundane a phrase. Since Silver kissed him and her magic made him a touchstone, he could hear music in everything. The whirr of insect wings, the whine of a radiator, the wind in the leaves of a tree. Even in her voice. Or perhaps especially in voices like hers. 'It is not usual for a mortal to wander here unattended.'

Dylan shrugged and turned back his attention to the new uncrowned matriarch. Not that matriarchs wore crowns. Well, some of them did, Silver had told him – really shiny ones – but they didn't need to. 'I'm here to see Silver.'

'Are you indeed?' She raised one perfectly curved eyebrow. 'My name is Meridian.'

She moved closer still. He could feel the warmth emanating from her skin and her scent encircled him like an enchantment – lavender from Provence, hints of honey, rich and warm.

'Look at me, Dylan.'

He didn't want to, but something compelled him. She was

79

too close for comfort, her eyes so very bright and entirely enthralling.

From very close by, Silver cleared her throat pointedly. 'I think you'll find that doesn't work so well on Dylan anymore.' Her voice sliced through the air between them. 'Or if it did, you'd rather wish you'd never done it.' Dylan flinched back nonetheless, because he wasn't entirely sure she was right. He was much closer to Meridian than he'd thought. Far too close. Her lips hung no more than a breath away.

Meridian smiled and glanced over her shoulder. 'You can't blame me for trying.' She didn't sound in any way alarmed or repentant. If anything she sounded amused. 'I've heard so much about him, about both of you. I wanted to see what it was all about, this fuss. A human touchstone, no less. The entire Sídhe race is agog.'

A cold hand closed on his wrist, pulling him back. 'He's nothing of the sort,' Silver snapped. Far too quickly. She was irritated, perhaps even scared, which made her even more dangerous than usual. Her other hand rested on her slender hip, her grey eyes narrowed dangerously. Not a good situation.

All the Market seemed to hold its breath, waiting.

Magic stirred beneath Dylan's skin, rising to meet her touch. Silver lifted her hand, moving it to his sleeve so they weren't touching skin to skin anymore and it subsided a little, just enough so that it didn't spill out of him.

Meridian ignored her. 'No one else has managed the like for over a thousand years, perhaps longer. And look at you –

overthrowing matriarchs and achieving the impossible all in one day. I am impressed, sister.'

Sister? Dylan looked at her again. There was no resemblance – neither to Silver nor Holly. But Silver didn't deny or, or refute the word.

'What do you want, Meridian?' Silver stepped up beside Dylan, reaching out blindly to take his hand. He threaded his fingers through hers almost without thinking about it, willing her the calm and strength she clearly needed. It seemed to work, because she settled a little more comfortably at his side and her fingertips caressed his slowly. The minute trembling he detected in her grip faded.

Meridian watched them with cunning eyes. For a moment she said nothing, but her gaze lingered on their joined hands.

Sisters. He knew Silver had once had a sister called Belladonna – Jinx's mother, who was now dead – but there could have been others. Holly, their mother, was old, even by fae standards. And they were hardly what one might call a close family. Not with Holly at the head.

'What do I want?' Meridian murmured. 'What do *you* want, Silver? That's the question everyone is asking. You overthrew Holly, shattered her touchstone with a fingertip and drove her from her own hollow. But now you do nothing. People need leaders, sister. Your people need a matriarch.'

'A matriarch like you, I suppose?'

'No,' Meridian chided, as if she was talking to a child. 'Like you.'

Silver flushed. Oh, she hid it, but Dylan could feel it in her skin. 'You well know that has never been my wish,' she said at last.

'Your wish? What does your wish matter? This is your duty.'

'My tree was destroyed. My touchstone—'

Meridian interrupted her with a laugh. 'And now you have another. You are a Leanán Sídhe, Silver, as I am, first and always. And miracles of miracles, your human is your touchstone.'

Silver surged towards her sister, tearing herself free from Dylan as if his touch burned. 'I have said it is not my wish, Meridian,' she yelled. 'That is an end to it.'

Power sparkled from her, anger making it manifest like lightning. Meridian's eyes widened in shock. She took a step back and her confident mask slipped. Dylan felt a smile crack his lips. He couldn't help himself. Having yet another relative of Silver suggest she suck him dry and cast his husk aside was getting old. Or that they would be happy to do it. That he was just a thing to be used. And he loved to see her kick ass. They all seemed to expect her to mutely accept their will as she might have done Holly's. But her mother had been more terrifying that any of them.

Except perhaps Silver herself.

Her mother's first daughter.

Silver turned back to him and pursed her lips as she read the look of admiration on his face.

'Come with me,' she told him and swept back towards her

private chambers. Servants and kith scurried around her, but she ignored them. At least here there was no one she didn't trust with her life. And his.

Dylan waited, watching her pace back and forth. But he knew in the end she would speak to him. This time.

'They won't stop unless I give in.'

'Then why not give in? Be their matriarch. I can't think of anyone else I'd trust.' Trust and the Sídhe didn't exactly go together. But strangely he did trust her – her and Jinx, just the two of them among all the Sídhe. 'Would it be so different from keeping your own hollow anyway?'

'I didn't manage that too well in the end, did I?' She shuddered. 'I got most of them killed.'

'That was Holly, not you.'

'It was both of us. And Izzy and Jinx. All that mess with Sorath. You didn't see it. You didn't see what Holly did.' He hadn't seen it, nor had he felt it as she had when her tree was broken and burnt, the source of her magic, a part of herself.

'It's over.'

'Holly's still out there somewhere. Oh, they're all so certain she's gone. But I know her. I've always known her. She doesn't just give up. Besides, if I were to use my magic it could destroy you, don't you understand? The more I use the power of the Leanán Sídhe, the less of you will remain. You can't be a touchstone for long. You won't survive.'

He'd known what he was getting into when he'd kissed her. The Leanán Sídhe's kiss was a gift as much as a curse, no ordinary thing. It empowered her and opened him up to the font of creativity, to the music of the spheres. It would consume him eventually, drain him dry, drive him mad ... Not for a moment would he take it back, any of it, even if he could.

But becoming a touchstone changed everything. And neither of them knew how much. Silver didn't like it one bit, which made him distinctly uncomfortable.

Being a touchstone made him a target, he understood that. It also gave him power over her and it didn't seem to matter. She fascinated him the way a flame enticed a moth. His world was so much bigger now. The music that poured out of him, the magic that allowed him to create it, he couldn't bear to be without that.

Life without Silver wasn't a life.

That was why he always ended up coming back to her. He needed her. Like an addict needed a fix, perhaps, but it was still need.

'You don't know that. No one does.'

'Why are you here, Dylan?' she sighed.

'I saw my sister. Or her ghost. Or ... or something. And Izzy said there were angels at her house, looking for one of their brothers. He's missing. Silver, what is going on?'

She stared at him for a moment, her gaze too intent, too lingering. Then she seized his hand and pulled him after her. Several of her people started towards them, disturbed by her sudden movement, looking for a way to be of service. Each one shied away at the last moment on seeing her expression,

TOUCHSTONE

which told him everything he needed to know. She was royally pissed off now.

They stepped into the one luxurious room she called her own and she pulled the curtained door closed behind them. 'Tell me everything.' She sat down on a low chaise longue, the one he remembered from her club. She must have brought it here. One last piece of her shattered home in the one place that was purely hers.

She perched there like a queen on a throne.

'What I said. Izzy said the angels came to her house, looking for one of their brothers who's missing. I saw Mari outside the gates to the college on Westland Row, opposite the station. And then ... then she was gone. A ghost?'

Silver shook her head, frowning. 'Are you certain?'

'Of course. Silver?' She looked even paler than usual, sickened, as if she'd been punched in the stomach.

'I fear that a door has been opened. A door that never should have been unlocked. That something got out. We have to tell Jinx.'

'Why Jinx?'

'Because something new is out there, stirring up ghosts like that. Or something very old indeed.' She shuddred suddenly. 'It's not just Samhain. It can't be. Amadán asked us to look into a murder, an impossible murder. And now missing angels? No. I need to talk to Jinx. He could be investigating the very same thing. They have to be connected. It can't just be a coincidence.'

85

There wasn't a queue or anything. Not at this time of the evening. The guy at the desk gave them a funny look, probably because he was hoping to close up as soon as possible. But Dad didn't bat an eyelid – just laid down the cash. When he took the tickets they headed on in through a narrow corridor lined with leprechaun memorabilia that made Izzy cringe with every glance.

'Seriously?' she said again, but Dad shushed her.

They waited for the door to be opened. The man who stepped through to greet them was a giant, ducking his head as he did so. When he straightened, he recognised Dad. Izzy saw the alarm in his sunken eyes, instantly quelled by willpower alone. He tightened a jaw that could crack walnuts.

'Mr Gregory, what are you doing here?'

His deep and echoey voice rippled through Izzy's chest in a disconcerting way. It wasn't loud, not as such, but it ought to have been. It ought to have her covering her ears and cowering, she knew that instinctively, but it didn't. As if it didn't quite sound the same in her world as it would in his. Another one of those tell-tale signs she was learning so much about.

'Just here with a few questions, Grim,' said Dad with such an air of nonchalance, Izzy almost believed him. If he hadn't been so worried about coming here. 'Nothing to be concerned about. Will she see us?'

Grim didn't look too sure. He glared at them both, clearly wishing they'd just go away, and then bowed his head. 'I'll check. If you'll kindly wait in the parlour?'

They followed him through the door, along the narrow winding passage like a tunnel beneath the Giant's Causeway, lined and capped with hexagonal columns. They emerged into a room with vastly oversized furniture.

'The giant's house,' said Dad after Grim vanished again. 'Cute, isn't it?'

It was kind of cute. Not tacky like she'd thought. But it made her feel like a child, and that vulnerability wasn't exactly welcome. Dad on the other hand seemed to be in his element, like a kid himself, gleeful as he wandered around chair legs and under the table. He stood in the fireplace and made faces at her.

So much for a serious situation.

'What is Grim?' she asked, walking over to the table, trying to see what was on top of it.

'A bodach. A giant.' He spread his arms wide. 'Welcome to his house.'

'He was tall, but not that tall.'

'That isn't his real height.'

She rolled her eyes to heaven. Sometimes she was certain Dad liked making her feel out of her depth. She was a novice, compared to him, as Gran was so fond of pointing out. Gran wasn't even a Grigori, but she'd been married to one for fifty years, as she liked to tell them, and 'bred one too', like they were pedigree dogs or something. It made Izzy grind her teeth. Her gran had always been aloof, when she was around, but now Izzy was seeing a whole new side to her, not a particularly charming one. Usually around that point in Gran's rant, she found some really boring tome and made Izzy read it from start to finish. It wasn't worth the argument.

Izzy wasn't actually sure which was worse, the endless lectures or the punishing drills and fighting techniques. She had danced for years in primary school, ballet training, some gymnastics thrown in because she'd found it easy in comparison. This, at least, gave her a chance to keep up. Flexibility and strength she wasn't aware she had inside her — because up until the age of thirteen she'd danced just for pleasure – resurged from muscle memory and old instincts. She had loved to dance. And then she'd given up, in that way many her age did. Not because anything happened or she'd wanted something else. She'd just fallen out of love with it. Secondary school made it harder to get to the classes, and ballet required more hours, more than she was able to give.

If only she'd known. If only Mum and Dad — especially Dad — had told her something to keep her going.

And now, she had terrible dreams about training, about the endless cycles of positions, blocks, defences and attacks. It infected every corner of her mind, waking and sleeping. But it was easier than the nightmares, where Holly tortured her, where Jinx despised her, where Sorath had won …

Sometimes she felt that training to fight was all she had left, the only way she could carry on. Sometimes she threw herself into it body and soul because it was the only way to numb her mind.

Behind Dad, in the fireplace, a door opened. The man standing there was no taller than Izzy, with hair almost as red as hers. His eyes were full of laughter, glittering with mirth, and when Dad turned around, he swept into a low and elegant bow.

'Grigori, you honour us with your presence. We have just a short window, but the Storyteller will see you now.'

Dad instantly sobered. 'Thank you. Cudgel, isn't it?'

The little man looked surprised and rather delighted to be recognised. 'Yes, sir. I am Cudgel and I have had the honour to be the Storyteller's sworn man for forty years now. Honoured that you remember me, sir. Truly honoured. Now if you will just follow me.'

'Of course. Come on, Izzy.'

But Cudgel didn't move. 'Alas, I regret to inform you that the Storyteller will only see you alone. Your daughter may have a separate audience afterwards. You may even leave her instructions, if you wish.'

'I'm not leaving Izzy alone.'

'There is no other way, sir. Two Grigori are too much of a risk to my lady's security, no matter how good the terms on which we find ourselves. You will please forgive us. Those are her requirements. Otherwise you are quite free to leave. Empty-handed.'

Dad hesitated. He glanced back at Izzy and she could see the doubt in his eyes.

I'll be fine, she tried to tell him with a look, with the way she firmed her jaw and clenched her fists. *I can handle this.*

She didn't add, *I hope.*

'Just give us a minute, if you will,' said Dad and Cudgel bowed again and stepped back through the door. Dad didn't waste any time. He crossed to Izzy and dropped his voice to a low whisper. 'They're probably listening so be careful. Don't promise anything, and don't trust anyone. She'll ask for something – a gift, a secret – or she'll ask you a question. Just … be careful what you think. Do you understand? You have to guard your thoughts, those things most dear to you, and be careful what you think in here.'

'Okay,' she said dubiously. She wasn't sure what he was actually trying to say. He wasn't being much help, twisting his words around so they wouldn't get his meaning. She didn't either. 'I'll try.'

'Don't just try. This is deadly serious. Thoughts have a way of becoming real in here. And they have a way of being stolen right out of your head too. Just promise me, okay kiddo?'

'I promise. But when you talk in riddles I don't—'

'It isn't a riddle, love. It's just what I say.'

'Sir,' Cudgel interrupted. 'Our time is short.'

'It's okay, Dad. I'll be careful. Promise. Go.'

He pulled her close and ruffled her hair. 'Good girl. See you on the other side. We'll nip over to Burdock's and I'll buy you some chips.'

He knocked on the fireplace door and it opened again. Dad squared his shoulders. Izzy watched him doing it. It made him look stronger, more dangerous, less like her dad. The Grigori walked out of the room and left her alone.

CHAPTER EIGHT

Unwanted Gifts

There was only one place to go for answers on this level of magnitude. Jinx checked in with Silver, a brief phone call which surprised him more than he'd expected.

'Listen to me,' she said, her tone curt. 'Dylan is here. He saw … he saw a ghost. I don't know for sure what it means, but …'

'Amadán said it's the Fear.'

She sucked in a breath of alarm. 'It can't be.'

'That's what he said. And the body he showed me—'

'All right, all right,' she said but she didn't sound all right. Not in the slightest. She sounded shaken to the core. 'Go. But keep your wits about you. They'll be expecting you. Make sure you have a gift of some kind prepared. She'll want something. Better make it something impersonal and physical.' Then she hung up.

A gift. Of course he had a gift. He carried a few trinkets

with him all the time now. The tourist shops were great for them. You couldn't ever have something for nothing. Just once, it would have been nice, just once for someone to say 'sure, okay, why not?' But life didn't work that way.

Not in his life anyway. Not among the Sídhe.

The Luas rattled by him, the bell clanging, and he stepped into the opening of an alley to watch it go by, while the press of pedestrians surged in to fill the space where he had been. A dark alley. One thing Jinx knew, nothing good ever came out of wandering into places like that after sunset on your own.

As he lingered at the opening, waiting for the tram to pass, he saw movement in the deepest shadows at the end of the alley. Homeless humans, probably, those lost at the edge of society, forgotten or dismissed, but nothing to concern him.

So why did he have such a powerful urge to go down there? His body, his mind, even his soul if he actually had one – every part of him wanted to step into the shadows.

But some small scrap of common sense stopped him.

The Luas passed him by, its lights gone, but he couldn't move. He felt like something had frozen him there. He couldn't leave any more than he was willing to enter.

'Always so obstinate,' drawled a voice riddled with bored amusement. He knew it. The sound of it made his heart spasm in fright, though he didn't show it outwardly. He couldn't do that.

But Osprey probably knew anyway.

'What are you doing here?' he asked as he turned to look,

but a strong arm seized his, twisting it behind him and up while at the same time propelling him around and into the alley.

Osprey forced Jinx to his knees.

'I'm delivering a message,' said Holly's chief assassin.

Jinx knew better than to beg. That tended to just make Osprey worse. 'A message?'

'Holly sends her love.'

Holly? Holly was gone. Holly had been defeated. He'd almost died and Silver had — Holly *had* to be gone. Everyone said it. Everyone. It was all he had.

He tried to look up at Osprey and received a kick to his back in recompense that drove him down to the ground.

'Holly's gone,' he said, his voice trembling, as if it didn't believe the words he was making it say.

Osprey laughed. 'Did you think it was that easy? Holly's an old power, Jinx. She isn't defeated if you take her touchstone away. She has her ways of getting more power when she needs it. She wanted you to know that, so you can tell Silver. And she wanted you to have a present.'

That didn't sound good. Holly had always referred to the piercings as presents. Like he was lucky to have them. Like she was doing him a favour.

He sucked in a series of rapid breaths and tried to make his heart stop stuttering too fast. 'I don't — I don't serve Holly anymore.'

'Of course you do. There's no opt-out clause, Jinx, no way

to leave her service. You know that.'

'There's death.' It sounded idiotic the moment the words left his mouth. Osprey gave that fearsome laugh Jinx knew too well.

'Such *bravado*. You don't want that, kiddo. You're way too young. Anyway—' he leaned in close until his cheek was right against Jinx's, warm and smooth, carrying the scent of cloves and nutmeg '—it doesn't help.'

He released Jinx, but before the Cú Sídhe could recover himself, Osprey stepped in front of him and delivered a savage kick to the stomach and up into his solar plexus. It drove Jinx's breath from him. His muscles spasmed and he fell back, gasping for air. Before he knew what was happening, Osprey knelt astride him, pinning his arms down with his knees, holding him there helpless. He looked the same. All the fae were eternally unchanging. A sharp, hawkish face, glittering golden eyes and sleek, swept-back hair flecked with brown and white. His skin wasn't just pale, but white too, bloodless, except for the streak of black crossing his eyes and the bridge of his nose. He grabbed Jinx's jaw and held it in a vice-like grip, pushing his head back to expose his neck.

'Hold still now. This is really going to hurt.'

He pulled out a thin line of silver, like a wire, which wriggled and squirmed in his grip. He flicked it and snapped it out into a line, which he brought down on Jinx's throat.

'Just let it work, that's a good boy,' he said as Jinx struggled and kicked, gagging against the tightening band of burning metal. His body ached to change, to transform, but the thing around his neck stopped him. He could smell the stench of burning skin – his skin – and the pain of it forced a howl from him. Jinx tasted blood and vomit, tears streamed from his eyes, blinding him, and then, abruptly, it was over.

Osprey released him, as if it was nothing more than a game. He even gave Jinx a good-natured punch to the shoulder. 'There you go. All over. That wasn't so bad, was it?'

Jinx rolled onto his side, coughing, fighting to hide his agony and humiliation even if it was already too late.

Osprey stood over him, his feathered cloak fluttering in the breeze stirred up by another tram. Sídhe women found him hopelessly attractive, at least at first. Not so much when they got to know him, when his sadism had already marked them forever. Jinx knew him far too well.

'What was that?'

But Osprey just smiled. 'Until next time, kiddo.'

'There isn't going to be a next time.'

Osprey shook his head, an expression that said Jinx had no idea what he was talking about. The smile was still painted on his mouth.

'Ah, Jinx,' he said darkly. 'There's *always* a next time. It's Holly, isn't it? She has plans for you. Mighty plans. See you.'

He strode out into the city lights, a fluttering, threatening silhouette that Jinx couldn't bring himself to follow. He waited until he was sure the assassin was gone and then raised shaking hands to his throat. A band of metal pressed tight against his neck and inside his guts something reared up, like a serpent waking from a long sleep, something golden and full of brightness. It burned the way a star burned, too hot, too bright. And he felt it take root, winding down within him and glowing there like an ember.

Something was wrong. Something was terribly wrong.

What had Osprey infected him with? What had he done? Holly had plans all right, he knew that. But he had no idea what they were. And he had no idea what this meant.

But Holly was gone. Holly was meant to be gone!

He curled in on himself and tried to make it not be true. The world was never on his side.

The ephemeral glow faded to a bleak and hollow emptiness. He didn't know if it was gone, or if it had even been real. Another of Holly's sadistic games, perhaps, leaving him lost. All the same it took time before he could bring himself to step out into the Dublin evening again. With his hands shoved deep in his pockets, he stalked, head down, until he reached the side of the Jervis Street Centre. And there he found the gate in the square that had once been a graveyard for the hospital, right in front of the display of gravestones lined up against the wall. He rubbed his neck again, the line still there, like wire in his skin.

He'd ask Silver later. She was the only person he could trust to give him a straight answer. Or indeed, any answer at all.

He knew he ought to tell her, that he should ring her again right away. But what could he say? Holly's back? She's as powerful as ever she was and I don't know how?

Oh yes, she'd love that.

And then he'd have to admit that Osprey had done something to him, marked him, branded him somehow. He'd have to describe that feeling, not just the humiliation, but the sensations afterwards. And tell Silver that Holly had a plan for him. That she wouldn't let him go.

Later. He'd call her later. When he knew more. He couldn't find the words now.

On the other side of the gate, the world of Dubh Linn was unlit and grim. This area of the city was virtually deserted. And the building before him, a warehouse from a bygone age.

The entrance stood empty, dark, a long snaking corridor vastly different from the entrance on the human side with its lights and pretty posters. He'd seen it once. He'd stared at it for about five minutes, unable to believe it was the same place.

There it was a site of amusement, entertainment. They charged entry to tourists, which, fair dues, was a nice money-spinner for them. They even served coffee and cake afterwards.

Only Dubh Linn showed this place as it really was. Dark and foreboding, terrible. Gnarled black tree roots surrounded the entrance, as if they would reach out and crush the unwary. The glass panelled door boomed like a drum when he knocked. There was no response for a few minutes and he was about to knock again when he saw a shape detach itself from the shadows on the other side. Twice as tall as he was, three times as broad. The words 'brick' and 'shithouse' sprang instantly to mind. He glanced down to see if the thing's knuckles were actually dragging on the ground. It looked like someone had shaved a silverback gorilla and shoved it into a suit.

The bodach stared at him — not a friendly stare — and Jinx wondered briefly if it was the uglier big brother of the one he'd fought at the Market. And if it knew what he'd done.

But it only produced a tiny golden key from its pocket and unlocked the uneven glass door.

'Welcome, Cú Sídhe. Lady Silver made the appointment so we are expecting you. If you would just wait in the ante-chamber while she sees her previous supplicant.'

Jinx nodded and followed the bodach inside. He wondered where the swarm of leps who usually ran the place had got to. Bodachs were the heavies, the muscle, a good idea to have on the door, but the leps were the brains. They knew how to spin money from old leaves. She relied on them.

Who else was visiting here this evening? But before he could ask the bodach, they reached the door to the ante-chamber and he found himself alone.

It was another gate. He knew that at once. So the ante-chamber and presumably the Storyteller herself were located in the human world. That made sense. He'd heard she shunned Dubh Linn. After all he had heard of her, the enemies she had made, the human world was probably safer for her.

Jinx hesitated. He didn't want to cross over any more today, the shiver over his skin, the vibrations in the pit of his stomach, the way the silver piercings and tattoos tightened on him.

It was getting worse. And now this new band at his throat. He didn't like crossing over. Not that he'd loved it before. Before Izzy. But since then, since the summer and all that madness that should have seen him dead, he hated it even more.

For a while, just a short while, he'd thought he had a future, but Dubh Linn and the human world of Dublin had snatched that away. It hurt him worse than Holly ever could.

Only Silver knew the truth.

Taking a breath he stepped through, entering the other side, the human plane, and a room designed to tease and trick the eye. It looked like the kitchen of a country cottage in a fairytale, but one made for giants like the bodach he'd just left, or maybe his even bigger brothers.

And worst of all, he wasn't alone. The face that looked at him as he stepped through the door, eyes wide, mouth open in shock, almost stopped his heart.

It was Izzy.

Izzy Gregory.

She froze, staring at him. The artificial lights overhead illuminated her like an apparition of something divine. Her hair flamed red, like the fire her natural mother could call up on demand, though a darker shade than Brí's own hair. Her skin was as pale as porcelain, her bone structure clearly denoting the beauty to come as she grew. All fae traits, but that was only one half of her heritage.

Her bright blue eyes came from her father. And she had oh-so-human freckles, like little flecks of gold all over her doll-like face. Her mouth hung open in surprise, the full lips painted a shimmering pink. The makeup was new. But then it had been almost three months.

Months without her. Months alone.

He hadn't seen her in so long, it hurt to look at her now, to see the flicker of answering pain in her eyes, the tightening of her jaw as she closed her mouth and glared at him.

'What are *you* doing here?' she asked. He wanted to cringe when he heard the venom in her voice.

Should have called her. Should have found a way. Should have done something. Anything. Should never have just accepted it and walked away. He silenced his racing thoughts, pushing them down into the depths of his mind where he could smother them. He had done the right thing, the only thing. It was too dangerous. Izzy shouldn't be in his life.

And yet here she was again.

'I could ask you the same question.'

She lifted her chin – proud and defiant, his Izzy. She always had been. A fighter to the core. 'My father brought me. You?'

'Silver sent me.' He didn't want to get into any more detail than that. She wouldn't understand.

'I see.'

The uncomfortable silence turned the air to lead around them. She didn't move, nor did he. As if neither of them wanted to be the first one to look away.

'Where is he? Your father.'

'He went in to see the Storyteller.'

They stared at each other, waiting for the other to talk, to say something, anything, to break this interminable pained silence.

She had balled her hands to fists at her side, released them and did it again. She always did that when she was nervous and trying not to show it, when she was unsure, but too proud to ask for help. He could read her so well.

He'd been trying to protect her when he'd cut off all contact. That's what he'd told himself. That's what Silver had said. What everyone said. They had to protect Izzy and Dylan, after all that had happened.

So how could he explain that to her?

'Don't have anything to do with the fae,' Dad had told her.

Right. Sure. Then he'd left her alone in some random leprechaun museum in the heart of Dublin, right on the edge of Dubh Linn. Don't have anything to do with the fae was easier said than done. Especially when, in the same museum, she'd found the one member of the fae race Dad really wanted her away from, the one she *really* didn't want to see ever again.

Except of course she did.

Her heart sped up when she recognised him, her breath hitching in her throat so that for a moment she couldn't say anything at all. She stared at those lips that had kissed her and longed to feel their touch again.

But Jinx – being Jinx – just had to open his mouth, say a few words and ruin it all again.

Or maybe that had been her, not that she was going to admit it. He hadn't changed then, she reminded herself. Nor would he. That was one of the lessons Gran kept repeating and repeating.

They are eternal and ageless. They cannot be trusted. And they never, ever change.

It worked on more levels than one. Who knew?

Of course, she should have known. Jinx always hurt her, whether he meant to or not. She really should realise that by this stage. She should have learned.

How could he be here now? Why? What did he want with the Storyteller?

'You felt it too?' she asked. 'Last night.'

He nodded. 'And there's more. Izzy ...' He fidgeted, uncomfortable. He wanted to say something, but didn't know how to, that was clear. She beat him to it.

'There was an attack at my school. Dad called them the Fear.' The words were out before she realised she was going to say them. Jinx's face paled, his bones standing out stark beneath the skin. In a moment he was right beside her, his arms rising around her but not quite touching her, not yet. His steel-grey eyes studied hers.

'Are you okay? Were you hurt?'

Swallowing hard, she took a deliberate step back. 'I'm fine. I drove them off.'

To her surprise he smiled. Just a flicker of a smile over his lips. Pride in his eyes. 'Of course you did.'

She wanted to kiss him so badly it hurt. Her heart was thundering inside her ribs, desperate to get out. But before she could do anything rash, like lift herself up on her toes and press her lips to his, someone cleared their throat rather pointedly behind them.

Cudgel was back.

Bloody leprechauns and their bloody timing.

'This way, Miss Gregory. The Storyteller will see you now.'

Before she could move, Jinx stepped in front of her. Still so close, she could feel the heat of his body, smell his scent, warm and beguiling, so familiar.

'Not alone.' She could hear the rumbled warning in his voice.

'Dad went in alone.'

'He knows what he's getting into.' He turned back to her, took her hands in his and gazed into her face. 'Izzy, don't go in there alone.'

'Jinx, it's okay.'

'No, it isn't. That's one of the Council of the Sídhe in there. Or at least she was, once upon a time. And she's dangerous. Like Holly, like Brí, and just as powerful. You can't risk—'

Enough. She had put up with this for long enough. She was thoroughly sick of being told what she could or couldn't do. She had to put up with it from her father, but not from Jinx ,who had given up any right to tell her what to do. Not that he'd had that right to begin with. She shook herself free of his hands and stepped away.

'I can take any risks I want to. I need to find Dad.'

'Izzy, please.' It was the concern riddling his voice that made her relent a little. That and the word 'please'. The Jinx she first met would never have said it, unless it was in the most sarcastic or threatening way possible. Certainly never in that tone of voice, as if he really meant it and that saying it was his last resort.

She stared at him, trying to figure out how he had changed. But then she remembered. On Wishing Stone, they both had changed. Changed utterly.

'Dad needed to talk to her. I need to talk to her.'

'I don't know what game your father is playing,' Jinx muttered with a hostility she'd never heard directed towards her dad from anyone. 'I'm coming with you.'

'The Storyteller will allow that,' said the leprechaun. 'Since you're both asking more or less the same thing. Follow me.'

Cudgel turned and vanished through the door in the fireplace before Izzy could ask what on earth he meant. How did he know what either of them was asking? She had to follow him and she couldn't exactly stop Jinx anyway if he chose to follow her. Infuriating hound that he was. It didn't stop her turning on him. 'Just don't interfere, understand?'

He gazed at her pointing finger and gave another half-smile. Such sorrow in that smile, along with bitter amusement. He reached out and pushed her hand gently to one side.

'I'll do what I must. I was once bound to protect you, remember?'

'Really?' Her voice turned scathing. 'Then where have you been for the last three months?'

The sadness hinted beforehand blossomed in his eyes, so close to pain that she instantly regretted it.

'You didn't need me, Izzy.'

But she had, she had needed him. More than she'd ever admit. Words wanted to claw their way out of her, words she couldn't say to him. Not now.

Biting down on them, she turned and stalked away, aware all the time of the treacherous warmth seeping from the tattoo on the back of her neck, and of Jinx following close behind.

CHAPTER NINE

The Storyteller

The inner chamber was lit from below, each stone and rock, each bit of gravel throwing shadows up onto the familiar bronze ceiling. They weren't in the museum now – at least not the museum as the human world knew it. Parts of it leaked through – the well in the centre of the room for example, and the blue spotlights set into the floor. Only here the well wasn't fake – Izzy could hear the slow drip of water somewhere in its depths – and the lights weren't artificial. They wavered like gas flames, like will o' the wisps out of old stories, fairy lights, the type seen at fairy forts and rings, whose only delight was to lure the unwary off their path and into danger. Trees pressed close around them, rocking and creaking in a breeze they couldn't feel.

Izzy knew the moment they stepped through the fireplace, that threshold, that place of betweens, that they had entered

Dubh Linn. Or maybe something like it. Jinx looked just as uncomfortable, but then he'd freaked out the moment he'd realised she intended to come in here alone. If the Storyteller was indeed like Holly or Brí, then maybe he had reason.

The warmth of having him there had faded quickly. That low-level warning of a chill on the back of her neck replacing it told her that something was happening, even if experience hadn't taught her already to pick up on the shimmering of the world as they passed between. Her body reacted, her blood flowing faster with the quickening of her heart. Each nerve ending charged with electricity. Her eyes picked out details she would barely register normally.

Dad had told her to expect this. Recognising it and using it was part of her training. Her Grigori senses would heighten at times of danger, help her react and help her survive. She had to trust them. She just wished they didn't make her stomach turn.

Glancing back at Jinx, she saw that he looked different too – harder, sharper. His grey eyes had taken on that metallic sheen of the fae, like steel. His bones looked more pronounced beneath his smooth skin, making the tattoos stand out in sharp relief. His black hair shimmered, iridescent as a raven's wing. He always had an air of danger about him. He was a hunter, after all, according to many a killer. Now it was just plainer to see. There was something new about him too, something she hadn't seen before. Harder, darker. Like something else lurked behind a mask, some new part of him that was alien, something she didn't recognise at all.

'Have you been here before?' she asked.

He nodded, just once. 'With Silver.' From the expression on his face it hadn't been a good experience. 'You?'

Izzy shook her head, wishing now that she hadn't agreed so readily to let Dad go on ahead. They would want something, he'd said. But what? And how was she meant to know what to ask?

'Why are you here, Jinx?' she asked.

'I needed some questions answered. There's something out and about that shouldn't be. It's my job to see to that.'

'You have a job now?'

A smile lifted the corners of his lips for just a moment and Izzy found herself starting at them with a fascination she couldn't afford to have right now. Especially not for him. It would, as Gran was so fond of saying, all end in tears. It already had.

'I have a job,' he replied. 'I'm Silver's emissary. It's the job she used to do for Holly.'

Izzy flinched. She couldn't help it. Her memories of Holly were not pleasant. 'Good for you.'

'How's school?'

'School's school.' Even as she said it, she realised he probably didn't even know what school was like when it was normal. Not when spectral monsters were popping up in the bathrooms. Maybe he'd be more comfortable with that than she was.

Grim appeared, opening another door, and a dark-robed figure glided into the room. She stopped, waiting until Grim closed the door, and then she sat down beside the well. The hood concealed her face, but her long-fingered hands were dark and the skin stretched tight over the bones like the skin of a drum.

'Well, now,' she said, in a sweet, musical voice. 'Here they are. You wandered. We had to come and find you.'

Izzy was about to say they only stepped through the door, but sense got the better of her. 'We wandered?'

'There are many rooms in this hollow, Miss Gregory. Some are as beautiful as this. Some are dark and terrible. You were fortunate your mind chose this one as the room you needed.'

Izzy frowned. Better to just go with it. That was the thing with Dubh Linn. Go with it and keep your wits about you. Otherwise it messed with you. It could screw you over completely.

'Where's my dad?'

'David went on ahead. He will meet you outside. I can't be having two of you in here at once. Two Grigori? *Anything* could happen. We should press on, so. You have questions, do you not? What are they? What will you give to have them answered? You have a gift for me, no doubt?'

The question hung heavily in the air and Izzy knew that it meant more than it appeared to. A gift? No one had mentioned a gift.

'I don't understand,' she replied warily.

'Of course you do. Every visitor brings a gift. Let's see, what shall it be? If you don't have something to give, maybe you have something pretty of your own. That hair … those eyes …' She leaned forward, hawkish in her examination of Izzy.

'I have a gift,' said Jinx sharply. 'I'll give it on Izzy's behalf.'

The Storyteller sank back sullenly. 'Let's see it then.'

He rummaged in his jacket pocket and pulled out a cloth-wrapped bundle. When he unrolled it, Izzy saw a little snow-globe with a green sheep in the middle. He handed it over as if it was a priceless treasure and the Storyteller ran her fingers over the surface, shaking it and holding it up to watch the little plastic flakes whirl around.

'This is a fine gift,' she said at last. 'So? Tell me why you're here.'

'I need to ask you about …' she glanced at Jinx again. She ought to thank him, but there wasn't time. His face was unreadable. 'About the Fear.'

'The Fear are a fairytale,' Jinx said quickly. Too quickly. Izzy knew when he was lying. That was one thing she had learned. And this wasn't entirely a lie. But it was denial.

'Jinx can tell you all about the Fear, can't you? They're a story to frighten fae children.' The Storyteller leaned in and Izzy caught a glimpse of a sharp nose and chin beneath the hood. Skin like coffee, features too pronounced.

'Something to frighten everyone,' said Jinx bleakly. 'And some believe they're less of a story and more of an actual threat. Here, now. Anyway, aren't you the Storyteller?'

She gave a short laugh. 'Who has been telling you tales, Jinx by Jasper? Why are you here?'

'Amadán asked me to look into something. A death. A young fae busker who worked for him. He's put out, which isn't good for anyone. He believes the Fear did it.'

Her tone sharpened to a knife point. 'That's impossible. The Fear are imprisoned.'

So, not a story suddenly. They'd gone from fiction to reality pretty quickly. But of course, Izzy knew that. She could still feel the touch.

Will you come to me, Grigori? Will you come?

She shivered. It was like they'd known her. And that name … they'd called her *Daughter of Míl*. 'They didn't look too imprisoned when they attacked someone at my school.'

'So your father said. Very well. I shall tell you what I know. But there is a price.'

'We gave you a gift. A fine gift,' said Jinx.

'You did, and I'm grateful for it. Now you need answers and there is a price.'

Izzy ground her teeth together. There was *always* a freaking price. Why did they always make such a big dramatic deal about it?

'What price?'

The Storyteller pushed back her hood and Izzy saw her whole face at last. Her skin was a deep, bronzed brown, like polished mahogany, and her eyes dominated her face, bright and golden, too big for the rest of her features. Unnervingly round and bright, a child's eyes in an adult face, but no child would wear such a look of avarice.

'A small thing,' she said, innocently enough. 'An entry to add to my book. A memory.'

Izzy frowned, doubtful as she registered the lie in the Storyteller's face. 'A memory?'

'Careful, Izzy,' Jinx warned in an undertone.

Oh, she needed him to shut the hell up. It wasn't his decision.

'Did my father do this?'

The Storyteller's lips quirked. 'We have other arrangements. David doesn't care to share his thoughts with me. So I require a lot more by way of shiny treasures and suchlike. From you, sweet child, I just want a memory. Or a secret. Often it's the same thing. Come now, everyone who passes through here writes in my book. There's no harm in it.'

'Is that why you're here?' Jinx asked. 'To feed?'

'Such an ugly turn of phrase, Cú Sídhe. But then, why are any of us here if not to feed on something? We all have needs. I'm the Storyteller, Jinx by Jasper. And this is a place of stories. They are the bricks with which it is built, the ghosts that linger after dark in the corners. Children flock here. They listen so intently when I weave my tales. Here, I am beloved.'

'What about their parents?' Jinx bared his teeth, disgust twisting his face. 'I can't imagine they're too keen on you anywhere near their kids. Don't they sue?'

The Storyteller said nothing in reply, but reached out her

arm and pointed a long, bony finger at him. Gold flecks glittered at her fingertips and Jinx froze, the arrogance draining from him in an instant. He sucked in a pained breath and stretched, his head going back, his chest expanding, his arms dragging out behind him, his face a mask of pain.

'Careful, boy,' she whispered, in her soft, lilting tones. 'I can pick your memories right out of your head. I can squeeze you dry and leave you with nothing.'

'Leave him alone,' said Izzy. 'Or I won't do anything. You'll get nothing.'

The Storyteller's head snapped around with uncanny speed, but she didn't release Jinx. When she grinned, all her whiter than white teeth were exposed. 'For most people, I charge nothing. It's a ritual, my book, nothing more. But from you, I want a memory. Otherwise, like I told your father, there is nothing for anyone and the Fear will run rampant. And whatever else is set free …'

A chilling clarity settled on Izzy's shoulders. 'What else? What else can be set free?'

'What else indeed. Now perhaps you're asking the right question. The Fear are terrible beyond words. But, there are worse things, little Grigori. Far worse. Do you really want to know what that is? Just look at the book. Give me what I want.'

Jinx whimpered – it was the only sound he could still make, but Izzy knew it wasn't through pain or terror. Not Jinx. He was trying to warn her. She ought to listen, but that had never stopped her before. She couldn't leave him like that.

'Let him go and I'll do it. I need to know everything — about the Fear, about the earthquake, whatever you can tell me.'

The Storyteller smiled. Not a nice smile.

'Very well. Do we have an accord?' She said it too quickly, eagerly, and Izzy knew she'd made a misstep somehow. She just couldn't work out how.

She held out her other hand and Izzy took it gingerly.

Jinx dropped to the ground as if a wire had been cut.

'All right,' Izzy said, trying not to think about him right now.

'You have to say it, sweet child.'

'I really hope you don't talk to mortal children that way,' Jinx groaned. 'Or treat them so roughly.' He struggled to his feet, trying to work out the cramps in his muscles. But at least he had regained something of his caustic tone. 'You'll get arrested.'

The Storyteller hissed at him, revealing more of her sharp teeth, and Izzy shied back, wishing she hadn't come in here or accepted anything. But she didn't retreat.

She needed to know. That was the problem. And to know, she had to deal with this creature and to let her do what she would to Jinx. And to her too.

What was this world making of her?

'We have an accord,' Izzy said, aware of the tightening of the air around her, the working of old magic. Magic to bind, magic to compel. 'This book, where is it?'

'Eager now? I like that. Grim, bring it in.'

Grim appeared as if from nowhere, followed by three smaller figures, each with a shock of red hair. One of them was Cudgel. They busied themselves setting up a table and chairs, paying no heed to the three pairs of eyes watching them.

Cudgel produced some grey foam triangles, which he arranged with great care on the table, a curiously practical and unromantic design.

'They came from the Bodleian Library,' he said, puffing his chest out as he admired his work. 'In Oxford.' When neither of them reacted, he pouted. He seemed to be waiting for something else and, a little belatedly, Izzy realised he wanted her to sit down. She slipped into the chair and the Story-teller placed a book in front of her, nestling it carefully, like a mother settling a baby.

Waves of cold emanated from the tome. It was over a foot long and half a foot wide. The cover was nondescript beige leather and something in her recoiled from it. There was a dark circle in one corner, like a mole.

It was human skin. She knew it was.

She didn't want to touch it, but she was going to have to.

'Who was it?' she asked, her voice emerging as a faint whisper.

The Storyteller gave her a look both puzzled and irritated. 'Who?'

'The cover. Whose skin is it?'

'Skin?' asked Jinx.

Izzy spared him a glance. He looked concerned now. 'It's human skin,' she told him. He curled his upper lip in distaste, but didn't otherwise react. He was probably relieved it wasn't fae. Just a human. Disposable.

'How do you know?'

'I've been working with Dad. Studying. Learning. I know all sorts of things.' His frown deepened as he considered her. Well, she wasn't about to enlighten him any further. 'What? Did you think I just sat around moping in my room for weeks on end because you buggered off?'

Jinx turned his death-glare on the Storyteller. 'Whose skin was it?'

'I don't know his name. No one does. All magic has a price, and great magic comes with a great price. I'm sure he knew that.'

Jinx circled the table, staring at the book. Maybe he'd wanted to go first. Maybe he didn't like what he was hearing.

Tough shit, Cú Sídhe, Izzy thought. Learn to use a freaking telephone and make some plans with people once in a while.

'The book will show you all you need to know,' said the Storyteller, clearly bored of their personal drama. 'And it will take the agreed payment.'

'My father—'

'Didn't do this. Not to worry. Your father knows all about the book. Didn't he bring you here? Don't be afraid.'

Afraid? She bristled. The fact that she was indeed suddenly afraid just made it worse.

'It will work for you,' said the Storyteller, her voice strangely hypnotic. 'Magic reacts to your mixed blood. Stirs it up, feeds on it and feeds it. It likes you, Isabel Gregory. And prices, memories or whatever, have to be paid.'

She understood that. She'd learned it well in the past few months.

The information she needed was so important, what was one memory? Dad hadn't told her enough. God, did Dad even know? He must have.

So why hadn't he done it himself?

What was one memory?

She fixed her gaze on the Storyteller. 'I understand. How do I begin?'

'Just open the book and find the page. Think of your question. An answer will come.'

Izzy closed her eyes, trying to centre herself. This kind of thing was what being Grigori was all about. She knew that now. She'd had enough long, serious conversations with Dad and Gran to know that now, to understand the implications. She wasn't a child anymore. She had responsibilities in the wider world. And if she wouldn't do it, who would?

Well, Jinx for one.

It wasn't like she could pick up the book and run. Jinx would probably stop her if she tried, especially if he was here for it as well. Why had Silver sent him? What questions did she have to which Jinx could find the answers? Was he really trying to find out the same things as she was?

She ought to ask him, but couldn't bring herself to do it. She had other matters to attend to, and couldn't let an ex-not-really-boyfriend get in her way.

Grigori watched the borders of the worlds, keeping the peace and solving the problems that arose. Problems like a missing angel. She needed to find out about Haniel, what had become of him. The angels were watching Dad too closely.

They couldn't afford the angels finding out about this book. That much Dad had made perfectly clear.

'Izzy?' Jinx's voice was low and gentle. It made a shiver snake its way up her spine, every hair on her skin prickling in a way that wasn't wholly unpleasant. It was warm, soft, like half melted chocolate. There might even have been a hint of affection in the word and that … that was dangerous.

She opened her eyes and fixed him with the hardest glare imaginable.

'What?'

'You don't have to do this. You shouldn't be doing this.'

So why was he here? If he had been prepared to do it, why shouldn't she? His double standards were infuriating.

'Don't tell me what I should or shouldn't do, Jinx. It never ends well.'

To her surprised annoyance, he grinned, that unexpected, fascinating grin that always left her disarmed. The words he said next sounded like an admonishment or even an admission.

'What are you trying to prove?'

She bristled. 'Do I need to *prove* something now?'

'That's not what I meant, and you know it. Why are you here? What are you after?'

She relented, just a little. 'There's a missing angel. Haniel, remember him?'

To her surprise, Jinx flinched; she didn't blame him, though. Haniel had not been kind to him.

'How long has he been missing?'

'A couple of days. A week? Who knows? The angels told us sweet eff all.'

'Then they're more forthcoming with you than anyone else.'

'With my dad, anyway. They seem to think I'm unclean, as if something I've come into contact with has tainted me.'

A shadow passed over his eyes and he looked hurriedly away. Izzy cursed herself. That hadn't been what she meant. Not him, not what they had once had. The angels might think that, but she didn't. She never managed to say the right thing with him. For a moment it had been fine, almost pleasant to talk to him. Then she just had to mess it all up again.

He cleared his throat. 'So you think the book will tell you where the angel is?'

'That's what Dad thinks, but he didn't want the angels to know about this, about the book.'

The book was a thing of Jinx's world, his people. Not angels or demons, not even humans, though it wore the skin of the human who'd made it. Or who it had been made out of.

'What about you?' she asked. 'Why are you here?'

'Me? Oh, I just came in to pick something up for Silver.'

He lied so very easily. She almost believed him, except she had sworn never to trust him again. But she saw the way he looked at the book, as if he wanted it just as badly as she did.

'So why are you still here?'

She meant it to hurt, and it did. He covered it well, but she saw the barb strike him. Revelled in it a little, even though her heart twisted at the flash of pain on his face.

'Izzy, I—' For a moment she thought he might break down, confess his transgressions and beg her forgiveness. She'd hear the perfect reason why he'd abandoned her, and he'd be so sorry. It had been such a mistake, and he didn't deserve—

She shook off the fae glamour before it could seize her rational mind and make her believe things that weren't true. How dare he? How could he?

The Storyteller spoke again, interrupting them before Izzy could tell Jinx in no uncertain terms what she thought of him, her tone sharp with impatience. 'Just concentrate on your question.'

'And how will I know what memory the book will take?'

The old fae grinned. 'Oh, you won't. But don't worry about it. You won't miss it.'

That was kind of what she was afraid of, though she would never admit it in front of Jinx.

Izzy closed her eyes and inhaled deeply. She fixed thoughts

of the angel Haniel and the anger of the other angels, of the idea that he was missing or lost, of all the terrible things that could have happened to him, of all the things she could imagine. And she looked down at the book, opening it randomly on a page and spreading it wide on the foam supports.

The pages crackled and sparked beneath her fingers. They were blank, entirely blank. She bit back a curse and blinked, trying to hold on to her question while at the same moment she saw ...

Her silver necklace arching out over the water, flashing as it caught the sunlight, like a lure for a fish. And the merrows, their hungry mouths and cunning eyes, darted after it, tearing at each other in their efforts to reach it first.

Something dropped onto the paper. A teardrop. Another splashed down from Izzy's wide eyes and spread out, turning the page black as she watched it.

She watched as the inky tendrils rushed out, filling the space with the blackest of night, with the stars overhead cold and uncaring. A fierce wind blew in from the sea, from the cold and endless sea. Izzy staggered back, but kept her mind fixed on the missing angel. She had to find him. That was all that mattered. She had to find him.

With a sob, Izzy fell to her knees. Stones bit into her knees but it didn't matter. Not now. She knew this place. She was sure of it. She had walked these paths with Dad, during their many Sunday afternoon rambles. Here and all the hills on the edges of the city. Never at night, perhaps, but she knew where she was.

The lights of Dublin, like the stars overhead, blazed too bright in the night, as cold as the wind. She could make out the chimneys of the Pigeon House, the broad sweep of Sandymount and the spindly fingers of Dun Laoghaire harbour stretching out towards her. Dalkey Island was a black void in the sea, and behind it the hill rose lightless and dark, Brí's home hidden and silent. In the far-off distance, Bray Head lifted like a leviathan from the sea, black and terrible, the Sugarloaf its dorsal fin. The boundaries of her world, all she knew. The lights and the darkness, gorse and heather, stone upon stone, the arctic wind and the sobbing cries of a lost angel.

The angel lay in the remains of the ruined cairn that covered the summit of Shielmartin Hill, sprawled helpless like a turtle on its back, his wings broken.

Holly gutted him, her blows swift and savage, her mind absorbed in her work, heedless of the blood that soaked her clothes. As Izzy looked on in horror, Holly ripped something out of him, something bright and glowing, a ball of white fire. She lifted it to the sky with her blood-drenched hand and then flung it down, plunging it into the earth beneath them.

She looked up, teeth bared, her eyes fixed on the hills and mountains to the south, across the bay. She was smiling. Even as blood splattered her face, she was smiling.

The ground shook, trembled, and roared, the rocks and stones grinding against each other, crying out in rage.

And a light, bright and terrible, broke free, engulfing Holly in blinding flames. She spread her arms wide, gathering the light into her hands, forcing it into a concentrated space, and stretching it out like a glowing wire that wriggled between her fingers until she brought it under control. Light reflected up into her face, made her eyes glow. Izzy screamed and hands seized her, strong, warm and wonderfully real hands.

'Talk to me. Izzy, are you okay? Izzy?'

It was Jinx. Her Jinx. He held her against his chest and she burrowed her hands into his clothes, tried to pull him even closer though that was impossible.

'It was Holly.' She finally managed to force the words from her mouth and Jinx froze, every muscle tightening beneath his taut skin. 'It was Holly. Oh my God … she … she … she's back. Somehow. Holly did it. She killed him. And she … she did something with his spark. I think it was his spark. She woke something up, something terrible. She made a thing … like a … a wire that glowed. And moved.'

He stiffened, but he didn't let go.

'Izzy, are you okay? Do you know your name?'

She shook him off and instantly regretted it as she wobbled on her feet. She felt cold. So desperately cold, as if she could never be warm again now she had made him let her go, as if he was the only source of warmth left in the world.

'Of course I know my name, and yours, Jinx.' She drew in a deep breath, which turned ragged and uncomfortable. The memory of the sea lingered, the rocks near Sandycove and the

Forty Foot, a flash of silver sailing out over the waves. Then it was gone.

The angel's despair filled her, his impotent rage. His terror.

Holly was back.

'The Fear aren't the only thing Holly let out,' she whispered. 'I think … I think … there's more.'

Jinx's hand closed on her arm, under her elbow. 'We should leave,' he said. 'Find your father and tell him.'

'It looked like Howth, I think. I could see the bay. And Bray Head. Up on Shielmartin Hill, I think. There's an old cairn. Dad said most of the summit was made up of an old cairn. Do you know what's buried up there, Jinx?'

'No,' he replied. 'But we'll find out.' That was what she was afraid of — that they'd find out far too soon, and in far too visceral a way.

'Jinx by Jasper …' The Storyteller sang his name in a teasing, musical way that couldn't mean anything good. 'You had questions too.'

'They don't matter.' He all but snarled the words.

'Oh, but I think they do.' She smiled, her eyes as hard as the stones scattered around them. 'As that was *so* entertaining, I'll give you some advice for free. That thing, around your neck? That's a noose. And it's going to tighten. Two more times.'

'And then what?' Jinx couldn't hide the shake in his voice. Izzy closed her hand against his, where it still held her arm gently. He felt so cold.

The Storyteller shrugged. 'Well that's a story for another

time. Isn't it?'

Jinx turned away abruptly.

'Farewell, little Grigori,' said the Storyteller. 'You have been most entertaining. Both of you.' She was smiling now, her eyes glittering with power. With Izzy's memory no doubt and those of everyone else she'd fed off. The book was her touchstone. It had to be. Izzy heaved in a breath, suddenly afraid she had done something really stupid. What would Dad say? Had he actually intended to let her do that? Oh God, she should have checked first. Somehow.

The Storyteller took Grim's arm while the others reverently carried the book back into the darkness of her hollow, and tidied away the table and chairs. But the Storyteller stayed, her eyes lingering on Jinx in a far from comforting way.

'Remarkable creatures, Cú Sídhe,' she murmured. 'They're about the only fae who mate for life, did you know that? But not our only shape-shifters. And the rest of them are not so faithful.'

CHAPTER TEN

What Is Lost

Jinx said nothing as he followed Izzy down the long, dark corridor, lit from below, which cast eerie shadows up onto the bronzed walls and roof. She wasn't talking and neither was he, although he was aware from the tightness across her shoulders and the way she held her arms that she was barely keeping it together now. Only the thought of finding her father again was keeping her going. Jinx hoped David Gregory was indeed waiting for them at the door back to the human world, or at least just beyond it. Not that he relished the thought of seeing her father again. It was all just too complicated.

And Izzy would never understand.

A noose around his neck, the glowing ember deep inside ... What had Osprey done to him? And at Holly's command. Holly, who was killing angels on hilltops, in sacred, forbidden places. Of course, she had always killed angels. It was her

127

favourite pastime, her hobby, but she'd never done more with their sparks than feed her touchstone, increase her own magic. She hadn't changed that much, so what was she doing now? What was she doing to him? He didn't know what was buried under any of Howth's hills, but he felt certain something was. Something terrible. And if what Izzy said was right, Holly had used Haniel's death to make the thing around his neck. His first noose. The first of three.

Holly was back. And he was lost.

'Which way?' Izzy asked, her voice wavering a little.

'Straight on,' he said and reached out. He didn't make contact, no matter how much he wanted to, but his hand barely brushed the material of her shirt. He didn't think she even noticed. It was enough. It had to be. He had to focus on here and now, on getting out. 'The tunnel bends a bit, but we don't turn off this path.'

To do so would mean being lost in the Storyteller's domain and that wouldn't be wise.

She set off again, without so much as a glance back at him. If Silver knew she was here, he'd be in so much trouble. If she knew he was anywhere near Izzy …

Everyone said he and Izzy should keep away from each other. Fate seemed to have other ideas.

Light seeped through the edges of the door that came into view. Izzy stopped, staring at it as if in accusation, but she didn't turn the handle.

'What is it?' he asked, coming to a halt behind her, as close as he dared.

'I … I don't know what memory I lost. It could be something important. What if it's my mum's face or something about Mari? What if …'

Then she did look at him and it was so much worse. Her eyes seemed huge in the darkness, pleading. Jinx took her hands in his without thinking and pulled her into his embrace.

'It will be okay, Izzy,' he whispered.

A brief, bitter smile flickered over her lips. 'People say that to me a lot. They're not often right.'

He couldn't help but laugh. 'Stop getting into trouble then.'

'Easier said than done.'

She leaned forward, rested her head on his chest and her breath evened out. 'I missed you.' The words were a whisper, a sigh, but he knew they were real and that she had really said them. Something hard and unyielding inside him melted. Just a little.

'I missed you too.'

'What happened? Why did you—?'

She was so close, so tempting. He wanted to lower his mouth to hers, to kiss her. He shouldn't be here, with her like this. He shouldn't be so close. But he couldn't move away. 'I had no choice. You belong in your world and I in mine.'

'No. I'm half fae, half Grigori.'

He had to fight for breath. 'That's not what I mean.'

'At least tell me why.'

'I can't.' That at least was true. The words would probably

choke him if he tried to say them. And she'd probably choke him again a second later for ever agreeing to abide by them. He sighed. It was all too late now. 'Your father will be waiting.'

'My father. Right.'

Was that suspicion? Izzy wasn't stupid and they always underestimated her. But instead of pursuing it further, she pulled away from him and opened the door. They walked through the shimmer of the portal and found themselves stepping into a bright open-plan café and shop, the walls wood-lined like a cabin. There were mugs, postcards, cuddly toy leprechauns and a host of books to buy too. And David Gregory sat at a table with a blue and white striped mug full of tea in his hand. There was no one else to be seen.

When he saw Jinx with Izzy, he got to his feet, his expression instantly suspicious.

'What are you doing here?'

Checking that there was no one else around, Jinx sketched a hurried bow. Formal. Keep it formal. It was his only defence. 'Grigori, it is an honour ...'

'I asked a question. Izzy, come over here. Are you hurt? Did anything go wrong?'

'Wrong?' asked Izzy. 'What could possibly have gone wrong with a matriarch picking through my memories for a juicy morsel, Dad?'

'She *what*?' He seized his daughter, pulling her into his arms and studying her face. 'Are you okay? What do you remember? Izzy? What did she do?'

Irritated, Izzy pushed herself free. 'I'm fine. Just fine. I don't know what she took, but it can't have been that big a deal as I don't know what's missing. Okay? I'm fine. I remember you, and Mum, and Jinx—'

David Gregory looked up, his eyes blazing, and Jinx wanted to drop through the ground. Pride made him put on his most arrogant face instead. He was still Silver's emissary. That had to count for something, even with the Grigori. 'Which doesn't explain why *you* are here?' Izzy's father said.

'Silver sent me. To investigate why the Fear are abroad. And now we have an answer. Holly.'

'Holly? But she was defeated. Silver drove her out.'

'It seems we were wrong. She has come back. And she is far from defeated.' The words hung like stones around his neck. David Gregory stared at him, unwilling or unable to believe the truth. That didn't make it less true though. Jinx knew that.

'Why would Holly come back to release the Fear?'

'It isn't the Fear she's after, Dad,' said Izzy. 'Or at least not just the Fear. She killed Haniel on the summit of Shielmartin Hill, on Howth. She's after something else. It was a ritual and she made something, but it wasn't the be-all and end-all. I know it.'

'She's always after something else,' said Jinx. 'And mostly it's revenge. As to why she'd kill an angel there ... I need to find out more. I'm just not sure where to go for an answer.'

'Would Silver know?' David Gregory asked.

'She might. Or Brí. If they chose to tell me. The Storyteller certainly didn't want to share. She seemed to find it all hilarious.'

'She would. She's safe locked inside her fortress.' Izzy's father cursed and she looked at him in surprise. 'I never should have left you in there. She tricked me and I was a fool. She said she'd just ask you a question as the fee.'

'Well, the question was, "*Do you want to read my book and lose a memory?*" wasn't it? That's a question.' Izzy's voice sounded like a harsh and distorted version of itself, as if she was forcing herself not to scream in his face

David Gregory looked furious. 'I'll deal with her later. And she won't think herself so bloody clever then.'

Jinx suddenly didn't envy the Storyteller one bit. The wrath of a Grigori was not something to be taken lightly. This one least of all.

Izzy opened her mouth to say something else when a rumble of thunder broke the air. The ground seemed to vibrate, the walls humming, and with a silent concussion of air, the room filled with angels.

The Grigori moved before Jinx or Izzy could react, pushing them both behind him and standing there like a human shield, his arms spread wide.

'Dad!' Izzy screamed.

'Get her out of here, Jinx,' was all he said in reply, never looking away from this sudden threat. 'Get her out of here now.'

'We must talk, Grigori,' intoned a golden-haired angel with

a song of menace in his voice. Jinx quailed at the sound. All he wanted to do was drop to the floor and hide. But Izzy was here, and her father clearly thought she was in danger. Or at least, didn't want to take the risk.

Izzy knew what had happened to Haniel. And that was information the angels wanted. They wouldn't ask nicely.

Jinx grabbed her arm and before she could protest, he ran, dragging her with him. The door outside rattled and banged on its hinges, and Jinx ploughed through the opening, Izzy on his heels. They plunged into the night-time world of Dublin city centre and didn't look back.

'Ghosts,' said Dylan, his fingers strumming the strings of the guitar. 'Tell me about ghosts then.'

Silver shook her head, her hair whispering over her shoulders as she moved. 'Ghosts are the provision of Donn, the Lord of the Dead. Play that chord progression again. I liked that.'

He obliged, concentrating on the music for the moment. It was working at last. But then it always worked best when she was with him. 'This?' He hummed along with it, the melody one that had been haunting him all day.

Like Mari's face. Like Mari standing outside the gates.

'Yes, that.' She smiled. 'Do you have lyrics yet?'

'No. And you're changing the subject. Why would I have seen her?'

'You ... you don't know that you really did. We all see things, Dylan.'

He glared at her. 'Yes. And they're usually real around here. I know what I saw. Please, Silver. Tell me.'

'I can't tell you if she was real. If you believe it ... well, then why not? Donn is Lord of the Dead, the keeper of the thresholds and the places between. He doesn't really socialise with the rest of us. Not exactly a partygoer if you know what I mean. Play the other one again. Have you tried to combine the two?'

The music filled the room again, reverberating off the ceiling and returning back down to them again, melody upon melody. Silver closed her eyes as it swept over her and he couldn't tear his eyes off her face. When he finished, she sighed.

'I think that's the best so far. Although I said that about the last two. What about the gig on Halloween night?'

'I don't know. We're just the support act.'

'A performance is a performance, Dylan,' she told him gravely. 'Support or not, an artist must always give their all.'

'The guys want me to play some of my stuff.' Not quite true. They wanted to drop all the covers and just do his music. But he wasn't sure.

'You should. I know a scout who works out of the club. I'll make sure he's there. No pressure. But do play that.'

No pressure. He rolled his eyes and she nudged him, silently enjoying his discomfort.

'Maybe it's just for you.'

Music, he had learned, was the one sure and certain way to get through to Silver. Play the right music and it acted on her like an opiate. It wouldn't make her do anything she didn't want to do, but it certainly improved her mood and made her more likely to listen to him. They were still learning how they could work with each other, the way they fitted together now, her magic in his flesh, what that meant.

'You've become quite the charmer, haven't you? Why?'

'Because I needed to know about Mari's ghost and what might have ... I know she was real. I just know it.'

'And what do you need?'

'I need ...' He put his guitar aside and leaned forward. 'How do I see her again?'

The amusement drained out of her face. 'We don't even need to talk about that. The living have no business with the dead. None.'

'Silver ...'

'No. It's too dangerous. Donn doesn't play games, he doesn't like visitors and he doesn't let anyone who strays into his realm out again. Not without a price.'

The fae always wanted something. There was always a price. Dylan knew that better than anyone. He had already paid the price. His gaze lowered to his hands resting on the guitar strings, to the light that danced beneath his skin like fireflies in the dim surroundings. He'd almost died. He'd been funda-mentally changed.

'What price?'

135

She leaned back, stretching out her legs and wiggling her bare toes in a decidedly distracting motion. 'Too high a price, I'm sure. Play again for me, Dylan. Please.'

Please? He wasn't used to hearing words like that. But her hand touched his and the light beneath his skin started dancing again. He could feel the music welling up inside him and he could barely contain it.

'Silver, why would Mari come back?'

'Maybe she has unfinished business. Maybe she has a reason to be unhappy. And maybe she wants answers of her own. Or perhaps she just wants to see you again, to hear you play. Your music is magical now. Perhaps it called her. Now please,' she leaned in against him, her body almost purring in the same vibrations that underpinned her voice. 'Play for me again. I want to hear it all.'

'You miss it, don't you?' he asked softly and her eyes opened, thin glowing slits.

'What?'

'Your voice. Having your voice as your power.'

'I have other powers … But yes. I miss my voice. I'd give *anything* to have it back.' It was the way she said 'anything' – the deep-seated need and desire – that made him really believe it. And that wasn't a comforting thought.

CHAPTER ELEVEN

Ghosts in the Fog

They sprinted down Abbey Street, along the side of the tram lines, trying not to look back, praying that no one was following. Izzy's chest felt tight and horrible, the same awful fear that had nearly crushed her into the ground when her father had been in the coma. Now he was in danger again, in terrible danger, because how could he hold off angels, of all things? Even him. He might be the Grigori, but so was she and that didn't seem to help.

Jinx held her hand in an iron grip. She probably couldn't have pulled free if she wanted to. But she didn't want to. He was the only thing real and strong around her, and she held on to him, as if he could keep her strong, keep her running. She just wanted to fall, to let the ground hit her like one of the silver trams that slid alongside them. She wanted to drop to the ground, curl into a ball and never move again. But she couldn't.

Jinx swung around the corner onto Capel Street and then again at the bookies, down by the old markets, red brick fronts and Victorian facades.

'It's not far,' the Cú Sídhe yelled. He didn't even sound out of breath, but she was already gasping. 'Just keep going!'

And suddenly she knew where he was heading. In one sense it was the last place she wanted to go, but where else was there? The Market might protect them from the angels. They couldn't enter there, could they? Though open to all on the horizontal plane, there were restrictions. There were rules to be observed. The Aes Sídhe's builders had been masters of their craft, physically and magically, and they had excluded those who might be enemies. It was a Sídhe place. It was a hollow and protected under the Grand Compact.

And everything revolved around that. Gran could quote the thing. Dad could too, but didn't bother. Izzy only wished she'd taken the time to learn it herself, but it had seemed so dull and boring at the time. Now she wished she'd made the effort.

Would it protect Dad though? Would it protect *him* from angels? He wasn't in a hollow, although the Storyteller's domain was right beside him. The shop stood outside it in her world. And she had left Dad there on his own.

'Jinx, I have to go back to him. What if he needs me?'

'They'll use you to get to him. He told me to get you away and that's what I'm doing. Now.'

Always obedient, she thought bitterly. *Always the good dog.*

They crossed the wider street in front of the Bar Council

138

building and slipped down the side where the road narrowed again and the grey stone walls loomed up over them, harsh and unforgiving. The streetlights flickered as they ran along the side of the Jameson distillery, and as they reached the end, flared to blinding incandescence.

'They're coming,' Jinx shouted.

But it wasn't the angels. Izzy stumbled, trying to stop. Fog tumbled out of nowhere, swirling through the air and cutting off everything ahead and behind them. Like the bathroom at school. And in that terrible fog there were figures forming. No, not figures, shadows made of mist.

The Fear rose all around the two of them as they faltered and stopped, back to back, trying to circle, to see it all at once, but their eyes couldn't penetrate the fog. Terror swept over Izzy, terror that made her stomach knot and her legs seize up. Jinx gasped out a curse, and his grip on her loosened. He faced the main group of Fear full on and dropped to his knees, staring at them, his mouth open.

The Fear bore down on them like a wave of fog. They materialised out of the miasma, laughing, their hands clawed, their eyes hungry, their teeth so sharp. Lightning leaped between them, sparkled in their eyes. Their power growing, fed by the terror rising in Izzy and Jinx.

What had Dad said? The Sídhe rhyme … *When the fog is dense and thick, when the whispers are all you hear* … There ought to be more. Everything she knew about poetry said there should be more, but Dad had never said it.

Izzy fumbled in her bag, tearing it open and digging in it for the knife. It was her only defence against the fae. Maybe it would work on the Fear too — they were still fae, weren't they? Or the ghosts of fae — but she had to do something. It made her strong, made her confident. It slipped into her hand as if it belonged there. Looking up, she saw they were almost at Jinx, almost there. She did the only thing she could think of and screamed his name. 'Jinx, change!' And she hurled the knife at their attackers.

Jinx shuddered, quivered and transformed. In a moment he flowed from one form to another and the knife sailed over his head, spinning in the air.

But there was nothing for it to hit on the other side. The Fear flowed around it, laughing as they did so, their bodies lithe and supple, made of mist. The knife clattered onto the stones. Useless.

The great green and black Cú Sídhe scraped steel-sharp claws across the road surface. His fur stood in hackles and he snarled at the figures dancing on air towards them. Izzy tried to shuffle back and came up against a wall. Nowhere to go. Rubbing her shaking hands together, she tried to conjure fire as she had in the school, but nothing would come. She swore and tried again while they slowly drove Jinx back towards her. Even in hound form, their fear infected him. One touch and he'd be lost.

One touch. And they'd be inside his head.

Just as they'd been in hers.

A single member of the Fear horde stepped forward and Jinx snapped at him, teeth closing on teeth as the creature flowed away, parted like fog, and then reformed, seizing the scruff of his neck. It brought him down with a yelp of rage and terror, pinning him to the ground, and raised its long fingered hand.

'*Well, Daughter of Míl? Is it time yet? No, not yet …*'

'Let him go,' she whispered, dredging her voice from the depths of her.

'*Is he yours? Then I'll take him. I'll take them all. All that is yours should be mine. You should be mine … But he's already marked, already another's. Don't you see it?*'

'Who are you? What do you want?'

'*Want?*' He laughed and dropped the Cú Sídhe. Jinx thudded to the ground as the ghostly figure swept over him. The features reformed, resolving to a handsome man, his eyes glowing an eerie green. Strongly pronounced cheekbones defined his face, and his mouth curved in a strangely sensitive way. But the eyes told her all she had to know. Cruel, heartless eyes. '*I want what I am owed, what I was promised. I am the king of my people. And I was promised much. I was cheated.*' He reached out to her, his hands stretched out towards her like those of a skeleton, reaching for her. '*But here you are now.*'

'Leave me alone.'

'*You will be mine, Daughter of Míl. By the cross on the head, by hellfire at Samhain. You were promised.*'

'No, I wasn't.'

'*Well, then* …' He stopped, turned back to Jinx's still form. '*I'll take another tribute instead. For now. If you don't come, I'll take them all.*'

'No! Let him go!' Izzy didn't know where her voice came from, but it shook the air. She felt the magic in the air all around them and fed on it. Flames lit up her fingers and she hurled the fire towards them. Suddenly energised, she lunged forward, throwing her other arm around Jinx. 'Get up and run. Please, please, please, get up and run!'

He staggered to all fours and they took off again, the hound leaping alongside her sprint. She only paused for a second, ducking down even as she moved to snatch the knife from the ground.

They skidded into the plaza at Smithfield, moving on blind instinct, running because there was only one place they could run from here and they needed to make it or die. Together, they plunged into the gateway to the Market, tumbling as they did so, skidding down the steep incline on feet that could barely keep up with their forward momentum.

Nothing followed. There wasn't a sound but their laboured breathing. Jinx groaned as he transformed back to Aes Sídhe.

'So they are real,' he said, his voice hoarse as if it grated on his throat.

'Too real,' she agreed. 'Are you okay?'

'I think so. I've never encountered anything so …' He shivered, not from the cold, though he'd left his clothes behind him. Something he only just seemed to realise now. 'Feck it, I

142

loved that shirt.'

Izzy managed a smile, even as her face burned. 'You can get another.'

'Yeah. I have a collection.' He nodded to an alcove a little further down the corridor. 'I usually leave a change there. Just in case.'

She couldn't tell him what the king had said. Or how close Jinx had come to being taken by them. Promised? What did he mean by promised? Promised by who?

By the cross on the head, by hellfire at Samhain. You were promised.

Instead, she turned it all aside with a joke. 'Is streaking becoming a habit?'

Jinx grinned at her then, a wild and dangerous grin that made her breath hitch in her throat, himself again. 'You could say that. I'm quite the spectacle some days. Even get fan mail.'

She tried to smile back, return the grin, but her mouth wouldn't work properly. Holly was back, the Fear were following them. She needed to let Dad know. She needed help.

And where was she going to get it?

She had no choice now but to make her way like a beggar into the Market, to rely on Silver.

And Jinx.

CHAPTER TWELVE

Silver's Market

The Market heaved with all varieties of fae life. Jinx was used to that, had known it all his life. With its cruel former mistress Holly gone, a new vitality had seized it, with an added element of lawlessness and abandon that set all his nerves on edge. Music rang out, echoing off the bronze domed roof, and the walls reverberated back with the bell-like acoustics. There were dancers and acrobats, jugglers and fire-eaters. From the moment they stepped through the entrance, he could tell that Izzy was distracted. So much to look at, so much to see. Or maybe she was just mulling over how close they'd come to falling victim to the Fear.

How close he'd come. He'd be dead now if it wasn't for her. Dead from the terrors they could plant in his head. Dead from the cold that came with them. Dead from fright.

He had to tell Silver. He ought to have kept running, stayed in hound shape and torn his way through the Market until he reached Silver.

But he couldn't leave Izzy.

Things had changed since they'd been together last. She seemed so much more confident, but he wondered how much of that was for his benefit. Or at least to protect herself from him, from letting herself trust him again. He couldn't blame her for that.

She'd spoken to the leader of that ghostly band. What they'd said he couldn't make out, but he didn't like it. Now she'd gone quiet. Far too quiet. It didn't do to dwell on the things some people said, especially not beings like that. But he knew Izzy was mulling the words over and over. She couldn't let them go.

Izzy wasn't the only thing that had changed. The Market seemed different now. Vulnerable. If the Fear came rampaging through here, what would stop them? Jinx could sense the vibrant atmosphere, the wild joy of freedom, the feeling that at any moment anything might happen, for good or ill. The Market was more than a little wild, as if infected with that older magic, devoid of the Sídhe hierarchy. It was the same thing that made him get into the fights, brawling like some medieval bear in a pit. But with Izzy here, it made him uncomfortable. Under Holly, the market had been safe enough, if you knew how to walk its ways and where to tread, if you were not unwary. Only its mistress stood above its laws. No one else.

Silver had defeated Holly, helped by Izzy, Jinx and the other Cú Sídhe, but she hadn't claimed the Market as her own.

In truth – though Jinx hated to say it of the Sídhe who had been his only friend through all the long years when he had been Holly's slave, his aunt, the beloved sister of his mother – Silver was struggling, and without a matriarch, the Market was running out of control.

He saw faces watching him as he and Izzy passed, faces with a schooled indifference that was anything but. They were beautiful and terrible, those faces. Some haunted his nightmares. But none so much as Holly's had.

She was back. The very thought made his chest tighten to the point of pain. Holly was back and she had a plan. A plan that included him. She had set loose the Fear. She didn't do anything without reason.

Izzy's hand tightened in his. Her touch alone kept him grounded, kept him from slipping into his hound-form and fleeing for safety. From the Fear. Even though they weren't here now, couldn't enter the hollow as far as he knew, or wouldn't, choosing to evade discovery instead for as long as possible. Even without their presence, their effect on him lingered like a hangover. He didn't like it.

When Izzy had taken his hand, he didn't know. He was just grateful that she had, and that she had yet to let go.

'Jinx.' She whispered his name, harsh with urgency. His instincts screamed alarm as he turned and saw her looking back behind them. Again.

At the end of the aisle stood two figures, identical in appearance, and dressed in perfectly matching black and white.

'Magpies.' The word was a hiss of disgust. He couldn't hide the relief though. He'd thought for a moment he'd been wrong, that the Fear had followed them down here, that at any moment they'd gorge themselves on the entire Market.

But it was just the Magpies. Checking up on him probably. It should never be a cause for comfort, but somehow it was. Because the alternative was just too terrible.

The Magpie brothers glanced at each other, sharing that strange unspoken communication, but they didn't move, just looked back at Jinx and Izzy as if willing them to approach, or as if their glares could hold the two of them there. It was a most uncomfortable gaze.

'We need to get away from them,' said Izzy on a single breath.

'They can't hurt us. Not here.' And wouldn't anyway. He was working for their boss. He couldn't tell her that. She'd never understand. Well, not working for him exactly. He was working for Silver. Now and always.

If only other people thought that. He could sense eyes on him, the other people of the Market, who would never trust him, who still saw him as Holly's through and through.

'They can hurt us *anywhere*.'

True enough now. The Magpie brothers were ruthless and cunning, experts at intimidation and pain. They served their master and their master wanted answers from him. They could hurt them, but they wouldn't. Not just yet.

'It's okay,' he said though he barely believed the lie himself. It wasn't okay. But they were safe for now.

Safer than outside.

'Sure,' she said, putting her head down and pushing forward through the crowd. 'Let's just find Silver and talk to her. We've got to tell her about Holly and the Fear. We've got to warn her.' She hung her head and muttered, so low she possibly thought he couldn't hear her. But fae hearing was more powerful than human, and Cú Sídhe hearing more powerful than all. 'I shouldn't even be here. Dad's going to flip.'

'He must have known we'd head here. It's the only safe place.'

She flinched, and gave him the death glare he knew too well. No, he wasn't meant to have heard that. 'I just hope he's okay. We shouldn't ... we shouldn't have left him.'

'And what would have happened had we stayed? They'd use you to get to him, if we're being optimistic. Or they'd just have a rummage through your mind and find out what Holly did.'

She ripped her hand free of his. 'God, you sound like Dad!'

A dark surge of anger speared up through him and burst in his brain, glittering and bright as a firework. He stiffened and fought the sudden urge to just walk away. Or worse, to turn on her. It was just for an instant, but it shocked him to silence, and was gone as soon as it appeared. Jinx forced himself to breathe. Like someone or something else lurked inside his skin, in the base of his mind. Burning bright.

She was staring at him, suspicion in her gaze. Had she sensed that burst of rage? He didn't know where it had come from, but it drained away just as quickly, dread taking its place. What had just happened?

He shrugged, trying to look nonchalant, spreading his hands out in front of her in what he hoped was a gesture of peace. 'He'll be okay, Izzy. They won't hurt the Grigori. Especially with the Fear loose and Holly killing angels. But they'll want to know everything and if they find out what she's done, what she could do ... I didn't live through the war in heaven, or our expulsion, but I've heard the stories. I've seen the ghosts in the eyes of those who did. No one can fight the angels.'

He didn't want to tell her any more, not about Holly and what she'd sent Osprey to do. He didn't want to dwell on the sensation that his mind and body belonged to her, that his life wasn't his own.

Silver raised her eyebrows to see Jinx with Izzy. He knew that look — surprise, yes, and displeasure, but also speculation. She could convey so much with just a look. So could her mother. But he didn't want to think of Holly. It made the line at his throat tighten. Jinx gave a respectful bow and Silver responded with a nod of her head. Izzy meanwhile bounded up the steps to Silver's private chamber, grinning broadly, and rushed by them both to hug Dylan.

Now it was Jinx's turn to glare. Whatever happened to *'stay out of their lives to keep them safe'*? Silver pursed her lips, chastened, and then rolled her eyes to the bronzed dome high above them. Apparently staying out of Dylan's life wasn't proving easy for her either.

Perhaps stubborn attracted stubborn.

'What are you doing here, Isabel Gregory?' Silver asked, her voice stern.

Izzy's smile faltered a little, but Dylan squeezed her hand. If it was anyone else – anyone – Jinx would have wanted to rip his arm off. The temptation lingered even though he knew he had relinquished all rights and demands on her. If he had ever really had any. Those were the wrong words to use around Izzy. Any rights were her own, not his. Any demands were met with strong resistance. He knew that and respected it. Other Sídhe would fight her just to prove her wrong. Jinx knew better. They would fail every time.

He'd given her up for her own safety and regretted it ever since.

'Lady Silver,' Izzy said, schooling her features and stance to formality. 'We need to talk in private. As Grigori, I offer my respect and my bond of peace while I stand within your hollow.'

Oh, she knew the words and the form all right. She'd been studying. Her father had drilled all the right words into her. But not the truth of it perhaps. He feared for her. Feared what this would do to her.

'Of course, Grigori,' Silver replied just as formally, though Jinx knew at once she was hiding her surprise. 'Come this way and take your ease.'

Once they were inside the inner chamber, Silver stopped by the door, handing out orders to those who attended her. Mainly orders of the *bugger-off-and-leave-us-alone* variety. They didn't look pleased. Eager ears wanted to hear what the Grigori's daughter had to say to the matriarch who would not be a matriarch.

Meanwhile Izzy stumbled to a halt, staring into the middle-distance, her eyes unfocused. She brought her hand up to her throat.

'What's wrong?' Jinx asked, instantly alarmed. The Fear had almost had them both. There could be repercussions, lingering complications.

'My necklace. Where is it?'

'Necklace?'

'Yes, the silver salmon pendant. Dad gave it to me.' She spun around, searching the ground, pulling at her clothes to see if it had caught in them.

'Izzy, you lost it months ago,' said Dylan, concern lining his face. 'Remember?'

She looked at him, blinked, her gaze sharpening. 'I lost it?'

The only thing that looked lost was Izzy herself.

'You gave up a memory to read the Storyteller's Book, Izzy,' Jinx said, as carefully as he could, unwilling to alarm her any further. 'Could that have been it?'

'I— oh, of course.' Her cheeks flushed red. 'Of course. That's what it took then? The memory of losing my necklace?' She sighed, but even that sounded shaky. 'That's not so bad, is it?'

Dylan looked bewildered, so that left Jinx to reassure her, something he wasn't particularly good at.

'I guess not. You gave the necklace up to save us from the merrows. Do you remember that?' Not so much 'us' as 'him'. The merrows would have dragged him into the water and torn him to shreds if she hadn't. Izzy might forget but he never would. She'd saved his life more times than she knew.

She frowned 'I remember the merrows. And I remember—' This time her cheeks flamed scarlet and she looked away from him. So she remembered him then, out of his mind with lust after encountering the merrows, lost in their magic, kissing her as if his life depended on it. Oh, yes, the Storyteller couldn't have taken that mortifying memory and spared him the shame. Just the necklace was gone. Just the way she'd saved them both. 'After,' she finished lamely. 'But not the necklace. Shit, that's strange. Like a whole section of my mind is blank.'

'And what did the memory buy you?' asked Silver. She settled herself on the chaise lounge in the centre of the opulent room, stretching out her long legs.

'Holly killed the angel Haniel. I don't know when exactly, although the night of the earthquake seems most likely. They were on top of Shielmartin Hill, in the broken cairn, on Howth Head. She took his spark and buried it and — and I think she woke something up, or started to.

She released the Fear.'

'Holly?' Silver stiffened all over and every trace of colour drained from her pale face. 'Holly's back.' She took a breath, a choked, desperate sound, and balled her hands into fists. 'But she wouldn't. She couldn't do that.'

Did she really doubt Holly's power? Or did she just wish it wasn't so? Was it just denial that made her say it?

'We've seen them,' Jinx interrupted, before Silver could continue. 'We barely escaped them. One of Amadán's people fell victim to them. And someone at Izzy's school too. Maybe more that we don't know about. I think they're on the hunt, Silver. I think that old story is very real.'

'What story?' asked Dylan.

'It's Sídhe mythology. Old stories.' Silver thrust her chin out, gritting her teeth, the picture of stubbornness.

'Silver,' Jinx chided. 'We *saw* them.'

'You don't understand. None of you do. The Fear weren't the only things imprisoned. The cairn on Shielmartin is only part of it, one weakened lock since it was broken down. And if they're out, if she has opened that first door … She knows where the others are. Everything else could get out as well.'

'Like what?' Jinx asked. 'Come on, Silver. What other imaginary things might get out?'

'The Shining Ones?' The words fell like stones from her mouth and Jinx sucked in a breath, his face pale as parchment.

'They… they *aren't* real.'

'The Fear *are* but not the Shining Ones? One story is but

153

not the other? Listen to yourself. Old stories can be true, Jinx, even if we wish they weren't. I know that. And the cairns held them in. But Holly would have to be … *insane* to do this.'

Insane? Didn't she know her own mother? If anything, 'insane' was an understatement.

'Silver,' he tried to make his voice calm, tried to make her believe him. 'It was Holly. She's come back. She's still powerful. She killed Haniel and took his power.'

'There was something else,' said Izzy, choosing her words with care. 'She made something – like a strip of metal, all silvery and blue. She took it with her.'

Silver frowned and her gaze fell on Jinx, so cold and hard that he couldn't help but squirm. 'Jinx?' He couldn't hide it from her. He couldn't hide anything from her and he'd known all along she would worm it from him. He lifted his chin and Silver scowled. 'Let me see.'

'See what?' Izzy asked, but Jinx couldn't look away from Silver now.

'It was Osprey. She gave it to him. He put it on me.' He stepped forward and knelt before Silver. She leaned in close examining his throat where, as he feared, a new line of tattoos had appeared, encircling his neck. A noose, the Storyteller had called it.

Silver touched his head with delicate fingers, brushed his hair back from his face as if he was still a child.

'Oh Jinx, that can't be good.'

'What is it?' Izzy asked again, impatiently this time. Jinx

looked up and Silver glared at her.

'Holly has ways of controlling Jinx, a very particular type of spell. This is one of them. A new one. A powerful one.'

'That's what the Storyteller meant?' Izzy asked, leaning in close to look as well. It made him uncomfortably aware of her. 'More tattoos?'

'What did she say to him?' Silver asked.

'I'm right here,' Jinx replied. 'I could tell you myself.'

'Not that we'd be sure you'd tell us everything,' said Silver. 'You have an appalling habit of trying to handle everything yourself. Izzy?'

'She said there would be two more and that each one would tighten it. She called it a noose.'

'Holly plans to kill him? No, I don't think so. She always valued him too highly for that.'

She did? That was news to Jinx. And worrying. Why? Why did she value him? Because Holly only valued things that were of use to her. And he didn't want to be of use to her.

'What's the Daughter of Míl?' asked Izzy.

Silver blinked at her, surprised. 'That would be you, although I haven't heard that name in many years.'

'The king of the Fear used it.'

'You met their king?' She went so still, all her attention focused on Izzy. 'You met Eochaid?'

'Yes. He said I was promised to him. What does that even mean?'

An awkward silence answered her, weighing on all of them

until Silver replied. 'That's something you need to ask your father. But Míl ... Míl was Grigori, like you. And he was the one who sealed Eochaid away. Only one of them could survive, if the Shining Ones were to be defeated. It's an old story, and not one for me to tell.' She sighed, the sound ragged, and sat forward. 'Jinx, call my messengers. We need to alert the Council and summon them. Immediately.'

A jangling tune interrupted Silver, silencing her and Izzy started. They all stared at Izzy as she flushed red.

'My phone.' She pulled it out of her pocket and answered the call, not caring who heard her relief. 'Dad! Are you – yes, yes fine. I'm in the Market – Yes.' She looked up, her eyes filling with doubt all of a sudden. 'Yes, Silver's here.'

There was a pause and then she held the slim phone out to Silver. 'He wants to talk to you.'

It didn't escape Jinx's notice that when Silver took the phone, her hand was shaking.

'Grigori,' she said. The deferential tone made Jinx uncomfortable, but he knew exactly why she used it. Even talking to David Gregory at a distance wasn't exactly easy. And Silver didn't like confrontation. 'Yes, we'll send her home at once. But I need to talk to you.' She spoke cautiously. 'I must call a meeting of the Council. Under the Grand Compact, I request that you join us.' She paused while Dad replied. Whatever he said, she didn't look happy. 'Of course. But – yes, Isabel can relate the details when she's back with you. My deepest respects.'

The Market was already peopled with diplomats and henchmen serving one of the council members. At least one of them, often more. They were each summoned and despatched with sealed letters, written in code despite the heavy wax seal the colour of blood. No fae trusted another completely.

And there was no one to act in such a way for the Grigori. No one but Izzy herself.

'Now we just wait to see if they will come,' Silver muttered, gazing across the now hushed and fearful Market. There was no hiding what they were doing. Not here. 'They have to.'

All of which left Izzy the unenviable task of telling her dad. It was too important to trust to a phone call. At least she knew he was okay. Not that he'd bothered to tell her that, or how he'd talked his way out of trouble. No, he'd see her at home and that was that.

Where she'd have to ask him to come to a fae stronghold and meet all the senior Aes Sídhe.

Jinx muttered something about needing to see someone before they left and, not having anything else to do, Izzy followed him, trying her best not to look like a stray puppy in search of a home. It didn't seem to bother him. In fact, he barely seemed to notice.

He walked through the Market with the air of someone on a quest, but headed for the fringes, those dark and ratty corners of the hollow where the stalls looked bleak, dirty and disreputable and the stall holders even worse.

'Don't say anything, okay?' he told her as they approached a stall staffed by a small red-haired fae dressed in a green hoodie, with the shiniest shoes Izzy had ever seen. 'He's a lep, and if they lose it there's hell to pay.'

'A lep? Do you mean a leprechaun?' She smiled. 'But aren't they ... I don't know ... lucky? Jolly?'

Jinx looked at her as if she'd never said anything so stupid in all the time he'd known her.

'You saw them at the museum, didn't you? Cudgel and his mob? Did they seem jolly? Look, ever seen a poltergeist?' She shook her head. 'Well, anyway, doesn't matter. He's way worse.'

The leprechaun scowled at them and proceeded to shove more things into a backpack.

'Where are you going?' asked Jinx.

'Puck's Castle,' he said. 'It's the only safe place. Something terrible is happening in this city and I don't want any part of it.'

'Oh, come on, Art,' Jinx began, but the leprechaun glared at him, then stared at Izzy, as if noticing her for the first time. He shook his head, blinking, and took a step back. Afraid. It was unmistakable.

'You need to stay away. I don't know what it is, but it feels wrong and it all centres on you. On the two of you, but mainly on you, Cú Sídhe. You're all about hollows, kith and kin, but we're not. My kind, I mean. We're solitaries, only tolerated because we're useful and do the jobs the mighty Aes Sídhe don't want to sully their hands with. When the shit hits the fan we're first against the wall. That goes for all the wanderers, the outsiders, the ones who don't belong. But listen, mate, the Cú Sídhe are usually next to get it.'

'But why Puck's Castle?'

'Don't you know anything? Puck's Castle? *Puck*? The Púca, Jinx, king of the wanderers, lord of wild magic. First among us? Hell's bells, Holly did a job and a half on you. Did she beat our stories from you? The Sídhe had their gods and we had ours. They're all gone, but they linger on. They can be called back. Sometimes. Some say they're just sleeping under the earth or in a hollow in the hills.'

'The Púca's a story.'

'Yeah,' said Art, zipping up the rucksack and swinging it over his shoulders. It was almost as big as he was, but didn't impede him in the slightest. 'And I'm off a bleedin' cereal packet. There's a lot of it about. Try to keep up, doggy.'

He pushed by Jinx.

'Hey!' Jinx caught him by the shoulder, stopping him.

'What? I've paid you all I owe you. My books are clear. No debts, Cú Sídhe.'

'I know.' He released the leprechaun and nodded to him. 'Just … take care, okay?'

It took Art by surprise. He stared for a moment, mouth hanging open. 'You too,' he said. 'Try to, anyway. Stay out of trouble, Jinx.'

And then Art was gone, lost in the milling crowd of the Market. Jinx stood there, almost looking bereft. If you didn't know he didn't have feelings, which Izzy did. Obviously. But he looked like he'd just lost his only friend. And perhaps he had.

'Jinx?' she said tentatively.

He turned sharply, his metallic eyes hard again.

'What?'

He hated it when she saw vulnerability in him. Izzy knew that, but it still hurt.

'I should go,' she said and Jinx took on that guilty, hunted look that made her squirm inside. This wasn't his fault. So why did he have to look like she was blaming him for something?

'I'll accompany you,' he said, all stiff and formal again.

'It's okay. I'm sure Dylan will come with me. He's heading home anyway.' They made their way back to Dylan and Silver in silence, Jinx mulling over Art's departure no doubt and Izzy wondering why his mood changed so quickly all the time. 'Dylan, ready to go?'

'Of course, whenever you're ready,' her friend replied willingly enough. 'Unless Silver—'

'No,' Silver interrupted sharply. Dylan looked devastated until Silver spoke again in a softer voice. 'You go home. And stay there. It's safer. Especially now. Jinx will go with you both. He has to see Izzy's father.'

'Fine,' Dylan replied. 'I'll be coming back with Izzy anyway. You need me here.'

'No, I don't.' But he only smiled at her. He was the source of her power. Of course she needed him when she was summoning the Council. 'Dylan … you must be careful. You know my people are not … not kind.'

'If one of your charming family tries to eat me again, I'm safer with you anyway, amn't I?'

Silver shook her head, more in defeat than denial. 'Take Jinx with you, Izzy, I beg of you. As a gesture of goodwill towards you and your father. He is my emissary. He shares my blood, my kinship, and he will keep you safe should anything untoward befall you on the way.'

Izzy didn't tell her about saving Jinx from the Fear. It didn't seem fair. Silver was adamant about this. And so formal it was getting worrying. What could she do but accept?

What would Dad say? He'd been freaked enough about Jinx turning up at the Leprechaun Museum. Who knew how he'd react to her bringing him to the house? Whatever was going on there, she'd need to get to the bottom of that as well. She wasn't looking forward to it. 'Well, okay then, I guess.'

Silver smiled. 'Please impress upon the Grigori how much my people need him right now. He must help us or the balance of all the realms will be in jeopardy.'

'I will,' Izzy promised solemnly, still not sure how this worked. But that was the role of the Grigori in a nutshell, to keep the balance of the realms. And she was, as everyone constantly reminded her, a Grigori now.

CHAPTER THIRTEEN

Ardat Lili

They left the eerily silent Market, its people huddled together whispering, their glances so very sharp. Those who hadn't already left like Art. Anyone who felt threatened had gone, and they were many. She saw the way they glared at Jinx and the way he struggled to ignore it. It had always been like this for him, or so he'd once told her, long ago. Now, all of a sudden, it seemed worse.

'Who's Osprey?' she asked softly.

'Holly's assassin.'

'And he didn't kill you?'

'No. Which could be worse for me.'

'What do you mean?' But he didn't answer.

There was no sign of the Fear outside, not now, just some drunken early Halloween revellers at the far end of the square, all face paint and fake blood. Jinx opened the gate to the Sídheways in Smithfield square. It was weak here, still damaged from Sorath's assault on it. The edges were frayed and ragged. On a sunny day it was almost visible to human eyes, an iridescent blemish on the surface of reality, like the little flecks of too-bright flashes in the field of vision before a migraine.

They entered the pathway between places and worlds, Jinx leading, Izzy and Dylan following close behind. He knew these paths, could navigate them without thinking about it. Izzy wondered if she got lost in here, would she ever find her way out again? And if she did how long would it take? The Sídheways twisted time, borrowing seconds here, hours there, and repaying them in complicated ways she couldn't make out.

Jinx was watching her again, glancing back at her from time to time, his gaze finding her whenever they paused. Izzy shivered because her Grigori tattoo's reaction to Jinx had always been warm and comforting. Never cold, never until now.

'What is it?' she asked.

He blinked, as if waking from a dream, and frowned at her. 'What?'

The cold faded away, replaced by the more familiar warm tingling.

'You were staring at me.'

'I was?' The frown turned puzzled and he had the good grace to look contrite. 'I didn't mean to.'

Oh, lovely. Such a compliment. Concern drained away to

irritation. Of course, he couldn't say sorry. None of them could. Except that he had, that night on the hill.

'It's rude to stare.'

He forced a grin. 'I'll remember that if you will.' That sudden teasing tone was going to get them both into trouble. But at least it sounded — and felt — like him again. Izzy wasn't sure what she had sensed looking out at her from the depths of his eyes, but for a moment it hadn't felt like Jinx at all.

The light bled and shimmered on the pathways. She could just catch snapshots and moments of the world beyond, snippets of sound amplified too loud, or delivered in a dead whisper. They stepped from place to place, an impossible route that made no sense, cobbles or grass one minute, concrete slabs and tarmac the next, while overhead strange birds reeled in the sky. The same sky turned black as night and stars shone far too brightly in complicated patterns. In the blink of an eye it turned grey as slate, the sky of a storm in the offing.

Izzy stumbled and Dylan caught her. She'd been looking up for too long and a wave of dizziness caught her.

'You okay?'

Jinx glared back at the two of them and opened the next gate, stepping out on to College Green. The clouds parted overhead, drenching the city in autumnal sunshine. He led them up the length of Grafton Street, making the crowds part before them by will alone.

'What was she talking about, Jinx?' Izzy asked, catching up with him outside Weir & Sons, 'What are the Shining Ones?'

164

'A fairytale,' he grunted. 'Made up to frighten children a long time ago. She can't really mean it.'

'She seemed dead serious,' Dylan said.

'I know,' the Cú Sídhe replied, doubt making his voice leaden. He reached up and rubbed his neck, where Silver had been examining the new tattoos. 'But it isn't possible.'

'What are they?' Izzy asked again. She was almost forced to run to keep up with his long strides now, he was so eager to be away from her.

She grabbed his arm to slow him down. He glared at her until she released him, but he didn't exactly pull away. Once he was free again he slowed his pace for them and finally, he started to talk.

'Old gods. Crazy gods. Killed and buried when mankind were still living in a garden paradise protected by angels. Well, not killed perhaps. Imprisoned. They were powerful and terrible, angels above angels. And after the war in heaven they went wild, feral. They knew nothing could stop them. And they didn't want to share with anyone, let alone each other. They only wanted to feed. Gods of chaos and darkness, gods of the void. They couldn't be controlled, only contained. No one could bear the thought of another war, so they were tricked, trapped. Because nothing could stand in their way except another god.'

'Like the Titans,' Izzy said.

'Every pantheon has them in some form. The first gods. Beautiful and terrible. We called them the Shining Ones and they were *our* gods. All the Sídhe loved and feared them. It hurt to look on them for too long. Their beauty burned the eyes from your head, the sanity from your mind. It was a time of blood and death. A time of horror outside of Eden. It's where we found ourselves. That's all I know.'

'She said the Grigori were there.'

'Yes. Or one of them was anyway, along with the Fear. That's the story. Eochaid and Míl … They were blood brothers, sworn to defend each other. But Eochaid became a monster, living off the terror of others. Míl had no choice but to overthrow him too. The Fear were imprisoned along with the monsters they'd fought against.'

'And now Holly has let them out.'

'So it seems.'

They turned into St Stephen's Green, walking by the duck pond and over the little humpback bridge to the central area of the gardens. People sat in sunshine, laughing, talking, reading in silence or just lying there, eyes closed, drinking it in. They could hear children in a nearby playground.

Suddenly, Izzy imagined ancient, hungry gods descending on this, gods too beautiful to look on, too terrible to endure. Phantom screams rose in the back of her mind. The tattoo chilled like ice or acid burrowed into her spine. She shook the sensation away. Or at least she tried to. It didn't want to go.

'Here,' said Jinx. 'There's another Sídheway gate up here. It'll take us most of the way Southside and we can pick up the next.'

But before they could reach it, the shadows surged out of the bushes like a wave of night. It wasn't the Fear this time. The sickening feeling in her stomach told her that.

'Shades!' Izzy shouted, and tore open her bag, reaching for the knife. Not to attack. For defence. The only way she knew how. She didn't hesitate, not for a second, dropping to her knees and driving the iron tip into the grass, drawing a circle just as she had on the hill when she first met Azazel. 'Dylan, here. Jinx—'

But Jinx had already shifted, a huge hound standing in his place, those long elegant ears, gleaming with silver studs and rings, flattened back against his head in anger. His green–black fur bristled, marked with the same dark–blue designs as the tattoos on his skin. Only his silver eyes remained the same, though they were narrow slits now. He snarled, all rage and muscles, long claws raking through the ground as he placed himself between Izzy, Dylan and the approaching shades.

The demonic creations hissed and writhed, unwilling or unable to come close, surrounding them all the same. Jinx prowled outside the perimeter, keeping them back. In the protective circle she'd drawn, Izzy stood up again, aware of Dylan at her back. She could feel him trembling, his breath harsh in his throat.

Elsewhere in the park, life carried on, oblivious to what was happening here, on this narrow patch of grass between trees and bushes, away from the path. A hidden corner that she feared would not remain hidden much longer. And when someone human stumbled on to the shades …

'Well, now,' said a smooth, cruel voice. 'Here's an interesting mix.'

The figure stepped out of the middle of the shades, shaking off shadows like dust. She looked like a girl Izzy's own age, sleek in the way the Queen Bees at school were, but with an innate sense of malice about her that they'd never hope to match. She was dressed in a school uniform very like Izzy's own, though it hugged her figure in ways it was never designed to do, and the skirt skimmed the top of her thighs. Her hair was a glossy sable, her skin deeply tanned and her eyes so dark they appeared black. Kohl rimmed them, making the shadows they contained so much more sinister. She parted her full, plum-coloured lips in a smile.

'What are you meant to be?' Izzy blurted out, belatedly relieved to hear her voice didn't shake as much as she would have expected. 'Lolita or something? Bad choice, it isn't on the lit course this year.'

The demon's smile didn't falter. It was a touch too wide, showing too many glistening white teeth. 'I was going for something a little more contemporary. I like your dog. Does he howl? If you don't call him off I'll have mine rip him to pieces, Isabel Gregory. I have a whole pack.'

'Who are you and what do you want?'

Jinx growled as the shades edged closer, driving them back. Despite her boast, they weren't eager to engage him. But they severely outnumbered him. If they really did all attack at once, he wouldn't stand a chance. Izzy reached out a warning hand, and he stilled, drawing closer to her, circling their position again. There was something eerily familiar about his presence. She'd missed him.

Focus, she told herself. You have to focus right now, on her.

'I'm Ardat Lili,' the demon said. 'But you can call me Lili.' She glanced around her, and then looked down at the uniform again.

She shrugged her shoulders and the uniform transformed into a t-shirt and jeans so stylish it would make those same Queen Bees, drooling over the autumn collections they'd never see for real, weep and rush to Dundrum Town Centre to lay siege to their beloved shops until they restocked.

Lili shimmied, getting herself comfortable in her new clothes, while all the time studying what Izzy wore, calculating every detail, and when her gaze returned to Izzy's face, the smile was even colder.

'We've been wondering what you're up to, Izzy. I can call you Izzy, can't I?' She flexed her perfectly and expensively manicured nails. They were painted gold and purple, the finish as glossy and perfect as the rest of her.

'None of your business.'

'Oh, but I think it is. I think it might be everyone's business. Demons have a right to be included. Otherwise we get tetchy.'

Izzy swallowed hard. The only demon she'd dealt with had been Azazel, who had a connection to her family and a positively charming demeanour in comparison. She didn't know what to do here. Helplessly, she glanced at Jinx, who was still caught up in the whole snarling and pacing, and not being a whole lot of use.

'This is Grigori business,' she tried again. Whatever the way out of this was, Izzy knew she couldn't tell the demon about the Fear, the Storyteller's Book, or the Shining Ones. So basically, none of it. Which was sure to be a problem.

'Grigori? Why? Do you think Azazel will leap in and pull you out of this? He has no power over me. I have no need to protect the Grigori. You lot aren't my concern. But knowledge is power. So spill, before I have to come over there and make you spill.' She took a step forward. 'All sorts of things.'

Another step. 'Secrets.'

Step. 'Blood.'

Step. 'Intestines.'

Izzy bristled. 'We're protected.'

She laughed. 'You've got to learn to draw a bigger circle than that. I mean, eventually, you're going to need to sit down. Or, you know, you could just fall over.'

Beneath their feet the ground bucked and shook, rearing up and tossing them aside. Caught off balance, Izzy and Dylan were pitched forwards and fell, sprawling on the grass outside the circle. The knife flew out of Izzy's hands.

Shades seized them, their grip cold but dry as old parchment, dusty and cloying. They wrapped themselves around her and she choked on them. She heard Dylan trying to fight, his struggles becoming strangled coughs. There was nothing to fight. Just smoke and shadows. Izzy couldn't see him. They were both swallowed up in darkness.

'Let them go,' said Jinx.

The darkness parted and Jinx was there, naked in Aes Sídhe form, holding Izzy's knife to Lili's throat.

Not that Lili seemed in any way concerned.

'Oh he's so pretty, this one,' she cooed to Izzy. 'And fool-hardy. Do you think you're fast enough, dog?'

'We can always find out. What do you want, demoness?'

'To find out what Isabel is up to, what the angels wanted. Fair's fair, after all.'

There could be no harm in that, could there? When Izzy thought about it, she was entirely reasonable. There was no need to panic. If it was Azazel she wouldn't hesitate to talk. But this one, this Lili … she didn't know.

No.

Charm, that was the thing. She was charming, using a spell, one that leached away healthy fear and even common sense. She was a devious one. And Izzy had almost fallen for it.

'Where is Azazel?' asked Izzy.

'My questions first,' Lili snapped. She was desperate, wasn't she? And maybe Izzy could use some information to defuse the situation. Just a little. What was the harm in that?

She could think of so many potentially harmful outcomes, but she pushed them to the back of her mind. She had to. She was Grigori. There had to be a way.

'There's an angel missing. He's called Haniel. The angels

wanted to know if I knew anything.'

Lili stared, her black eyes flicking through her options. 'Truly?'

The shades tightened their grip. Dylan gave a gasp of real pain. Jinx pressed closer with the cold iron knife. If she had been fae, Lili would be screaming by now. But she wasn't fae. Though she hissed at him when the blade pricked her skin, she didn't flinch.

'Truly,' panted Izzy. 'That's all.'

'Very well,' Lili relented and she sounded rather satisfied, which wasn't comforting at all. The shades loosened their grip just a little, just enough so breathing was easier. 'Haniel, you say. I remember him. A little scut if ever there was one. Well, here's hoping it's something unpleasant and permanent.'

Oh, it is, thought Izzy but she said nothing. Holly could be very permanent indeed. One angel wouldn't stand a chance.

'Shining Ones?' Lili drawled, tasting the words, as if she'd overheard a snippet of conversation, as if she'd reached into Izzy's head and plucked out the thought. Izzy stared at her, horrified. 'Didn't I mention I could do that? Silly me. So, what's a—?'

Jinx struck, plunging the knife for her throat, but she side-swiped him before he could connect. The blow lifted him off his feet and sent him crashing back against the nearest tree trunk.

'No!' Izzy yelled, but it was Dylan who moved. Light burst from his skin, shucking off the shades like discarded leaves.

He glowed with Silver's magic, every pore bright. The shades screamed and recoiled. Even Lili staggered back.

'*What are you?*' she asked, her voice a drawn-out hiss of pain.

'Leave her alone,' Dylan said. His voice reverberated through the air, doubling back on itself in impossible harmonies. 'Leave them both alone.' The shades fled to surround Lili, forming a shield, a defence of wavering smoke around her. She glared at Dylan, ignoring the other two completely, her gaze like a predatory animal at bay. For a moment Izzy thought she was looking at a double exposed image – a beautiful girl, and something else, something of scales, horns and teeth, something terrible.

Behind the dark veil, Lili drew herself up to her full height, shaking off fear and preening herself back to perfection, hiding the cracks in her image.

'Very well,' she said. 'I have enough for now. We'll meet again soon. Very soon, Isabel Gregory.'

And then, the demon and her shades were gone.

Dylan sagged forward, the light blinking out. He looked dazed and appalled, staring at his hands as if they weren't part of him at all.

'You okay?' Izzy whispered, not sure what to say to him. Not entirely sure what had happened.

'I'm ... yeah. I think. Where's Jinx? Is he hurt?'

Izzy ran to Jinx, who was already trying to pick his groggy and probably concussed body off the ground.

'Was that Dylan?' he whispered, his voice hoarse.

'Yes?' She wished it didn't sound like a question but couldn't help herself.

'Silver's powers, they're getting stronger if they're manifesting without her touch.'

She glanced back to Dylan, who looked pale and shaken, but otherwise unhurt. He too was picking himself up, with more success than Jinx. She could breathe again, could allow herself to actually ask the question. 'Dylan, are you sure you're okay?'

'Yeah.' He tried to grin, but it looked more like a grimace. 'Fun times.'

'Always.' She tried to laugh, but couldn't quite manage it. There were no signs of the light left on her friend. Silver's magic might be kept inside him, but it wasn't making another appearance right now at least. He seemed good. She'd have to ask Dad to check later. He'd know for sure – or then again, better not, given how Dad felt about the Sídhe. Dylan didn't seem hurt at all.

But he didn't seem right either. There was something about him that was completely different. If he could manifest Sídhe magic as well as storing it, that made him even more than a human touchstone. She wasn't sure what it made him. He'd been pinned down by demonspawn and yet he was unhurt.

What would the Sídhe say about that? She didn't want to think about it.

Jinx on the other hand had a gash running across his forehead that was pumping blood, bright and glossy, so very red.

His eyes had that unfocused look.

'Grab his clothes and pass them over, will you?' she asked Dylan. It wasn't the first time that she wondered if there was anything quite so useless as shape shifting that left him naked and vulnerable afterwards.

Then her body caught up with the thought that here he was, naked and in her arms, and that excruciating embarrassment was back again with a vengeance.

'Get dressed,' she told him brusquely, grabbing the clothes from Dylan and shoving them at him.

'Here, take this,' Jinx replied, just as mortified by their position as she was. He handed her the knife, carefully turning it hilt first towards her, equally careful not to touch the iron. He wasn't a fool, her Jinx.

And he wasn't *her* Jinx either.

She relieved him of it and shoved it deep into her backpack again. One of these days, she was certain, she was going to end up having to explain it to a cop. She'd rehearsed excuses, but none of them sounded convincing. The best she'd managed was 'it's an antique', and it looked far too sharp for that. Same with 'it's for cosplay' and 'it's a prop for the school show.' She really wasn't looking forward to that conversation.

Jinx pulled on his clothes in silence. He was fast, practised, but he winced with every movement.

'She was a demon, Jinx. Not one of the fae. A full-on demon, even if she looked like a girl. Would you have tried to hold Azazel like that?'

His eyes blazed. 'If he threatened you like that, yes I would. You know that.'

'Yes,' she admitted, even though she didn't want it to be true. Azazel would destroy him without a qualm. Izzy took his hand, squeezed it tight, even though she didn't want to. At least that was what she told herself. 'But don't. Please.'

He studied her face for a moment. What he was looking for, she couldn't say, but she wished she could lean closer and kiss him, wished he'd just lean towards her.

'Here,' she said, rooting in her backpack for some tissues. 'For your head. You're bleeding.'

He took them from her, his hand brushing against hers and she pulled back sharply. Too sharply.

The look of rejection on his face made her instantly wish she hadn't. But it was too late. What else did he expect? Forgiveness? He'd dropped out of her life, left her without any explanation. He didn't deserve forgiveness. 'We should get going. We need to see your father. And quickly. Before we run into any more unexpected and unwanted company.'

CHAPTER FOURTEEN

Tales of Old

The house looked much the same to Jinx as it had the last time he had come here with Izzy and Dylan, but this time there were lights on, and an unmistakeable presence that set Jinx's nerves on edge, tingling with alarm.

The Grigori himself was in there.

Jinx didn't like to think about the sudden instinctive response to that realisation, the way his heart pounded and his throat tightened. The fear reminded him too much of what he had been – Holly's slave, and then Izzy's slave. But he didn't know if it was an inbred fae respect for the Grigori, or just that this was Izzy's father.

But at the same time, he would do anything for her if she asked. Even go into this house with her when the Grigori was there.

Izzy opened the door and the unexpected smell of freshly

baked goods assaulted him, making his mouth water and his nostrils flare.

'I'm back,' she called. 'Dad? Mum?'

'I'm in the kitchen!' her mother shouted.

David Gregory came out of the living room, already talking to his daughter without seeing her. 'She's stress baking, Izzy. I didn't tell her everything but she knows enough to—'

And he stopped. Staring at Jinx. His expression turning thunderous.

'What's he doing here?'

Izzy closed the door behind her and Dylan shuffled his feet. Jinx didn't know what to say or do, so he just stood there, feeling awkward. Only Holly had ever made him feel quite so much like prey as he did in that moment. The Grigori's gaze pinned him in his place like a spear.

'He's hurt, Dad. Hurt defending me. There was a demon.'

Concern drained the anger from the Grigori's voice. 'What demon?'

'Lili … something. Or *something* Lili … Ardent? Or—'

'Ardat Lili?' He sucked in a breath, his jaw tightening. 'Izzy? Was it Ardat Lili?'

'Yes. Dad, she was waiting for us. Following us, I think.'

'Did she see where you went? Did she find out about the book?'

Izzy shook her head and David Gregory sighed in relief. His eyes flicked furtively over to Jinx.

Was he still bleeding? He couldn't tell. Right now he just

wanted to lie down and close his eyes. His head felt like it would burst open like over-ripe fruit.

Izzy was still speaking, explaining what had happened. 'It was after that. After we left you. After the Market. Silver—'

And suddenly he remembered why he was here. Not for Izzy, not for her father. Silver had sent him for a reason, for his own people. Silver needed him to do this, and to succeed.

'Silver begs you to help us,' Jinx interrupted. 'She sent me here, as a surety, an ambassador, as hostage if you will.'

'I'm not dealing with any of your kind, Cú Sídhe. I made myself perfectly clear.'

Yes, the only time they'd ever been alone together or spoken one-to-one, Izzy's father had made himself perfectly clear. The hair on the back of Jinx's neck came up in hackles. He opened his mouth to reply even though he knew this was all spiralling towards disaster. But he never got a chance to speak.

'Oh, stop it, both of you,' Izzy interrupted. 'Dad, about the book. Haniel's dead. Holly killed him. She's doing a spell. Silver ...' She glanced at Jinx, who didn't know where to look and so stared at the floor instead. 'Silver freaked out. Who was Míl, Dad? Why does King Eochaid of the Fear think I owe him something?'

There was probably no moment quite as awkward in Izzy's life as sitting there in the kitchen, watching her parents and Jinx.

'The angels,' Izzy asked at last. 'What did they do? How did you get away?'

'I didn't. I negotiated. Carefully. Sometimes talking works so much better than fighting. Really. I'm trying to stop a war. Tell me everything you discovered. What happened?'

She related everything she'd seen, every detail. Holly, the broken cairn, Haniel's fate. And the light, the trembling deep, deep underground. The gleam in Holly's eye as she looked across the bay. The wire she had fashioned from whatever she'd drawn out of the earth after the angel's death. Jinx sat in the chair beside her, fidgeting while Dylan sprawled on the couch, more at home than any of them.

'Silver said that Holly isn't just summoning the Fear,' he told Dad solemnly. 'That's a side effect. She's after something else. The old gods.'

Dad shook his head. 'The Shining Ones? Not even Holly would risk raising that kind of power – it took a host to put them down the first time. It took a supreme sacrifice and a … a … it doesn't matter. She wouldn't. She couldn't.'

'It also took a Grigori,' Jinx said. He fell silent again as Dad glared at him. Instead, he averted his eyes, clearly wishing he'd never said it.

'What Grigori?' asked Izzy.

Jinx looked up and met her eyes. The words came hesitantly and he kept his gaze fixed on her and her alone. 'They called him Míl, the soldier. He was the first of you.'

'It's a myth,' Dad said.

Jinx lowered his gaze once more. 'If you say so, Grigori.'

'Of course I say so.'

'Dad, don't be a bully,' Izzy told him. Although why she felt the need to jump to Jinx's defence, she didn't know. But Dad wasn't being fair. He'd never talk to Dylan that way and Dylan was right there, equally in the firing line. She knew that much and it irked her in a way she couldn't quite describe.

'I'm not being a bully,' said Dad. 'Míl is a myth, a garbled pre-Christian version of the early settlers of this island, reverse-engineered onto history. Pseudo-mythology, not even the real thing. He was an origin for the Milesians. *Míl Espáine*, the soldier from Spain.'

She knew her dad was stubborn. She hadn't picked it up off the stones in the road. But he wasn't even listening to Jinx. That didn't seem to bother the Cú Sídhe. Jinx acted like he was used to it and just ploughed on in anyway. Maybe stubborn infected them all.

'He's none of these meagre things to us,' said Jinx. If he was trying to choose his words carefully, Izzy thought, he wasn't doing a terribly good job of it. He was angry, that was the problem. Angry, but trying to be a good emissary. She squirmed on his behalf. He didn't want to blow it, but he was struggling. She wished it wasn't so obvious. 'He was the first Grigori to come here. He split the island, or it was done in his name. All that stuff about Spain and the Milesians? I don't know that. Time twists history to stories. But I know Míl was a soldier. What do you think the Grigori are?'

'*Soldiers*,' said Dad in a grim and equally angry tone. 'We're a little more than soldiers.'

'If you say so. Míl aligned himself with Eochaid, King of the Firshee and one of our most powerful warriors. They were brothers in arms, sworn to each other. And Míl promised his daughter in marriage to the king. And he broke that promise. It was the same time that Míl and his magicians cheated the Sídhe. Your ancestor promised us that you would share this island, but instead of giving us a share of the land, he split it into two planes and exiled us to Dubh Linn. We made it our own, but in the beginning, in the very beginning, it was a ghost world, an empty rock, a shadow of this island. Míl cheated us, and he cheated Eochaid.'

Dad shrugged. 'It's old news, Jinx. We don't even know how true it is. Like you say, time changes history to story.'

'If there weren't those among my people who remember it clearly.'

'People like Brí and Holly? They have their own version of history, believe you me. Alright, I'll tell you what I was told, what the Grigori know. In order to lock the Shining Ones away, one of them had to remain with them. The plan was that Eochaid would stay and Míl would take his place in a year, or one of his children would. The life Eochaid had given up would be restored to him by the sacrifice. But Míl only had one child and when the time came, for whatever reason, he left Eochaid there.' Dad glanced at Izzy and she squirmed a little. The look said it all. She suspected Míl could no more hand over his daughter than her dad would hand her over. He just had to act this way in front of Jinx, didn't he? Over-protective and so embarrassing.

'Míl tricked him,' Jinx said. 'But he couldn't break the spell that tied them together, the spell that sealed the Shining Ones away—'

'Old stories—'

'David,' Mum's voice was perfectly calm and cut through the tension like a hot blade. 'David, enough. You're right. They're old stories, which probably don't mean what we think they mean. But they do mean something, deep down, a kernel of truth that led to the tale. We're arguing semantics and we don't have time for that.'

'She's right, Mr Gregory,' said Dylan. Izzy had almost forgotten he was there. 'Silver needs your help. To ask like this, to send Jinx. I've never seen her so shaken. If Holly is back ... They all thought – *we* all thought that she was defeated, but she isn't. She can't be, but she's desperate. She has to be if she's planning to release the Shining Ones. We have to help.'

Mum smiled at him. There was nothing in the world so comforting as Mum's smile, Izzy knew that. 'Of course we're going to help. We owe Silver and Jinx a great deal. More now.'

They all looked at her, sitting beside her husband, neat and ordered and perfectly unruffled. She couldn't have surprised anyone more than Izzy, but at the same time Izzy knew if she could rely on anyone, in any circumstances, it was her mum.

Jinx looked awestruck for a moment, but when he turned

to look at Izzy's father again, his eyes were steely with determination. 'Silver begs you, Grigori. You're sworn to protect all, even us, the lowliest and the forsaken. We're fae. We're the outcasts, the scraps off the table. But you're meant to help even us.'

'Very well,' said Dad grudgingly after a single glance at his wife. 'Tell Silver I'll come to her Council meeting. I'll listen to them talk. Or argue, more like. And I'll see what can be done. But the angels aren't going to like it. And the demons have sent the shades sniffing around so I'm going to have to have words with them too. Serious words. Ardat Lili's a loose cannon. And right now, all I have for Zadkiel is that Holly killed Haniel to let out an army of ghosts and maybe raise an ancient god or three? Oh and by the way, the most terrible thing the angels ever faced? The things they had to call on outside help to deal with? *Our* help? The help of upstart humans and fae? That's going to go down well.'

'Maybe you should leave that bit out for now,' Izzy said, trying to ease the tension. 'Just in case. It might annoy him.'

Dad gave her that flat, humourless look. 'Really? Do you think so? Holly let out the Fear.' He sighed. 'The Fear never cared about the human world. They made the fae look like the epitome of altruism. They'll fall on it like a ravening horde and all the protection and balance we've worked for all these years will literally go to hell. No. They won't like it. Go on then, Jinx by Jasper, go home and tell Silver I'll cover for you now. Because I really don't have a choice, do I?'

'I'm to go back? But Silver sent me—'

Dad looked exhausted, like he had when he first woke up from his coma, battered and bruised. 'As a hostage, I know. But I have no need of hostages. This isn't the dark ages. Go back to the Market. And you should get home too, Dylan. Your parents will be worried sick. Izzy, you should be in bed.'

Damn it, did he have to make it sound like she was a child?

'Dad,' she protested, the word dragging out in a whine, before realising that she'd just completed the image for him. Mortifying, that's what he was. Utterly mortifying.

Jinx unfolded himself from the chair and gave a neat bow. The cut on his head had already healed but it left a red mark and still made her stomach twist unpleasantly to think about it.

When he spoke it was all arcane formality again. 'My thanks, Grigori. I regret the intrusion and apologise. I would not have come here again, against your express word, had Silver not requested it, had it not been so urgent.'

Izzy stared. His express word? *What* express word?

'I realise that. The circumstances are exceptional. The last time, I—'

'What last time?' Izzy asked, interrupting Dad before he could finish. 'Dad?' He had that instant guilty look to him. He never could lie. He was hiding something. 'Dad, what did you say to Jinx the last time he was here?'

The last time she had seen him before today. The last time … just after the hospital … Just before he'd completely vanished from her life without as much as a whisper of farewell. What had Dad said to him? Her stomach tightened, her breath hitching in her throat. He couldn't have. He wouldn't have …

But neither of them answered. That horrible silence muffled all her senses, smothered all her feeling in despair. Jinx, par for the course, barely offered her a goodbye. Dylan promised to ring later, but seemed as perplexed as she was by it all. And then they were gone.

Once they were alone and the door firmly closed against the night, Izzy turned on her parents.

'What happened *last time*?'

Mum sighed. She looked exhausted, wrung out. 'Your dad was worried, that's all. Things had moved so fast. And you're so young.'

With dawning horror, Izzy backed away from them towards the stairs.

'You didn't. Dad, tell me you didn't.'

He pursed his lips and then gave her a defiant look she was pretty proud to wear herself at times. Like father like daughter. Everyone said that. And she knew what she'd try to do if she thought there was even a chance someone might hurt someone she cared about. She knew.

'Izzy, I had to do what was best for you. You're my daughter first and foremost.'

'Did you warn him off? Did you pull some sort of Grigori superiority thing on him and tell him to leave me alone? Dad, tell me you didn't?'

'I had to.'

It felt like a punch to the stomach. And here she'd been blaming Jinx all along. Poor Jinx. Of course, said a small defiant voice of her own, deep down inside her, he could have ignored her father and come to see her anyway. He could have arranged stolen moments and secret meetings. It might even have been romantic, sort of *Romeo and Juliet* without the gory bits and the grisly end. But that wasn't what either of them were like. And Jinx, all bound up with Cú Sídhe honour and duty – it would have destroyed him.

'You knew he'd obey you,' she said, unable to keep accusation from sharpening her voice. 'Because he's Cú Sídhe.'

'It's what they do. I know Brí's pack and Jinx is still one of them at the core. Even Silver agreed. She said it was safer for you and for Dylan if you had nothing to do with any of them until you have to, when you're older. I know them. I knew Jasper, Izzy. He was a killer, an assassin. Did Jinx share that with you?'

'No one seems able to let Jinx or me forget it. So his father was a killer – Jinx isn't! He's done nothing but protect me.' Okay, so that strictly wasn't true but they'd worked that out, hadn't they? And now, now … Now Dad didn't want a Cú Sídhe hanging out with his daughter because of what his father might have been?

'What is it, Dad? Isn't he good enough for me or something? Eochaid says I'm promised to him – is that something you want to share? Do we have to keep the bloodline pure?

Oh no, wait. You were happy enough to fuck Brí when it suited you.'

A stunned silence crashed down around them. Izzy couldn't believe she'd said it, but the words were out, like a physical assault on her parents' marriage.

Mum sucked in a breath. Her voice shook wildly, but it was loud and firm. Not to be argued with. 'Go to bed, Isabel. We'll talk in the morning.'

The enormity of what she'd said slapped Izzy in the face. She needed to explain, to apologise. She'd meant to hurt Dad, not Mum. She'd meant to show him what a hypocrite he was. She never meant to hurt her mother. 'Mum, I—I didn't—'

'Get out of my sight! Right now!' Mum's voice broke as she shouted the last words and Izzy turned, fleeing up the stairs and slamming her bedroom door behind her. She fell, sobbing, onto her bed, burying her face in the pillow to smother the sounds, hating herself, hating them, hating everything in her life. And hating being Grigori more than anything else.

CHAPTER FIFTEEN

Shades and Regrets

Dylan wasn't sure if Jinx walked with him to be companionable, to make sure he actually went home, or for some other reason he didn't know. Perhaps Jinx didn't have anywhere else to be. Perhaps he didn't know what to do now. After all, Silver had sent him to the Gregorys' as a surety, a hostage. What was a hostage to do when he wasn't wanted?

They walked in the shadow of what had happened, and the brewing storm they had left behind.

'Did he really warn you off Izzy?' Dylan asked at last.

'Yes.'

'And Silver?'

Jinx gave him a long look, a do-you-really-want-to-do-this look, but when Dylan didn't back down, he answered. 'Silver said it was for the best. That you'd both be better off without us in your lives. So we stayed away. You didn't though.'

'No. I didn't. But I'm the pushover, not Izzy.'

'A pushover?' He looked genuinely shocked at the thought someone would say that about themselves. Or maybe, that he would say it about himself. Which left Dylan a bit surprised. Jinx didn't think of him as a pushover. That was somewhat gratifying.

'Yeah. When you vanished, it devastated Izzy, but she's proud. She wasn't going to run after you. Whereas I needed some explanations for what was happening to me. The magic, whatever it is, ended up in me, that makes me the touchstone ...You saw, didn't you? I don't know how to control that. It's like... like it's leaking out of me.'

'Silver is Leanán Sídhe.You couldn't have stayed away from her if she'd locked you up behind iron bars herself.'

Dylan laughed, in spite of himself, surprised to find the sound still in him. He wouldn't put it past Silver. There was little he'd put past her if she was determined enough. She was terrifying. And more dazzling than anything he'd ever seen. She was addictive and dangerous. He'd do anything if she asked. And that was the most frightening part of all. 'True.'

'She wanted you to be free to study your music.'

Dylan stared at him. 'Really? I thought she just—' That she'd just done it to get rid of him, in the hopes of distracting him. Until she needed him, of course. He hadn't imagined that she'd talked about it much, let alone to Jinx. Mind you, who else did they have to talk to? They didn't trust anyone else, that much was clear. 'I didn't know.'

'I would have liked to study,' said Jinx. 'History. I like history.' It sounded like the type of admission he didn't make very often. And the mental image of Jinx sitting quietly in a lecture theatre, making notes on the Renaissance, or the French Revolution didn't form easily.

'You would have studied history? Human or Sídhe?' Jinx didn't answer and another thought struck Dylan. He'd heard Jinx play, knew what his guitar meant to him. He'd recognised the raw talent that ran throughout the Cú Sídhe when he'd played in Silver's club so long ago. 'What about your music?'

Jinx hesitated, and instantly his shields went back up. 'It doesn't matter. It's never going to happen. Holly had plans for me, but it wasn't an education.'

'What sort of plans?'

He shrugged, and his eyes had that hooded look. 'I don't know. Don't want to know either. But she planned everything. Always did. Nothing has changed. I still think … no, I *know*, she's just waiting. Everything she planned will still unfold as she intended. She was always like that. She planned far in advance, every eventuality covered. We should never have discounted her. It was stupid. So stupid.' He rubbed his neck as if trying to get rid of an ache he couldn't quite touch.

They walked on in silence again, down the hill, through the orange glow of streetlamps.

'So Izzy's dad really warned you off?' Dylan asked again. 'I can't believe he'd do that. He's a nice guy … usually.'

Jinx's mouth tightened to a hard line. 'Maybe you're just

more what he was thinking of when it came to a mate for his daughter. *Or maybe no one will be good enough. I've heard that of the fathers of daughters.*

Dylan remembered his dad's face whenever Marianne turned up in the mini skirt and high-heeled boots she loved. Or when she'd wanted to go to some club that had been on the news for a riot the night before. Compared to his sister, Izzy was an angel. The right kind of angel.

But Mari was dead now. And he still blamed himself and wondered if his parents did too. He was there. He hadn't saved her. If anything he'd led the banshee to her. Silver could be right, that he and Izzy were better without the fae in their life.

Too late now. Far too late. Mari was dead. Izzy was half-fae anyway, on her birth mother's side and he … he couldn't have left Silver for anything in the world. The idea that Jinx could have given up on Izzy so easily was beyond belief.

They turned into his road and he saw the porch light still on. They'd been waiting up for him again. Only they weren't. Not really. It just looked that way to everyone else.

They weren't waiting for him to come home at all. He was eighteen, an adult, by all standards. He'd even seen death. He'd been there when it happened, and he'd let his sister die.

'Dylan?' Jinx's voice sounded far away. 'What is it?'

Dylan hadn't realised he'd stopped walking. He stood there, unable to take another step. 'Nothing.'

But it wasn't nothing.

Bathed in the silvery light of the blub in the porch stood

the figure of a girl. She was waiting for him, her hands on her hips, her chin up, itching for a fight, as she usually was.

'Mari?' he whispered. And he thought he saw a smile flicker over her ghostly face.

A knowing, satisfied smile.

'Jinx, do you see her?'

Tell me I'm not going mad.

'Who? Where?'

Dylan glanced at the Cú Sídhe, confused, but saw only blank incomprehension. When he looked back to the house, Mari was gone.

Dad sat on the end of the bed and Izzy ignored him.

'We'll have to talk eventually.'

She rolled over, glaring at him. He'd do this all night if he had to. Stubborn, that was the problem.

'No, we don't.'

'I beg to differ. Well?'

'Why did you do it?'

He sighed, a deep sigh, full of regret and dismay. 'Because … because I didn't want you hurt.'

Hurt? She wasn't just hurt. She'd been hurt. Now it felt like something had ripped her chest open and dragged out every iota of pain she'd managed to lock away.

'Yeah. Great job there.'

'I thought you'd get over it.'

Tears stung her eyes again. 'This is worse, Dad. This is so much worse.' He just nodded, but didn't say anything. She thought of Mum's face, of the pain and anger there, the long-ago agony of knowing her husband was with someone else, of agreeing to raise Brí's daughter, of having that thrown in her face. 'Is Mum … is she okay?'

'She's upset. Do you blame her?'

'*Her*? No.' She glared at him until he looked away, guilt carving lines in his face.

'The past is the past, Izzy. It has to be.'

'Someone ought to tell it, because it keeps coming back to bite us all in the ass. This Eochaid thing …'

'I'll go talk to your grandmother tomorrow. She might be able to shed some light on it. You can come if you like.'

'No, thanks.' She didn't say she'd rather learn to kick herself repeatedly in the head.

'Izzy, please understand—'

'You keep saying that, but there isn't any sign of you extending the favour to me, is there?'

A loud crash downstairs brought them both up to their feet. The kitchen, pans clattering on tiled floors and then, nothing.

'Mum?' Izzy yelled, but Dad was already out of the room and down the stairs. She followed, using the bannisters to propel herself forward. Their argument forgotten, the two of them sprinted across the hall and Dad flung open the door of the kitchen.

Mum stood in the centre of the room, very still, her shoulders hunched awkwardly, her eyes wide with terror.

Shadows coiled around her, twisted in and out of the mess of cake tins, saucepans and shattered plates all over the floor. The biscuits and cakes she'd been baking were strewn all over the place, mangled crumbs and sticky burnt messes on the countertops and tiles.

She opened her mouth, a thin, frightened breath escaping as she stared at them both, her eyes huge, her pupils dilated wide. But she didn't say anything. She couldn't.

Shades filled the kitchen. They clung to the walls and dripped from the ceiling. The demonic servants coiled around her, holding her in a tight embrace. But they hadn't taken control of her, not yet. Izzy remembered the empty eyes of those she'd seen at the hospital last summer, possessed and beyond help. Mum was still Mum.

'Well now, we have a predicament,' said a familiar voice.

Azazel stepped out of the shadows, brushing wisps of darkness from his long black coat. His dark and endless eyes fixed on the two Grigori and he smiled.

'What are you doing here?' asked Dad in the coldest, calmest voice imaginable.

'It's a matter of leverage really. We have a stake in this matter too, you know. The Fear, the Shining Ones ... Oh, it has been most enlightening. Lili may be an idiot, but she got on the trail fast enough. She just doesn't know you like I do, Gregory. She doesn't know what buttons to push.'

Mum gasped again as the shades around her tightened their grip. They coiled about her body, creeping up towards her mouth, threatening to smother and consume her in an instant if anyone made the wrong move.

'Let her go.'

'In time,' the demon said, his voice still sweet with reason. 'But I want something in return.'

'And what's that?'

'Little Izzy here is going to face Eochaid. She's going to put him back down in the ground for once and for all. Just her.'

'She can't do that, she's just a child.'

It stung, but at the same time, she agreed with him. This was crazy talk.

'Oh you'd be surprised what she's capable of. I've seen her stop angels while you were tucked up in bed. Eochaid is trouble, you know it. That psychopath can't be allowed to go free. And if you do it, David … well, there will be untold consequences. Very angry angels, for example. Not to mention what might happen to you, and to poor Rachel here. No, Izzy does it. She's strong enough.'

'Except I don't know what to do.'

'Better find out then, hadn't you? If you want to see mother dearest again.'

'You want me to kill Eochaid?'

'Did I say that? Kill Eochaid and you defeat the Fear, but you know what else will get out. That's the thing with Old Magic. It's tricky.'

'You're talking about the Shining Ones?'

He laughed. '*The Shining Ones*, such a fae name. Call them something pretty and maybe they'll be flattered and leave you alone. The fae worshipped them, you know? But I suppose some people will worship anyone if they're frightened enough. There were other names too – Crom Cruach, Crom Dubh and Crom Ceann. They fed on blood and death. We had names for them too, didn't we David? The angels have names for them you pray you'll never hear. But look to your legends and see if you want them back.'

Crom Cruach, she knew that name. A dark god, a drinker of blood. Old stories of saints and sacrifice. The others didn't sound much better. Three demon gods who were defeated long ago.

'They're the Shining Ones? But … they talked about Seraphim, about angels higher than angels …'

'Like I said, call them something flattering and they might just leave you alone. Seraphim—' He said the word like he was naming a plague, '—they never had a sense of proportion.'

'And what do you want me to do?'

'What you were born to do, Isabel Gregory. Isn't that obvious? Stop this, contain them, by whatever means necessary. Even if it means giving yourself up to Eochaid of the Firshee.'

'No,' said Dad suddenly. 'Izzy, don't listen to him.'

'I've never lied to her, David. Unlike you.' He reached out and stroked the back of his gnarled fingers along the side of Mum's face. She squirmed, her whimpers muffled. 'We're going to be going now. But these are my demands. David Gregory, you stay out of this. You keep the angels out of it. And Isabel, you go and find the Fear. You put them down by whatever means necessary before Samhain lets them take full form. Or you take their place. Whatever happens, the Shining Ones cannot be released.'

With a flurry of shadows and twisting darkness, they were gone, and Mum with them. Dad yelled her name, throwing himself forward, but he was too late. He crashed onto the tiled floor where she had been.

CHAPTER SIXTEEN

Trying Normality

Mum's phone kept going to voicemail, but Izzy kept ringing, just in case, despite knowing it was pointless. Wherever they had taken her, there was no signal.

Dad hadn't slept any more than she had.

This was all her fault. She should have done something, anything, but she'd let it happen.

What if the demons kept her? What if they possessed her? What if they killed her?

She pushed the thoughts away. She had to. How could she do anything useful if she thought about Mum? She wanted to curl up on her bed and weep, take the foetal position and never move again. Not until her Mum was back. But that wasn't an option for her.

She had to be a Grigori now or she'd fall apart.

'Dad?'

He grunted at her, so focused on the pile of books in front of him. Trying to find something, *anything*, to help.

'Dad, we have to do something.'

'I am. I will. I'm going to find her, Izzy.' He sat back, pinching the bridge of his nose and frowning. 'I'm going to get her back.'

'I can help.'

'No.' It was instant, and devastating. She stared at him, mouth open. 'You have to carry on as normal. If the angels realise that Azazel has your Mum, that he has such a hold over you and me … they won't trust me to be impartial. They won't negotiate.' He shook his head and groaned. 'I've got to go. I can't do anything here. If I can track them down, maybe …'

'So I'm to do nothing?' She couldn't believe what he was saying. Surely there was something she could do? She could help him.

'You're to provide a smoke screen. Look, you've work today, haven't you?'

'They asked me to cover at the coffee shop but—'

'Good, do that. Stay out of trouble. Have the most boring, normal day known to mankind.'

'You think they're watching me?'

He smiled. 'I know it. Angels and demons alike. The fae too, probably. And I'm counting on it. Okay?' He pulled on his jacket and dug out his car keys. 'Please Izzy.'

'You get her back. Promise. No matter what it takes.'

He hugged her, held her close. For a moment she could

almost forget everything that was happening, forget the horrors she had seen, the agony she'd felt. She could just be his daughter. Be the little girl who didn't know any of this ....

But only for a moment. The reality of it crushed her with his next words.

'I will bring her back. I swear it. Go to work. Get lunch. Go to town and see Dylan and his band play this evening. Just be you. Old you. And I'll find her.'

After last night she didn't know what else to say. Mum was gone. Dad was frantic. 'Sorry' didn't seem like anywhere near enough. And besides, part of her was still angry – raging in fact – that he could have treated Jinx that way. That he could have treated both of them that way. At least Jinx had got an explanation, of sorts. She'd warranted nothing at all. Just left in ignorance to think the worst of someone innocent in all this.

But that all seemed to pale into insignificance now.

Mum was gone and somehow it was her fault. Azazel wanted her to face a monster she couldn't beat. Every time she thought of it she got angry all over again. Spitting angry. Door slamming, incoherent, righteously angry.

And all she could do was shut it out, close away her feeling and try to pretend everything was normal. Just imitate her old life and hope no one noticed.

At least the coffee shop was busy, crammed with mums who had dropped kids at the local GAA grounds for training, seeking comfort from the bitterly cold morning in coffee and gossip. The whole place had been decked out in orange and black, with little witch and cat dolls. Carved pumpkins filled every window ledge, the tea-lights inside them flickering whenever the door opened. She hardly noticed the hours slip away until it was after lunchtime. She checked her phone. There was no word from Dad.

Izzy grabbed a sandwich and sat at the back of the shop, trying to be as inconspicuous as possible. Clodagh phoned, gabbling on about the gig Dylan was playing tonight with his band Denzion and Izzy let her railroad arrangements to meet without knowing if she'd actually go.

Act normal, Dad had said. They can't suspect anything.

So she just agreed to everything Clodagh said and hung up. If Clodagh thought that was weird she didn't let on. She seemed delighted.

A short, redheaded man watched her from the far end of the shop. His eyes glinted in a fae way that instantly put her on edge. When he noticed her looking his way, he got up. As he crossed the shop to where she sat, she recognised him as Art, the leprechaun who had spoken to Jinx at the Market. He looked taller outside Dubh Linn, more human than he had. A glamour, no doubt. A way of blending in.

'Miss Gregory? Do you remember me?'

'What do you want?'

'I need your help. It's rather difficult to explain, but I can show you. It's to do with ... ' He looked around furtively, ' ... with the issue of the Fear. I think I've found something. Will you come?'

All her instincts told her it was a bad idea. Her tattoo felt cold, and her skin tight around her.

'I think you need to leave.'

Unexpectedly his eyes brimmed with tears and his mouth wobbled. He looked like a lost child. 'Please, Miss Gregory ... there's no one else I can turn to. And as Grigori, surely ... ' His voice cracked and the air shook. Cups and saucers clattered on the shelves behind the counter and Izzy surged to her feet. Jinx had warned her. The last thing she needed was a hysterical lep in her workplace. Hours were hard enough to come by as it was and Carla could barely manage since the rebuild. Fae emotions could be devastating to the world around them. All they'd need would be for Art to lose it and the whole place could be wrecked again.

'Calm down. People are watching.'

'You have to come with me, Miss Gregory. Please. I think they know, I think ... '

She grabbed his arm and hauled him towards the door. 'All right, all right. I have another couple of hours here and I can't just leave right now. But afterwards, okay? Meet me outside at four.'

Art babbled out his thanks and sped for the door as fast as he could. Izzy turned back to see Carla looking at her with raised eyebrows.

'Everything okay?'

She pasted her brightest, fakest smile on her face. 'Sure. Just ... you know ... ' What could she say? The only explanation that might work felt excruciating. But she jumped on it anyway. 'Boy trouble.'

Carla rolled her eyes and turned back to the milk frother. 'You want to get a better class of boy, Izzy.'

Izzy tried Dad again as the day wore on, but got voicemail every time. And when four rolled around and she knocked off work, Art waited across the road, pacing back and forth like a nervous cat.

'What is it?' she asked, zipping her coat up to her neck and shoving her hands deep into her pocket against the cold.

'Here, come this way. There's a gate.'

'Here?' But she followed him nonetheless, up the busy main street and into an alley by the barbers. There was graffiti here too – human graffiti though, not the remains of an angel, unless angels now looked like babies wearing boxing gloves. Izzy took a deep breath as the lep opened the gateway and they stepped through the Sídheways, emerging onto a wooded hillside, through a gate between a pair of trees growing together, or perhaps one tree that had been split in two when it first started growing.

Izzy looked around, trying to place herself. The light was already fading. This was wild land and the way up was steep. Looking around she could see the sea far below her, through a gap in the trees. And she knew the place.

'Up here. Quick, this way,' said Art, scrambling up the steep slope ahead of her. She followed, until the path grew more even and the trees thinned out again, leaving only the rocks, gorse and shadows.

Bray Head. She was on Bray Head, looking back towards that Dalkey Island and Killiney Hill. Izzy could even see the white point of the Obelisk. She thought of Brí, reigning uncontested beneath that hill, her birth mother, volatile and cantankerous, but good, deep down. If you could reach that far. What would she say about the dead and whatever Holly was doing? Should they have gone to her first? But then, all the Aes Sídhe had their own agenda and Brí was no different. Izzy didn't know exactly how she fitted into Brí's machinations and she wasn't exactly keen to find out.

They all had plans, didn't they?

'Izzy?' A lone jogger came to an abrupt halt on the path below her and squinted up. 'What are you doing here?'

Ash smiled brilliantly, a little out of breath and clearly delighted to see her. She pulled her earbuds out and wound them around her hand. She was still jogging, bouncing on the spot although she wasn't going anywhere. Who jogged uphill? Who jogged up hills as steep as this?

'Ash?' Izzy said, not sure what to say in response. What *was* she doing here? How did she answer that one? '*An ancient psycho fairy is sacrificing angels and I want to know why*' didn't really sound like an explanation many people would be comfortable with. 'I could ask you the same thing.' She looked around for Art, but he was nowhere to be seen now. Figured.

The air turned even colder but Ash didn't seem to notice. 'Yes, I live here. Well,' she laughed. 'Not here. Back there.' She

205

waved a hand vaguely down towards the town. 'Are you going up the Head?'

'I'm … um …' Izzy looked at the steep slope above her. 'Walking?'

'Bit late isn't it? It's a long haul up there.'

'Yeah … I just wanted to um …'

Ash shrugged. 'I know a shortcut. Come on.'

It wasn't really a shortcut. Well, if you moved at the super-fit pace that Ash seemed capable of maybe every way was a shortcut. Izzy bet they loved her on the hockey team at school.

Still no sign of the lep. He'd gone.

They made their way through the trees, soon out of breath but laughing and passing comments back and forth. Strangely there was no one else around. It was half term, but no one seemed inclined to this walk this afternoon. The cold wind didn't help, or the early twilight. Finally they broke clear of the trees and pushed their way along paths cut through head high gorse and up the rocky slope until even the gorse fell away, leaving the bare bones of the hill exposed.

By the time they reached the top and looked back down at the sweep of the bay, the mountains and the sprawling town, Izzy was exhausted. The lights were starting to come on below them, glowing red before turning to yellow and white, an ocean of lights picking out the streets and houses. The sea looked dark and endless in comparison, the hilltop deserted. Out towards the horizon, the lighthouse began to blink.

And there was clearly nothing out of the ordinary up there.

Wind pulled at them. Ash grinned with exhilaration, her long black hair whipping out behind her. 'Isn't it gorgeous? It's so beautiful up here, like standing on the edge of heaven.'

'Yes. Fab. Best sight ever.' She didn't even try to make it sound like she meant it. She sat down on the edge of the plinth where the stone cross was planted. And then she felt the air shift, chilling even further. Everything changed, charged with electricity. The mist was crawling up the sides of the mountain. The shadows were getting darker, longer.

'So that's it,' said Ash, oblivious. 'Not a lot up here really, other than the view. It really is getting late. Want to go back down? We could get a coffee?'

Coffee was the last thing on Izzy's mind. The earth was humming under her feet, the air charged with static. And it was getting colder by the second. Long shadows stretched from the rocks and stones, spreading towards them, faster and faster. It was getting dark, so dark.

'Yeah, coffee. Coffee would be great. Let's go.'

'Under-caffeinated or something?' asked Ash, still smiling.

'Horribly. Come on.' Izzy made to hook an arm in hers, but she was too late.

A blast of wind struck the ground behind Izzy like an explosion, flattening the heather and grasses. She could feel them behind her, feel the cold emanating from their shadowy bodies. And then she heard Lili's voice.

'Going so soon? What a shame. And I haven't even met your new friend.' Shadows surged up around them and the two girls backed up towards the cross.

'Ash ...' Izzy tried to say something, anything that would get her out of this unscathed. But she couldn't think of a way. 'Ash just stay still, stay behind me.'

Lili smiled, showing all her teeth. 'Well now ... Tell all Izzy. Who is this?' The demon circled her and Izzy could see her rictus skull grin again. The girlish face was still in place, still perfect and chilling. She wore a suit this time, black and expensive from the cut and the lines. Too expensive for Izzy to know the make, that was for sure. Her long hair was plaited in countless little braids that hissed like snakes as they brushed against each other.

Had Art known she'd be here? Had he brought her here for Lili? Where the hell had he gone?

'Lili, I don't know what you want from me, but she has nothing to do with this. Let us go.'

'Poor little girls, is that it? Innocents abroad. My favourite kind.'

The shadows rushed closer. 'Don't let them touch you,' Izzy warned. She felt for the knife, knowing that if she pulled it out she'd freak Ash out completely. But what else could she do. 'I should never have brought you with me. I should have come alone.'

Ash didn't answer. She'd managed to back up onto the plinth beneath the cross.

Lili ignored Ash now. Perhaps in the shadow of the cross she was untouchable to the shades. Izzy fervently hoped so.

This left her with the demon grinning in her face. 'Well, yes. You here alone would have been the simplest solution, but no matter. Here you are and here we are. So why exactly *are* we here, Izzy?'

Oh, God, she couldn't tell Lili that. Even if she had a solid answer. She couldn't tell Lili that Holly was killing angels and why, that Eochaid was after her, and that Azazel wanted her to confront him. Somehow. She certainly couldn't mention the Shining Ones. 'I just … I was just … I wanted to walk.'

If she pretended to be terrified, incoherent, and useless to her, would the demon let her go? Would she back off and release Ash? She couldn't lose someone else to demons and their shades. Her hand closed on the hilt of the knife deep in her bag. It was no use against a demon, she knew that. Their last encounter had proved it. Not unless she could draw a circle and there wasn't time for that.

There wasn't time for anything.

An icy cold hand grabbed her throat, cutting off the air and burning against her skin. Izzy gasped, struggling to pull away, but Lili was too strong. Dark eyes filled her field of vision, dark eyes all she could see. They swallowed her up, blotted all thoughts from her mind, and smothered her will with their darkness.

'The truth now, sweet child. Tell me the truth. You know it's for the best. Trust me.'

The scrabbling terror in the base of her throat clawed to escape, like a rat trapped at the bottom of a well. But she couldn't. She couldn't break away from the demon, couldn't even close her eyes.

And the words came, grating from her throat, ripping their own way out in spite of her.

'I saw Holly looking here. When she killed the angel.'

'Which angel?'

'Haniel.'

Lili laughed, a bright, girlish laugh that rang out across the hillside. 'How marvellous. I wondered what had happened to him. So, Holly's killing angels. But why, Isabel? Tell me why?'

The ground shook beneath them and abruptly the spell holding Izzy shattered. Lili staggered back as the air beside them trembled and shimmered. Flashes of lightning cut the distortion, making it look like a localised thunderstorm, and the smell of ozone filled the air, making the hair on Izzy's arm straighten.

'This is why,' said Holly, stepping out of the vortex. It was a gate to the Sídheways, Izzy realised, like the one Sorath had used on the hill, broken and distorted and bent to Holly's will.

Holly, wild-eyed and dangerous, moved so fast Izzy could barely follow her. She grabbed Ardat Lili by the hair and pulled her onto the foot-long knife she carried. The demon only made a hiss, the air forced out of her lungs, bubbles of blood frothing from her lips. The shades surrounding them howled as they vanished, twisting to scraps of smoke and then they were gone as if they'd never been.

Izzy screamed, recoiling. A hand grabbed her, warm and

trembling. Ash's hand pulling her back and out of the way. No one was looking at them now. The shades had scattered.

Holly threw the demon down and leaped astride her, her face focused entirely on her work, gutting and butchering her body without a glance at Izzy or Ash. Blood splashed up onto her flawless face, just as Haniel's had before, drenching her hair, so dark a red it was almost black like tar. But there was no mistaking it as anything other than blood. She gathered up something from the gaping hole in Lili's chest and lifted it. Shrivelled and black, like a dried-out, over-roasted cut of meat, it took a moment before Izzy realised what she was seeing.

Lili's heart.

Holly smiled triumphantly and kicked the corpse aside. 'I thought she'd never bloody get here. And thank you so much for making it happen, Isabel Gregory. I couldn't have managed without you. You and little Art of course. Where has he got to? I promised him a reward.' She grinned wildly and pushed her golden hair back from her face with her free hand, leaving a smear of red on her skin. Izzy's stomach lurched in disgust. 'Oh, don't look like that. She was following you. What better way to get her here, I thought. So I lured you here as she tracked you. And now it's done. An angel's spark, a demon's heart.' She thrust the knot of desiccated meat into the ground, which opened beneath her touch, swallowing both the offering and Holly's arm up to the elbow.

The rumbling in the ground started again, a roar like a great beast trapped. But there was no cairn here, no lock to open. Was there? Or maybe there had been, so long ago that no one remembered it anymore, on this high point of land, in line with Howth and who knew what else?

Holly pulled back, shaking dirt off her clothes. From the ground she drew a line of light, just as she had in Izzy's vision. As she watched, the line moved like a dowsing rod, as if looking for something to touch, as if it was a sentient thing. It glowed.

'Stand back. They're coming and they're dying to get their hands on you. The king most of all.' She paused, thinking about it, a cruel smile spreading over her face. 'Or better yet ...' She leaned in close, driving Izzy back further so she bumped into Ash. 'Run!'

CHAPTER SEVENTEEN

Old Haunts, New Fears

It was afternoon by the time Jinx persuaded Silver to go with him and she could find time to get away. He couldn't go alone. The old hollow was a broken and grim place, filled with traces of pain and misery, the memories of much happier times shredded to rags and tatters by all the things Holly had done there. Jinx stood in the laneway outside, the cobbles loose beneath his feet like old rotten teeth. Even now, no one had dared recolonize the place. The door hung limply on one hinge and the taint of blood – old, congealed, rancid blood – filled his nostrils.

'We shouldn't be here,' said Silver again. She hung back, her arms wrapped around her body to hide the shivers. She had grown weaker, her need for sustenance growing by the second. Perhaps it was the proximity to her old touchstone, the tree Holly had torn down and burned. Perhaps it had just been far too long since she had dared to touch Dylan.

He'd tried to talk to her about that before, but she didn't want to. Silver had glared at him and gone back to whatever she was doing at the time. When he pressed her – because he was the only one who could press her on delicate subjects and get anywhere – the glare had turned to iron.

'He's ... he's too much, okay? I don't want to be beholden to him.'

'And you don't want to lose him either.'

'I don't want to kill him. Say it as it is.'

'But he's getting stronger. Like ... like the magic is seeping out of him. Don't you see that?'

'Of course I see it. But ... I can't explain it. I don't under-stand it. And that scares me, Jinx. Everyone expects me to know everything, and I don't. Okay?'

The death glare he knew. It wasn't actually dangerous – not like Holly's – but he knew it as a signal to back the hell off.

Everyone expected her to know everything. Like now. Like he did.

And she didn't. She was lost, which was why she had him. They could only trust each other.

'We need to take a look at least,' was all Jinx could say in reply. It had taken a solid hour of arguing to get her to agree to come with him. She wouldn't let him go alone. He'd already explained his theory to her. It sounded feeble to him now, standing here in front of the place where so many of their friends had died. But if Mari was back, why not the others? Why not someone who would know more? They had to look. Holly's victims were so many, and Mari had been but one incidental death along the way. One that closely affected Izzy. Could Holly pick and choose who was raised? Was it just her victims? Or were all the dead coming back? The veil between life and death was always thin so near to Samhain. That was why she'd chosen now to open the gates of the prison holding the Fear. And the Shining Ones.

He needed to find out. If it wasn't for him this wouldn't be happening. If it wasn't for him, the friends who had died here would still be alive.

'This wasn't your fault,' Silver said to him. 'You know that, don't you? You didn't cause this.'

That was the thing with Silver. Sometimes it felt like she could look straight into his damaged soul to winnow out his secrets, his guilt.

'Would she have doubted you if it wasn't for me?'

'Jinx, don't. I refused to tell her where you were. If that was anyone's fault—'

Yes.

The door of the hollow breathed the word, a long, low sigh, agony and hatred combined with longing. Silver took a step back, shivering like a deer poised for flight.

Silver, the voice came again. *We begged, we bled, you did … nothing!*

'I couldn't,' she whispered. 'I didn't know what she wanted to know. She saw through any lies. But I … I avenged you.'

A figure resolved itself from the shadows in the doorway, one that Jinx hardly recognised at first. The last time he'd seen that face it had been broken, those laughing eyes had been like glass marbles, gazing at eternity.

'Not very effective, your vengeance. She's as strong as ever she was. Maybe stronger.'

Sage tried to step through the doorway, but something unseen held him back. Such was the way of spirits until the nights when the veil was thinner, the turning days. Samhain was barely a day away, but still the veil held. Frustration darkened his features.

'Come in then,' he said. 'And ask your questions. We may not answer though. And you may never leave.'

'Sage.' Silver reached out her hand as she staggered forward but Jinx caught her, holding her back. The dead never released things they could grasp easily.

'Don't,' Jinx whispered.

'You wanted to come here.' Her voice came out in a hoarse sob.

'To see if what I suspected was true. To be sure. It's almost Samhain after all. No good comes from talking to the dead, nor from entering their hallways. You taught me that long ago, remember? Among all the old poems and songs of our people. *When the veil is weakest—*'

'*The dead will walk abroad.*'

'The veil grows weaker every day,' Sage interrupted. 'We'll all walk free again come Samhain. That night is our night. And if Holly succeeds the veil will be no more. The Shining Ones will tear it to shreds on their way through and burn the world to ashes. The Fear are already abroad. When their king trades places with the Grigori and becomes flesh again, all the dead will walk free. There will be no rest for any of us then, dead or alive.'

Rage set fire to Silver's voice and her hand tightened on Jinx's arm. 'What do you know of Holly's plan?'

Sage shrugged, a gesture so familiar, so like *him* that it felt as if Jinx had been punched in the gut. He held Silver tighter still. This had been their friend, their companion. Together they had made such music that mortals had wept, enraptured and bewitched. They could raise the Sídhe to a frenzy of lust or violence, or lull them to a calm so perfect they'd never want to disturb it. He'd been part of their lives for much longer than Izzy or Dylan.

'Holly will do as Holly always does — what Holly wants. But I know that this is the optimum time for her to raise a Shining One. She has everything she needs to hand. She has prepared for millennia, just in case the opportunity every presented itself, just in case she ever needed them. You spoke of vengeance, Silver. No one knows the nuances of revenge like your mother. She'll tear you all to pieces. She'll use you to destroy all those you love. Only the Lord of Death can help you stop her, but he's holed up in his hollow, up there in the hills.'

'Donn?' Silver's nails dug into Jinx's arm and she shuddered.

She hadn't truly seemed afraid until this moment, or rather the fear that emanated from her now was far sharper, so much more terrible. 'Why would we deal with Donn now? After so long.'

Sage laughed a bitter laugh. 'What choice do you have? The Fear are ghosts. Who knows more about ghosts than Donn? Who else is the Lord of the Dead?'

'And you know all this, how?' asked Jinx. 'When did you become so wise?'

Sage tapped his nose and grinned. So like himself. So like the being he once was. 'Sage means wise.'

'Yeah mate,' Jinx replied evenly. 'But it's also a type of herb.'

To his surprise the drummer laughed again, a genuine laugh this time. 'I've missed you, Jinx. Be seeing you soon. Real soon.'

The ground shook, rocking and bucking beneath them and Jinx felt something he had almost forgotten spear through him. Fear. Not for himself. For her. Izzy's fear infecting him like a poison.

Silver saw it, saw him stagger back. 'What is it? What's wrong?'

'Izzy. Isn't it always Izzy?'

'Where?'

He could feel it, could follow her fear like a scent, like a trace of vivid colours on the wind. 'This way. Quickly. She's in danger.'

'*Run!*'

The word echoed after them, cut with laughter and the two girls sprinted for the trees, scrambling downhill and trying desperately to keep their feet underneath them. Up ahead they saw a group of lads, laughing, passing a beer can between them and Izzy knew it was all going to go wrong. She knew, even as she hurtled towards them, that this was going straight to hell.

And there was nothing she could do to stop it.

Because morons were morons wherever you went.

'Hey, girls, where're yous off to so fast?'

'Keep going,' Ash yelled, her voice barely out of breath. How fit was she? 'Just keep going, Izzy.'

'Get out of the way!' Izzy tried to avoid them, but they spread out, ready to catch her. Clearly this was hilarious. Couldn't they see how serious it was? Couldn't they tell? 'There's a psycho up there. Get out of the way!'

And before she could slip by one of them grabbed her, his hand like a clamp on her arm, fingers digging painfully into her muscles. Her feet went out from underneath her in spray of dirt and stones and she landed full on her back, winded.

'You little bastards!' said Ash. 'Let her go.'

'Or what? What are you going to do, darling? Come here, let's look at you.'

There was a dull thud and a gasp of breath forced from a pair of lungs.

'Jaysus, bitch!' The one holding Izzy hauled her up by the arm. His friend was rolling down the hill and Ash had taken on a fighting stance, fists up.

'I said let her go. And you'd all better get the hell out of here too because—'

A wall of fog rolled down the hillside. And in the fog ...

The boy holding Izzy's arm dropped her and she scrambled back, trying to put as much space between herself and these scumbags as possible. But they weren't interested in her now.

They seemed mesmerized, transfixed by the sighing, singing voices coming from the fog. Stronger than ever, both the mist and the voices. She could see their faces, terror draining the colour away, leaving them gaunt and pale. Aged.

'We've got to go,' said Ash, reaching her side and pulling her forward, down the hill, away.

But the Fear were coming out of the fog now, no longer indistinct. They wore more solid forms this time. Their hands were long and their nails sharp as knives, as sharp as their grimacing smiles, which drew up too wide on their skeletal faces. Their eyes, hollowed out pits of darkness, fixed on the group before them and Izzy knew what they were thinking. Just one word. Prey.

'Izzy, please. We have to run.'

'We can't leave them. Ash, we can't just—'

But it was already too late.

Eochaid peeled back his lips from bone white teeth and spoke. 'Daughter of Míl, come to me now.' He seemed more solid now, more real than when she'd seen him before.

His voice sounded like tortured piano wires. When no one answered, he reached out, as he had reached out to Izzy in the school, and touched the nearest thug on the forehead.

The boy let out a strangled sob, his eyes bulging until they looked like they were half out of the sockets. Izzy watched a dark stain spread down the leg of his jeans, and the stink of piss reached her.

'Barely enough to feed a viper.' Eochaid's voice was an irritated hiss. 'Let alone all of us.' He tightened his grip and the boy went rigid, colour draining from him. He shuddered, once, twice and screamed, his hands stretching out like claws. Eochaid loomed over him, his mouth opening in a snarl, or a smile as he drank down his victim's terror. The scream tailed off, and left him gasping, whimpering and then silent. Ice crusted on his skin, in his eyes and he fell still. Eochaid shook him once, checking to see if there was any life left in him and then threw him aside like a discarded toy. He crashed against the nearest tree and landed heavily, rolling down the slope. Eochaid nodded to the other Fear who fell on the other terrified boys in a rush of screams and freezing terror. It was over far too quickly.

Eochaid watched in silence. And then he turned to Izzy, his cunning eyes fixed on her.

'Run!' Ash screamed and pulled her down the hill. This

time Izzy didn't hesitate.

Half way down there was a tree. It might have been two trees or one split apart when it was just a sapling. Whatever it was, they grew side by side, almost forming an oval as they curved back towards each other.

It jerked back and forth in her view and Izzy fixed all her attention on it as if it would help her, as if it would save her. She threw herself downhill with Ash beside her. She could feel them coming, feel the wall of cold and terror behind her, rolling down towards them, towards the unsuspecting town.

'Oh God, oh God, oh God,' she could hear Ash beside her, the words like a mantra, forcing her to keep going, to keep running.

And the air between the trees shimmered. It moved in that way she knew too well. It was the gate to Sídheway, the same one she'd come through. And even as she threw herself towards it, the air parted.

Jinx stepped out, and caught her in his arms.

It was so sudden her feet swept on, as if she was still running, and nothing could stop her. Off balance on the hill, she fell, taking Jinx with her and they rolled, body over body down over rocks and tree roots.

The fog followed them, sweeping over the steep slope, carrying nightmares with it. It was going to get them. Her and now Jinx too. And it was all her fault. The Fear were going to get them.

But nothing happened. She looked up, tears blinding her,

the thundering of her heart inside her drowning out everything.

Holly walked down the hill, the Fear parting for her like an honour guard. She smiled at them, not a good smile. But then Izzy had never seem Holly smile what she'd term a good smile. This was laced with venom and the triumph of revenge about to strike.

'Well now, I was wondering when you'd get here, Jinx by Jasper. It's about time.' She stopped, regarding the two of them tangled together. Ash crouched off to one side, half hiding, unwilling or unable to leave. Holly ignored her for the moment.

'Holly,' whispered Jinx, as if his breath had been knocked from him. 'Grandmother …'

Her smile widened still, but didn't reach her eyes. 'Yes. Get up, boy. I have need of you.'

'No.' But he got up all the same, disentangling himself from Izzy as gently as he could. His every movement was wary, guarded. But she could sense the way he vibrated with alarm. 'I don't serve you anymore.'

'Oh Jinx, you silly boy … you will *always* serve me. Whether you want to or not. I thought we'd established that already.'

She stretched out her hands and whispered something. It made the sound of leaves blowing in the wind, rustling against each other. The Fear drew closer, hungry again despite feeding already. Izzy saw them as they circled the gate, making Ash creep reluctantly forwards.

'Do we need some incentive?' asked Holly. She snapped her

fingers and a shout went up from the bushes. One of the Fear rushed out of it, hauling a small, struggling figure with it.

Art, it was Art. The leprechaun sprawled in the leaves and mulch, squirming in an attempt to get away, and failing.

'Let him go,' Jinx said.

Holly shook her head. 'He's a traitor, Jinx. Isn't he? Tell him, Izzy.'

Jinx stared at her, and read whatever Holly wanted him to see in her face.

'Please Jinx, please,' Art howled. 'You know me. You know how it is. I tried to make it to the castle, but she had me. She made me. Please Jinx! I had to bring the girl here. I had to!'

Jinx shuddered and Izzy scrambled to her feet, wrapping her arms around him. 'Don't listen to them. Please Jinx. Don't—'

His body turned hard as iron and just as cold. Izzy looked up into his face and didn't know him. His eyes froze and darkened, the bright silver dulling, that rebellious gleam fading. He looked confused, like someone waking from a dream. Around his neck the new line of tattoos glowed with a terrible brightness.

'Jinx?'

'He can't hear you, Isabel Gregory.' Holly's voice rose in a chant. 'Jinx is mine, my blood, my bondsman, always mine. I made you, Jinx by Jasper. I made a vessel of you, a thing that could hold a primal god. I took a broken, useless runt of a child and I made you for a purpose and now it's time. My magic doesn't just surround you, you are riddled with it, right to the core of your being. It isn't just in your tattoos and your piercings.' She tapped the side of her head with one perfectly manicured fingernail. 'It's in here. Forever.'

Jinx pushed Izzy aside without a word and walked up the hillside. He dropped to his knees at Holly's feet and bowed his head.

'My Lady Holly,' he said, and it sounded as if he had to force the words out through clenched teeth. 'I am yours to command.'

She glanced at Art, who was still trying find a way out, a way of escape.

'Kill him,' said Holly.

'No!' shouted Izzy and Art at the same moment and she lurched back to shield the leprechaun. Not for his sake perhaps, but for Jinx's. She couldn't let him do it.

But Jinx didn't move. He shivered again and Izzy knew he was trying to fight. Trying and failing, but trying nonetheless. While he couldn't break free, he still didn't obey her, not completely.

Holly scowled and then nodded to Osprey. The Aes Sídhe assassin covered the ground in seconds, his feathered cloak whispering as he moved. He seized the gibbering, pleading, sobbing Art in strong and implacable hands and deftly snapped his neck. Then he flung the body down in front of the Fear and turned back, bowing to Holly with elaborate grace.

'He's still got a lot to learn,' he said.

'And we'll make sure he learns it, my dear,' she replied, her gaze fixed on Jinx, aglow with malevolence. 'The hard way.'

CHAPTER EIGHTEEN

Falling Apart

Onstage, the lights were bright and the crowd beneath him bucked and surged like an animal to the music. Dylan could feel it, their energy, their response to the songs they played and it was addictive. His songs, his music, and they responded immediately. Like magic.

He glanced to the left of the stage, where Clodagh was dancing, swinging her hair out, twisting to the tune and he smiled. He couldn't help it. She'd come in alone, unable to get Izzy on the phone even though they'd planned to come in together. Clodagh wasn't happy about it, but the music made her forget. So did access to the green room.

The strange melancholy haunting him ebbed away with Clodagh around. She didn't know that last night he was seeing off demons with magic that shouldn't even be his. Seeing her simple enjoyment made him feel normal again. Just for a moment. Like the old days. Before Silver. Before everything got so complicated.

Only it wasn't like the old days. Not really.

Dylan and his band might only be the supporting act, but everything was falling together. The audience was right there, held with music and magic. The power hummed through his body and out into the world around him. It changed everything, coloured everything with the Silver's presence.

No sign of Silver either. It made him sure that something was going on, but he didn't know what. It couldn't be good.

Winding up the number, he met Steve's gaze and saw him nodding furiously towards the bar where there were more guys in suits. The scout stood with them and gave them another of his enormous thumbs-up gestures. It was looking good. Really good.

He switched tunes and started the one he'd written for Mari. It took everything down a level, softer, gentler, melancholy, building to tragic once Steve's vocals kicked in, harmonising with Dylan's.

When he concentrated on the melody, and the elusive harmonies that went with it, he could almost sense her standing nearby.

Mari.

His little sister. The one he had failed to help, to save. The one he had let die.

The music called her, charmed her, and he knew it was a song for her and her alone.

It was Mari's song.

It flowed like a dream, bright and dainty to begin with, but then smoothing out, a sweeping melody that undulated through the refrain.

Mari's song. He wasn't sure about this. Hadn't been, from the moment the lads had told him that they had to include it in the set. And then more and more of his songs. Fewer covers now, more original songs – that was Steve's mantra – *'cause your songs kill.*

Lots of things killed, but not in the way Steve meant.

And that was when he felt it – a chill, as if he stood in a pocket of arctic air in spite of the heat in the club generated by exertion, the crowd and the lights.

He glanced at Clodagh, to see if she felt it too, but she was swaying, eyes closed, tears on her cheeks.

Mari stood behind her, as if he had summoned her with the song.

She smiled at him this time. So much better than the scowl he'd seen before when she'd stood in the doorway under the light, or outside the college gate. And he'd forgotten the effect of her smile. Mari could make anyone forget all their troubles when she smiled. She made him forget guilt and doubt. The world seemed to separate, like a waking dream, and while he sang, part of him stood still, enthralled by her presence.

'*I like it,*' she whispered, her voice so faint. He shouldn't have been able to hear it over the music, but he could.

'*Good,*' he replied – in his mind rather than with his voice.

Dizziness swept over him, a strange sense of double exposure, as if part of him was there on stage, playing and part of him looked on, talking to his sister. Dylan glanced down. His fingers glowed. Traces of light clung like dust to the strings. He had to keep playing. He couldn't lose her again. He couldn't stop in the middle of a number, especially not this number.

'*The only way to stop it is to visit the halls of the dead,*' she said in answer to a question he hadn't asked.

'*Stop what?*'

And she smiled. Without answers this time. Infuriating, difficult, dangerous Mari. He knew her of old.

'*Where are the halls of the dead, Mari?*'

'*I'll be waiting there for you. For you and for Izzy.*' She brushed her hand down the length of Clodagh's hair, not quite touching it. As if she couldn't bear to touch it and she couldn't bear not to.

'*Mari, where is it? Why would we go there?*'

'*Because you'll have to. She'll have to. And so you'll go too, whether Silver will let you go or not. They'll all want you, you know? All that magical power locked inside you. You're just like a ripe fruit to them, Dylan. Even to Silver. Just you wait. She'd drain you dry in a moment if she had to.*'

Dylan shuddered as she spoke that one terrible truth. '*I know that.*' he replied.

Mari studied him for a long moment as if she could see into his mind and pick through the thoughts there as easily as she picked through his vinyl collection. '*Maybe you do. But I* wonder if you really believe it.'

'Why are you here?'

'You called me. Music and magic are a powerful combination, Dylan. Always have been. That's what makes you so dangerous. And in such danger. And besides, I wanted to come. I wanted to see you play. I wanted to warn you.'

'Really? Why?'

'You're my brother, duh. Besides, the things that are coming ... no one should have to face that. Especially not you. And if Izzy heads into trouble like that, you'll follow, won't you?'

'What do you think Izzy's going to do?'

Mari shook her head. 'What she always does. And you'll be right there with her.'

She froze for a moment and a brief trace of fear flowed over her face.

'What is it?'

'They're here. You have to leave now. They're here.'

Dylan shuddered and snapped back into his body, like an elastic band stretched too far that slips free. His gasped breath misted in front of his mouth. The notes almost faltered as his fingers shook. He covered quickly and blinked as the lights swung around to pick him out. Dry ice swirled around his feet, spilled over the edge of the stage and into the audience. It snaked around the edge of the room in a way it shouldn't. It really shouldn't.

It wasn't dry ice. It was fog.

The Fear filled the club. He could see them now, forming

out of the mist, wandering through the enraptured crowd, invisible to them for now. Just for a little longer. Invisible and waiting, ready to pounce. Oh God, this was bad. Because the moment they felt strong enough, they'd tear through this place, this crowd. They'd feed.

He knew it.

Mari's voice came very close to his ear, her colder than cold breath playing against his cheek. He couldn't see her now. *'You can't help them. The Fear are here. You have to go.'*

'Go where.'

'Where you always go. To Silver. To Izzy. You have to leave, Dylan.'

'Mari—' he began, trying to find a way to say thanks or sorry, or anything coherent, but she cut him off.

'Keep singing. The moment you stop, they'll attack. I think you're all that's holding them back now. Go to the House of Donn. He's the only one who can help you. The dead belong to him. You're a target too, Dylan, with all that magic in you. Don't you get it? Go!'

One of the Fear rose in front of him now. Through the semi-transparent body he could see the others and then he couldn't. The body turned solid and the song came to a stop. He couldn't keep singing. His voice died in his throat, choked with fear. Unable to think of anything else to do, Dylan swung his guitar around at the amp and feedback screeched through the club. People screamed and the Fear attacked – he couldn't tell which happened first. Everything blurred. Dylan dived to the side of the stage where Clodagh backed away, her face white with terror. She could see them too. All of them.

He landed heavily, awkwardly, knocking the air from himself. But he couldn't let that stop him.

'Clodagh. We have to get out of here. Now.'

'Dylan. What's going on? What are they—?'

Her voice died in her throat. Mist poured towards them while all around them the Fear drew terror from the shattered audience, those they'd fed on, those they turned on now. The strength it gave them made them coalesce, take form. Clodagh could only stare at one, transfixed as it coiled up before her and loomed over her, forming a figure.

The Fear surrounded the two of them. There was no way out. Clodagh sobbed something almost incoherent and Dylan pulled her against him, burying her face in his chest so she wouldn't see them.

The face in the mist leered at them and then turned its full attention on Dylan.

'Lady Holly said you would run, but that we should chase. She said you would beg, but that we should not heed you.'

'I don't care what she said.' And he wasn't begging for anything.

'She said you should come with us, pretty shining boy. She said if you fight us we should make you.'

Holly wanted him. That couldn't be good. None of this was good. 'If she wants me she wouldn't let you hurt me.'

It reached out a long clawed hand and brushed its knife-like fingertips against Clodagh's hair. 'She didn't say anything about not hurting your friend. The second prison has been opened. We're free to feed now. And these other cattle make us strong. So strong.'

The other Fear drew closer, clustering around their prey.

Clodagh sucked in a breath and turned in his arms. Power-less to stop her, Dylan tried to say 'no', but the word died in his throat. The creature's nails scraped her cheek, drawing a thin line of blood.

It bared its teeth and Clodagh screamed. The spell holding Dylan back shattered with the sound. He seized her arm, pull-ing her clear, and ran for the fire exit, dragging her after him.

'What was it? What was that?' She panted as she ran, but still tried to get the words out. 'What was that thing?'

'I… I don't know.'

'It's something to do with Izzy, isn't it?'

Izzy… and him. They'd come for him and Mari had tried to warn him. Mari had come back from the dead to warn him. 'Something. Maybe. Just run.'

'They're coming after us.'

Of course they were. And how could you outrun some-thing like that?

They reached the main road outside and almost fell under a passing truck. The lights flared, bright and blinding, but Dylan kept going, skidding around the corner. Everything fell still. Quiet as anything. As if waiting for something worse.

Alarms blared everywhere, the fire alarm, he hoped. Some people burst out of the doors of the club, screaming, pulling at their hair and clothes. He'd left everyone in there. Dear Jesus, he'd left the guys and all those people …

But he couldn't go back. Holly wanted him. Holly had sent them for him.

Two figures stood on the other side of the road, watching the chaos with glee, dressed in black and white, perfectly turned out and pristine. Magpies. Izzy's description had been clear enough. So had her warnings.

But they were probably his only hope. Because getting out of here any other way wasn't going to happen.

'Hey!' he yelled. 'Magpies. Hey!'

They started towards him, grinning like the nightmares they were. Like they'd been waiting for him.

'Who are they?' she shouted. And then stopped, digging in her heels, her hands like claws on his arm. 'I remember them. Jesus, Dylan, what are you doing?'

'Clodagh, there isn't time.'

'They're monsters.'

'Yes. But they're better than what's behind us. We don't have a choice.'

'But … but Izzy said …'

'Clodagh, look.' The mist was gathering, rolling from the fire exit and the main doors of the club and in it, he could see a horde of monsters. Teeth and clawed bared, eyes fixed on the pair of them, on their prey. They had claws like knives and mouths like voids, ready to suck them both in.

Other people could see them now, so great was their power and strength. Screaming, panicking people, feeding them with terror, making them stronger even as they rolled out over Dublin. Death and devastation would follow. And the Fear would follow him.

Clodagh sucked in a breath and gripped his hand even tighter.

'Okay,' she said. 'Okay.' She swallowed hand and looked up into his face. 'You'd just better be bloody right. Or if they don't kill you, I will.'

Jinx struggled against the spells but they closed around him, tighter than an iron maiden. They burned beneath his skin like iron too. The silver that pierced his skin flashed, bright points of agony, and he couldn't help himself. Couldn't stop. Holly spoke … no, Holly *commanded*, and he had to obey. His body and mind, so used to doing her will, complied at once.

Magic. It had to be magic. Her magic, which had woven itself around him, through him for his whole life. She was his blood, his kin. It only made her hold on him stronger.

Somewhere far off Izzy was shouting his name. He could hear her and it tore him apart inside to hear the anguish in her voice. Izzy, who wouldn't give up on him, who wouldn't leave him, not like he'd left her.

He looked up into Holly's face, her perfect, impervious face and saw the loathing in the depths of her eyes. And the triumph. She had him. She knew it.

And so did he.

'Doesn't she understand you yet?' asked Holly, almost gently but with an all too familiar mocking lilt.

He wanted to answer. He wanted to tell her to go fuck herself, but he couldn't move. His voice didn't belong to him now.

'Jinx, please ...'

'Still begging. Do you ever do anything else, Grigori-child?'

'I never begged *you*.' Izzy said it with a matching venom. 'I never will.'

'Oh, you will. If not for yourself, then for him.'

'What are you going to do to him?'

'What I always intended to do to him. He's mine. My property. He could have just been an unwanted runt, a by-blow, but I've given him purpose.' She reached out and stroked his hair. Jinx wanted to recoil, to throw himself away, to change and run as fast as he could in the other direction, but he couldn't.

Instead, he had to endure her touch. She took the second wire, slender and glowing like the one Osprey had wrapped around his neck. This one joined the first. It sizzled against his skin, but this time he couldn't scream, couldn't tear at it. He couldn't move. Only suffer in silence and frozen stillness. And that terrible brightness surged up inside him again, engulfing him, threatening to blot him out completely.

'Let him go!' Izzy cried, her voice filled with the echo of his anguish.

'Or what? What exactly will you do Grigori? Surrounded

by the Fear. Eochaid can take you now if he wants. No one will stop him. You're alone. Useless.'

And then there was another voice. 'Not quite alone, mother.'

Silver stepped from the gate to the Sídheways, magic already kindling at her fingertips. Holly's own magic, stolen from her when Silver broke her touchstone.

But Holly didn't seem perturbed.

'You? Grown a spine now, have you?' Holly stepped forwards, past Jinx. He lurched to his feet and turned, ready to follow her, though it was the last thing he wanted to do. Light coursed through him, Holly's power surrounded him. He had no choice. 'Let me tell you, Silver, I'll have it all back in no time at all. Now, Jinx and I are leaving.'

'Over my dead body.'

'That can be arranged too. It would be a pleasure. But a waste I fear.'

'I'm not letting you take him anywhere.'

'Your precious little nephew? Or my weapon. That's what he is, remember? That's what I made him become. And now it's time for the next step. Get out of the way, Silver. Or I'll unleash the Fear on you, daughter or not.'

Silver just smiled. It wasn't a pleasant expression. It mirrored Holly's. Mother and daughter. Closest they could be among the Aes Sídhe. Matriarch and heir.

'You forget something, as usual, Mother,' said Silver. 'I have something you'll never have.'

'And what's that?'

'Friends.'

The Portal rippled behind her and the fae came through, more of them than Jinx would have expected. There were banshees there, and leps, quite a few bodachs. And Cú Sídhe. Silver must have sent word to Brí to have that many of his people behind her. How she did it, he didn't know. He'd only been minutes ahead of her. But with the amount of magic Silver now controlled — housed in Dylan, but hers nonetheless — anything was possible.

Holly didn't flinch, but she hesitated. That alone should have given Jinx a glimmer of hope. But it didn't; he couldn't hope.

He was trapped. If she left, she'd take him with her. Holly would never forgive him for almost breaking free of her. He stared at Izzy, tried to tell her with his eyes alone, prayed she'd pick up his thoughts.

And behind her, the other girl reached out. She took Izzy's hand in hers and leaned forward, whispering something. Jinx strained to hear but he couldn't. Slowly, Izzy nodded and returned her gaze to him again.

'Jinx, if you can hear me … remember the hill? Remember what you said to me that night? You can remember, can't you? Please.'

She sounded so desperate, so afraid for him.

Remember? It was seared into his memory. He'd thought he'd lost her. He'd thought he was lost himself and that they had unleashed hell on earth in the form of two vengeful fallen angels.

He'd said he was sorry. He'd begged her forgiveness. He'd told her he loved her. He'd said all those things that the Sídhe could not say, and only Izzy's magic had let him do it.

Did she think that had changed? After the way he had treated her, it was a fair assumption. But he hadn't changed, his feelings hadn't changed. He just couldn't move.

Then he saw what Izzy was holding. The knife. The one she'd used to stab herself with on the hill. And previously… previously, she'd tried to kill Holly and almost killed him in the process.

Or the angel had. He wasn't sure any more.

Was she trying to warn him? Why would she warn him when she knew what happened before? Did she want him dead? That was it. He was Holly's again, and she wanted him dead.

Izzy moved, just as quick, with all the training that her father must have put her through. He wouldn't have thought her capable, but the hard glint her in eyes told him all he needed to know.

She flung herself at Holly, who folded back out of reach, the leader, letting others fight for her. Jinx did the only thing he could imagine doing, the thing everyone seemed to expect of him – he threw himself between them.

The knife glanced across his side, cutting but not stabbing. Not like before. A line of pain rather than the agony of the last time. She twisted aside at the last moment, pulled the strike and her elbow caught him right in the solar plexus.

Breath went from his body and she landed on him, pinning him down, Holly forgotten. The other girl dived on him to help her.

'Silver!' Izzy shouted. 'Get us out of here. Now!'

Holly turned on her with a rage, but they were already up, dragging him with them, heading for the gateway. He tried to struggle, tried to break free. He couldn't let them take him. Not like this.

He needed to stay with Holly. She owned him, she commanded him. If he left her —

The bodach that met them at the gate loomed over the two girls, and when he took hold of Jinx, there was no hint of escape. It was like being seized by stone. And Jinx recognised him — the one he'd fought. The one he'd beaten. He didn't even know his name.

'Get him through,' Izzy shouted. 'Get him to safety now.' She'd tricked him, he realised that now. She'd counted on him needing to protect Holly because of all the obedience beaten into him over so many years, because of all her spells and enchantments, because Holly still owned him, in spite of his will and his heart. And Izzy, had counted on that and used it to trap him.

To save him. But she hadn't. She couldn't get Holly out of his head, could she?

Jinx by Jasper ...

He glanced back, and Holly was there on the rise. As the other fae faced off against the Fear — not engaging yet, but ready if the need arose – Holly lifted both her hands out to either side and whispered words. Words that carried on the breeze, but words meant for him alone.

Words that struck him like a physical blow.

Jinx felt the piercings in his body turn white hot, the tracery of tattoos twist and tighten, digging barbs into and beneath his skin. Her curse winnowed into his veins, plunged into his mind. The wires that had burrowed beneath the skin of his neck ignited like strips of potassium. He arched his back as agony shook him like a terrier, and then he crumpled into darkness, welcoming oblivion.

CHAPTER NINETEEN

Beyond Dubh Linn

They emerged onto a crowded College Green, right under the looming edifices of the gate to Trinity College and the Bank of Ireland.

Life swirled around them. City life, Dublin life. Someone started pointing and shouting, but to be honest most of the people just ignored them.

'He's seeing through the glamour,' said Silver. 'Must be a bit of old blood in him. We ought to check him out.' She nodded to one of the Cú Sídhe – not Blythe or her brother, Izzy was sure she would remember them.

'Leave him,' Izzy said, in a voice much louder than she'd intended. She was shaking again. She couldn't stop. 'No one will listen to him anyway. He's just high or something. Why bother about it?'

The guy had stopped shouting now. He'd noticed that they

were watching him and backed away, terrified. Of course he did. Izzy knew how scary they could be. Even Silver.

Especially Silver.

The guy turned and ran, cursing and shouting as he did so, dodging in and out of the pillars of the bank. People folded out of his way, desperate to avoid him, and Izzy felt a pang of pity. Did he start taking drugs because he could see the fae around them? Or did the drugs have some weird cocktail effect on his mind, opening up his perception to the world of Dubh Linn and its inhabitants? Which one messed with his sanity more?

'This way,' said Silver. 'Quickly, we don't have much time. The door is a fixed point, but it'll only open to where we want to go for a little while.'

Izzy sighed. Of course it would. Why would anything be easy? But they needed to get out of sight. And they needed to get help for Jinx.

She reached out for his dangling, limp hand and squeezed it gently. He felt so cold.

If they told her he was dead, she'd believe it. And it would shatter her to tiny pieces.

'Let's go then. Lead the way.'

Ash came up beside her. 'Are you okay?'

'Yeah, I ... are you?' She was taking all this remarkably calmly.

'I guess.' She looked around nervously but she hadn't freaked out yet. 'They're friends of yours right? I mean... I know they aren't ...' She swallowed the words she wanted to say. Normal, perhaps? Or human? She'd seen everything. She'd used the Sídheway with them, seen them as they actually were – Silver lithe and graceful, shimmering with power; the Cú Sídhe animal in humanlike form; the bodach, a towering hulk of muscle and brawn that could be a tree or a rock formation. And Jinx of course. Jinx all hard lines and paler than pale skin, with his metallic eyes.

But then she'd seen every nightmare in that mist. She'd seen Eochaid just as clearly as Izzy had.

'They're good, aren't they?' Ash tried again. She stared at Silver's back, the way her hair shimmered as she walked.

'Good.' Izzy wasn't sure she'd use that word. 'Maybe. Sometimes. But I think ... they're kind of on our side for now. So long as we're on his.' She nodded at Jinx. And so long as *they* were still on his. Izzy didn't know how long that would be.

And which side was Jinx on?

He'd bowed down to Holly, knelt before her, her servant again. He'd looked at Izzy like he didn't even know her, and at Holly like she was a goddess. And they'd all seen that. She knew Jinx had struggled to be seen as more than just Holly's assassin. Her dog. Had he just undone it all? From the glances some of the fae were giving him, they thought so.

They crossed the road, Silver stopping the traffic by will alone it seemed, and headed up until they were almost at the place where College Green became Dame Street. A few horns blared, a few voices cursed, but no one seemed to quite know why. A freak traffic jam, a brakelight backlog without obvious cause.

Silver stopped. The pedestrian crossing signals flashed wildly behind her, the beeps loud and insistent, but she didn't pay it any attention. They stood outside a doorway. Just an arched wooden door in a redbrick building squeezed between two entirely different grey ones, one pale and ornate with black metalwork, the other windowed in a regular pattern. But this building was different, a strip of red bricks set back, barely wider than the door itself, as if the building had been pressed together between the tectonic plates of its neighbours. Over the door, a white – or rather off-white with pollution – plaque depicted a ship. There were no windows. Nothing else. Just a strip of redbrick, all the way up.

The Tiny Building, people sometimes called it. A Dublin oddity. Izzy always assumed it was part of one of the buildings on either side, when she ever thought about it at all. Now she wasn't so sure.

Silver wasted no time. She knocked rapidly – a quick staccato rhythm both purposeful and whimsical – and from inside came an answering knock. A code, Izzy realised. Silver knocked again, just once and this time the knock boomed, drowning out even the noise of the traffic right behind them.

The door opened. 'Inside,' said Silver. 'Quickly.'

What else could they do? Izzy glanced at Ash, who looked resolute but freaked. Of course. What else would she be?

Izzy nodded to her, and stepped inside.

Into Dubh Linn. Into something more than Dubh Linn.

The fading evening light streamed around her, multi-coloured as if it fell through stained glass. She'd only seen that effect in churches before. All around her, huge ferns and exotic palms shifted in a breeze she couldn't feel, cutting that rainbow. High overhead she could see a dome, made of scalloped slivers of coloured glass, the source of the amazing light. A greenhouse, she realised, but huge and ornate, like the ones at the Botanical Gardens but with the glass coloured like the canopy of the Olympia theatre. It stretched up above her, maybe a hundred feet.

'Where are we?' she asked.

'We call it the Liberty,' said Silver briefly. 'A sacred space, a place of freedom, of our own Sídhe jurisdiction, where we are answerable to nowhere and no one else. Once we had many such Liberties but now ... well, this is all that is left. A little bubble of safety. At least we should be safe here. I've asked the others to meet us. Your father included.'

'And Jinx?'

Silver glanced back at him and there was no disguising the concern on her face. 'I hope one of them can help him.'

'One of who?'

'The Council.'

'*Your* Council? Brí and Amadán and all that lot? Are you crazy?'

'Maybe. But I don't know what else to do. There are few as skilled as your mother in the arts of healing—'

'She's not my mother,' Izzy interrupted, almost automatically.

Silver ignored her, '—but those who are, I've asked them to come too. There is magic here far beyond anything I know. Holly... Holly didn't share.'

'I imagine.' She couldn't. Not having Holly as a mother. Holly had infiltrated every aspect of Silver's life, controlling every tiny detail. That was what Holly had done, wasn't it? She'd given Silver just enough rope and then tied her up with it.

If it hadn't been for Dylan.

Speaking of whom, 'Where's Dylan?'

Silver flinched at the mention of his name. 'I don't know. He has a gig tonight.'

'I thought you'd be there. I thought—'

'That I follow his every move? Hardly. Neither of us are there, are we?'

Izzy regarded her carefully. It wasn't the whole truth. Silver had to know something. Dylan had become the reservoir of all her power. She *ought* to know where he was. For that reason alone.

And Izzy wasn't sure which frightened her more – that Silver clearly didn't know where he was, or that Izzy could see through her so clearly.

They reached the centre of the Liberty and the jungle of plants thinned out to reveal a lawn. Chamomile, she realised, as they walked over it. The scent rose as their feet crushed the plants, which bounced back up as if they'd never been there once they had passed. Here and there exotic flowers burst out of the earth in clumps, bright and violent, the colours clashing. Some of them Izzy could name – bird of paradise flowers, oriental lilies, and about half a million different orchids – and others that she couldn't, because she wasn't sure they really came from her world. Or if they had they'd gone extinct thousands of years ago. But here, they bloomed, they thrived. There was no sense of season. Just life. Wild and dangerous, life.

In the centre of the green a single pillar of stone rose from the grass. It was twice her height, at least, and bigger than she was at the base, but it tapered as it went up. Not to a point. This wasn't a stone version of the Spire on O'Connell's Street. This was something else. Much older. She could tell, just by the vibrations in the air around it.

'The Vikings called it the Stein,' said Silver. 'They used it when they settled here, as a place to meet, to discuss, and to find a workable solution with us. It wasn't easy. Not one of us had any time for them but life has to go on. Peace had to be negotiated so we did that. The Long Stone… it's so much older though. It once stood alone here and no one would dare come near it. This was our place, our Liberty. The Milesians had more sense. Even the Nemedians … anyway, it was long ago.'

'Why is it here? Why does no one know about it?'

'We moved it here, out of Dublin and in here. To make a

sacred place, a meeting point. To be the focal point of the Liberty, to hold it in place. Weren't you listening?'

'There's a Long Stone pub,' said Ash, her voice unexpectedly near. Izzy and Silver stared at her. 'It's just over by Trinity. And a stone there too.'

'It's a copy. A bad one,' Silver replied. 'Come, we need to get Jinx looked at and to get on with this. Follow me.'

Izzy frowned at Ash for interrupting. She'd been getting somewhere. She wasn't sure where exactly, but Silver was talking. For once. And now she wasn't any more.

Brightly coloured silk tents had been set up at various points around the central lawn. It looked like some kind of medieval fair. The material moved in the breeze as well. A breeze that didn't touch them, that didn't seem to touch anything but the plants and the tents. Silver led them to a pale blue one and the bodach laid Jinx down on the low bed covered in more sumptuous fabrics.

'I'll bring help as soon as it arrives,' she told them. 'And I'll send refreshments, if you need them. Don't leave. This place … it may look beautiful, but it's dangerous. Understand?'

Of course she did. Izzy knew that about everything connected with the fae. Every last one of them. Even Jinx. Even Silver.

Perhaps, especially Silver.

And like that, she was gone.

'Right,' said Ash. 'Well, great.' She tried her phone and cursed at it. 'No signal. Figures.'

Izzy swallowed hard. 'I should … I should probably explain.'

Ash gave her one of those looks, almost worthy of Mari. 'Really? Do you think? That'd be great. Because at the moment it's all kinds of crazy and I can only go so far with the flow. Want to start at the beginning?'

Dylan knew this was so far out of 'not good' that it might as well have been a budget airlines arrival point somewhere on the continent. He'd need to take the handy shuttle bus to get even in the vicinity of 'not good', and pay twice over to reach anywhere near 'all right'. But he couldn't let Clodagh know that. She was barely holding it together as it was, and he couldn't let anything happen to her. She'd been Mari's friend since junior infants. They'd always been together, a pair of little princesses. While he'd hung around with Izzy, Clodagh and Mari had spent their lives like sisters. The sister she never had, but always wanted. The sister who would do whatever she said.

Which meant, by extension, Dylan needed to look after her. Because he'd failed to look after Mari, and Izzy was nowhere to be seen.

The Magpies drove way too fast, while Clodagh and Dylan slid from side to side in the back seat of a car that had never heard of a seatbelt. They hung on to each other, trying not to listen to the conversation up in front.

'So I says to him, 'are you starting?' And then he did. So I brutalised him.'

'Y'did not.'

'I did too. And then his old wan starts in as well. But I wasn't taking her on, was I?'

'You'd be mad to.'

The car screeched to a halt, almost throwing both Dylan and Clodagh into the front seat. 'So what did you do?'

'Nothing. She started in on him, not me. Crucified his sad little arse.' He turned back, grinning madly at them both. 'We're here. Time to get out.'

Here was the middle of nowhere, a jumble of rocks and gorse and overgrown green that couldn't decide if it was going to be one thing or another. Here was the tail end of a mud track up a mountain with nothing but the odd sheep around for miles. But what choice did he have? He'd asked for help. And this was where it led him.

'Right then,' said Clodagh when he didn't react. She opened the door and stepped out, stabilizing herself against the car. 'Damn it, I'm meant to walk in this? Are you, like, totally mental?'

'What do you want, love?'

'Do you want us to carry you?' They sniggered as they said it.

She just gave them a withering, princess glare. 'Like I'd let you.'

Dylan got out of the car, ready to defend her if he could. But what could he do if they tried anything? He'd do something though. He knew that.

His fingers itched and he could sense the swirling warmth beneath his skin, just as when the demons had threatened Jinx and Izzy. He'd used the magic inside him then. He could do it again, if he needed to. Couldn't he?

He could feel it there. Just out of his reach. All he had to do was grab it.

'Well now,' said another voice, a booming voice, bright with jollity but laced with something darker. 'What have we here? Friends, I hope.'

The nearest rock slid back and a man stepped out of the darkness beyond. He wore a suit so beautifully tailored it didn't need to say bespoke. That was a given. His hair was silver grey, but his face wasn't particularly old. It wasn't young either but rather had a kind of unearthly smoothness about it. The kind he'd seen before in Brí and in Holly.

He was fae, and he was old. One of the oldest.

He remembered Izzy talking about them, and Silver had mentioned him. It couldn't be anyone else.

'Amadán?' he said, in as respectful a tone as possible. 'We need help.'

'So I believe.' He waved a hand at the pair. 'They called ahead and told me all about it. They saw the Fear as well so don't fret.'

'You know about them?'

'Oh I know *all* about them. And that they're on the loose. Who do you think told Jinx?'

'What are they?' Clodagh asked.

Amadán peered at her, like a kindly old uncle until you saw the piercing sharpness of his eyes. 'Monsters, my dear. The very definition of monsters.'

'And what are you?' she asked. She tightened her arms around her body in a self-hug that Dylan wished didn't make her look so vulnerable. It was never good to look weak in front of the fae, especially the Aes Sídhe.

'Oh, I'm a monster too, dear.'

'Leave her alone,' said Dylan.

Amadán's attention swung around to him and Dylan wished he'd shut the hell up instead, just for a moment. Until he realised that Clodagh was in the clear now. Relief and fear made his skin tighten on his bones and the magic fizz up like a bottle had been shaken. 'I haven't seen you in months, Dylan O'Neill. Did Silver keep you so very close all this time?'

He knew that wasn't true, of course. He knew far more than he was letting on. 'I ... I've been around. I have a life.'

'For now. Until she needs much more from you than you're prepared to give. Now, shall we go?'

'Where?'

'Where indeed? Silver has called a meeting and I am most eager to attend. Particularly with you at my side.'

'I'm not standing beside you.'

'Oh I think you will.' He nodded. One of the Magpies grabbed Clodagh, jerked her close against him and grinned, all his teeth on display. 'So, shall we go?' asked Amadán.

CHAPTER TWENTY

Monsters

Izzy paced back and forth, waiting for Silver to return. Jinx slept on, but it didn't seem like normal sleep. He just lay there, still as a corpse. She had to keep checking that he was still breathing, holding her hand against his chest, bending down so she could feel the faint whisper of his breath on her cheek.

'Please wake up,' she said. 'Please, come back.'

But he didn't respond. He didn't even seem to hear. It had been hours and he never moved.

When Ash pulled a pile of cushions down and curled up on them, quickly falling asleep herself – but a normal, noisy sleep – the weight of it all made Izzy crumble. Suddenly they were alone and she didn't know what to do. She watched Ash carefully, but the other girl didn't stir. She was exhausted too. Only when she was sure that she wouldn't wake her friend,

Izzy moved closer to Jinx.

She lay down beside him, held him in her arms and breathed in and out, trying to match her breath to his, her heartbeat to his but it wouldn't work. When she pressed her face into his back, he felt so cold.

The tent was of the Arabian Nights variety instead of the bogged down seaside campsite. Lush fabrics surrounded them, silk and satins, all the luxuries the Sídhe lavished on themselves. And beyond those insubstantial walls, the grounds of the strange greenhouse buzzed with life, with that same wild and unpredictable chaos on which the Market thrived. To find it here made everything feel all the more alien to Izzy. She'd thought of it as a peaceful place when they arrived. More and more of the Sídhe were arriving with each passing minute. She could feel it in the air around her, like electricity.

No one came in. No one dared. Silver had commanded it and suddenly, with the reality of Holly back once more, of Holly raising monsters and killing where she would, no one defied her. Not for an instant. Silver was all they had.

She could feel their expectation as well, as if they sensed … maybe not what was happening exactly, but the fact that *something* was happening. The tension was hard to ignore. Added to that, Silver suddenly seemed galvanised, issuing orders and commands, acting like the very thing she denied being, a matriarch.

Reaching out tentatively, Izzy stroked Jinx's hair, his forehead, but he never responded. His skin felt cold as ice and it made her shiver inside. She couldn't lose him. It wasn't fair.

Tears stung like needles in the corner of her eyes. She'd shed too many already and the thought of more made her burn with anger, but she couldn't seem to get rid of the stupid things. This was her fault. All her fault. She wasn't entirely sure how but she knew it was true. If she'd just stayed home this morning or gone straight home after work, if she hadn't listened to Art and gone to Bray Head, if she hadn't been so determined to prove herself …

She wished she'd done what her dad had said right at the beginning. She wished she'd stayed the hell away from Jinx because if she had he wouldn't be in this state now, would he? He'd be Silver's emissary. He'd be safe.

Instead, he was unconscious, trapped in some spell of Holly's. Izzy had put him right back in Holly's path, and now he was lost again. She held him close and shut her eyes. Even though tears leaked from the corners. And Mum would be safe, not a hostage to demons. It was all her fault.

She tried to sleep, but how could she? If she slept, something even worse might happen to him. None of the fae really cared about him. Anyone could walk in here. She had to guard him. Especially now.

Izzy bit her bottom lip and held Jinx's icy hand even tighter. Dad was going to flip. There were no two ways about it. If someone had already told him, he'd never forgive her. How had she gone from being ideal daughter to this in so short a time?

Noise outside grabbed their attention. Ash woke up at once, if she had ever really been asleep. She glanced at the pair of them, without any judgement passing over her face, but didn't speak. Instead she stepped forward, as if to shield them from whoever was coming, and Izzy stood as well. Ready for anything.

The curtain door was pulled open and Silver entered, followed by the fiery figure of Brí, her red hair aglow, her clothes a million shades of scarlet, orange and gold.

'It's okay,' Izzy said to Ash, who nodded, though she didn't look entirely convinced.

'I should step outside perhaps,' she said.

'That would be best,' Silver replied firmly, though not unkindly. 'I'll have someone find you some food. You must be hungry. Both of you.' She looked pointedly at Izzy, but Izzy, just as deliberately, didn't move.

Ash slipped by the others, getting out of the way as deftly as possible. Izzy just stared at Brí, waiting. And Brí stared back.

Izzy's birth mother made a striking figure, but she wasn't alone. A young man followed her, his skin very darkly tanned, almost black contrasting with hair of a vibrant unnatural blue, the same hue as his eyes. He paused in the doorway, gazing at her long enough to let her know that he was studying her, taking in every detail he could see. He smiled, but it wasn't a warm expression.

'He's here,' said Silver. 'If you would …'

'Of course,' said Brí. 'Hello, Isabel. In trouble again, I see.'

She couldn't back down in face of that. Every instinct in her screamed that she had to defy it. 'It's hereditary, isn't it?'

Brí shrugged, a beautiful gesture, nuanced and elegant. Dancers would kill to be able to move like that.

'Perhaps. You should ask your father. It seems to be his idiom.' But she smiled and her eyes glowed like the huge amber gemstone in her necklace, her touchstone and source of her power.

'Izzy, please,' said Silver, shifting nervously. She didn't want any trouble. Not now, not here. Not if it might cost her Jinx. She turned to the young man, who was already grinning. He wasn't even trying to hide his amusement. 'This is Isabel Gregory. She's the daughter of the Grigori David and … ' she glanced at Izzy's birth mother, '—Lady Brí.'

The blue haired boy raised one perfectly arched eyebrow and darted a wicked glance towards Brí. If anything, the matriarch was looking rather smug, although she said nothing. If she didn't know better Izzy would have said her mother looked proud.

Silver continued with her introductions quickly, eager to get them over and done with. 'Izzy, this is—'

'Call me Reaper,' he interrupted, his voice rich and molten, so deep it reverberated through her like the earth movements of earlier. 'Well now, what has happened to you?' He held up a hand when Silver started to speak, silencing her. When she obeyed, closing her mouth and stepping back demurely, it was Izzy's turn to stare. 'It's fine, Silver. You explained everything.

Several times actually. We know what's happening. That's why we're here after all. It's just an expression.'

He moved all at once, surging through the space between the door and the bedside like a flash of light. But as he reached Jinx's side, he knelt down and seized his hand in a fierce grip. Izzy gave an involuntary cry of alarm. Reaper looked up at her, the amusement still glittering in his blue eyes.

'Don't fear, little Grigori,' said Reaper. 'I'm sworn to do no harm. I live my life by that code.' He stared at Jinx, studying him. 'Oh, but this is remarkable. Who marked and bound him thus? The working is masterful. It must have taken years.'

A painful silence answered him.

Izzy glared at him. The tattoos and piercings on Jinx's body were Holly's work and had kept him enslaved to her for most of his life. They still did, or so it seemed now. Reaper didn't have to sound so impressed by it. It was horrible.

There was new line around his throat, just below the first, a band of Celtic knotwork in the deepest indigo blue, with hints of silver embedded in it, exactly where she'd wrapped the wire around him. Izzy felt her eyes sting and ache just looking at it.

'Holly,' said Brí at last, her tone thick with loathing. 'She had him pierced and tattooed all the time she held him. She said it was to stop him favouring his hound form.'

Reaper ran his hands up Jinx's arms and across his chest. He framed Jinx's face with his long-fingered, graceful hands. 'Oh, it was more than that. She worked this for years. Planned it.

It's too perfect.'

Izzy's voice trembled as she spoke. 'She said he was a vessel. She controlled him completely, in an instant.'

'Indeed she did. There's quite a power struggle going on in there. Brí, I may need your help here.'

'Me?' Brí snorted in a completely unladylike manner. 'This isn't my area—'

'The Cú Sídhe are. You know more than anyone, my Lady.'

Brí preened herself a little, mollified by his flattery. Izzy gave her a plaintive look that also seemed to help. At least she hoped so.

'I'm forever healing you and your companions it seems,' her birth mother grumbled as she approached the bed. 'Well now, Jinx by Jasper, let me look at you.' She breathed in deeply and released the air in a long, low hiss. Her fingertips rested lightly on the faint pulse in his neck. 'So cold,' she said. 'Usually Cú Sídhe run hot. Poor baby. What has she done to you?'

Izzy wasn't used to hearing such compassion in Brí's voice. Usually she was screaming blue murder, or being snide and superior. Now she used the tone of voice one would use with a beloved pet rather than a person.

'Can you help him?' asked Silver. 'Can you release him from this spell?'

'Holly is so skilled. We may be able to wake him, but to separate the two? It would take a much sharper blade than I have to hand.'

'What do you mean?' said Silver warily. 'What sort of blade?'

Reaper gave her a speculative look and Silver instantly bristled. 'What do you mean, Reaper?'

His voice when he spoke was soft and seductive. 'Lord Donn's sword, so sharp it can cut through a whisper or a sigh. He keeps it inside his hollow, deep underground, beneath the mountain, far from the eyes and hands of mortals, angels and demons. And very far from the hands of the fae.'

'Because it's too dangerous,' said Brí. 'Far too dangerous to be free in the world. And far too dangerous to let any of us near it.'

'Why?' Izzy asked.

That awkward silence settled again. Everyone tried to avoid making eye contact with Izzy. Except Reaper. She looked up and met his gaze, his piercing blue eyes that looked right inside her. He stared at her for long minutes until she felt weighed and judged. And found wanting? The moment dragged on.

Finally Reaper answered. 'They call it The Blade That Cuts. Donn is the oldest of the Aes Sídhe. The very oldest. Once they called him the Angel of Death. He repelled Adam and Eve from the Garden. He torched the cities that are now drowned beneath the Dead Sea. He tore down the tower to heaven. And that sword gave him the power to do all that.' He turned to look at Izzy and his eyes were so bright, like the gas flame in the boiler at home. They hypnotised her, held her gaze and she couldn't look away. 'It also gave him the power to heal. When we were expelled from heaven, he alone brought his angel sword with him. Because no one – not Zadkiel, not

Gabriel – none of them would dare to attempt to take it from him.'

Passion filled his voice as he spoke. His eyes gleamed with an eerie brightness, and Izzy shivered, dragging herself back from him.

'They say if he chose, Donn could use that sword to open heaven's gates to us again.' Brí's voice sounded strangely distant and weak with longing. That wasn't like her. Izzy felt an urge to look at her, but she couldn't seem to tear her own attention away from Reaper.

'Then why doesn't he?' Silver snapped, her fragile patience shattering. 'If he really could. Because we don't belong there anymore. We've changed and he knows it. We belong here, not in heaven. If we went back we'd break it to pieces in less than a day. We'd pick it apart just for fun. Enough. You have work to do, Reaper. You promised to help. You can glorify your master's name some other time.'

Reaper laughed and the spell on Izzy shattered. A glamour? It left a sensation like cobwebs trailing over her skin. She'd been standing there spellbound and he could have done anything to her. She backed away, appalled that he could work a glamour on her so easily. If Donn was powerful, so was his servant.

'Whatever you need is at your disposal, Lady Silver.'

She nodded and turned to go.

'Wait!' Izzy said. 'This sword can heal him, but we can't go and get it? Can we take him to it? Would that help?'

'Enter Donn's hollow? Are you mad?' Silver asked.

'I'm completely serious.'

'Izzy, with everything that is happening, with Holly and the Fear, with the threat of the Shining Ones … it's far too dangerous.'

'I'll do whatever I have to.'

They all looked at Reaper who seemed to consider the matter for a moment and then spread his hands out wide, his long, elegant fingers unfurling like delicate plants.

'It's not impossible. Difficult, but not impossible. At Samhain the door to the hollow stands open. All may come and go. But there will be a price.'

'Isn't there always?' Izzy muttered.

'We'll discuss it later,' said Brí, moving to Jinx's side. 'He needs us. We have work to do here.'

'I want to stay with him.'

Brí glared at her. 'Why am I not surprised? Thankfully for us, it is not your decision. Outside Isabel. All of you. Leave us to work.'

Left with no choice, Izzy reluctantly left Jinx in their care. As she closed the door behind her she saw the way they circled him, wary as cats around a cobra.

Ash waited for her outside. They locked together, a unit, and for that Izzy was grateful. If she was alone with Silver right now, she'd lose it. She knew that. And she wasn't entirely sure what Silver would do.

'Your father will come soon,' was all Silver said. 'I can get you some food. You must be hungry.'

Izzy shook her head. Her father wouldn't come. He'd be negotiating for her mum's release. He had to be.

But part of her was afraid he would. And if he did, what did that mean for Mum? That he'd done it? Or that he put his duty as Grigori higher than his wife? Once she would have sworn that nothing was more important to him than Mum but now …

'We're good,' said Ash when Silver didn't move, waiting for something.

Silver glared at her, eyes narrowed. 'Somewhere quiet, out of the way?' She really had no idea how to talk to teenaged girls. Amazing, cool and magical as Silver was, she didn't have a clue in this situation.

It felt strangely powerful to stand beside Ash and face Silver down. Like she was in control for the first time in days. The feeling was exhilarating, but undercut by the thought that she could lose it all in moments. And she would, if Dad arrived. Then she'd just be his daughter.

But she wanted him there. Because if he came, Mum was safe. Wasn't she? He wouldn't come here if she wasn't. At least she hoped so.

A queasy feeling in the depth of her stomach wasn't so sure.

'Silver, I … I just need to unwind a bit. I just need … it's peaceful here.'

'For now. All right. Just stay away from the Sídhe, okay? Stay away from anyone you don't know. More and more are coming all the time. Not everyone — many of the solitaries are fleeing, trying to find other places of sanctuary, although I fear there's nowhere else left.' She stopped, apparently aware she was rambling. 'Just stay together and don't go wandering.'

'Sure.' That was easy. It would be a pleasure.

Silver stared at Ash again, as if trying to figure her out. She looked unsettled, as if having the girl there was making her skin crawl, but she couldn't say why. 'And keep her away from them too. They're too dangerous. You know that.'

'You're *all* too dangerous. I know *that*.'

Silver snorted and turned away, marching over the lawn. Her heels didn't sink in to the surface, Izzy noticed, even though they looked like spikes.

'Whoa,' said Ash, exhaling the word in a rush. 'They are freaky.'

'They're Sídhe.'

'I gathered.' They turned away, heading for the centre of the lawn where the Long Stone stood all on its own. 'So, not made up stories.'

'Not as such. Though the stories aren't always that accurate, you know?'

'And Jinx?'

Izzy bit her lower lip. 'Jinx too.'

'Thought he was too hot to be real.'

A little twist of something like jealousy appeared for the first time, deep in Izzy's gut. 'Oh he's real. But he's Cú Sídhe.'

Ash frowned, thinking about the translation. 'Hound? Like

Cú Chulainn?'

Legendary Irish hero, stubborn and pig headed, thought he knew everything, stood his ground fighting everyone else on the island, ended badly … yeah, that sounded about right. That sounded just like Jinx.

'Something like that,' she muttered.

'And what's your in on all this?'

'I'm … I'm kind of … related. To them. To some of them.'

'That red-haired woman back there?' Brí. Of course she'd picked up on that.

'Yeah. Her.'

They reached the stone. The air was even stiller her, calm and muffled, as if they were closed off from the rest of the world. Maybe they were. The aura of peace wrapped itself around them and for the first time in days Izzy felt the tight line running through her shoulders begin to relax.

'And Holly?'

'God, no. I'm not related to her at all.'

'But Jinx is.'

'Her grandson. Apparently. Silver's his aunt.'

'Not exactly a loving family then. Poor guy.' She bent down, checked the lawn with her hand and then sat down, crossing her legs. 'It's nice here.'

Izzy sat down too. 'I guess. You're taking this well.'

Ash shrugged. 'I'm not. But there's no point in freaking out, is there?' Then she looked up, a frown breaking over her face. Izzy followed her gaze to where a group was arriving into the area with a great deal of kerfuffle. She recognised the Magpies at once, and her tattoo turned cold. The man walking in front of them was property developer smooth, with slate grey hair and piercing eyes. He wore a three piece suit and his shoes shone. But when she looked at him she saw something old and terrible, Sídhe. He was the Amadán, the Old Man, the Trickster. She knew it in an instant.

And that wasn't the worst thing. The two figures with them. That was the worst thing. 'Hey,' said Ash. 'Isn't that *Clodagh*?'

CHAPTER TWENTY-ONE

Wild Magic

It was a dream. It was just a dream. He had to keep telling himself that because if he didn't, if he believed it was actually real …

It wasn't a dream. It was a nightmare.

And at the same time he knew it was real. So very real.

Because standing in front of him was a horse taller than he was, twenty-two hands at least. Taller than any natural breed. Its obsidian black coat gleamed and the wild tangle of its mane and tail streamed like black ink in water behind it. Its eyes glowed with a yellow sulphurous light and they fixed on him and on him alone.

Jinx tried to breathe, but the stench of death swept over him and choked him. His head swam like he was drunk or delirious.

The Púca watched him silently. Slowly, carefully, he dropped to his knees, bowed his head and tried to fight the instinct to run.

You didn't run. You never ran. They loved it when you ran. Because then they could chase you. You'd wake up broken, exhausted, covered in sweat with your heart racing and your blood thundering.

If you woke up at all.

If your heart didn't explode inside you. If the shock didn't kill you.

'Jinx by Jasper, are you still hers?'

Its voice was like wind through autumn leaves, rustling and sighing. It reached inside his mind and talked to him there, in the still small place at the base of his brain.

He tried to find his own voice, but failed. Terror smothered him.

'Tell me now, Jinx by Jasper. Are you still hers?'

Holly's? He didn't want to be Holly's. He didn't want to belong to anyone. No one but himself.

'Tell me,' said the Púca.

'I … I'm not …'

The Púca snorted and a smoky billow of breath uncurled from its nostrils. Its left hoof scraped the ground beneath them and sparks shot up like embers from a fire, drifting away into the night's sky.

'Then to whom do you belong?'

He didn't know the answer to that. Still he knelt, curled up beneath the great beast, his body bare and shivering, unable to find words.

The Púca lifted its head as if scenting something.

'Jinx, can you hear me?' It sounded like Izzy's voice. It lingered on the air from somewhere far away. He could almost feel her presence, almost. Her touch, her scent, her body pressed against his, warm and tender. So afraid.

Her fear fluttered through him and lodged deep inside him. It found something to answer it there.

'Please hear me. Please. Wake up.'

Fear. Terror. Loss. All those and more. A desperate need. A hollow, empty void that sucked everything inside it and left him even emptier. The thought of not being there for her, not being with her. The thought that Holly had reached out and seized him like that. In an instant. She'd snapped her fingers and he had been hers once more.

Even if inside he had screamed and railed. Even if he hadn't had a choice.

He had been Holly's.

Holly knew it. And so did Izzy.

'I don't want to.' His voice came out, forced through barbed wire in his tight throat.

'Whose are you?'

'I'm my own person. I want … I want to be my own person. I want my life.'

'Then take it. Or lose it.' The great black horse bent its head towards him. Its mane fell forward into his pleading hands. He gripped and the Púca pulled him up. Up onto his feet, up

onto its back. *'We ride into the nightmare. Hold on or be lost.'*

Its muscled body bunched beneath him and it leaped forward into the night, taking him with it. And all he could do was hold on.

The wind froze him, tore at his hair and the heat in the creature beneath him wasn't enough to warm him. It moved across an empty, darkened land, where nothing grew. Nothing moved except them and the shadows like tar clinging to the dips and hollows, to the undersides of stones. He didn't know how long it took, how far they went, but the Púca didn't slow, not for a moment. It showed no sign of tiring. But why would it. This was a creature that didn't tire, didn't fail.

It was also something dead – a spirit. The Púca were all gone, centuries ago, wiped out. Or so they said. Shapeshifters, kings, the lords of wild magic. He rode a ghost.

The Cú Sídhe whispered stories of them. In the darkness, late at night. That once they were kin and now they were no more. That they were wild, filled with wild magic, and that they alone of the fae ran free.

'Are you kin to the Cú Sídhe?' he asked, breathless.

'We are.' The Púca laughed inside his mind. *'You're not surprised. That's good. That will make everything easier, won't it?'*

'Easier?'

'We are things of between. Things of change, on the boundaries of all things – now and then, one thing and the other, yesterday and today and tomorrow. We are the changers, the shifters. So of course, we are kin. All shifters are my kin. And you are closer than any other.'

'Where are we going?'

'The pool. You want to see the truth, don't you? This is the only way.' Jinx struggled, knowing right away that this was fatal. He tried to throw himself off, but his hands were tangled in the thick black hair. It clung to him like tentacles, wrapping around his fingers and hands the more he tried to free himself. *'Whatever are you doing?'* The Púca laughed, never missing a pace in his wild gallop. *'You'd die in an instant. I'm no waterhorse, Jinx by Jasper. Not a kelpie or anything of that sort. You're safe with me. There's no need for me to kill you. You flirt so often with death that sooner or later you'll get there without my help. Fall though, and nothing could save you. Ah, here we are now.'*

And with that he slowed to a trot and then a gentle walk. It drew to a halt by a deep, circular pool, the surface still as a mirror. But the water was black, reflecting a starless sky. Released, Jinx slid off the Púca's back, feeling the touch of the earth like a welcome embrace.

'Where are we?'

The horse snorted, thick mist billowing from its nostrils. Jinx could see its golden eyes in the water. And then it wasn't a horse anymore but a man. Thick hair the colour of ebony tumbled down his back and cast his face into shadows. But the eyes were the same. Golden, sulphurous, glowing. He still had the horse's ears, Jinx realised, and hooves instead of feet. The thrill of wild magic shimmered in the air around him. A man stood beside him now, but not really a man. The king of the Wanderers. A Púca.

'*Look, Jinx. Look and remember and see.*'

The voice flowed around him, through him, familiar as air, soothing every jarred nerve.

The water on the surface of the pool shifted, rippled, but there was no wind. Not even a breeze. The water was still as death.

'Where are we?'

'*Look into the pool, Jinx.*'

He knew he wouldn't get an answer but he didn't need to hear it. He knew. The Púca had said that they were creatures of the between and Jinx had a good idea which between had him in its clutches now — if he was lucky the space between sleep and waking, otherwise … the space between life and death.

The water moved and the reflections moved, changed… Or his reflection did. The Púca was still the same, dejected and heartbroken, watching everything. A woman stood with him, also dark haired but beautiful, so beautiful it almost hurt to look at her for more than a moment. He didn't know her. And he did. He knew her like he knew his own face, for his face carried traces of hers.

His mother. A sob jerked up inside him, unexpected and violent. He tried to swallow it down and it came out strangled. Her face. He'd never thought to see her face. Tears stung his eyes.

'Bella,' the Púca whispered, his voice so full of longing and despair like a reflection of all that Jinx felt. Through long years and smothered memories, Jinx knew that voice.

Jinx shivered, blinked to regain his vision more clearly. The image didn't falter. The woman smiled and his heart filled with something unknown, something he had never felt before. Jinx reached out, without thinking, his fingers almost touching the water. The water that moved and boiled beneath them, that rose as if weightless to meet them.

The Púca grabbed Jinx by the shoulder, pulling him back as the eels burst from the depths, snapping at him, hissing wildly.

'I didn't say it was safe here, Jinx. I just told you to look.'

He nodded, terrified and weak with it. The water stilled again, and the image had changed. Holly stood there, pristine as she had always been, dressed in a tailored suit, her blonde hair sleek and shining, not that blood-stained monster from Bray Head. She looked just as Jinx remembered her.

Because a small, pale figure lay at her feet, beaten and broken, the first of so many tattoos decorating his skin, still red and raw and fresh.

Jinx bit into the inside of his cheek to keep from crying out as he saw himself as he'd been, when she first took him.

He remembered fighting. Fighting and fighting until he couldn't fight anymore, until all the fight was beaten out of him.

'She made you hers,' said the Púca. 'Just as she tried to do before, to me. But with you she finally succeeded, didn't she?'

'No.'

The kindness bled from his voice. 'Oh, really?'

He waved one hand over the surface, wiping away the image of Jinx as a child and showing him Jinx now, or earlier today on Bray Head. He was kneeling at Holly's feet and though Izzy shouted his name, he didn't respond. He was Holly's, through and through. He knew how it must have looked to everyone else.

His throat closed on the word. One word. One plea. 'No.'

'It looks very much like it to all of them. You know what they'll say. All the Sídhe. Treachery is in your blood. Your mother, your father …'

'No,' he didn't want to hear about them, not anymore. Not after seeing her. 'Belladonna was my mother and she—'

'You didn't know her,' said the Púca. 'You were just a babe. I knew her. I loved her—' Jinx shied back. These were words he didn't want to hear. Couldn't allow himself to hear. Because if the Púca loved Bella, he had to be—

'Don't say that.' It came out too sharp, too harsh. The Púca would be offended. Instinct coiled up inside him, the need to survive at any cost. But he couldn't hear. It couldn't be true. If the Púca loved Bella, then he could only be one person. 'Please …'

'Oh, *please* is it?' He laughed and his hands closed on Jinx's shoulder, hands cold as ice, clawed below the knuckles where nails should have been. They dug into his skin and the tattoos hissed and writhed beneath his touch. '*Please* is all well and good but it doesn't do anything for me. Or for you, it seems. They'll call you a traitor again, Jinx. They all saw you kneeling there. Down on your knees in front of your matriarch. Son of a traitor, son of a murderer, Holly's assassin. Holly's dog. All those names will be back, if they ever really went anywhere. She's taking you back without even trying.' He leaned in close, his breath so cold against Jinx's cheek, but Jinx didn't dare to turn and look at him. He stared at the water where something else was unfolding. 'She has a plan. She wants the wild magic, wants control of it. It slipped her grasp before, you see. She couldn't control me, so she couldn't control it. But now she has you. She's waited so long and she made you for this. She took you and she made you a tool, a vessel. She thinks to control it through you.'

He stood on a hilltop, city lights spread out below him like a billion fireflies. Light rose from the ground, like a wave, a tsunami, golden and terrible as it engulfed him. It burrowed through every pore and winnowed its way deep inside him, changing him as it went. Filling him until he blossomed with light, blinding and golden as the Púca's eyes. The same light filled his own eyes, eating away at the silver he knew and replacing it until they were the same as the being that held him. And worse, much worse. Shining tears spilled down his face.

'It's coming,' whispered the Púca. 'And there's only one way to avoid it. Death.'

Jinx opened his mouth to deny it, but nothing came out.

Izzy marched across the lawn, everyone else forgotten as she saw her friends flanked by the Magpies. As she drew up, Dylan looked completely panicked, glancing at the older man with them. Clodagh stayed by his side, her expression dazed. That couldn't be good. It really couldn't be good.

But Dylan stepped forward to meet her, his hands raised as if in a gesture of peace. 'Izzy, just hang on a second.'

'I'm not in the mood. What are you two doing here? What happened? What did you do?'

'The Fear,' he said and her heart shuddered inside her. She stopped, staring at him. 'They were at the club. All those people … We had to get away. And now …' He glanced back at Clodagh.

It wasn't good at all.

'Who is he?'

'My Lord Amadán,' said Silver, her voice clear and delicate. She didn't appear alarmed as she glided towards them. Everything about her was calm and collected. 'I'm so delighted you could make it. And thank you so much for returning Dylan and his friend to us.'

Amadán swung towards her, Clodagh on his arm, which put her between the two Magpies. Out of their reach.

'Delighted to attend. Especially as the nature of the invitation was so urgent. And my boys found your touchstone in a spot of bother.'

'So I see.' Silver reached out for Dylan's hand, threading her fingers through his. Izzy didn't like the possessive glint in her eyes. 'And you also brought … um …

'Clodagh.' Dylan finished for her when the pause went on too long. His voice sounded flat. Annoyed. Silver didn't appear to notice, but Izzy did. She knew that tone. It was the one Dylan would use when Mari was being a bitch but he wasn't quite ready to engage.

Strange to see the same expression echoed on his face now.

'Clodagh, yes …' Silver tilted her head. 'Let her go, my Lord. She doesn't have a part in this. She shouldn't even be here.'

'Ah, Silver, but she's so pretty. Such a sweet, mindless little thing.' He smiled at Clodagh and she giggled, as if proving his point. 'I thought I might keep her. I do like my pets.'

But Silver didn't return the smile he graced her with. Her face turned still as stone. 'You asked for our help with the Fear. We complied. I sent Jinx to you. Don't return a favour with a slight, Lord Amadán. Let her go.'

Amadán paused for a moment, his expression one of specu-lation. Finally he sighed and pulled Clodagh close, planting a kiss on her forehead. 'Bless you, little one, you'll need the luck. Go on then.'

He twirled her away, releasing her and Clodagh spun free, all grace and elegance for a moment before his spell wore off and she stumbled. Ash caught her, steadied her.

'What are you—?' She looked around, dazed and confused. 'Ash? Where are we?'

Ash shushed her, drawing her gently back and away from the Sídhe, but Izzy didn't move. She folded her arms and the

Amadán looked her up and down.

'Well now,' he said. 'You're David's girl, no mistaking that. Where is he? And where's his charming wife, eh? I haven't seen her for an age.'

The filthy snickering of the Magpies swooped around them, but Izzy ignored it. She couldn't let them get to her now. Thoughts of Mum made her heart race. Where was she? Was she okay? And what had Dad done in the meantime to try to get her back. She only hoped he had succeeded.

'He's coming,' she said calmly. And this time she prayed she was right.

'Come, Lord Amadán,' said Silver, her voice soft and placating. 'Later Dylan may be persuaded to play for us. You've never heard music like it, I promise you. Let me find someone to attend you.' She beckoned three Sídhe towards them. 'There are refreshments—'

A scream broke the quiet, terrible and desperate, filled with agony. It made them all turn, all the power games forgotten.

It was Jinx.

CHAPTER TWENTY-TWO

Invasion

Izzy jumped up as if dragged by wires, her eyes wide in panic. She ran from her friends across the Liberty, blindly, until she reached the blue tent where she had left Jinx earlier. And suddenly, terrified by the new silence beyond the thin walls, she hesitated.

She pushed the flap aside with a hand that shook so much she could barely use it.

Jinx sat on the edge of the trestle bed, his head in his hands, his eyes closed. His shoulders hunched up, tight and painful.

Reaper looked up as she entered, but Brí didn't. She knelt at Jinx's side, one hand on his tense arm, all her attention on him and him alone.

'It's going to be all right,' she said in a strangely gentle voice, not the voice Izzy expected to hear from Brí, especially not to Jinx. 'There is a way. No matter what, we will help you. I swear this, Jinx. I will find a way.'

That meant something, Izzy knew, something serious. A Sídhe oath could not be broken.

'Grigori,' said Reaper. It might have been by way of greeting but it was fractionally too late. It sounded like a warning, the tone not lost on Izzy. Brí fell abruptly silent and then looked up at Izzy. 'He is awake at last.'

'I know,' she replied, though she didn't step further inside the tent. 'I heard the screams.'

Jinx lifted his head and stared at her, his expression hollow, haunted by pain. His eyes gleamed even more silver than normal.

'Izzy.'

It sounded like a prayer. She couldn't think of anything else now. Brí and Reaper might not have been there. All that mattered was him.

She stopped, the image of him kneeling at Holly's feet too keenly etched into her mind. It shook her but she couldn't move.

'We need to speak to Silver,' said Brí.

But Izzy didn't move. 'Tell me first.'

'Isabel—' she began, impatiently.

Izzy folded her arms across her chest. 'Tell me, mother. What did Holly do to him? What is she after?'

Brí stared at her, open mouthed, her eyes blazing with anger. But she still didn't say anything.

'Wild magic,' said Jinx, so quietly. She couldn't resist the lure of him anymore, but crossed to his side, kneeling down where Brí had been a moment before. He was still shaking, but struggling to control it. He looked wretched, like some kind of junkie, thin and wrung out, sickly pale but sheened with sweat.

'What is?' she asked.

But with her so close, he couldn't seem to form words. He hid his face again and his shoulders tightened.

Silver arrived, throwing the door back as she entered. Dylan followed and Clodagh and Ash came after him. The little tent was suddenly very crowded.

'What happened?' Silver asked.

'Jinx dreamed. The Púca appeared to him.' Brí brushed her hands together, as if wiping off something distasteful. 'It showed him what Holly wants. And it isn't good, but then, we didn't really expect it to be if your sainted mother is involved, did we?'

Silver glared at her, but said nothing. Brí smiled nastily.

He wasn't telling them everything. Izzy wasn't sure how she knew that exactly – something in his eyes perhaps? Something in the way he wouldn't quite make eye contact. There was more to this. 'What does she want from Jinx?' Izzy interrupted, sick to death of their games.

Jinx himself answered, his voice hoarse and broken. 'She wants me for the Shining Ones. I saw myself drowning in their light. They're things of wild magic, of the first magic. She thinks the spells she wove on me will make it possible

282

to control them.'

'What *are* the Shining Ones? What do they want?'

'The highest of the orders,' Brí answered for him. 'Beings with power beyond anything we wielded. Thousands died in order to bind them. Tens of thousands.'

'And why did they need binding?' asked Dylan.

Brí tilted her head on one side, studying him. 'Have you ever seen a creature that's seen too much death and killing? A soldier perhaps, or a dog from a fighting pit? Something that has seen too much horror to ever be able to function in normal society. They were the Seraphim, the Shining Ones, our very own nuclear option. They tamed the chaos. But when the war was over, when they were no longer needed ...'

Clodagh snorted. 'So they were discarded. Lovely.'

'Not discarded,' said Reaper in an apologetic tone that didn't sound wholly sorry. 'Decommissioned perhaps. Put out of harm's way.'

Izzy tightened her hand on Jinx's. 'Out of harm's way? Under a mountain in Ireland?'

Brí barked out a laugh. 'To be fair, there was nothing here at the time. An empty island. A rock in the ocean. And then a prison. It was the only reason we were allowed to come here, so that we might do some service even in exile. And apart from the rare occasion where people stumbled on to the wrong place at the wrong time, when they lost their mind or their way ... There was never any need, until now. But this is our duty, those of us who were exiled, those of us with the strength. Whether we like it or not.'

Izzy stood up, turning to face her birth mother, feeling stronger with Dylan and the girls here. She didn't want another lecture on duty. It was all she ever heard of these days, from both her families. 'Is Jinx okay?'

They both looked down at him, which Izzy couldn't decide was a good or a bad sign.

Thankfully, Jinx answered for himself.

'Yes. I'm okay.' He got to his feet, spread his arms out wide. He breathed in deeply and then exhaled. 'Or at least I think I am.'

Izzy couldn't help herself. Relief broke over her like another blow robbing her of the strength she'd been relying on to keep going. She threw herself at him, wrapped her arms around his neck and pulled him against her. Burying her face in the warm scent of him, she felt her whole body shake.

'I thought you were gone again,' she told him. 'I thought I'd lost you.'

His arms enfolded her, his touch unsure. But when it was clear she wouldn't pull away or mock him, that this wasn't some sort of elaborate trick to make a fool of him, his embrace tightened. He kissed the top of her head, folding himself around her, his breath warm and gentle on her as he sighed.

'I'll never leave you again,' he whispered as quietly as he could. 'Not unless … unless you make me.'

She gave a bitter laugh. 'Why on earth would I do that?'

But Jinx didn't join in, didn't laugh, bitter or otherwise, and there wasn't even a smile in his voice. 'Holly planned all this. And Holly's plans are rarely flawed. You may have to, love. You may not have a choice. The Púca is a ghost, a spirit that knows far more than it should. And more than it told me, I'm sure.'

Izzy stared at Jinx. He'd called her 'love'. Did he even realise he'd said it? But before she could even begin to see what she felt about it, another blow fell.

'Like Mari,' said Dylan. 'Like her ghost.'

Jinx nodded. 'Maybe. The dead are stirring, there's no doubt about that. It's Samhain, but it's more than that. Whatever Holly has done has stirred them up.'

Dylan ignored him. 'She said we had to go to Donn's hollow.'

'Don't even think that,' snapped Silver. 'It's too dangerous. If anything happened to you—'

'You'd lose everything!' he shouted. 'I know that. But you don't own me, Silver.'

She glared at him, her eyes narrow slivers of light, dangerous. 'What does that mean?'

Dylan jutted his chin forward, but kept his teeth clenched tight together, glaring back at her.

'Young love everywhere,' Reaper murmured. 'It's so sweet. And tragic, of course. Doomed, one might say.' He gave a bow to Brí and Silver. 'I should go. I'll be needed elsewhere soon. Lady Brí, an honour to work with you, as ever.'

She didn't reply, but watched carefully as he turned towards the door, moving like a ballet dancer, not quite right for someone just walking.

The tent door fell back behind him. 'What is he up to now?' Brí murmured.

The air seemed to suck out of the tent, poised for a moment and then, like a silent explosion, a concussive force slammed through the space around them. The earth shivered underneath them, hummed with warning.

'No,' Jinx gasped, his eyes wide, fixed on Brí. 'Izzy, you have to go. You can't be here for this.' He waved a hand towards Clodagh and Ash. 'Get them to safety.'

'For what?' she asked, still holding him close.

All around them alarms began to ring, some shrill wails, others booming claxons, air raid sirens and inhuman screeches.

Silver cursed, pushing by the two of them and heading for the door. 'They wouldn't dare!'

'Oh, they would,' said Jinx. 'You know they would. Especially now.'

Silver ignored him. Brí, on the other hand turned to Izzy, her face like stone. 'Isabel, keep him in here, whatever happens. Can you call your father? I fear we will need him.'

'My father?' She stared at the matriarch, as if she had gone out of her mind. Of all people, Brí wouldn't want to see Izzy's father, or admit that he was needed. Izzy knew that. 'But why?'

'He is the Grigori,' she replied. 'And a Sídhe stronghold has just been breached. They've broken the Compact and they're inside.'

'Who are?'

'Angels,' said Reaper, as he struggled back inside the tent. 'The angels have invaded Sídhe grounds. They're here.'

Dylan's hands trembled and he stared at them, willing them to be still. Nothing happened. They shook again and he couldn't control it, couldn't stop it. And it was happening more frequently. Was this what he had to look forward to? Was this what would happen?

They'd been lucky. Or Amadán was playing with them all. He wasn't sure which and neither thought was comforting. Not to mention what he'd seen in the club, the way the Fear had fallen on the audience and spilled out into the city. What were they doing?

But with Silver making demands like that, with her possessive nature to the fore, he couldn't concentrate. Anger made the magic inside him seethe and coil. Her magic, reacting to her and her anger.

With the arrival of the angels, it became a white-hot sheet of rage and terror, slicing through him. She risked spiralling out of control and the magic with her.

'Are you okay?' Clodagh asked.

No. He wasn't.

Silver looked shaken, her hands trembling like his were, just from being near to each other. The anger was gone now, or had transformed to something else. Nothing petty or selfish. The situation had turned to one of grave seriousness. 'Stay inside, out of sight. Don't come out, understand?'

They watched her return to Brí and Reaper, to the argument with Izzy and Jinx.

'Oh, charming,' said Ash. Clodagh sank on to the low divan, her complexion grey. Ash was the first one to her. 'How are you feeling?'

'Feeling? I'm not … I'm not feeling anything. I just … what did he do to me?' Her wild gaze locked on Dylan. 'What happened to me?'

'They're … they're fae. He enchanted you.'

'Can they do that?'

'Well, duh,' said Ash. She stood up and crossed to the door, gazing out through the gap. 'What can't they do?'

'Apologise,' he said, as if it was a joke. But it didn't feel like one.

The Sídhe were fighting.

Silver's voice rose over all the others. 'I'm going to face them. Yes, of course I am. I called this meeting. They've no right!'

'Something's wrong,' Ash said. 'Can't you feel it?'

He tried to push the bleak thought out of his mind. Nine years, that was the deal. But everything was happening so quickly now. Maybe because he was a touchstone. Maybe because his luck was shot. Maybe because Silver didn't know her own strength.

'What is it?' Clodagh asked. Only when she spoke, did he remember that he wasn't alone, that Ash and Clodagh were both watching him.

'Trouble.' What other answer was there? Everything was trouble.

The noise outside reached a crescendo of panic. Ash retreated, cursing under her breath and Silver turned back to them without a moment's hesitation.

Izzy got it first. She was always quickest.

'Leave him alone!' she shouted at Silver, beginning to move in front of Dylan, but Jinx held her back. Gently, perhaps, but with arms she couldn't break free from. Immobilised, Izzy stared at Dylan desperately afraid. Appalled.

And he knew what was going to happen. What *had* to happen.

Silver's voice hooked his mind, focusing all his attention on her instead. He couldn't ignore her. 'Dylan, I need you.'

Maybe that hook was in his heart instead. More meat hook than fish hook.

So much for foreplay. So much for promises. His regret must have showed on his face and something flickered across her features – doubt and regret finely mixed. She felt it too then, the fear that he would never be more than a tool to be used. The guilt that went with it. She didn't want this any-more than he did. There just wasn't any choice left to them. Everything she said, every word, was true. He knew it before she spoke.

'There's no time. There are angels here. The Fear are on the loose and they aren't the worst thing we can expect. Holly is trying to destroy everything and it looks like she's going to succeed. I know what I said, but I need to be strong now and you're my touchstone.'

'What do they want?' he asked, clenching his hands into fists to hide the trembling from her.

How long until he became expendable? The treacherous thought in his mind laughed at him. The more he tried to push it away, the louder it got. How long until the power became more important that the vessel? And how long until she wouldn't let him leave at all?

He'd always known Silver was dangerous. He'd only tried to kid himself that he could handle that. Now he knew he'd been wrong.

'I don't know what they want.' She stepped towards him, so close that they could touch at any minute, but she didn't actually reach out and touch him. Her hands hesitated above his arms. In the skin beneath whorls of light started to glow, drawn out by her proximity. The power inside him wanted her, wanted her touch, wanted to be used by her.

Even his body betrayed him.

Dylan looked deep into her eyes, recognising the hunger there, like an addict looking for a fix behind her perfect façade. But knowing what he knew of himself, feeling what he felt, which one of them was the addict? Perhaps both of them were.

'Have you tried asking them?'

'Please, Dylan. I must protect my people.'

That was it really, the difference he saw between Silver and the rest of the Sídhe who would throw anyone else under a bus the moment it suited them. Or just for laughs.

Silver and Jinx. That was it. He didn't care about the rest of them. Did such creatures even deserve to be saved?

And who was he to be the judge?

And what if he was the one going under the bus? *Her people*, she said. That was who she was interested in. *Her people*. Not him. Unless he was hers.

As gently as he dared, Dylan reached for her, turning his head slightly to avoid Clodagh's appalled expression. But he had to say something.

'Take care of me when I go under, Clo. Okay? I'll be … I'll be counting on you.'

'Under? What do you mean?' Her voice choked in her throat. She was freaking out.

Dylan tried to smile, unable to tear his eyes from Silver's. 'You'll know.'

It was Ash who answered, her voice strangely assured. 'We'll be here.' He might not know her, but the sound was a comfort. It was the type of voice you could trust. Older, wiser than it should have been. 'No harm will come to you. I promise.'

He pressed his lips to Silver's in a kiss. For a moment it was just that, chaste and simple, but then the magic inside him built up like a wave about to break. It grew and kept on growing, a tsunami of power. Silver gave a little moan of desire that wasn't for him alone, opening her mouth against his. Her hands seized his arms, slid to his shoulders, dragging up along the muscles of his neck and to his head where she held him, her long and elegant fingers knotting in his hair.

The magic burst through him and with it came the music, wild and passionate, tearing through him. Dylan cried out, the sound smothered by her lips, as Silver devoured what she needed, his cry swallowed up in the maelstrom that engulfed him.

As she let him go and he collapsed to his knees, someone else caught him and cradled him, someone he knew to whom he should be grateful. He wanted to say her name when she called him, but the music had taken his voice and his conscious thought. He was lost.

CHAPTER TWENTY-THREE

Stand Off

Silver pushed by Izzy and Jinx as she left, glittering with power. Brí took a hurried step after her and then stopped, looking back at Dylan. Her own touchstone, the amber pendant at her throat, glowed like the inside of a volcano.

'Izzy!' Clodagh's voice sounded frantic. 'Dylan ... She did something to him.'

'She needed her magic and he's the source,' said Jinx brusquely.

Clodagh shied back from Jinx, but didn't say anything. Ash was trying to hold Dylan up, to get him onto the bed, but he had that dazed, spaced out look that couldn't be good. His gaze was fixed on the ceiling and he grinned at something they couldn't see while tears streamed down his cheeks.

'Fabulous,' Izzy muttered.

She had no idea what the angels would make of a human

touchstone. Nothing good, she was sure. Probably something very dead.

'Can you help him?' she asked Jinx. He stared at her. 'You know Silver and her power better than anyone. Come on, Jinx. Please. How do we snap him out of it?'

He knelt down by Dylan's side and gazed at his beatific features. 'I don't know. I reckon Silver doesn't know either. Not this time. I mean, her previous touchstone was a tree. It didn't tend to wander off by itself. Lady Brí?'

But Brí didn't move. 'I don't know. He's an unknown thing, altogether new. I thought there was a way to break it but now … now I'm not sure. And this is not the time. We are in great danger. There's a whole host out there. Zadkiel and his kin.'

Reaper stood behind her. 'I'll try.'

'You leave him alone,' Brí snapped. 'Not one step nearer, understand? I saved him once. I don't want to have to expend all that energy again for the sake of Silver's touchstone.'

'I've got to do something,' said Izzy. She looked to the door as an idea began to form. 'I've got to talk to them.'

Jinx shook his head. 'You said they hate you.'

'Yes. But, Jinx … I have to. I'm a Grigori. I was born to this.'

'Of course you were,' said another voice. Her father's voice. 'But I was there first.'

'Dad?' She couldn't quite get the word out. Her voice cracked as she turned and saw him there. And then she was in his arms, having somehow passed through the space between them without thinking about it, throwing herself across the tent and through the door to the place where he stood. He swept her up in strong arms, arms she could always depend on, and held her to him.

'It's okay, love,' he whispered. 'It's going to be okay.'

'Where's Mum? What's happening? Did you find—?'

'Shh.' His embrace tightened. Which told her all she needed to know. He hadn't found her. He didn't want anyone else to realise. He was compromised. They both were and they couldn't risk anyone finding out. But where was she? What were Azazel and his demonspawn doing with her?

'What are the angels doing here?' she asked.

'I guess they found out what happened. Holly has raised the Fear and loosened them on the city. But that's just a distraction. She's trying to raise the Shining Ones and she's going to use Jinx to do it. If they get out, the war in heaven will look like a playground brawl. Not even the angels can stand against them. The time for reticence is over.' He looked in the room, straight at Ash. 'Someone reported in.'

The dark-haired girl rose to her feet, her eyes darker than ever and her face defiant. 'Grigori,' she said with a curt bow.

Izzy's chest squeezed in as her new 'friend' seemed to transform in front of her eyes. The girl was gone. This was something else, something tall and imposing, something as old as time. But Ash had helped her on Bray Head. How could she deceive them this way?

'What the hell?' Clodagh growled. She backed away, her eyes wide with rage.

'Not hell,' said Dad. 'Never hell, isn't that right, Ashira?'

Ash smiled then, a slow knowing smile, her teeth very white against her lips. 'Never Hell, Grigori.'

'Did you betray them?'

She cocked her head to one side, as if questioning him with a look. It was too quick a moment, unearthly. 'They are Sídhe. There is no *betraying* them. They are the betrayers, not I. It has always been this way.'

'Ash?' Izzy took a step away from Dad, towards her. 'What's going on? What – what are you?'

'She's an angel,' said Jinx. She'd never heard his voice sound so bleak and lost. Not even when Holly had him. 'And she must have told them everything.'

'I did my duty,' said Ash. 'I also saved your life. Another part of my duty. Both your life and Jinx's.'

'And you brought Zadkiel here? Why?'

Ash shook back her dark hair from her face and shoulders. 'I think you know why, Izzy. You remember what Sorath was like. Jinx is a vessel. He's dangerous. Far too dangerous. His body could hold a Shining One, and Holly has the means to control him. We deal with him now, before it's too late.'

Jinx. She was looking straight at Jinx.

'No. No way.' Izzy moved back towards him, as quickly as she dared, reaching out for him and no longer caring if Dad saw. He didn't seem to react, though his gaze followed her every movement. When she reached Jinx, she stretched out for his hands, wrapping his arms around her, holding him as close as she could.

Dad's jaw tightened. She was pretty sure a vein in his head was about to explode, but he didn't react in any other outside way.

She could hear Jinx breathing, could feel the warmth of him, and the answering warmth that lingered in the tattoo on her neck whenever he was near. Comfort. Safety. Like coming home.

'Enough,' said Dad. 'Come with me, Ashira, and we'll see if there is a way to negotiate our way through this. You aren't so reckless. I take it Zadkiel is alone behind this ill-thought-out incursion. You haven't done anything yet, nothing to tip us into war at least, nothing that cannot be repaired. There's still time. And you lot—' He glared at each of them, '—stay here. Stay out of sight. No matter what. Understand?'

Figures surrounded the Long Stone, great and small, all those fae who hadn't already fled, which wasn't many. They parted as David Gregory approached, Ash his shadow. They didn't close the gap again. The fae didn't dare step where he had stepped. So they formed a gap through which Izzy could see the Stone and the lawn around it. Silver stood there, glittering with power. And on the lawn behind her, Izzy could see the other angels.

The brightness that came with them made everything sharper. It hurt to look for too long, but she forced her eyes to adjust. Through her tears, she made herself watch as Ash joined Zadkiel and stood there. They spoke only briefly, a curt exchange and Ash frowned, biting her lower lip.

A host of angels stood in the wrecked encampment. They'd lost some of the pleasant disguise with which they presented themselves in the mortal world. They weren't here as guides and guardians. This was all about threat.

Jinx muttered an expletive or two and tightened his grip on her as Silver joined Izzy's Dad. She walked carefully, with dignity, head erect, shoulders back. She glowed, almost as brightly as they did.

'She's channelling her magic,' said Brí as she joined them. 'Nearly all of it, if I'm any judge.' The calculating tone of her voice made Izzy glance at her but Brí didn't seem to notice. Her eyes had turned avaricious and dangerous. They weren't fixed on Silver either. Her gaze was full of David Gregory.

Just when you thought you might be able to trust them, Izzy thought ... But then she couldn't trust anyone now. She knew that.

'A brave man,' said Reaper. His skin took on even darker tones in the brightness. When he smiled, his teeth were so very white. 'Maybe we should join them and show our support.'

But Brí raised a hand to stop him. 'Not just yet. Let's see how this plays out first.'

'Typical,' Jinx muttered. 'Abandon everyone at the first sign of trouble.'

'I didn't bring this trouble upon us,' Brí told him sharply. 'That would have been ... oh, yes, you. You and your friends, walking in here with an angel in disguise. Now shut up and listen.' Then her voice caught in her throat. 'Oh, David—'

Dad was talking fast, trying to negotiate, but they could see on Zadkiel's face that nothing was going to placate him.

'What do we do?' Izzy asked Jinx, torn between following them and staying, unable to abandon her Dad. She wanted to run to him, but was too afraid. Supposing she distracted him, or said the wrong thing? She knew Zadkiel loathed her and blamed her for everything. He'd all but told her that her association with Jinx tainted her, and yet here she was with his arms around her. She tightened her own grip on him. She wasn't letting go. Their contact might have been all that was holding the two of them up.

Zadkiel held up his hands. Anger crossed his face and he turned away from Izzy's dad and pointed up. The huge glass and metal structure shook, as if the building was being rocked by an unseen force and the ground bucked beneath them.

Silver glanced over her shoulder and the light in her seemed to brighten still further. She glowed. Even her eyes were filled with incandescence. She opened her mouth in a gasp of surprise.

'What's happening to her?' Jinx whispered. 'Look at her.'

Izzy couldn't tear her gaze from her. Silver pushed past Izzy's father and faced Zadkiel with something like murder in every line of her body.

'I don't know,' Izzy whispered. 'What do you mean?'

'She isn't a diplomat any more. That's my job, and one at

which I am failing. But still, she's playing with fire. Heavenly fire.'

Her voice shook the air, louder than the muttered exchange of before so they could all hear her clearly. She was projecting it on purpose no doubt, for the sake of everyone inside. 'You are here without leave, archangel, come unbidden to our place of peace against all our accords. There must be a reason or there will be retribution.'

Zadkiel cast her a contemptuous and dismissive look, but ignored her. When he spoke, his voice was as loud as hers. But he directed it elsewhere.

'David Gregory, rein in the Sídhe bitch. Why are you standing with her?'

'I stand here as the Grigori,' Dad replied. 'And as Lady Silver rightly points out this is a grievous breach in the Grand Compact. My role is to see this situation does not degenerate further. You should not be here, Zadkiel, so kindly answer the question.'

All pretence of courtesy and respect bled from the angel's voice. His voice was cold with loathing and disgust. 'You overstep your bounds, mortal.'

Dad took a deliberate step forwards, his every nerve tense. His voice was thunderous, his glare like murder. 'No, Zadkiel. *You* overstep your bounds. This is an invasion of sovereign space. The Sídhe have not invited you here, but they invited me to safeguard them. Answer her. Why are you here?'

'This stands far outside the Grand Compact. It overrides

every agreement made then or since. This is a matter of divine order and nothing stands higher. It concerns the Shining Ones, the Seraphim.' He pointed right at Silver. 'Your dam would release them. She has already let the Fear out among the mortals. They revealed themselves in many places tonight, causing chaos and panic, feeding and killing. Indiscriminate carnage. The more they feed on terror, the stronger and more dangerous they become.'

'This is nothing to do with us,' said Silver. 'Holly has been cast out. You know this.'

'And yet you harbour the vessel she created, into which she would pour the most terrible power. Where is the Cú Sídhe called Jinx?'

Ash stiffened, glancing towards Izzy, and leaned in close, saying something to her superior. Was she trying to help them now? Was she trying to defend them? Not that it mattered. Zadkiel didn't listen, but waved her aside.

Jinx tensed and Izzy pushed backwards in case he got some mad idea about going out there. She all but dragged him into the tent.

'Brí!' Izzy shouted over her shoulder.

'Stay where you are!' her birth mother yelled. She and Reaper crouched on either side of Dylan, their hands pressed to his chest. He was aglow with power, as was Silver. They were channelling their power through him and into Silver.

'You can't have Jinx,' said Silver. Her voice wreathed with anger, ringing out around the Liberty. 'He is my emissary. He is protected.'

'He is an abomination. Give him to us, Grigori. Make her comply. Or we will burn the ground of Dubh Linn. We will destroy every hollow and leave the Sídhe who survive wanderers forever.'

'This was not the plan,' Ash shouted suddenly, trying to pull Zadkiel back. 'Isabel Gregory is my charge. You promised protection. Our role is to protect the innocent, at all costs. We cannot attack the Sídhe. It would break the compact, Lord Zadkiel.'

'Be silent,' said the archangel.

'I'm silent too often. If he is a vessel, perhaps we can make him not a vessel—'

He raised his arm and struck her, sending her sprawling backwards and down to the ground.

'Enough,' he growled.

The light in the rest of the angels grew even brighter and Silver and Dad made pitiful shadows against it. But that didn't stop them. They didn't back down or even appear dazzled. They held their ground, black rocks against a sea of light.

'No,' said Dad. Izzy couldn't believe it. She loved him for it, but the words didn't sound like her dad at all. Not when it came to Jinx. But at the same time, it was. It was every inch her father. 'You won't be taking anyone anywhere. Jinx by Jasper is protected, as are all his kind.'

'Enough of this,' Zadkiel roared. 'Give him to us now.'

'No one should be handed over like that.' Her dad stood

his ground. 'Ashira is right, Zadkiel. We can find a way. We can undo this spell. There has to be a way.' Izzy could not have loved him more in that moment.

'He's wrong,' said Jinx, which made anger flare inside her. 'They'll kill you all. Let me go, Izzy.' She pushed him back inside again, looking frantically to Brí for help.

'Jinx by Jasper,' Brí shouted. 'You stay exactly where you are. Don't make me restrain you. Watch them, Isabel. We need to know what they're doing.'

She pulled the door open again just in time to see Zadkiel try another tactic. He smiled and somehow that was even more frightening.

'Come, Lady Silver,' he said, all charm again. 'If we are to negotiate, then let us negotiate. You have something we want, namely Jinx by Jasper.'

'My kin and my kith. If you think I'll bargain him away—'

'And we can restore something lost to you. Something important.'

'What?' Disbelief dripped from her voice.

Behind them, Dylan cried out, sobbed and lurched to his feet. 'Silver, no,' he said, staggering towards them while Reaper and Clodagh struggled to hold him back. 'Silver, please. You can't.' He dropped to his knees and his gaze fell on Izzy and Jinx. His voice grated in his throat. 'You have to get out of here.'

'Silver won't let them take him,' said Brí. 'She's too noble by far.'

'There's a weakness,' said Dylan. 'Something she wants more than anything. More than any of us.'

Zadkiel reached out his hand, unarmed and elegantly unfurled his fingers. Light swelled there and Silver's eyes widened. Everyone stared, captivated by the light blossoming in his hand. Even Silver seemed hypnotised by it. Zadkiel touched her throat and her eyes widened as the light blended with her own, bright and beautiful. Her hands flew up to her neck as if to touch the gift and assure herself that it was real.

Dylan collapsed, like a marionette with severed strings.

'What is it?' asked Clodagh. 'What did he do?'

'Her voice,' whispered Dylan. 'He's given her back her voice. The only thing she wants.'

'He can't do that,' snarled Brí. 'That's mine! I bought it. I traded it fair and square. Damn them. Damn them *all*. They need me out there. And Reaper, if this goes pear-shaped, get them out of here. All of them. These two, my daughter and Jinx by Jasper as well. Understand?'

He nodded. 'Yes, Lady Brí.'

She faltered and wrapped his hands with her own. Her voice dropped low and solemn, her eyes fixed on his determinedly. 'You have my debt then.'

Brí swept past them, out in the light and the boiling air. Fire ignited around her, her magic at full force, her touchstone blazing at her throat. Like a being made of fire itself, her hair the flames, her skin glowing like embers, she crossed to the Long Stone, the assembled crowds falling back from her path, angel and Sídhe alike. She joined Silver, taking the other matriarch's hand in hers.

Silver stared at her in shock, her other hand still on her neck as if she couldn't drop it for fear this was a trick and the voice would vanish. Something passed between the two of them, but Izzy had no idea what that might be.

'Don't promise things that are not yours to promise, angel,' said Brí.

Zadkiel seemed to falter. 'Lady?' His voice was a whisper that carried like distant thunder. 'Lady, you of all the Sídhe know this must be.'

'I know many things, Zadkiel. More than you. But you will not take Jinx by Jasper. Not while I exist.'

'Lady.' His odd deference seemed to shock the other angels. Even Ash took a step back, staring at Brí as if trying to work out a puzzle. 'I *beg* you, step down. Give us the Cú Sídhe. We will purge him, set him free of the bonds that control him. We will—'

'You will *kill* him, Zadkiel. Use your words. And the answer is still no.'

They moved more quickly than thought, angels roaring through the air. Not like people anymore, but flaming swords, great Catherine Wheels, gaping mouths filled with teeth and eyes. Only Ash stood unchanged, looking still as human and vulnerable as ever, a girl amid horrors. Lost in dismay.

A rushing wind swept across the lawns, sweeping up the remains of the tents in a maelstrom. The earth shook and the shadows unfurled wings of darkness. Eyes brighter than stars burst from the blackness and shades spilled from everywhere. The angels faltered, turned towards new arrivals on the field with murderous eyes.

A terrible crash shattered the air. Glass fell like rain, tiny shards so brightly coloured and so beautiful that it was only in the moment before they struck that the beings beneath thought to look away. Screams filled the air, glass tore into Sídhe flesh or melted and evaporated as it stuck the angels. Zadkiel raised his hand, shielding himself and those immediately around him – Silver, Brí and Dad.

The stench filled the air and the verdant plants blackened and shrivelled. The perfect chamomile lawn beneath their feet turned to ashes.

The demons had come.

Another figure joined the group on the steps, dressed in his customary black, his long coat spread wide like bats wings in the wind. He smoothed back his hair with gnarled, claw-tipped fingers. When he smiled, his teeth were very white and sharp.

'Well, this is quite a gathering,' said Azazel. 'Sorry to gate-crash, but we felt left out. After all, we've lost brethren too.'

'Abomination,' snarled Zadkiel.

Azazel shrugged. 'You're so fond of that word. He's an abomination. I'm an abomination. It used to be a privilege. Now everyone's at it.'

'I abjure thee, demon—' Zadkiel began, but Azazel stepped

right up to him and grabbed him by the throat, silencing him.

'Go on, please. Give me a reason, little brother. I've been dying to snap your pompous neck for millennia.' He looked over at Izzy's dad. 'Where's our girl?'

The shades hissed, faces looming from the depths of their darkness as they spread around the doorway to the tent, trying to get in. Something held them back still, some last trace of Sídhe power.

Reaper. It had to be. Izzy could feel the vibrations of magic in the air around her, in her blood. But Reaper was watching her, a curious expression on his face, the way an expert might study an anomaly.

'Ah, there she is,' said Azazel, letting go of the angel and smiling broadly. 'And the boy with her. We're good to go then.'

'No!' said Dad.

'No?' Azazel paused, his eyes narrowing. 'Are you forgetting something? Or rather someone?'

He snapped his fingers and Mum appeared, swathed in shadows. Dark circles ringed her eyes and her skin was pale as parchment. She looked terrified, helpless. Izzy screamed, and this time it was Jinx who had to hold her back, pulling her against him.

'This isn't a request, Grigori,' said Azazel. 'Give up the boy to them and it is war.'

'Give him to the demons and we will rain fires of vengeance on this world.' Zadkiel swept his arms out wide, ready to strike.

Azazel shrugged. 'War, chaos. We're good with that too. But we want him.' He pointed right at Jinx. 'If you want her back, David. Ever.'

'Isabel,' said Dad. He never called her that. Never. But his voice carried through the chaos and protests as clearly as if he whispered it beside her. He swallowed hard, glanced at his wife, and then looked at Izzy again. 'Isabel Gregory, you know what you have to do.'

She did know. She hated herself for it. But she knew. 'We have to get out of here,' she whispered.

'Your wish,' said Reaper, 'is my command.' He stood behind them, with Clodagh at his side and Dylan slung over his shoulder like a sack of flour. Like he'd been ready all the time. 'This way.'

He rubbed the finger and thumb of his free hand together and blue on the spark that formed there. Suddenly the tent filled with lights, dancing, swirling, a firework display of chaos.

The world ripped open, the ground heaving. 'Follow me,' said Reaper and stepped through it. The tent material bil- lowed out, ballooning around them.

'But we can't leave them,' said Jinx.

Mum. She couldn't leave Mum. But she couldn't stay either. She couldn't hand him over. And Dad had told her what to do, hadn't he? This had to be what he meant. It had to be. She pulled Jinx with her, through the portal Reaper had opened. Who know he could do that? Who knew anyone could do that? Just open ways on a whim. Brí for one, Izzy supposed.

Maybe her dad too. Or at least, she hoped so.

'Dad can negotiate. The very sight of you is driving them crazy. Without you, they don't have a reason to fight. Maybe they can stop arguing and work together to find a way to stop the Fear and Shining Ones.'

'You heard them. They have a million reasons to fight.'

'They don't have a prize then. Just shut up and run. Don't lose Reaper.'

They caught up with Clodagh first, gasping in panic as she ran. But still running hard, not giving up and dissolving in tears. Izzy pushed onwards, her feet pounding on stone now. There were cobbles underneath her, the Sídheways winding on ahead like a narrow alleyway she almost knew.

She had to find Donn, find a way to help Jinx because otherwise the angels and the demons would come for him again. And there would be war.

The telltale glimmering of another Sídheway opening filled the far end of the alley. They plunged through and let it take them wherever Reaper was heading.

CHAPTER TWENTY-FOUR

Hunted

Jinx tried not to think. It was so much easier not to think. The angels and the demons were after him and whatever Holly had done to him was clearly so dreadful that they were prepared to break the most serious laws of all to get to him. They'd violate every treaty, go to war. They'd tear the world apart to capture him. And if he was lucky, capture was as far as it went. He didn't think that likely. Neither would allow the other to take him. He knew that. And if they thought he was lost ... or a threat ... And even Silver could no longer be trusted. They'd promised her the one thing she wanted – her precious voice. She'd lost it to free him from Brí, given it to the other matriarch. Given the chance to get it back, he knew she'd take it. Nothing had ever hurt her like that except perhaps the destruction of her tree. When Brí had taken her voice, she'd weakened her so much that Holly could get to her touchstone and shatter it. Only Dylan had saved her. No one truly understood how that might work out, what it was doing to either of them. And now... now she could be more powerful than ever. With Dylan *and* her voice, she'd have the power she thought she needed to really be a matriarch. Without realising that she already had it. And that her power wasn't the thing that mattered.

Only Dylan wasn't with her. He was lying there on the other side of the cellar where they hid, unconscious still.

Jinx had dreamed when he was unconscious, strange and terrible dreams. It hadn't just been the Púca, not when he'd looked in the pool. The Dubh Linn was a seer's pool. He knew the old stories. What you saw in there was always true. The voices in his mind had been too harsh, too real. They'd invaded every molecule of his body, leaving barbs of memory behind when Brí had forced it to withdraw. How she'd done it he had no idea and didn't want to know. It didn't do to dwell too closely on the ways of matriarchs and their abilities.

Or the amount of power Brí could command when she put her mind to it. Even the angels had been scared of her. He'd seen that. From the moment she stepped out. Sorath hadn't wanted to confront her. Neither did Zadkiel. What had she been to them?

And now Silver.

He didn't know where they were. Reaper had brought them through the Sídheways by paths he didn't know. Paths he couldn't hope to know, for they were old indeed, their edges frayed and worn which meant, to know them, Reaper had to be very old as well.

And now they huddled in a cellar, under the ruins of some old house burnt out almost a hundred years ago. Dylan slept peacefully, though he'd woken when they first arrived, wild and raving, hysterical. Reaper and Clodagh had calmed him, the girl still holding him close and Jinx suspected that Reaper had used some magic as well.

'You couldn't have done anything,' said Izzy. 'They would have killed you.'

'I don't know what they would have done. Perhaps it would have been a good thing.'

'No.' She drew close in the darkness and pressed her lips to his. 'That would never be a good thing.'

'Izzy,' he started, but her lips were in the way and he'd dreamed so long about kissing her again that he couldn't pull back. He wrapped his arms around her, touched her face and her hair. All the while she kissed him, that sweet, delicate way she had of kissing, like she was tasting him, that drove him out of his mind with need. He couldn't seem to let go, to move back, or to be anywhere but there with her. She tugged at his shirt and slid her hands underneath it, her hands so cold against his hot skin, so soft against his muscles.

She brushed against a bruise from the fight the other day and he hissed with the shock of it.

'What is it? What's wrong?'

'Nothing. Nothing at all. Izzy—'

One of her hands pressed against his cheek then and she stared up, her eyes so bright and blue that he felt like he was falling into the summer's sky. 'I won't lose you again.'

The sudden rush of anger in her voice made him smile and the smile made her angrier still. 'You won't, won't you?'

'You think I'm joking?'

'No.' But he couldn't keep the laugh from his voice. He should have, he knew that. It never did to laugh at her. And that fiery temper was never easily quelled. But at the same time he couldn't help himself. He threaded his fingers through her bright fire-red hair, soft as silken strands.

In all this danger and terror, this moment was perfect happiness. How could he not laugh?

She punched his shoulder. Surprisingly hard. She'd been practising, leading with the first two knuckles, the hardest bones of all. 'Shut up.'

'Yes, my lady,' he murmured, lowering his mouth to capture hers again.

'Oh, God, get a bloody room,' Clodagh snapped from the other side of the cellar where she sat beside Dylan. 'It's nauseating.'

Izzy opened her eyes, so blue, and laughed. Probably not the sound Clodagh was expecting but after a moment she joined in as well. A bright sound in the darkness. Jinx could only stare at them, bewildered.

'You're so weird, Izzy Gregory,' her friend said.

'I know. What're you going to do about it?'

'Embrace the crazy I guess.'

'You okay? Really?'

Clodagh shrugged. 'I'm still here, aren't I?'

'Mari wouldn't be.'

'Of course she would have been!' she scowled. 'Maybe you didn't know her. Mari was complicated. She could be a bitch, sure. But when she had your back ... and she had our backs, Izzy. Always. Remember when Sarah Blake started that rumour about you in second year?'

'No.'

'Yeah, because Mari told her to shove it or the world would know about her secret fluffy unicorn collection. See?'

Jinx listened, bemused. It was like another language, words from another world. He envied them.

'Where is Reaper?' he asked.

Izzy shook her head and the brightness in her dimmed a little. She didn't know any more than he did. 'He said he'd be back.'

'How's Dylan?'

'Awake,' he said, his voice ragged. 'My head wishes I wasn't.'

Izzy got up and crossed to him, kneeling down beside him. 'Are you okay?'

Dylan struggled upright, swinging his legs down, but clearly he thought better of it a moment later as he dropped forward, head in his hands. 'No. Not really. Give me a minute.'

'What happened?'

'They gave Silver back her voice. Temporarily, I expect.

Nothing's for nothing or what's the point? But it broke our connection. I lost the music. All of it.' He sounded bereft. 'But they won't let her keep it. Not unless she hands over Jinx.'

There was no doubt in any of their minds that she would. That was the worst part. If it got Silver her voice back, it was worth it. That was all she wanted, after all. She'd given it up to save him. In a way it was only right.

If it meant this would end and Izzy would be safe…

'You ought to have left me there.'

Clodagh tutted. 'Suicidal, are we? Great. That'll help. That'll help loads.' Jinx just glared at her, putting every bit of malice he could into the expression. She arched one perfectly shaped eyebrow. 'I'm not scared of you, you know?'

He glowered even more. 'You should be.'

Clodagh just rolled her eyes, already bored. 'Please, tell him, Izzy.'

'Yeah, she's not scared of you,' said Izzy. 'Years of Mari. That's why—'

'Do you mind?' said Dylan, sharper than Jinx would have expected. He'd lifted his head again, blinking in the dim light. Mari had been Dylan's sister, his kin. Jinx understood in an instant, even if the girls did not. Kin were everything … or at least, they were meant to be. 'Where are we?'

Clodagh answered. 'Hiding in a cellar. A really funky smelling one. It's brilliant. Not. I don't think he's coming back, Izzy.'

'All right.' She stood up, stretching out her back in that hypnotic way he couldn't help but watch. 'Reaper wouldn't just leave. He made a deal with Brí. You don't do that lightly. And if you do, you certainly don't double cross her.'

The door scraped open behind them and Jinx slid to his feet, ready to fight if he had to. But the figures that entered on silent feet weren't a threat. If his heart could speak it would have sobbed with relief.

'What have you got into now, Jinx by Jasper?' asked Blythe. The other Cú Sídhe laughed. Blight always had a better sense of humour than his sister. That wouldn't be difficult as Blythe probably couldn't break into a smile without cracking her face. But she was the most skilled Cú Sídhe he knew, leader of her pack – his pack – and she had never let him down. Or indeed, let him forget it.

Behind them, Reaper stepped into the room and shut the door. 'We need to move on. It's chaos out there. The rumour mill is running riot. And there are rather a lot of fae saying we should hand you over. They can't decide which side gets you though. The Fear killed many tonight, and drove more out of their minds. Humankind cannot cope with such things. They have their excuses already – gas leaks and rioting, such things – but it won't be long until they strike again.'

'Where's my dad?' asked Izzy.

'That I do not know. I ran into these two and—'

'Lady Brí sent word,' said Blythe. 'She told us to track you and guard you. So here we are.'

'And if they did, others can as well,' said the blue-haired Aes Sídhe.

'Not bloody likely,' snorted Blight. 'No one tracks like Cú Sídhe.'

'Some do,' Reaper told him solemnly, not amused by his bravado. 'Perhaps not as fast, but just as accurately in the end. We should go.'

'Where are you taking them?' asked Blythe.

'To My Lord's hollow. That's where you want to go, isn't it?'

'And who's your Lord?' asked Clodagh.

'Donn.'

'Oh, good,' said Dylan. 'Just what we need. Yes, let's go and pay the Lord of the Dead a visit. That's what Mari said we had to do. Why the hell not?'

'Hell,' said Clodagh. 'Funny.' She nudged Dylan, who only winced.

Jinx frowned. She had the strangest sense of humour. Maybe proximity to the fae was turning her mind. Maybe Amadán had done something to her regardless of his promises. 'Izzy?'

'Yes. That's what Mari said. That's what everyone said. The only one who can help us is Donn. If Reaper can take us there, then that's where we go.'

The night air felt cold when they stepped outside. The cellar had offered shelter Izzy hadn't realised. Now a fine misty rain made the Dublin streets grey and dull. It haloed the street-lights in yellow, the ornate black lamppost casting a strange multi-shadow of swirls and shamrocks. Izzy paused, leaning against the cold metal.

Nothing felt right. She wanted to phone Dad, but she didn't dare. He'd tell her not to do this, she knew it. He might even tell her to give Jinx up for the greater good, and she couldn't do that. He might even say it was the only way to get Mum back and she couldn't make that choice. She just couldn't.

'Isabel, you know what you have to do.'

He only used Isabel when she was in trouble and they both knew it. And she was in trouble now. Maybe that was what he'd meant? Oh God, had she done the wrong thing? Had she abandoned and doomed her mum?

'Izzy?' said Reaper. 'We have to move.'

'I know.'

The Cú Sídhe skirted the sides of the wide pavement, herding the group, the two of them more effective than any other guard. The brief discussion about whether they should split up and take Clodagh and Dylan home had been shut down pretty quickly. Clodagh wasn't going anywhere. She wanted answers in the same way Izzy had all those months ago. She had shed the ditzy façade and replaced it with a steely determination that Izzy wished she shared.

Although the question of Amadán's effect on her friend still bothered her.

Reaper took Izzy's hand, drawing her towards him and Izzy heard Jinx's growl, low in his throat, dangerous. Reaper just smiled and bowed.

'All due respect, Jinx, but I have a lover of my own. I have no designs on yours.'

Lover? Izzy's face flamed hot. 'We're not—'

'We aren't—' Jinx exclaimed at the same moment and then stared at her, appalled.

Reaper grinned. 'Of course not. Silly me. Shall we go? The night moves on. It's almost Samhain.'

'Samhain? Halloween? Isn't it already Samhain?'

'The day, yes, but not quite the hour. The time when the veils are at their thinnest. When the Sídheways are most malleable. When the door to the land of the dead stands open and anyone may enter. We shouldn't waste time.'

Up ahead, the mist was getting thicker. Clodagh and Dylan stopped with Blight in front of them. No one moved.

Izzy had a bad feeling. 'How far is the next gate?'

'Not far. In the Castle grounds.'

She shook her head. 'Too far to run then?'

'Why?'

She pointed. Something was coming out of the mist, something fluid and shadowy that drifted from place to place. The temperature plummeted and left them shivering, teeth chattering. The rain got heavier, drops splashing in puddles, throwing up sparks into the night.

'There are seven of us. Stay together.'

But Izzy wasn't listening to Reaper now. His voice was just a whisper behind her. The world shifted, becoming less real, less solid. Or maybe that was her. She felt dizzy, vague. Not herself.

Up ahead, the Fear swirled out of the mist, bearing down on Clodagh and Dylan. Blight and Blythe crouched low, every muscle alert and poised.

But it was clear that they were terrified. How could they not be? They were creatures of instinct.

'Get away from them!' The voice rang out behind her and before she knew what was happening, Jinx leaped by her. She moved after him, afraid that something would happen to him, that somehow she'd lose him again. And she couldn't. She just couldn't.

'Izzy?' Clodagh said, and her voice strained almost to the point of breaking. 'Izzy, this isn't good, is it?'

Izzy could hear it in her voice. Fear. That was it. What these creatures thrived on and all they wanted, the other origin of their name.

'No. Just don't panic. Don't be afraid. That's what they want.'

'Seriously?' Clodagh gasped, barely able to get the word out. 'Shite advice.'

She tried to force herself to be still, to concentrate on the fire inside her, the birthright from Brí that sometimes worked and sometimes — most of the time — didn't. It was all she had. And when she faced them it seemed stronger. She had to believe that.

The figures in the mist coalesced, forming a solid mass. More of them than Izzy had ever seen and at their fore, the king. Eochaid.

'Isabel Gregory,' he hissed, drawing out the 'z' sound in her name like a curse. 'Lady Holly sends her greetings. She bids you come.'

'I'm not going anywhere with you.'

'Then your friends die. They die screaming.'

'Don't listen to him, Izzy,' said Dylan. And then one of the Fear was on him. It seized him by the throat and dragged him to his knees, turning him around to face her. Long, clawed hands ran over his face and neck, threaded through his hair until he was gagging on unvoiced screams. His eyes strained from the sockets, the pupils pinpoints and his mouth opened too wide in a silent scream, too terrible to escape from his tortured mind.

'He's strong. Amazingly strong. A unique mind. How much can he stand, do you think?'

'Let him go.'

Eochaid stretched out his hand, slowly unfurling long bony fingers in enticement. 'Come with us.'

'Not on your life,' said Jinx.

'Jinx by Jasper,' the king of the Fear laughed. 'So strong, so bold. Remember though, we've seen inside your head and your heart already. You belong to her.' Jinx glanced at Izzy and Eochaid laughed. 'No, not her. To Holly, you fool.'

'No, I don't. Never.'

'You don't have a choice in this, boy. You know that in your heart of hearts. Holly's magic is already upon you. The Shining Ones are already inside you. You heard the angels and they don't lie, do they?'

Angels never lied. Izzy sucked in a breath. They'd promised Silver her voice — given it to her in advance of payment, so sure of their success. They wanted Jinx. Everyone did.

'Why?' Izzy asked. 'Why does Holly want me, when everyone else wants Jinx?'

They laughed, all of them. Snide and knowing snickers echoed around them.

'Not Holly. Us. *We* want you. Only the child of Míl can free the king of the Fear. Your strength is my strength. And if you are ours already … well … I'll walk free and live forever, won't I?'

'Let me go and I'll show you how cooperative I can be.' Her hand itched to plunge into her bag. She only had to get her hand on the knife and she'd kill him all right. In a moment.

'*Ah-ahhhhh,*' he sighed. 'You can try. But not with that knife. Pretty though it is, it won't kill me. The Blade that Cuts, on the other hand …'

He saw the understanding in her eyes and his own expression turned dark with malicious glee.

'Why would you tell me that?'

'You won't use it. The Blade can only be used to do one thing or the other — to kill or to cure. Not both. Not for you. Once the choice is made … well … ' He smiled, baring his yellowed teeth, more like a snarl. 'And you need it for something … and someone else.' He leered at her, at Jinx. 'Are you prepared to pay that price, little girl?'

'I will do what I must.' But she swallowed hard. It was true, she didn't want to sacrifice anyone, especially not Jinx. The Blade was one shot only! No one had bothered to mention this before. Just all that sword of light bull. Bloody Sídhe.

She'd killed herself, or tried to, to get rid of Sorath. She'd tried to sacrifice herself. But that was different. That was her choice, her decision. She wouldn't give up someone else – Mum and Dad, Jinx, Dylan or Clodagh? No, never.

'Will you, indeed? Very noble. Just what I'd expect from a child of Míl.'

'Stop calling me that.'

Eochaid reached out, his cold hand resting tentatively on her skin. She shivered, terrified, but it wasn't the same sort of smothering panic she'd felt before. This was sharp and painful with clarity.

'Daughter of Míl,' he sneered. 'Where is your fabled strength now?' His eyes flickered, following movement behind her. 'Come no closer Cú Sídhe, or she will see you die screaming before she follows you to a cold oblivion.'

'What do you want from me?' she managed to say.

His fingertip traced an icy trail along her neck and the tattoo on the back turned even colder. 'What do we want?' The laughter of the other Fear whispered around her, across her skin like cobwebs. Her hair rose on end and her chest tightened around her skeleton, tight and painful. 'This was our land before you came, and before the Sídhe came. Ours. And when they came we helped them. We made a deal, just as you made a deal. We were part of the Compact, part of the defeat of the Shining Ones. We betrayed our gods for you and your friends. One of us to cage them – you or me. I mean to see that it will be you. After all these millennia, it's only fair. And we will have vengeance on the de Dannan and on their pawns too. All of them. Holly promised us that.'

'Holly lies all the time. She's never kept her word, or if she has it has been twisted beyond all recognition.' Jinx again, trying in spite of Eochaid's warning. Izzy heard him draw in a brief gulp of air before the Fear struck. With a thud, he hit the pavement and then he screamed. Not high and sharp. Not a scream of terror or panic. This was wrenched from him, forced between clenched teeth and given only after there was nothing left to stop it.

Eochaid turned Izzy around, keeping his hand at her throat. Jinx lay on the ground, pinned there by mist and violent hands.

Dylan and Clodagh were struggling against their captors. Reaper stood back, arms raised to the level of his eyes, which darted from side to side, looking for an out. Blight and Blythe were unconscious. Whatever it had taken for the two of them to be beaten down, Izzy didn't want to think about it. The faint and frantic stirring of their chests as they breathed betrayed the nightmares wrapped around them. They were helpless.

And she was on her own.

Jinx's gaze met hers, broken and angry, filled with despair. He was in so much pain. She could sense it like her own.

'Let him go,' said Izzy.

'He'll be the death of you,' said another voice, a female voice filled with amusement. Not in the position to feel amused at anyone or anything right at this moment, Izzy scowled, knowing that voice. Recognising it right away. 'Give him up, Isabel Gregory.'

'Never.'

'Ah, well,' said Ash. 'It was worth a shot. Your father said you knew what to do. I hope he's right.'

Light burst from her fingertips. Bright white light. She opened her mouth and it was like listening to a choir, to a multitude of choirs. The Fear screamed, their voices warped in dissonance, breaking through the beauty of Ash's song.

Izzy felt the fire inside her flame up at last, the fire quenched and dwindled almost to embers by terror flamed fresh and new, terrible in its brightness. It almost stopped her heart, as if it was burning away inside her but that didn't matter.

Fire had worked on them before. It was the only thing that had worked. She called it, her birthright from Brí, her natural mother's only real gift to her.

Flames burst from her pores, caressed her in a warm embrace, wrapping her in golden light while the Fear screamed and retreated. What must she look like to the people coming out of the bars and theatres, the people in town to party or late finishing work? To the bus that screeched to a halt, to the driver blaring their horns. But if she didn't ... if she couldn't stop them … the Fear would destroy them all.

Happy Halloween, Izzy thought bleakly and let herself burn.

CHAPTER TWENTY-FIVE

The Black Pool

The Fear released Jinx and retreated, rushing away from Izzy's fire and the angel's song like startled cats. He heaved in a breath, and another, and then forced himself to stand. His treacherous body trembled and shook, wanted to collapse and sob out his terrors. But he couldn't allow that. Not while Izzy was in danger. Not while—

He tried to reach her but the fire was too hot. He could see her in the flames, like Brí, engulfed in them, but untouched, her red hair flowing out around her head, lifted by the heat and the boiling air, her eyes so bright it hurt. She was looking at him. Just staring straight at him. But he knew she couldn't see him.

Lost. His Izzy. Lost in flames and darkness. And alone.

It was like the hill all over again, the hill and the Wishing Stone and Sorath consuming her, controlling her. But this time she was lost in her own power, her own magic. And if she couldn't lose him, he couldn't lose her either. Not again. Words he couldn't say reached up from deep inside him with needy grasping hands, but he still couldn't give them voice.

'Izzy,' he cried instead and reached out for her. The fire licked against his hands, blistering him, hurting him, but he didn't care. He grabbed her hands and pulled her towards him, embracing her and the fire that was part of her.

It died before it consumed him. Her skin felt warm and damp, as if she had a fever. She blinked at him and then pulled him the rest of the way into her arms.

'Are you okay?' Her voice sounded hoarse and exhausted. 'Jinx, please, tell me you're okay.'

'Yes. I am. Are you? What happened? Izzy ...' She didn't answer, and his alarm escalated again. He stared at her but she just stared into the middle distance. 'Izzy, talk to me.'

Her magic terrified him. There was no getting away from that. It was too powerful. When it flowed through her like that, he feared he'd lose her completely.

She blinked, the little sparks in her eyes fading now. 'I ... I'm okay. I think I ... oh, God, Jinx! Your hands!'

The skin was black in places, violent red in others, blistered already. The pain hadn't hit yet, but he knew it would. Jinx knew burns. And even magical fire burned.

'It'll fade.' A lie, but the dismay in her eyes was too much to bear. He couldn't make it worse.

Izzy held his wrists gingerly, turning his palms up.

'We have to do something. Get you to a doctor or—'

'What doctor would see me, Izzy?'

He tried to smile and the first wave of agony hit. He bit on the inside of his cheek and tried to ride it out. But from the look on her face he failed.

'What if I get some water? Maybe I can—'

'Leave it.' He sighed as the pain receded a little.

'How will you play?' she asked.

It seemed like such a non-sequitur that he stared at her in silence, unable to understand what she meant.

'Play? Play what?'

'The guitar.'

For a moment he didn't know what to say. In all this, she thought about his guitar? His music, which had once meant more to him than anything else in his life. He'd thought of it as his one freedom.

He shook his head. 'I haven't played since ... since ... I left you. Silver had no voice, and Sage and the others were dead anyway. There were so many other things to do ...'

He hadn't even thought of playing guitar as any more than a half-remembered dream, forgotten in the harsh light of a new reality.

Reality without Izzy.

There had been no need for music. No chance of joy.

There were tears in her eyes now, glistening like dew. They hadn't fallen, but caught on her long lashes. Realising he'd seen them she turned her face away.

'Ash?'

The angel stood several feet away with Dylan and Clodagh, talking gently to them, making sure they were okay, Jinx realised. At least her attention was off him for a moment.

Just a moment until Izzy called it back.

'Please,' Izzy said. 'Help him?'

Ash tilted her head to one side. 'Why would I do that? I'm here to retrieve him. To hunt him, I believe you thought.'

'He's in pain. And if you're hunting us—' She stressed the '*us*', '—then why come alone?'

A brief smile flickered over Ashira's dark features, wry amusement making her eyes sparkle. 'Well, yes, there is that. All right.' She walked towards them, but Jinx pulled back. Only Izzy's grip stopped him bolting altogether. 'Don't fret, fae. I won't hurt you.'

'Much,' he added bleakly and that strange smile quirked her lips again.

'I came because I value reason over force. My brethren can be rash. Zadkiel is an angel of battle and that's all he understands. I try to work with them, but I'm not so good as part of a host. They don't entirely trust guardians because we spend so much time with mortals. And when I try to introduce new ideas I get that look. It's maddening. Plus, he doesn't know you, Izzy. Not like I do.'

'And how do you know me?'

'Better than you think. I know, for example, that if someone tries to command, bully or force you one way, you'll go in the other as fast as possible. I know that your friends mean everything to you. I know how much you love Jinx. And how much he loves you. Whether that's wise or not.'

She took Jinx's hands from Izzy, her grip firm but not uncomfortable. She had the hands of a fighter. He could feel callouses from handling weapons. But her touch was cool, almost like polished stone. He flinched in spite of himself as she closed her eyes and her lips moved, though he heard no sound. A prayer or a spell, he wasn't sure if it made a difference.

'What are you?' asked Izzy. 'My guardian angel? Because if you are you totally suck at the job.'

That smart mouth of hers again … He'd never tire of that. He could hear the nerves and tension it masked but he'd bet few others would.

Ash's expression didn't change. If anything the subtle smile warmed further. Maybe the angel appreciated her too.

'You're still alive, aren't you?'

'So where were you on the hill with Sorath?'

'I'll repeat my previous question.'

'You're impossible.'

'Yes.' Ash released his hands and pressed her palm against his cheek. He flinched that time, surprised at the unexpectedly tender gesture. 'We're well matched, Izzy and I.' And to his further surprise she winked. 'They say a guardian becomes like their charge, or a charge like her guardian.'

'I think you'll find that's dogs and their owners,' said Clodagh in a dry tone. 'The problem is, we still can't trust you.'

Ash turned to face her, startled, perhaps even dismayed. 'Why not?'

'You lied to us. Hid who you were. Pretended you knew nothing about … all this.'

'Would you have believed who I am?' She took a step nearer to the girl. Angry and defiant, Clodagh didn't move. 'We *all* hide things about ourselves.'

Clodagh lifted her chin. 'Not something that important.'

Ash looked around at each one in turn, before looking back at Clodagh. 'We all hide things. Please, I only did what I thought I had to do. I had no idea Zadkiel would demand Jinx in that way, or of any of his plans. I thought we could undo what has been done to him, or at least try to find a way. I thought, if we worked together—' She spun back, impossibly graceful. She'd be a formidable fighter, Jinx thought, fast and merciless, insightful. If she had wanted to kill him he would be dead already. She didn't play games. '—but it seems I was overruled. So that's that.'

'You ignored him.'

'Yes. I do things like that.'

And she had spoken up for him at the Long Stone, earning a blow for her pains. Zadkiel had admonished her. He could see the mark on her face and jaw, already purple. It would fade soon. Angels healed even faster than the fae.

He glanced down at his hands. They didn't hurt anymore, but the skin was still dark, as if all the ink in his tattoos had run together, coating his skin. For a moment the image stirred a memory, of the Púca's black, clawed hands on his shoulder. They weren't unalike. That thought chilled him.

'I think you should go,' said Izzy, her jaw set and determined.

'I'll only follow you. It's my duty. Since the summer.'

'I won't let you take him from me.'

'I understand that. Though I think it's a terrible mistake. We could keep him safe, out of harm's way. But I will protect you, whether you want me to or not. I am your guardian. Besides, I have nowhere to go back to. Zadkiel has cast me out for insubordination, for speaking on *your* behalf if you recall. So here I am.'

'Let her stay,' said Jinx suddenly, only aware that it was his voice when the words came out. Because, for some impossible reason, he believed her. 'Please, Izzy ...'

'But—'

He reached out for her and she took his hand tentatively, as if testing it really was healed in spite of appearances.

'Are you sure, Jinx?' asked Dylan.

'Yes.' His gaze met the angel's and he was surprised to read relief there and gratitude. Nothing angelic had ever looked at him that way before – maybe there was more variety among them than he's thought. In fact, few beings had ever shown him kindness of any kind, other than those already around him. Izzy and Dylan ... and Silver, although he didn't dare to hope that would still be the case.

The thought of losing Silver stabbed inside him. She'd been more to him than an aunt. She'd been like a mother and her kindness for so long had been the only kindness he knew. Now, with Zadkiel's promise, he had to assume that was gone.

He might still hope, but he needed to smother that. Hope was for the naïve when it came to the Aes Sídhe and the things they wanted.

'We should go,' he told Reaper who watched all this impassively. 'All of us.'

Donn's servant bowed his head. 'Very well. If he will allow the angel to enter his halls, of course. If not … well, the gate isn't easy to pass though if not. And if he does welcome you in, Ashira, you will face the same thing as the rest. You will have no power there, no strength. You'll be as a mortal. There is a real chance you will not leave.'

The Chester Beatty Library housed treasures from all human history and a few Sídhe things that it shouldn't, or so Silver said. Dylan knew it well, had wandered its exhibition rooms soaking up the unexpected peace and inspiration found there. He'd sat in the sunny roof garden composing in his head but he had never thought about it at night. They got there through the old castle gate by the City Hall, looked down on by the edifice of the Sick and Indigent Roomkeepers Society building, and office blocks without the souls of the earlier buildings.

They passed the gothic Chapel Royal, through cobbled yards, walking into the garden where brick paths wound like snakes through the manicured grass.

'They're meant to be eels,' said Reaper. 'People think the original Black Pool that gives Dubh Linn its name was here. It wasn't though.'

'So where was it?' Clodagh asked. But he ignored her. They were all doing that. Dylan knew it wasn't wise. Clodagh noticed a lot more than they gave her credit for. Sídhe arrogance, perhaps. It maddened him.

Reaper pointed at the library building – half old Georgian, grey with regimented windows, half modern steel and glass.

'It's locked.'

'Is it? Oh dear, silly me.' The Sídhe spoke without a trace of humour. 'We're talking about using the very first gateway the Sídhe ever created, the one all Dubh Linn was named after. But let's just give up because of a few human locks, will we?'

'It is forbidden, that gate,' Ash interrupted.

'So are a lot of things,' Reaper replied coldly. 'Like you being here with us, probably.'

Even before dawn stained the sky the city was starting to come back to life around them.

'We don't have time,' said Jinx. 'What about the security?'

'I have an arrangement with security.'

'Do you have an arrangement with monitoring systems, locks, shutters, the Gardaí and electronic alarms?' asked Clodagh.

'Aren't you the smart aleck, Clodagh?' Reaper gave her the broadest smile. 'Of course.'

He turned away from the main entrance and walked down to a smaller, nondescript door in the older part of the structure, which didn't look as if it had been used in more than a century, long before the library was here, when it was just the Clock Tower building . Someone had tried to paint it white but the paint was already flaking off, like dead skin. There was no sign of a handle or a keyhole, just eight wooden panels. He knocked, a swift rhythmic knock – similar to the one Amadán had used to gain access to the Sídhe sanctuary – and after a moment's pause knocked again. Just once. The last knock boomed as if he had banged on a kettle drum and the door opened silently. There was no one to be seen.

They walked through a stainless steel kitchen tiled in the purest white and out into the deserted café, chairs stacked upside down on tables so the floor could be washed to spotless perfection.

Reaper opened another locked door and led them into the main hall. It still gave the impression of being a street with a glass roof high above them showing the night's sky. The original buildings, a Georgian cul de sac, painted white and in the centre a fountain, long and thin as a reflection pool from an Andalusian palace, tiled in the brightest peacock colours.

That was where Reaper headed, the far end of the pool, where it was at its narrowest. He stopped at the foot looking back at them.

'It is the first Sídheway,' he told them solemnly. 'It is untouched by the taint in the outer paths. So far, anyway. It leads to only one place, the entrance to Donn's hollow. There are no other ways there save the long road and death itself. This is an old path and old paths affect those who take them, changing them, judging them. You will see things you do not want to. You will see things you fear. Do not under any circumstances leave the path. Do not look back. It is Old Magic.' He paused looking at them each in turn. 'The oldest. Do we have an understanding?'

Everyone nodded. Some less enthusiastically than others.

Jinx stood with the other two Cú Sídhe right behind Dylan, but he didn't move. He looked at home with them, Dylan realised, with his own kind. If he ever looked at home anywhere.

'We may be followed,' he said to them. 'By things in there as well as things out here. Perhaps by things worse than we can imagine.'

'I don't know,' said Blight. 'I can imagine some terrible things. I have a vivid imagination. Everyone says so.'

Jinx frowned, the joke sailing directly over his head as most jokes did. Dylan shook his head and turned around, watching them. Blight grinned happily. Blythe scowled. They didn't appear to have changed in the least. At least she was clothed this time around.

'Ignore him,' Blythe said calmly, looking at Dylan as if she could read his thought, an unsettling proposition. 'It's nerves.

We'll take up the rear and hold the gate at the other end for you, Jinx by Jasper.'

Jinx shuddered at the sound of his full name on her lips and a shadow passed through his eyes. 'You knew my father, didn't you?'

'Yes.'

Dylan saw Jinx hesitate, but whatever was on his mind, he decided to press on with his questions. 'Was there something … anything … well, strange about him, maybe?'

Blythe opened her eyes wider in a curious mix of disdain and amusement. 'Apart from the *apparently* hereditary ability to ask stupid bloody questions at inopportune moments? No, why? Whatever do you mean?' The last two questions were asked with humourless candour.

Jinx looked furtively towards the others and lowered his voice. 'Blythe … please …'

She groaned. 'Yes, there were things about him that were strange. He joined our pack, I suppose, if you want to be picky about it. But that's nothing strange. You don't have to be born one of us to become one of us. And pack is pack. Once part of it, the past is the past. He thought there was nothing he couldn't overcome. And he never *never* listened. Do they count as strange?'

'What colour were his eyes?'

She paused, frowning again, the flippant answers gone as she studied his earnest face. Dylan watched as she chewed on her lower lip.

'Gold,' she said at last. 'Like the setting sun. Why?'

But Jinx didn't answer. He stalked away, back to Izzy, as if he could escape the answer.

The two Cú Sídhe stared at Dylan in silence until he couldn't bear to stand there anymore and he turned away, making for Clodagh and Ash at the edge of the shallow pool. They were looking at the mosaic and he thought again of the garden of a Moorish palace in Spain, the representation of heaven on earth. That was one of their sayings, those kings of Al-Andalus of long ago – 'Heaven is a garden.'

He glanced at Ash again, still worried, and he wondered. She didn't look like she belonged in a garden – a boxing arena or a dojo, maybe, or flicking through a catalogue with Clodagh over coffee. She stood awkwardly at the edge of the group, beautiful in the way fire or a lightning storm was beautiful.

'Is she telling the truth?' Clodagh's voice was very quiet, shaken. She stepped in close to him and dropped her voice so it wouldn't carry.

'I don't know. I think so.'

'Not a lot of help, Dylan.'

'I'm full of that these days.'

'Do you have any idea where we're going?' He shook his head and she sighed. 'Mari would have been able to find out. I'm useless.'

'No you're not. And Mari wasn't all that. I mean – yeah, she could be charming and stuff, but – '

Clodagh was smiling at him but he could see tears in her eyes. 'I sometimes think you didn't know her.'

'Are you okay?'

She rubbed her hand across her eyes briskly. 'Sure, why not? Why wouldn't I be?'

'Mention of Mari?'

'Yeah, well ... She was my – my best friend.'

'She was my *sister*.'

'It ... it doesn't get any easier, does it? I keep thinking that maybe it is just time to move on, but ...' She sighed again. 'It's not fair. To meet someone, to share so much, to discover that you, that you both ... and then she's just gone.'

Dylan tried to hug her, but it felt awkward halfway through and ended up giving a pathetic half-hearted pat on the back. He was missing something. He knew it. When they parted though, he saw her watching the angel with suspicious eyes. And Ash was watching Clodagh in return.

CHAPTER TWENTY-SIX

The Darkest Path

Izzy eyed the shallow water dubiously. The coloured mosaic tiles shimmered as if it was much deeper, reflecting light from other places and other times up into her face. The eeriness of the library at night was infecting her. Not a library really, more like a museum. Like so many things here — where 'town' was a city, where the hills were called mountains.

This was fae magic, she could sense that, but also something far older and wilder. Dangerous. Worse still, something in her responded, a thrill of excitement where there should surely be terror.

Reaper raised a hand, gesturing to them to step in.

'Walk to the end.' His voice was gentle, like melted chocolate. 'Don't look back.'

'Wait,' said Jinx and stepping in beside her. 'You aren't going to go through on your own.'

'You're the one they're after,' she said, grateful nonetheless for his hand in hers, the way they fitted together.

'I think we both have that dubious honour. Together?'

They walked forward and the water rose like glass walls around them. Light and dark inverted for a moment and all those swirling colours merged to white, then broke apart to slide through the water like oil.

Izzy had the suicidal urge to throw herself in, even though she knew it was madness. But she still reached out to touch the water, hardly aware of her actions until Jinx said her name.

'Izzy, don't. Look.'

Her eyes adjusted to look past the wall of water. Merrows cut through the ocean beyond, sleek and beautiful as sharks, their scales glittering like rainbows, their long hair trailing after them. Lovely faces with lethal, hungry eyes.

Izzy shuddered and looked ahead again. Not back, never back. She wasn't rescuing Jinx from Tartarus, or wherever Orpheus went to find Eurydice, but rules were rules especially when it came to the Sídhe and their old magic.

'I can't hear anyone following,' she said.

'I know.' He sounded as worried as she did and now she knew why he'd come with her. If he hadn't been right behind her, she couldn't stop herself looking over her shoulder, to see if he was all right. She couldn't have gone on without him. And a stumble or wrong turn here would be worse than fatal. She tightened her grip on his hand and his fingers responded. A blessed relief.

She couldn't lose him. Not again. She wouldn't be able to bear it. Focus, that was the key. She had to focus.

'It'll be okay,' she whispered to herself. Jinx bent down to kiss the top of her head. She jerked up to look at him in astonishment, the unexpected and not unwelcome moment of intimacy surprising her. But he didn't look happy, or even content. If anything, he looked at her with a longing that wouldn't find fulfilment. 'Do you know this place?' she asked.

'No. I've never been here. It was ... it *is* forbidden.'

'By Holly?'

'And Silver. And Brí. By everyone.'

'For good reason I expect.'

'The best. Donn. He doesn't like visitors.'

'I hope... I hope this is worth it.'

'Me too.'

'I thought it was coming out of the land of the dead that was the problem,' she said. 'Not getting in.'

'Getting in under circumstances where you *can* get out again, perhaps?'

She tried to lighten the mood. 'It's Samhain. The doors are open, isn't that what they say?' She failed; he just grunted and squeezed her hand. 'You're the optimist today.' And failed.

He stiffened, staring ahead into the deepest shadows. 'Such is my life. Do you hear that?'

Another sound, something behind them where there had been nothing. The darkness ahead transformed and light reflected up onto a stone ceiling, unnatural underwater light filtering through from an endless ocean that couldn't be there.

There was only herself and Jinx. And the sound behind that didn't come from the sea. It sounded rhythmic, hollow, like… like hoof beats.

'What is it?' she asked, starting to turn her head, starting to …

Don't look back.

That's what Reaper had said. *Don't look back.* This was it. The test, the way in, the entry to the underworld. *Don't look back.*

Even as she remembered, so did Jinx, his voice sharp and sudden. 'Don't look, Izzy.'

The sound of a huge horse thundering down on them filled the air. Izzy pulled Jinx forward, into a sprint and he came, off balance, twisting as he moved. Had he looked? Oh God, had he looked? She dragged him with her, all the time yelling at him, running through the stone chamber that stretched out before them, the dimensions suddenly impossible, like a dream when the destination kept moving away faster than she could reach it.

'Don't look back. Don't look back, Jinx. Don't—'

A sound like thunder boomed around them and the air turned from merely cold to arctic. Izzy tried to cry out, but her voice froze in her throat. She scrabbled for Jinx's hand, tried to hold on to him, but it was torn from her grasp.

Everything went black.

The music swallowed him. Dylan felt the world twist and re-form around him. The lights came up and instead of the pool edge and the empty library, he stood on a stage in front of a screaming audience, cheering, crying his name. The guitar was oddly heavy in his hands, the strap tight against his neck. Sweat fell into his eyes and he blinked it away.

Exhaustion swept over him. How long had he been playing?

'One more tune! One more tune!' They chanted the words over and over.

'Go on,' said a familiar, teasing voice. 'Play.' He turned to see Marianne standing there beside him. She wore her uniform from the coffee shop, the clothes she had died in, but she didn't look dead now. 'What are you afraid of?'

'This isn't real, is it?'

She smiled then and faded away. Silver stood in her place wearing that glittering wisp of a dress that he'd first seen her in, her long hair like gossamer tumbling behind her.

'You have to play, Dylan. Or every one of us is lost.'

His fingers slid painfully against the strings that, like razor wire, cut into his skin. 'I can't.'

'Do it!' She bared her teeth and he saw the monster behind the façade.

Dylan stumbled back and the music soared around him –

his music, a melody he had written that seemed to be part of him. But he wasn't sure now. Maybe it was hers. Maybe it was all Silver.

'You don't own me,' he told her.

Silver stalked towards him, eyes blazing, Holly's child through and through. He could see the malice, the hunger. The screaming crowd got louder and louder, frenzied in their need for his songs. They'd tear him apart if they could lay hands on him.

'Like Orpheus,' said Silver. 'That's how he died. And you'll go the same way. Won't you?'

Orpheus … why would he think of Orpheus? The musician, the poet, the prophet who lost his wife and couldn't bring her back from the underworld. The land of the dead …

'You aren't Silver.'

'Silver's gone. You think you know her, but you're a fool. The Sídhe will tear you apart to get at the power inside you. Without Silver's protection, you're fair game.'

'So what? I should just give up? I should let her do whatever she wants? I'm not a slave.'

'You're not even a slave. You're a battery.' The laugh didn't sound anything like Silver's laugh.

'Who are you?'

The image wavered and changed until his own face looked back at him. Once more Dylan swung the guitar like a weapon and ran.

All Jinx knew was pain and darkness. The cell door opened and Holly stood over him, in his nightmares, in all he could remember. It was always Holly.

'What's your name?'

'Jinx by Jasper.'

She shook her head and the lash descended, cutting his skin, tearing it open until he screamed.

'What's your name?'

'Jinx by—'

She struck again and again. He was only a child, barely more than an infant. He remembered this, right from the start when she took him. He'd never known pain or misery. But Brí had cast him out, cursed him and now, in spite of Silver's promise to look after him, he lived in darkness and pain.

'What's your name?'

'Jinx,' he gasped, unable at last to say the rest.

'Jinx,' she said. 'How apt. A jinx indeed, to all who have known you. Come here.'

He had to crawl because he didn't have the strength left to stand. She bent down and stroked his head, then grabbed him by the jaw, hauling him up for a moment before letting him drop back down in a heap at her feet.

'Well, you'll have to do. Bring the equipment. We have work to do. You.' She pointed to Osprey. It was the first time Jinx could recall seeing him – huge, towering over him, his feathered cloak fluttering, his hands impossibly strong. 'Restrain him.'

'Don't fight, lad,' he whispered in that soft, terrifying voice. But Jinx couldn't help it. Osprey held him down on the stinking floor, in pools of blood and piss and who knew what. Some of the others gathered around them laughed, Osprey was silent and Jinx sobbed until he had no voice left. No one helped him.

Where was Silver? She had promised. She'd said she'd look after him, protect him. She'd *promised*. The promise of one of the Sídhe was meant to mean something, wasn't it?

'We need to get control of that wild magic in you before it leaks out,' said Holly, brandishing a tattoo machine like a gun designed by Jules Verne on acid. Not that he'd known about Jules Verne then. Or acid. He'd been an innocent. He could see the indigo ink swirling around, mixing with silver. It would hurt, had hurt. He recalled the agony, because all this happened years ago. And it was happening again.

Every detail.

'Please. Don't, please.'

'Are you begging, Jinx?' She sounded amused.

Would it work? It never worked. But he couldn't help it. 'Yes. I'm begging.' Maybe this time. Maybe this one time … 'Please, Grandmother, please don't.'

She stepped on his face, grinding him into the ground, the heel of her shoe perilously close to his eyes. Just a slip and she'd blind him, intentionally or not. And she wouldn't care.

'No true grandchild of mine would beg. Now, hold still. This is going to hurt. A lot.'

He didn't want to scream. He didn't want to beg again. He didn't want to be weak and plead.

But he did. He kept on screaming, pleading, begging and promising anything she wanted until he passed out.

That didn't bring peace though. It was like waking to something else. The black horse with golden eyes was waiting for his pathetic and broken soul.

'You aren't a horse,' said Jinx, gathering something of his own present self to guard himself.

It slid into the form of a hound effortlessly.

'You aren't Cú Sídhe either.'

It took on that long eared, hooved form that was almost human but not really. It would never be mistaken for human.

'Neither are you,' said the Púca. 'Not entirely.'

He swallowed hard. 'I'm… I'm Jinx.'

'Yes.' The Púca smiled. 'Always. Until she has her way, and then you won't even be that anymore. The angel gave her the idea I think, that she should move now, that she couldn't wait anymore. She'd taken you, prepared you, moulded you and she nearly lost you to Sorath. It must have driven her wild.'

'How do I escape her?'

'You die.'

Jinx sighed. 'I've done that. It didn't help.'

The Púca shook his head. 'You didn't stay dead. That angel

again. You never even made it to Donn's halls that time, it was so quick. Barely a missed breath. There has to be a sacrifice, Jinx, and once there is wild magic will take over. Dying alone doesn't help. You change, transform. That's how we work. We aren't born Púca, you know? Nothing is.'

'So you were Cú Sídhe?'

'Once.'

'And you – you were my father?'

He reached out his hand, black and scarred from fires, the claws instead of nails repulsive and strange.

'*Was* and *Is* and *Will be* get confused here. When the time comes, you'll have to choose. If you choose unwisely, Holly will win. Chances are she will win anyway. Nothing in life is fair and Holly knows it. She covers all her bases, boy. She has plans within plans and a thousand contingencies. I felt it moving, taking shape. All things of wild magic did, all the solitaries, all the people of the edges. I came for you, Jinx, but I can only do so much. You are the one who must act.'

It sounded as hopeless as he had feared. How could he stand against Holly? 'Then what can I do?'

'There was a moment—' said his father '—a single moment when you were more yourself than ever before. You need to hold on to that. Do you remember it?'

On the hill, that terrible night, holding Izzy as she lay dying in his arms, begging her to forgive him, telling her he loved her. He couldn't say it now though. He couldn't heave the words into his mouth.

The Púca smiled sadly and vanished without giving an answer. Darkness closed in around Jinx.

'Shall we begin again?' asked Holly and Osprey's violent, uncaring hands seized him, pinning him down.

CHAPTER TWENTY-SEVEN

The Blade That Cuts

Izzy found herself on a rock surrounded by the sea, the waves churning and splashing, sending spray up into the air around her. She knew the place. She was sure she knew it, but a curious haze settled on her brain whenever she tried to focus on it.

In the water beneath her, the merrows were circling. Their song rose through the water, beautiful and hypnotic, but she knew she couldn't listen to it. She knew they'd kill her in an instant if they could. She remembered that much.

The rest was foggy.

It was worse than coming through the gate. This time there was no Jinx there with her, no one to rely on but herself. She was alone. Stranded.

'Remember this?' said a voice.

She looked around to where a slender man sat in a little

round boat made of willow and animal skins. He wore black from head to toe, modern clothing starkly contrasting the ancient vessel. He had dark glasses with little round lenses on and his auburn hair glowed in the light of the setting sun.

'Remember what?' she asked.

The wind blew louder, sharper, and the song of the merrows grew even louder. She had to shake her head to fight off its effect.

'This.' He held out her salmon necklace and she felt her neck, surprised to find it wasn't there. It was gone.

'That's mine.'

'No. You threw it away.'

To save herself and Jinx — she remembered him telling her that if she didn't remember the actual event. It was scrubbed clean from her mind by the Storyteller's book. But she had last had it here on this rock and Jinx had been with her. Where was he now? What had happened to him? 'It's still mine.'

The man dangled it out over the water. 'Come and take it then.'

The water churned beneath his boat, and it rocked precariously. She saw the merrows fighting up from the depths, ready to tip him, seize the necklace and the man. They'd rip him to bloody shreds in the water.

'Look out,' she shouted, starting to her feet, reaching out for him.

And they weren't in the sea anymore. The rock she stood on was surrounded by gorse and scrubby grass. She stood on

Killiney Hill, not far from the Wishing Stone.

'You should have died there,' said the man, looking at the step pyramid where she and Jinx had defeated Sorath.

'Believe me, I tried.'

'You don't mean that. You didn't want to die.'

'Who does?' She climbed down gingerly, relieved to have her feet back on land.

'You'd be surprised.' He joined her, a willowy figure still dressed all in black, the small round smoky-lensed glasses like something from long ago. She couldn't see his eyes beneath them. Though he moved smoothly, with an easy and elegant grace, she sensed something off. He moved by instinct rather than sight, feeling the world around him.

'You're blind,' she blurted out and instantly regretted the rudeness. Her face burned scarlet with embarrassment. What was she thinking? You didn't just say things like that.

'My eyes cannot see,' he corrected her, completely unruffled. 'But I am far from blind.'

'You're Donn.' And she knew she was right, the moment she named him. Donn was still smiling. The smile never faltered.

'You see more clearly than most.'

'I have to stop the Fear. Their King Eochaid – if I don't—'

'The angels and the demons will fight no matter what you do. It is their sole purpose in life.'

'What about Jinx?'

'What about him?'

'Can I save him?'

'Yes. But you may not like what you have to do. And saving ... saving comes in many forms. But you can save him. Look—' He pointed to the Wishing Stone and flames erupted into the night.

She saw herself wreathed in fire, her magic, controlled by Sorath, lit up the night and Jinx on his knees, helpless before her. She reached out, drew him to his feet and kissed him.

'Forgive me,' he had whispered, his lips against hers. *'I'm sorry. I'm so sorry.'*

The image paused, like a still frame in a movie and Donn peered closer.

'There's hardly anything left of him really. He'd already died in the Market and your angel dragged him back. Maybe she didn't bring all of him with her. She should have killed him again right then. He ought to have been mine. Maybe he still should be. Did she know what he is? Do you think?'

'What do you mean?'

'Always with the questions, Isabel Gregory. Jinx is barely there. Holly spent years scourging the spirit from him, entwining him with her spells. He's more empty than anyone I've ever seen. Probably why he can betray so readily.'

'He doesn't betray—'

'Really? If I'd asked then on the rock, what would you have said? He can't be trusted because he's barely there. Pour something into an empty vessel and what does it become? Does the substance change because of the thing holding it? Why do you keep returning to that moment with the merrows? What *then*, exactly? You saved him. He kissed you. And—?'

She remembered. His kiss had been savage, out of control, but more honest than he had ever been with her up to that point. It had been made of raw need and desire and she had wanted it. And then—then—

'He used you, Isabel,' said Donn.

'We couldn't have got out any other way. His piercings couldn't be taken out.'

'He didn't try. Faced with the prospect of using you or removing one scrap of Holly's magic on him, he chose to use you.'

'It's history.'

'History repeats. He left you. He didn't even explain.'

She straightened up, her hands on her hips, her head held high. Enough was enough. 'What do you want?'

'The truth,' he said. 'Look at him. Know him.'

Golden light filled Jinx, seeping out of his pores, blazing from his eyes. She could see the other inside him. Wild magic, they called it. The Shining Ones – no wonder they were called the Shining Ones. Seraphs were barely controllable, the nuclear option …

So dangerous that even the angels were willing to do anything to stop their escape.

'How do I stop it?' she asked. 'How do I save him?'

'Have you thought it might not be possible to do both?'

Questions, questions and more questions. How was she to

get a bloody answer if he just asked more questions?

'I have to try.'

'Try. But don't expect to win. Not this time. Sacrifices have to mean something. Ask three questions. I'll answer then for you.'

'How do I stop the Fear?'

'You imprison Eochaid. Or kill him. Like any ancient monster. Cut off the head and the rest will fall.'

'That's what Holly wants. If I kill Eochaid, the Shining Ones go free and Jinx is lost. I won't do it. I won't kill him. I can't. If I do the Shining Ones will get out and we all lose. Isn't that the way it works?'

'Are you sure that's your question?' He laughed, a dry, bitter laugh and answered before she could change her mind. 'There's a way out. For a price.'

And what's the price? That should have been the next question. But she hadn't asked about Jinx yet. She didn't know how to stop the Shining Ones if Holly did call them. She didn't know how to stop the angels if they came for Jinx after all. She stared at Donn, helpless in indecision.

'What ... what would you do?' she blurted out.

The wind stopped, the hillside slipped away into darkness, the visions faded to nothing.

She found herself kneeling on a stone paved floor her head tilted back as if in supplication. High overhead, the dull bronze ceiling barely reflected the light. But there were candles everywhere. Half melted, candles upon candles, towers of old wax. They clung to the walls, to the crevices between the stones and dripped down to form stalagmites on the ground.

Jinx lay beside her, still as death. Dylan was sprawled a little further off, near Clodagh. None of them moved.

Izzy pulled herself up shakily and searched the long flickering shadows.

'I told you she was different,' said Reaper. He stood by a dais dominated by the statue of a man in a throne.

No, not a statue she realised. A man, dressed all in black, slender and pale. He had auburn hair and wore wire-framed dark glasses with blacker than black lenses, just as he'd had in his vision. He didn't move. He didn't even seem to breathe.

Izzy faced him, her hands balled to fists at her side. 'Well?' she asked again. 'You didn't answer. What would you do?'

'What would I do?' The voice echoed around them, though Donn didn't move his lips, didn't appear to speak at all. There was no doubting the source though. She knew the voice by now. Donn, Lord of the Dead. 'I'd follow my conscience, Isabel Gregory. Take the Blade then. Make it the weapon you need. Or use it to heal your beloved. The choice and the Blade are yours, but don't say you weren't warned. Use it at your peril. It will only work once, do you understand? Only once. And there is a price.'

'What price?'

'I said only three questions. You asked them. Reaper, take them to rooms and let them rest.'

'I won't kill Eochaid. I won't kill Jinx or hand him over. We don't have time to rest. We—'

Donn moved then, suddenly, lifting his hand and snapping his fingers. The click echoed loudly off the bronzed ceiling of his hollow. Izzy crashed into unconsciousness.

Jinx woke to find Ash looking at him, her face up close to his, her expression one of intent study. He held her gaze until she looked away.

'It's rude to stare,' he said. 'Did no one ever tell you that?'

'I've been waiting for one of you to snap out of it, locked up here in the darkness. Our hosts are less than charming.'

'Can't you just fly out of here?'

'I have no power here. Donn is … well … he's more powerful than I imagined.'

'Where's Izzy?'

She just gave him that knowing smile again. 'You really do care for her, don't you?'

'Not that it's any of your business.'

'Ah, but it is. My business, I mean. She is my business.'

'And here I thought you'd been sacked.'

'People think all sorts of things. Are you going to tell her?'

'Tell her what?'

But he knew what she meant. Angels saw far too much. He hated her for it.

'I think she deserves to know, Jinx.'

'I'll tell her when I need to. There's no point yet. It'll just give her something else to worry about. And she doesn't need that.'

'Did you see him? Your father?'

He nodded carefully. 'Did you know?'

'We … suspected.' So no, was the actual answer because otherwise she would have just said it.

'What does it mean?'

'That you have the same potential inside you. Or perhaps less because of your mother's blood. Although, with all Holly did to you… it's hard to say.'

'A great help, Ash. Thanks.'

'I try my best.'

Sarcasm wasn't her strong point was it? Or maybe she was better at it than he was. He swallowed hard and glared at the angel with determination. 'Keep her safe, Ash. Don't let her do anything stupid. Just tell her … just keep her safe.'

'I will,' said Ash solemnly. 'I promise.'

Could he trust that? He ought to be able to do so. She was an angel after all. But he was Sídhe. The two didn't exactly go together.

'You're different from the others.'

She smiled then, a brief, almost sorrowful expression. 'I hope so. Zadkiel and his host are zealous in the extreme. They want order. They're obsessed with it. They don't always see the bigger picture. They can't see the value of the individual as I do. That's a problem.'

'You see value?'

'In Izzy? Of course. And in you as well.'

'That must be popular among your fellows.'

'Not terribly,' she admitted. 'But it is not something I have ever tried to be.'

He looked around the room, at the too-young Grigori, the touchstone and the human girl, at himself. 'A misfit, then. Like the rest of us.'

The others were stirring, although Izzy slept on. For that at least Jinx was grateful. She needed sleep. As far as he could tell she had been almost twenty-four hours, or perhaps more, without rest. He sat beside her, watching carefully, and thinking of all the ways things could have been different. He wished he'd had the courage to defy her father and Silver, to tell them to go to hell. He wished he had stayed with her. Because every lost minute felt like a lifetime.

'If there is a way, she will find it,' said Ash.

'I know that. There's nothing she can't do when she puts her mind to it. You didn't – you weren't there on the hill. You didn't see her wrest control back from Sorath. She was ... she was amazing.'

To his surprise, the angel pressed her fingertips against his cheek, a curiously empathetic gesture. Her touch felt strangely comforting, her skin soft and warm. 'I was there. I saw it all.'

Reaper came for them shortly after Izzy started to wake, almost as if he had been waiting for her. He led them out of the little room, Izzy at the front of the group, and back to the candle lit chamber. She expected it to be frightening, creepy, this place of the dead, the fact that she was here on Halloween, but there was something curiously peaceful about the place instead, like walking through one of those ancient Abbeys in France, still in use after centuries and crammed throughout out with the sense of all that time. The atmosphere entangled around her spirit and made her feel comforted.

Donn was still seated like a statue. Oldest of them, he didn't touch anything of the modern human world. Even the glasses were something of an earlier time. She couldn't tell how old. He barely moved and whether he could see though the dark lenses covering his eyes, he didn't react. Maybe he really was blind. Perhaps he had seen everything already and didn't need to.

When they were gathered, he nodded to Reaper who vanished off again. Did he have other servants or just Reaper at his every beck and call? It didn't seem like much of a life for either of them.

And then something moved in the corner of Izzy's vision. She turned and saw her there – Mari, standing in the shadows looking wan and fragile.

'Mari?' Before Izzy could react Clodagh pushed by her, heading towards the ghost without any trace of fear. Mari smiled and held out her arms in greeting.

'Clodagh, no!' Ash cried out, but Clodagh paid her no attention. She embraced Mari, holding her close.

'I missed you. I missed you so much.'

'And I've missed you.'

'There's so much I should have——' but Mari held a finger to her lips, silencing her.

'You have to let go, hon. I know it's hard but you've got to let me go.' She looked up at Dylan and Izzy. 'All of you. I'm stuck here because of all that grief. Yours, our folks ... Please.'

Dylan let out a strangled sob and Ash caught him in her arms, holding him close as he finally broke.

'It wasn't your fault, Dylan,' said his sister softly.

Izzy took a step forward. 'It was mine.'

Mari stiffened, suddenly glittering with anger. Something passed over her face, something of the rage and darkness her ghost had manifested before. 'Everything in this world is not your responsibility, Izzy. It isn't actually all about you. Holly was looking for you, sure. But the banshee was *her* servant and she found me. *She* killed me. Not you.'

'If I had been there——'

'You'd be dead, thicko. Anyway, coulda-shoulda-woulda,' she sing-songed. 'You weren't. There was nothing you could do.'

'But I was,' Dylan said, his voice thin and tortured.

'You were busy having your own ass saved,' said his sister. 'Dylan——' She reached out and touched his face. He flinched back, shivered and went still. She looked disappointed. 'You just keep punishing yourself and paying for something that wasn't your fault. Let go.'

He closed his hand over hers.

'I can't.'

'You have to. It's going to kill you. *She's* going to kill you. And if she doesn't one of the others certainly will. The music is wonderful, Dylan, but so are you. Let go.'

'Just like that.'

'Because I say so. And I'm a bossy cow, remember? Honestly, the state of you all without me.'

'There has to be a way to bring you back. To bring you home. Mari!'

She shook her head. 'Of course there is, but it's been too long. Far too long. You can bring the spirit back but what good is it without the body. And can you imagine? Ew!' She screwed up her face and then laughed out loud. The sound shook through them all and all the grief and pain seemed to loosen and fly apart.

'It's time, child,' said Donn. 'As you say, there is no going back for you. You've been dead for far too long. Only someone newly dead can be reborn. Like Jinx by Jasper was. But I don't like it. I look on it as cheating. Time to move on.'

Mari stepped back. 'I know,' she replied, with a surprising amount of respect for her, although she still lingered another moment. Even the Lord of the Dead had only a tentative control over Marianne. 'Gotta go, guys. See you.'

She smiled and began to fade, until, as they watched she

came apart. Hundreds of fluttering scraps of colour became hundreds of butterflies that scattered into the high dome, swirled around once in a wave of rainbow hues, and then were gone.

She was gone.

'Time is almost up.' Donn broke the silence, his dry voice echoing through the dark. 'Samhain night draws on. Don't you want the Blade? That's why you're here, isn't it?'

A shimmering line appeared in the air between them, like a crack in the air, breaking through reality to reveal another sun on the other side, just a glimpse of it, so impossibly bright. It bled through the darkness, staining this world with something else, something untamed. In an instant it would consume everything, if she took her eyes off it ...

'There it is,' he said. 'Take the weapon. Make it yours.'

'Be careful, Izzy,' said Ash.

Donn hissed at her and the angel stumbled back, her face suddenly pale. 'You're already here against my better judgement. Have a care, Ashira, or you will never leave. Isabel Gregory, my patience wears thin. Take it, if you can.'

She could. Of course she could. Izzy knew that now. It was fire and she knew fire. It was part of her, Brí's legacy. It lived in her blood. Still, she hesitated.

'Just like that?'

'Yes. It is your choice how you use it. But you cannot heal anyone here. This is a place of the dead. Reaper will show you the way out. In the world above, beneath the Samhain sky, there you can help him. Is that what you wanted to hear?'

No. She wanted to do it now, right away. But it made a twisted kind of sense, a fae logic, that she couldn't heal in the world of the dead. 'And if I heal him, it's gone again? It just returns to you?'

But Donn didn't answer. He just watched her, waiting.

'What's the price, Donn?' she asked.

He smiled, a thin, arrogant expression. So knowing and cruel. She hated him for it.

'You were so eager before, Isabel Gregory? Second thoughts?' He gazed at Jinx. 'I want what I was cheated of before. Jinx by Jasper belongs here. You'll send him to me. And you'll follow.'

He thought she'd kill Jinx? Some kind of murder–suicide deal? No way on this earth. She opened her mouth to say so, but another voice interrupted.

'You think you know her,' said Jinx. 'But you don't.'

'I'd never make a deal like that.'

Donn laughed. 'It's not a deal. I don't need to make deals. Call it a prediction if you like. I don't know where, when or why, but it will happen. I promise. Go on then, take the Blade.'

Izzy hesitated, her hand trembling.

'Do it,' said Jinx. 'He can't predict the future.'

She reached out for the blade and felt it curl into her grip. It warmed her palm for a moment and then found the Sídhe fire in her blood and merged with it, like calling to like.

It rushed through her, heady as a burst of adrenaline and she felt herself waver, as if her body and her spirit were knocked out of alignment. It faded into her, hidden from view. But she could still feel it there, tempting and addictive.

'Use it wisely,' said Donn. 'It will defend you, but it will also beg to be used. And holding it chips away what you are little by little. If you use it to heal him, you can't use it to kill, Isabel Gregory. Remember that. It will be no defence against the King of the Fear. Be careful how you employ it. And as for the future … we'll see, Jinx by Jasper. We'll discuss it one day, just the two of us. Soon.'

Her head still swimming from the effect of the blade inside her, she nodded. 'You have my word. But I'll never kill Jinx.'

'So you say, Grigori. But I know what that fire inside you does. You say it now, but it is not always so easy to give it up again. Heal or kill. That's your choice. Remember, you must do your duty first and foremost, or everything falls apart.'

He inclined his head towards her, not quite a bow but clearly, from the look of shock on Reaper's face, more than he had done for anyone else in a long time. 'Now go. Or the time will be lost.'

Reaper led them from the hall, his expression guarded but as he stopped in the winding corridor, he beckoned to Izzy.

'A gift, before you go.' Though he smiled, he glanced back towards the hall where Donn sat. 'May it guide you.'

'A gift?' she asked and felt Jinx step closer. 'What sort of gift?'

'And why?' asked Jinx. Reaper ignored him, his smile only

wavering for a moment.

'This.' Reaper opened his hand to reveal her salmon necklace. 'It was lost. It won't bring back the memory the Storyteller took, but here at least is the thing itself.'

Izzy smiled and took it in grateful hands. 'I never thought I'd see this again. Dad gave it to me. A birthday present.' She put it around her neck and pressed her hand against it. Where it touched the Grigori tattoo it felt unexpectedly cold, but familiar for that. Mum and Dad were a world away, perhaps more. She didn't know. But having this one piece of her past back made them feel closer. 'Wow, Reaper, thank you.'

He didn't reply as he turned away and began opening the gate for them. The way out. Izzy's heart blossomed inside her. She slipped her hand into Jinx's again, squeezed his fingers.

'I'm not sure about this,' he muttered.

'What do you mean?'

'Doesn't it feel ... easy?'

Couldn't it just be easy for once? Just this once. They were almost there. Once they were back in the library, she could us the blade heal him, to free him of Holly's spell, and then they'd find a way to deal with Eochaid without the threat of the Shining Ones. It had to work.

CHAPTER TWENTY-EIGHT

Hellfire

They stepped out into fresh air, a cold misty rain and damp grass. The smell of it hit the back of Izzy's throat, made her skin tingle. It was real. So real. Her world, not that of the dead. The relief that she stood on solid ground and breathed real air made her head spin. The sky was huge and black overhead, the colour of coal. Not the library. Somewhere far from the city centre.

'Where are we?' asked Clodagh.

The city spread out below them, lights sparkling like stars overhead. Howth was barely visible behind a bank of rain, but she could make out the silhouettes of the chimneys known as the Pigeon House at Ringsend.

'It took a lot of time from us,' said Jinx, his gaze fixed unswervingly on Reaper. 'Hours. It must be almost midnight. I thought you were an expert.'

'Well, you're here and you're in one piece. A few hours is a small price. I said it was old. With age come a less than perfect reliability. Call it eccentricity. It's a gate that knows its own mind and sometimes it takes more than anyone can control. Everyone all right?'

Shaken, that was the word for it rather than all right. All the same, Izzy nodded.

'But why are we here?' she asked. 'Why not at the library? Come to that, *where* are we?'

'I know this place,' said Dylan. He pointed to their left and the squat, grey structure on the crest of the hill. Graffiti sprawled across the lower half. The stone roof covered a deep darkness and the arched but empty doors and windows looked like demon eyes. So black. 'The Hellfire Club?' said Dylan. 'Who said you lot don't have a sense of humour?'

'No one. We're hilarious. But we didn't build that here. A cairn stood guard over our gate and a supremely arrogant man had it taken apart and the stones used to build this, his hunting lodge. Imagine. Our own back door. Needless to say, he never had much pleasure of it. No one has since either. My Lord Donn does not take kindly to interlopers, or thieves.'

'Take note,' said Ash bleakly.

'We didn't steal anything,' Izzy said. She closed her hand and felt the warmth of the fiery blade in her skin. A curiously comforting feeling.

Izzy had been to Montpelier Hill before. Half the kids of Dublin had, clambering up the steep sides to looked across the city. Dad had been there, filling in the details, as always. The hill belonged to one William Connolly, called Speaker Connolly, and he had the barn-like hunting lodge built on the site of a cairn, using its stones. The first disaster, a gale, blew the slate roof off. More stones from the cairn were used to construct a stone roof and nothing brought that down, not even arson. Nothing would bring it down. That was Dad's side of the story. Things took a darker turn, entered into the realm of the urban legends she had loved before she knew how true they were It became the Hellfire Club, used by the notorious gamblers and profligates of that name, and the woods below it were renamed Hellfire wood. There were tales of satanic masses, murders and rapes, debauched and drunken nights where fortunes and souls were gambled and lost. The devil himself was said to have appeared in the form of a great black cat. Those who saw it went mad and died.

It was a ruin now, but a solid ruin. One that would not fall because Donn didn't want it to fall, she got that now. It was a threat, a reminder and a message from Donn to everyone else. Menace still rolled off it in waves. Graffiti, litter and the remains of fires dotted inside and out. Burnt down candles and messes of animal remains indicated that some practices were not as long forgotten as others.

Did people still practise black magic up here, Izzy wondered? If so, they had no idea what they might disturb. She hoped for their sakes that their magic was all sham and wishful thinking.

Real magic came with a price.

A wave of intense cold sucked all warmth from the air. Izzy could sense unseen eyes as old as the stones and just as unyielding watching her. She shivered and then heard the sound of someone clearing their throat.

'Well, it's about time,' said Holly. There was a flurry of movement as Sídhe of all kind materialised out of the darkness.

The need to run, to escape, swept through her. But only one of them could get away with ease. She knew that even as she said it. 'Ash! Get help now! Find Dad.'

The angel turned back to her, her face full of shock, but her hesitation was only momentary. Light surrounded her, and the noise of unseen wings almost drowned out the sound of attack. Then she was gone. Something hit Izzy hard in the small of her back, bringing her to her hands and knees. She saw Blight and Blythe transform to hound shape, furious creatures of teeth and claws.

But Jinx didn't. Izzy looked up to see him trembling from head to foot, filled with rage but unable to do anything. She couldn't leave him. Not like this.

In moments, the attack was over, the Cú Sídhe overwhelmed and beaten down to unconsciousness. Dozens of Sídhe stood around them, banshee and bodachs for the most part and a small group of Aes Sídhe. No sign of Clodagh and Dylan, thank God. But she couldn't spare more than a glance for them now. She hoped they were hiding. She hoped they were safe. But no one was safe.

Holly was there.

Jinx fought to transform when Blythe and Blight did, but the silver and the tattoos flared to life, holding him captive. They didn't stand a chance, not against those numbers. In moments they were defeated and bound, Blight unconscious, his sister still struggling, but unable to break free.

Holly advanced on Jinx with a smile. 'There you are,' she said. 'We thought you might miss the whole thing.'

Jinx edged back, trying to change because it was easier to fight or flee in hound form. But he couldn't. With Holly there, exerting whatever control she had on him, his body wouldn't obey.

'Reaper? What have you done?' said Izzy, appalled. But Jinx could guess.

'I didn't have a choice.' He turned to Holly, his head held dangerously high. 'Where is he?' No one with any sense talked to her that way. But then, Jinx was beginning to think Reaper had lost every scrap of sense he ever had. 'You promised. We had a deal. Where is he?'

Holly gave Meridian a nod, and her daughter clapped her hands. A young man struggled free of the rest, golden where Reaper was dark, and so beautiful even the Sídhe couldn't help but watch him as he moved forwards, graceful as a dancer.

As it was, Reaper sobbed, a sound that might have been a name or merely incoherent relief. He threw himself forward wrapping his arms around the newly freed captive, shaking from head to foot.

'It's okay. You're safe now. I have you. You'll—'

The knife flashed between them and Reaper froze for a second, shock and horror spreading over his face with the same speed as the blood gushing from his throat. He sank to his knees, his hands trying to stop the flow and failing.

Holly smiled, not even sparing him a glance. 'Good, Coal. Well done. A clean kill. Welcome to my kith. Now that's out of the way, let's see to you, shall we my hound? After all, you wouldn't want to miss your moment, would you?'

'Leave him alone!' said Izzy. She stepped between them, furious and fearless, her hands balled to fists in that way she did when she was picking a hopeless fight. Jinx wanted to tell her to run, to get away, but he couldn't. He was lost in Holly's magic, woven around him, through him, inside his skin.

'Ah, there you are,' Holly sneered. 'I'll get to you in a minute. First we have someone to fetch here. Someone we're missing. Stay right there. Shan't be a minute.'

She waved her hand at them and Izzy let out a shocked gasp. He could see her struggle, but she was helpless as he was, locked in position, held in a web of Holly's magic.

'What have you done?'

'Me? Silly girl. Don't you know not to take gifts from strange men?' She flicked one finger under the pendant at Izzy's neck. 'I like you on your knees, Grigori. It's more fitting, don't you think?' Izzy's legs gave way and she dropped before

Holly, who laughed as she turned away, ignoring the girl's sob of frustration and Jinx's silent, impotent rage. 'Meridian? Where are they?'

Her daughter Meridian, as beautiful as Holly and Silver, as all of them, smiled a cruel smile. 'Osprey is just rounding them up now.'

Mist curled around the grass, freezing it where it touched. Dylan pressed against the shadows of the hunting lodge, trying to hide himself and Clodagh. That was how he found the bonfire, a stack of old pallets and bits of furniture, odds and ends gathered together to make an as yet unlit Halloween bonfire.

But it should have been lit by now, shouldn't it? Like the thousands blazing in the city below them. Bonfires were as ancient as the land, an old tradition of harvest and spring. A celebration. A sacrifice.

With a screech like a demon a firework went up, bursting in a shower of scarlet and yellow. Others followed, the city of Dublin throwing fire into the sky.

A terrible feeling of dread swept over him and he knew he shouldn't be here, that he shouldn't be on this hillside, that they should never have split up. Holly was here. It was a trap.

A thud and a snarl sent Dylan to the ground in a tangle of limbs and teeth as something dark as night slammed into his side. He fought, trying to throw the thing off, but was caught in battle so savage that there wasn't time. Clodagh screamed his name.

The figure hoisted him to his feet and dragged him across the grass. He could see Clodagh in the creature's other hand. His fingers knotted in her hair as he hauled her after them, kicking and struggling, in spite of the futility. The ground turned rougher, pitted with overgrown rocks and banks as they were dragged to the remains of the cairn.

'Enough, Osprey,' said Holly, her voice coloured with amusement. 'Don't kill him. He's valuable, you know.' Dylan's captor dropped him and left him to find to his own feet. The tall Aes Sídhe dressed in shining feathers dusted himself off, preening as he re-joined his mistress.

Another firework sent shards of blue light through the sky overhead and Holly stood there, watching, her arms folded, her eyes like nails in the night, her mouth a hard line of triumph. Izzy was on her knees, Jinx standing helpless beside her. The Cú Sídhe were imprisoned and angel was gone.

For help. He had to hope they'd gone for help.

'Here we are.' She smiled. 'All alone. Did you think you were going to stop me all by yourselves?' Her guards spread out of the shadows, mostly Aes Sídhe, cruel and beautiful, sleek predators. Dylan and Clodagh were quickly surrounded. Holly approached them, reaching out to lift Clodagh's chin, studying her face the way a butcher studies a calf. 'I've never understood how humans work. It doesn't matter how many

I've taken apart to find out. Who knows though, maybe you will provide the answer.'

'Leave her alone,' said Dylan, sounding braver than he felt.

'Welcome, Dylan O'Neill. I've been expecting you. Awaiting you, in fact. You're just in time for the main event. In fact, we couldn't start without you.'

'Isn't he just delicious?' said Meridian, joining her mother and smiling like a vixen in the henhouse. They both eyed him hungrily. 'All that power in him.'

'All *my* power,' said Holly, a note of warning in her tone. 'And all Silver's too. Stupid girl. What a colossal mistake. And then she just leaves you wandering around in the dark where ... well ... *anything* could happen. If it was me, I'd have you locked up where you'd never see the light of day again. In fact ...' She clicked her fingers and the guards stepped forward.

Dylan grabbed Clodagh's wrist. If he darted to the left there was a sort of gap. They might make it though. If he was fast enough, if Clodagh could keep up, because he couldn't leave her. If he could get to Izzy. If he could just distract—

'Oh, don't run,' Holly told them in a bored voice, and started to check her manicure instead. The others stiffened, like hounds on point, ready and eager for the hunt. 'We'd only have to chase you. And that *never* ends well.' She raised her voice, calling over the hillside. 'Are you here, Lord King?'

And Eochaid's voice rippled over the hillside, mocking and laughing, loathsome.

'Come out, little Grigori. It is the appointed place and time.

We should end this. Be mine or die. It is time.'

'No,' Jinx said, the words harsh and guttural, forced through his tight throat. 'You can't do this.'

'Jinx, my dearest, surely you know by now I can do whatever I want. Bring him here.'

Osprey seized Dylan again, throwing him to his knees before Holly and holding him there. His grip felt like metal, fingers digging into Dylan's skin through his clothes. Holly circled him, studying him with that cool, terrifying gaze. She stopped behind him.

'Now, let's see how this works,' she murmured. 'It may hurt …' She paused, as if considering that. 'A lot.'

She pressed her hands on either side of Dylan's head, dug her fingers into his hair and scalp, and dived into the well of power inside him.

Mist rolled up the hillside, filling the last gap in the flames and Eochaid materialised out of the darkness, horribly real. He unsheathed a sword and pointed at Izzy where she knelt in the middle of the shattered cairn.

'It is time.'

'Take her,' said Holly. 'She's yours. Just as I promised.'

Eochaid reached for her, one clawed hand closing around her neck. He lifted her until her feet left the ground. She hung there, helpless as the King of the Fear pulled her face towards him, his fetid breath washing over her.

'So at last we are here.' The sword hung from his free hand. He wasn't even bothered using it. Izzy choked, tried to keep breathing, but his touch robbed her strength. He drained her life, making it his own. She could feel herself fading away, even as he got stronger. She would be the ghost and he would be free.

'No!' Jinx's voice came out in a strangled cry. From the corner of her eye, Izzy saw him surge forward, from human form to hound in seconds. He lunged at her, snarling and leaped for them, jaws wide. Eochaid staggered back and Jinx slammed Izzy down to the ground. The air burst from her lungs and she stared up into his face, the growling striped wolf-like creature, a different kind of terror making her blood surge through her like flames.

He transformed again, her Jinx once more and grabbed the necklace from her neck, breaking the chain. He hurled it away.

'Izzy, remember ... remember that I ...'

A black shape in a flurry of wings burst through the air. Osprey grabbed Jinx, and the two of them rolled across the ground in a whirlwind of kicks and punches.

And in an instant, Izzy could move again. She pushed herself onto her feet. Her bag lay not far away and inside it... inside it ... She threw herself for it. But too late, Eochaid moved to intercept.

A blade of fire burst from her hand. As Eochaid lunged at her, she parried and twisted away.

Jinx, where was Jinx? She tried to look for him but didn't dare take her eyes off the king.

Izzy's blood sang in her veins, laughed with an unearthly joy she had never known. She knew it wasn't right, that she shouldn't be feeling this. She shouldn't be able to move like this. Training with Dad was one thing, but a few months didn't make you into a fighter. It certainly didn't make you into a killer. But she wanted to kill him. She wanted him dead. It didn't sound like her or indeed feel like her. But her body seemed primed, the moves so easy, so fluid and the energy that coursed through her overwhelmed the small voice of common sense still straining to be heard.

She couldn't kill him. She had to remember that. Kill him and the Shining Ones would be out. Kill him and they'd take Jinx and she'd lose him forever. And if she used the Blade to kill, that was all it would do and she'd never be able to help Jinx anyway. She had to think. She just needed a moment to think.

The sweep of his sword made the air scream. Something tangled around her feet, like mist suddenly turned tangible and she stumbled. Just in time, she brought the Blade up to stop his blow taking her head off. It caught her shoulder as she rolled away and the shock of pain as it cut her made reality slam back into her brain. Hot blood soaked into her shirt.

She landed heavily, stones biting into her, and saw what else she'd fallen on. Her bag. The strap still twisted around her foot.

This was real life. What was she doing? No amount of training with Dad had prepared her for this because Dad would never actually hurt her and she knew it. But Eochaid would. Eochaid would enjoy it.

He lunged towards her. 'Ready to end this now?'

She couldn't answer. She had to focus, to get away from him. She had to—

He struck and she parried, letting the fiery Blade move for her. And within her she could feel it directing her. The Blade that Cuts, the weapon of angels, one of the oldest weapons there was. It was part of her. She could feel it, sense what it wanted and could move with it, anticipating his movement.

Her other hand pulled the iron knife from her bag, the bone handle fitting into her left hand flawlessly. She could only use the Blade that Cuts once. But this one ... this one was an old friend. She'd thrown it at him once and it hadn't been able to hurt him. But that was then. He was solid now. Proximity to her, the life – hers and how knew how many others – he'd drained through terror, his feet on this earth, rock strewn and unstable as it was ... it made him vulnerable. It wouldn't be enough to kill him, but she could hurt him. She could drive him off.

She led with the sword made of flames, but she struck with the knife made of iron.

Eochaid screamed, a terrible cry that shook the world around them. The knife cut through skin, muscle and sinew. He flung her away with a strength she couldn't hope to withstand.

Izzy fell back, staggering, but keept her footing on the icy stones and grass, taking the moment to regain strength and catch her breath. The cairn shuddered beneath them, rock grinding against rock.

For a moment the air shook with his scream and then something else took over. The air trembled and with the concussion of a silent detonation, a shockwave bursting around them, they were no longer alone.

The gate opened and Silver burst through, followed by a group of Cú Sídhe and other fae, an army. The rest of the Fear turned on them, savage on the attack.

Eochaid moved faster than she thought possible, his sword slicing towards her. She jerked herself back, but not fast enough. Her foot slipped on a stone. The tip of his sword caught her shirt and tore through, sliding across the skin of her stomach beneath.

'Never stop. Go for the kill. If you rest so does your enemy,' said the king. 'Didn't he teach you that one basic lesson?'

Pain followed, white hot and acidic. She gasped, no time or energy to cry out. Her knees went from under her and she fell.

'Isabel!' Far off she could hear her someone shouting her name. Dad. How was Dad here?

Izzy struggled to roll, but made her body move. Sound distorted around her. Her own breathing sounded loud and ragged, almost deafening. 'Get up, Izzy!' Dad's voice, as clear as if he stood beside her. 'You have to get up or he'll kill you. Keep moving Izzy. Keep moving!'

The blade in her hand pulsed with magical fire, warning her, waking her from her dazed state. The energy hummed back into her, stirring up the flames in her blood that came from Brí. The bone handled knife felt so cold.

Get up. Get up. You have to get up!

Why wouldn't her body do as she said? Was it Holly again? It didn't feel like Sidhe magic. Not this time. This was pain, exhaustion. This was dying. She pushed her hands into the earth and tried to force herself up, but she hurt everywhere, her shoulder and stomach most of all. Why had she ever thought she could do this? She was going to fail. She was going to die.

Eochaid's feet crunched the frozen grass as he came nearer. Solid now, so solid, feeding off her death, becoming real as she faded from life.

'You would never have done it,' he said. 'You should have just let me drain you and become the ghost I was. But at least when you die, Holly won't be able to raise Crom. She can't do it without you.'

'Without me? Why not?'

'You and I are part of it. Always have been. It took our combined efforts – Míl's and mine – to lay the Shining Ones to rest. And he betrayed me. Such are the ways of mankind. To me. To the Sídhe. To yourselves. So it will take our combined blood to free them again.'

He reached down and picked her up, his hand around her throat again. A solid grip, she couldn't escape. 'Look at them.' He swept his other hand towards the battle around them. 'Do you know why the Grigori hid the Sídhe? Why they built Dubh Linn and separated the fae from the humans?'

She waited for the answer. She didn't have breath to form words and he'd give it anyway. And it hurt too much to speak. Her soul ached, thin and stretched too far inside her. She was a bag of skin and bones, and he would drain every scrap of energy from her.

'To protect the Sídhe,' he whispered, his voice soft as a lover. 'Look at all humankind has done – your weapons, your knowledge, your lust for bloody devastation. Can you imagine if the world at large found out about them? About their beauty, and their talents, their devious nature and terrible deeds ... The world is going to find out, Isabel Gregory. I'm going to show them. I'm going to unleash my army of ghosts on the human world and the fae with it. What we did in Dublin this evening was just a taste. We'll feed on them all. No more hiding. No more imprisonment. And the fae can take the blame.'

Over his shoulder she could see the Sídhe who had arrived through the gate. They hated the Fear and came with weapons ready, holding Eochaid's troops back. Silver was there, moving like a queen at the head of an army, beautiful and terrible. She saw other faces she knew – angel, demon and fae ...

But she couldn't see Jinx. She couldn't see him anywhere.

If the Fear attacked the human world, so many people

would die or go insane. And it would only get worse.

She could imagine what the world would do if they found out about the Sídhe, things none of the fae would believe – hunt them, prostitute them, experiment on them, dissect them, destroy them.

What it always did to something it didn't understand.

She couldn't let that happen. Finally she understood why Dad and Gran had tried to teach her so many of those old stories. Finally.

But Eochaid didn't care about keeping the otherworld secret. He wanted to see everything burn. She couldn't let him. But she only had one way left to stop him.

'No,' she whispered and reached out a hand, her fingers splaying against the rotten finery of his robes.

He froze, staring at her in bewilderment.

Take the weapon. Make it yours. That's what Donn had meant.

Kill him.

She could only use it once. Use it to heal or use it to kill. Kill him and the Shining Ones would be free to take possession of Jinx, loose in the world with only Holly to control them. But if she didn't kill Eochaid, it was over for all of them. For the human world, for Dubh Linn and all its inhabitants. They'd know everything, and destroy it all. War was coming, no matter what. That was the sacrifice he spoke of. That was what she had to give up. It had to have value or it was worth nothing. She had to give up everything. And everything was Jinx.

'No,' she said again, and let the blade go. Something no one thought she would do. You didn't release the Blade that Cuts. You didn't let it have its own will. But she did. She let go, let it decide what it was, what it would do. And she hated herself for that. It shot forward from her hand right into his chest, light exploding inside him, not a sword, but a bomb.

It wanted to kill.

Trade one evil for another, maybe. Face the danger here now before her, rather than the danger down the road. Hope and pray that she was right, and trust. Trust Jinx, because that was all she had.

The Shining Ones might be worse, but they weren't here yet and Eochaid was. The Fear had to be stopped now. 'Cut off the head and the rest will fall' Donn had said. She just prayed he was right.

The King of the Fear flung her away from him, but too late, far too late.

Izzy crashed onto the ground as Eochaid flailed backwards and burst into flames.

Izzy staggered as she rose, head reeling; the king fell, the fire consuming him joining Holly's barrier holding back the others. The blaze drenched the hilltop in heat and infernal light.

Dylan was on his knees, helpless while Holly held his head in her hands, channelling power from him. His face strained in agony, mouth and eyes wide, a silent scream as he twisted beneath her touch.

She had his power, all his power.

Pain lanced through Izzy's body, her muscles convulsing as the fiery blade returned to her, the backlash sending her stumbling, and she saw the look on Holly's face, the triumph. Jinx stepped up beside her. Blood and bruises covered him and his eyes glowed with that unearthly golden light. Osprey limped behind him, grinning like a maniac.

She'd done it. She'd given them everything. God, she'd hoped it would take time but she'd been wrong. Her chest crushed in on top of her heart, smothered her breath. She'd been so terribly wrong.

Around them, the world slowed to a crawl. The fire leaped and danced in stop motion around the edge of the cairn, every other image making it through, the rest lost to the darkness. Through the distortion, she could see her dad, trying to reach her. The sound, muffled, only reached her as if from far away. But Holly's voice, within the circle of power, was crystal clear.

'At last,' the matriarch said.

'What have you done?' Izzy gasped.

'Me? Nothing at all. This is all you, my dear girl. You've opened a moment, created a rather special Sídheway all your own. Well, the start of one anyway. You just have to complete it now. Jinx?'

He moved like an automaton. Not unwillingly though. She could see no struggle in his face. It was as if he didn't know what he was doing. As if Jinx, her Jinx, wasn't there at all.

He glinted in the firelight, all those piercings, all those excruciating points of control on him. All the things Holly had bound him with over all those years. And more. So much more. Light sparked across his skin, like lines of current, a walking plasma ball in human form. The two lines of tattoos at his throat glowed brightest of all.

'Jinx, please,' she whispered. 'You have to fight her. You have to beat her.'

Jinx moved irrevocably forward. Izzy could see the same glittering darkness in his eyes, the glow that welled up inside him. He didn't even look like Jinx, not anymore. The cold, implacable face, the arrogance of the highest of angels, the hatred of a lower life form… all those things she had seen in Zadkiel and his kind were amplified a hundredfold.

'Don't you like him anymore?' asked Holly, laughing beneath the words. 'What a shame. He's quite taken with you. All that fire and spirit. You shine, Isabel Gregory. Not in the same way as Dylan here perhaps.' She tightened her grip on Dylan who was lost in pain and misery. 'And Shining Ones do so love things that shine. They need your energy, your fire. It's barely holding on to him now, only here with my power, but one taste of you and the spell will be forever.'

'What do you mean *taste*?'

'Just look at him, Isabel, and you won't care. The Sídhe blood, the fire in you … you want to serve him. Just give in.'

Her eyes caught on the light that encircled him, that flickered over him. Bright and golden, so beautiful to behold. She stared at him in wonder, captivated by the vision. Fire walking on the hilltop. More than fire. Pure light. Everything in her wanted to please him, to serve him. All the fire in her surged wildly and she couldn't help herself. She would have dropped to her knees but it would mean moving. And she couldn't move and risk losing sight of him. The Shining One, the seraph, the most wondrous thing she'd ever seen.

Jinx stopped in the centre of the ruined cairn, towering over her so that she had to tilt her head back to keep looking at him. And she *had* to keep looking at him. He smiled, a slow, lazy, knowing smile that reached inside her and made her helpless. He was beautiful, more beautiful than anyone or anything she'd ever seen, more beautiful than he'd ever been before. And at the same time, when she looked into his eyes, she knew he was terrible as well. Beautiful and terrible, all rolled together. He seized her hand and the bone handle of the knife, bringing them together with a determined slowness. The iron sliced into her skin and blood welled up in the wound, covering the metal where Eochaid's blood still stained it.

The spell on Izzy shattered. Far too late. She sobbed out his name, recoiled from him in horror.

Jinx – or the creature that had been Jinx – raised the knife to his mouth and licked it clean. In front of her eyes, a third line blossomed in the skin of his neck, binding the other two together like a barbed vine.

'Now!' Holly screamed in delight. Power detonated around

them, power in the ground, power in the sky. Dylan screamed as it raced through him and coupled with the power in him. The strange barrier wobbled and distorted, breaking apart and where it fell, flames roared across the ground, a white hot inferno on the edge of the circle of stones. Izzy threw herself at Jinx, bringing him to the ground in a tangle of limbs.

The moment broke and noise fell over them in a wave like physical pain. She grabbed him, shook him.

'Jinx, please. Listen to me. Don't … don't go. Don't change. Please fight it. Please. Please!'

The flames closed behind them, a wall of fire cutting them off completely. At the last second a figure burst through the last gap, leaping over them before they could rise high enough to catch her. She landed deftly and put herself between Izzy and Holly.

'Stay behind me,' ordered Silver. 'This might be the only chance we have.'

CHAPTER TWENTY-NINE

Sacrifice

The voice in Dylan's mind demanded more and more, everything. He couldn't fight. Not now. Holly reached inside him and took it all. He understood now how gentle Silver had tried to be by comparison, even if he hadn't appreciated it at the time. There was no consideration for him now, no sense of him as a person, as an individual. He was a thing to be used, a source of power and nothing more.

And, God, it hurt. He'd never known pain and humiliation like it.

Into the blur of light, of agony and misery, came another voice.

'Dylan? Dylan, love, listen to me …'

Silver. It was Silver. But how could it be? And Silver had never called him 'love', not even as a general endearment, not even by accident. It had to be a trick, a hallucination. It couldn't be real.

'Dylan, you are the only one who can stop this. Please, listen to me. You have to take control back from her. She's using the magic inside you to cast this spell, to raise Crom and kill Jinx. To bind them as one. I can't stop her, but you can. Listen to the magic, to the music it makes. Please, listen.'

Music. He knew music. He could understand music and there was music all around him. In him. Running through his veins, whirling through his mind, making his heart race and his skin shiver.

'Silver?' he whispered.

Holly's fist in his hair tightened painfully. 'She should have gone back to a tree or picked out a pretty, shiny rock. What was she thinking, picking you?'

But she hadn't been thinking, he remembered. He could picture, in vivid detail the cell in Holly's Market and Silver dying, raving, lost. Silver hadn't been thinking. And she hadn't chosen him.

Dylan's eyes snapped open and his gaze fixed on her, trying to protect Izzy and Jinx from Holly's spell, trying to stand in the way of her own magic wielded against her. Trying to reach him.

Silver hadn't chosen him as her touchstone. She wouldn't have been able. She was dying. She'd told him to go. She had said no.

He'd chosen her.

Mind and body, Dylan seized hold of the magic pouring

out of him and pulled it back. Holly's spell snapped like old elastic, the backlash sending her stumbling across the grass where Osprey caught her.

Someone grabbed him, pulling him up and then they were running, half stumbling, but always moving. Clodagh, it was Clodagh, dragging him across the open ground while his mind pinwheeled and exploded like the fireworks over the city.

He collapsed as he reached Silver, who cried out in a language he couldn't hope to understand, lyrical and beautiful, but torn in pain.

The earth shook underneath them. The fires dropped.

'Leave him alone!' Izzy screamed at all around her, holding Jinx as if to shield him from the world. 'You just leave him alone!'

Angels, demons and fae all around them surged forward, without Holly's spell to hold them back. Dylan didn't hesitate, even though he was acting on instinct alone. He reached for Silver's hand.

'Have to stop them.' He pushed the words through his numb lips. 'They'll kill him. Now they know for sure.'

She nodded and closed her eyes, concentrating. A shimmering wall arose around the five of them. Ice, he realised. It was a wall of ice, cutting them off.

And then Silver looked at him. There were tears on her face. 'Dylan, I thought you were gone.'

'Well, you were swanning around with the angels,' Clodagh snapped. 'With your voice back and all. What did you need with any of us?'

'My voice?' She stared incredulously at the girl, too shocked to be angry at her tone. 'I would never do a deal with that pompous, stuck-up ass.'

'He thought—'

Silver sucked in a tight breath and stared at him. Guilt made the heat drain from his face. He'd doubted her. He'd thought she'd give anything to have her voice back, and that included Jinx. And him. They had all misjudged her and to see that knowledge on her face cut him to the core. 'You didn't. Oh love, tell me you didn't. Don't you know me yet?'

'Hardly,' he whispered and let her pull him close, to hold him because there was no more fight left in him. 'You never let me get to know you.'

'That'll change. I promise, that will change.'

Jinx curled against Izzy. She shook so hard, her whole body trembling, but she wouldn't let him go. Her blood was on his hands again. He could smell it, warm and strangely sweet. He could taste it.

Oh God, he could taste her blood. What had he done?

And deep inside him that dreaded glow of sentience stirred up again, responding to it. Much as he might struggle, he could feel it now. Crom Cruach, first of the Shining Ones, planted as a seed inside him, fed and watered by the deaths of angels and demons and now by the very beings that had contained it long ago. His blood, surging in his veins transformed to light, to a blinding, terrifying light. He was changing, and when it happened, he would be gone.

Púca were meant to change. His father had been trying to tell him that. Holly was counting on it. And with the process having begun, what could be done to stop it?

The last noose tightened around his neck. He felt it, closing in, moment by moment.

Wild magic. He was a thing of wild magic, of chaos. So were the Shining Ones. They were kin.

Sorath and Lucifer had been nothing to this. Buried in the land, constrained for millenia, the rage of the Shining Ones knew no bounds. And in him, they had an escape. The spark of an angel, the heart of a demon, and the combined blood of two sworn enemies – the Grigori and the Fear.

'Izzy,' he said. 'Izzy, help.'

'I'm here. It's going to be okay. I'll find a way. I'll use the Blade.'

'You used it. It's gone.' That didn't stop her trying. He could see her frown, that knot of frustration making lines between her eyebrows. 'Izzy, it's too late.'

'No. It isn't over. It can't be. I have to try.'

She studied him, her eyes so blue, flecked now with those strange touches of gold the blade imbued in her. She was changing too. He could feel it. She needed to return the blade to Donn before it consumed her and wiped out all that made her human. She'd used it to kill. Donn had warned her what that could do to her. They were both slipping away and he could think of only one way to stop it.

'Jinx, Dad will negotiate with them. We'll find a way to stop this, to undo her spells. Please. I only did what I had to do. I had to stop Eochaid.'

'You haven't done what they asked.' No, she hadn't give him up. She still refused to do that.

She glared at him, angry, ready to fight. God, he loved that about her. Always ready to fight. Even if the fight was impossible.

But this fight she couldn't win. Not this time.

He took out the iron knife with the bone handle. Izzy stared at him as if he was crazy and perhaps he was. But he could feel the creature inside him, could feel it rising up like a shark from the depths. He could sense what it wanted to do. The world really would burn and Izzy would be first.

He couldn't let that happen.

'You did this once,' he told her.

'And to myself, but that's not the way. Not this time.'

'What'll the angels do to me, Izzy? What'll the demons do? If they even have time and a chance. I can't let them take me. You can't let me go. What'll I become? He's coming and I can't stop him.'

'Jinx, this is insane!' Silver interrupted. 'You don't know what you're saying. Holly can't be trusted—'

'But I can. No one believes it, Silver, except perhaps you.

Look at me. Look inside me. Tell me what I'm becoming?'

Silver frowned, but she bent to study his eyes. He saw her blanch, her gaze turn wide with fear and dismay. 'Oh… Jinx …' she whispered. She sank back beside the others, holding Dylan tight. 'He's right, Izzy.'

'No!' Izzy protested, even as he pushed the knife handle into her grip. Her fingers closed around it compulsively. She looked appalled. 'There has to be another way.'

Jinx shook his head and pressed the point against his chest, just under the ribs, angled up.

Professional, clear minded intent, that was what they needed here. He locked his emotions away and thought about the logistics, how to make it easiest. He knew how to kill. Holly had made sure he knew how to kill. In oh so many ways. 'Quick and clean, Izzy. You'll get my heart. Straight in. Give it a slight twist to get the air in. It'll be over almost at once.'

'Jinx, I can't.'

'Look at me. Just at me.'

And then she did. She really did. She looked deep into his eyes and he knew she saw the coming horror, so bright and terrible it would scourge the earth. She saw the terrible revenge it would inflict on her, on her family as Grigori, on everything she knew and loved. What he knew she would see.

It broke his heart to see the hope die in her. Worst still knowing he was the one to kill it. He had to do something to comfort her. He had to try. 'It's like Donn said. You'll send me to him. I'll wait for you, remember? Just like always.' Even that didn't bring a smile. Perhaps she knew it was a wish rather than a promise. But what could he promise her now? Jinx pressed his free hand against her cheek, cupping her face gently. 'Izzy, you couldn't let Sorath destroy the world. You couldn't let Eochaid and the Fear do it. You can't let me do it either.'

'But you wouldn't do it. It won't be you.'

He smiled. 'No. It won't be me. Very soon now. It's almost … He's almost … Please, Izzy.' He felt the strength draining from him, or rather perhaps his ability to control his own strength. The fingers of his hands flexed against her skin, ready to rend and tear, to hurt and he could barely stop them. 'Please, Izzy. Please.'

'I'm sorry,' she whispered and kissed him, leaning in, pressing close. Her lips were so soft, so gentle. The knife between them made him stiffen. He felt it bite, felt the acidic touch of the iron against and then inside his fae skin. This knife had cut into him so many times that now it almost felt like part of him.

The beast inside him howled, not the death howl of the Cú Sídhe, because the Cú Sídhe wanted this death, but a cry of rage and frustration that ripped through the fabric of reality. Holly's scream married with it, as if somewhere out there she felt it too as she fled from Silver and Dylan, from the world of pain the rest of the races had in store for her after this. He hoped it hurt. He hoped it seared through her flesh and into her shrivelled heart. He hoped—

Izzy sobbed, her lips still pressed to his, and Jinx's last

thought was that he should have told her he loved her.

One last time.

Everything turned to snapshots. She felt so cold. So cold and the lights kept bursting around her and fading away, like camera flashes. Brighter than fireworks. The bonfire crackled and roared but Jinx was turning cold and so was she. The stones beneath her sucked out every last drop of heat. The shadow of the Hellfire Club trapped her in darkness. Everything was cold.

She'd seen it in him, the monster she'd only glimpsed before, that thing that had lurked inside him since Holly first killed the angel and bound him with its spark. That creature that had been eating away at the Jinx she knew, the Jinx she loved.

She couldn't breathe. Her chest was caught in a vice and her heart hammered at it from the inside. It would break apart one way or the other and there was nothing she could do to hold it all together. Everything was pain.

Strong arms closed around her, crushing her until she fought against them. They tried to pull her away from Jinx but she ripped herself free and threw herself back on his unresponsive body. His corpse. He was a corpse.

'Izzy,' said Dad. 'Isabel.'

Voices like far off screams battered at her but they were drowned out by the fireworks and the bonfire. By the constant shriek of pain in her head.

Holly and her kith were gone. Silver barked out orders, arguing fearlessly with Zadkiel and Azazel as if she had done it all her life. But suddenly she arrived beside Izzy, kneeling by Dad.

'Grigori,' she said. 'Please. We need your help.'

Of course they did. They needed her Dad as peacemaker. That was his role. The balance in between all the worlds, like he'd shown her on the Celtic Cross so long ago, keeping it all together, no matter what.

Mum gathered her in a familiar embrace. Bruises coloured her porcelain skin and there were livid scratches on her bare arms. But that didn't stop her taking one of Izzy's hands and pulling it oh so gently away from Jinx.

'You have to breathe, love,' she said. 'Look at me. Look at me and breathe. In and out. Ignore them. Ignore all of them. Just breathe.'

Mum was okay. That should have mattered. Dad had rescued her, or the demons had let her go when they didn't need a bargaining chip anymore. She didn't know and it didn't matter. It should have made her heart sing with relief. Mum was safe. But Jinx wasn't. She couldn't focus on anything but that. Jinx was gone.

He was gone. His eyes, dull and staring endlessly upwards. No light in them. No light at all. This wasn't like before. He hadn't actually died in the Market. She hadn't seen him dead. Sorath had healed him right on the edge of death and saved her the agony. If only he could have waited, a moment longer. Given her time to think, to work something out, to find a way to save him. If only he had waited.

And then it hit her.

He'd said he would wait for her.

Adrenaline hit her like a jolt of electricity.

He was waiting. He had to be waiting. It was still Hallow-een so the rules of Samhain still applied. The doors would be open. The veil was thin. The dead could walk free if someone came for them, if someone could lead them home. She just had to get in and find him.

Just like Donn had said – she would send Jinx to him, and she would follow.

She was up and running before she knew it, sprinting across the grass to reach the Hellfire Club. She threw herself inside and dived through the gate.

The hall stood dark and empty. The smell hit her first, a smell she knew, metallic and earthy. The smell of death. She called up a flame that flickered at the end of her fingers. Not the blade. This was her own power and it took all her efforts to keep it alive in this place of death. Her frail light bounced off the walls and ceiling, revealing part of what she already guessed. Blood splattered the bronzed walls but there were no bodies. Not that she could see in the half light. Even in the realm of the dead, the smell of death hung fresh and violent as a physical assault.

'Jinx!' Her voice echoed off empty chambers, bounced

back to her, mocking and empty. 'Jinx! Where are you?'

'Gone,' said a broken voice. 'They're all gone. She killed what she could kill, and took him.'

Donn's throne had been shattered, stone pieces scattered over the dais and his body lay amongst them, as broken as the throne and his voice.

Izzy dropped to her knees beside him.

'I brought it back. Your blade. I brought it back. So you have to give Jinx back to me. Please, where is he?'

Blood trickled from the corner of his mouth as he tried to find breath to speak. Bubbles filled it, almost a foam. He opened his eyes and they were like holes in the sky, endlessly black. She looked away, horrified, and found his glasses on the ground, twisted and crushed. It looked like someone had stamped on them. She had a good idea who.

'She took him. When she broke me. Such power. None of the Aes Sídhe should have such power. We can't handle it. We become monsters.'

'You're all monsters anyway.' Distracted, distant, she couldn't find the sympathy for him she knew she should feel. He had been cold and cruel. Never kind.

He laughed and the blood bubbled up from his lungs again, spilling over his chin in a glossy wave.

'Where did she take him?'

No need to ask who. Holly. It had to be Holly.

'How do I know? Holly goes where she will. If she is still the same. The spell she wove broke and rebounded on her.

You and your friends broke it. Killing Jinx ... the spirit of Crom ... the backlash ...'

'What do I do?'

'Guard the Blade. You're going to need it. Using it as you did, with all that fire inside you ... It is part of you now. And it will change you.' His hand closed reflexively on hers, leaving them covered in fresh blood, his as well as her own and Jinx's. So much blood.

And Donn died.

Izzy threw back her head and screamed, howling in denial and despair.

Time moved in fits and starts. Dylan gave up trying to track it all and focused on Izzy instead. She'd stumbled back to them and dropped to the ground like a stone.

'He's dead,' she whispered, her voice broken.

'Oh, Izzy,' said Clodagh. 'Jinx wouldn't want—'

Her face transformed for a moment, her eyes blazing. 'Not Jinx. Donn. She killed him and took Jinx with her. She—she—'

Words failed her and she sank in on herself, silent and still. Broken. Dylan knew he ought to go to her, to comfort her but he couldn't move. Everything hurt, every part of him inside and out. His head pounded, his muscles ached.

Placated, the various supernatural beings left. Amends were

promised, peace restored. Somewhere along the way, when time came to lay out the dead, they discovered that Jinx's body had vanished and no one knew where. No amount of ranting and threats of dire retribution from Silver revealed anything. Not even David Gregory could find out anything.

Izzy had just sobbed when they told her and wouldn't answer any questions. Or perhaps she couldn't. With Donn dead, the Sídhe seemed at a loss. He was one of their oldest Lords.

Dylan sat with Izzy and Clodagh, watching, unable to do anything to help, half afraid of getting in the way.

'Ash has gone,' said Clodagh morosely. 'Said she needed to report in. Said Zadkiel is in massive shit and she intends to make sure it all hits him and nobody else. Fair and square.'

'Good,' Dylan replied. Zadkiel deserved everything he got.

'So Holly—' she began.

'I don't want to talk about it.' He didn't think the feeling of Holly in his head, using him, would ever go away to the extent that he could talk about it. Not even to Clodagh.

Izzy sat staring into space, watching the stars overhead. The mist had gone with the Fear, leaving a clear still night full of stars. The city below was like a sea of yellow and orange lights. No fires now, no fireworks. It was too late. The Samhain revels were over and everything was broken. Izzy turned the knife over and over in her hands. Her Dad had tried to take it from her. She'd just held on even more tightly. Every so often she would shiver from head to foot, but she didn't speak. Whatever she had seen in the hollow, whatever Donn had said, she wasn't sharing, no matter who quizzed her. Not matter what clever questions they asked.

'Izzy?' he tried again.

She closed her hand around the iron blade of her knife and pulled it sharply through her fist, opening the same cut again, the one Jinx had given her. Shock turned her face from a mask to a real face once more. She felt it. It looked like it was the first thing she had felt for an age.

Blood splattered everywhere.

'Shit!' Clodagh exclaimed, jumping up. 'Jesus! Help! Someone help!'

Dylan grabbed her wrist, holding it tight in an effort to staunch the blood. He pulled the knife away from her and dropped it on the grass.

'What are you doing? Are you trying to hurt yourself?'

She blinked at him as if she had only just noticed he was there. Tears filled her eyes. 'Everything hurts, Dylan. Everything. I don't know how to feel it all.'

'Here, let me see,' said a familiar voice, as three shadows fell over them. Amadán knelt down, damp grass staining the knees of his expensive suit darker. He took her wrist from Dylan's unresisting grip. The Magpies flanked him, grinning their sinister grins. They didn't kneel, but one of them bent down and picked up the knife. He held it with a terrible ease. Amadán made her uncurl her fingers and tutted as he studied the deep ragged cut left behind. With a single touch, he healed it. Dylan felt the surge of magic like fingers down his spine and Izzy sobbed.

'What happens now?' Dylan asked. 'To Donn's realm. If he's dead, what happens to the dead?'

'It's never happened before,' said Amadán. 'I don't know. Maybe someone else will take his place. Maybe it's the end of days and the dead will rise up. We'll have to see.'

'Not comforting.'

The old man smiled a brief and humourless smile. 'That's not my job, touchstone. I'm no oracle. Not that they're comforting either. Aloof gobshites, usually. Smug with it.'

'What about Jinx?' Izzy whispered suddenly, as if she had just found her voice again. It was harsh and ragged, but determined.

'When you're ready,' said Amadán, after he had studied her for a long moment. '—I'll help you find out what happened.'

'When I'm ready? I'm ready now.'

He shook his head and smiled at her, for a moment every inch the loving godfather he sometimes pretended to be. Dylan wasn't fooled. He could see the heartless bastard underneath the exterior. 'I think not. Rest, recuperate, and see how you are tomorrow. And the day after. I cared for that boy, you know? Admired him. All he's been through, all he has risen above ... I don't like the thought of Holly getting her hands on him again. When you're ready, Izzy, we'll be around.'

'How will I find you?'

'Ask the magpies, of course.'

And then they were gone, just as her father came running towards them, yelling at the Amadán to leave his daughter alone.

It took a week before she could get out of the house by herself. Just as well really, because she spent it sleeping, or waking up screaming from nightmares anyway, but she rested. Because she had to. Because she needed to get ready. Her parents were always around, keeping an eye on her, fussing over her. Not that she blamed them. But eventually, even they slipped up. Her parents didn't want to let her out of their sight, but they couldn't keep it up forever. Real life intervened. Gran came by, but didn't speak to her. She watched Izzy while Izzy pretended to sleep. And then she left. Izzy learned to be devious. She learned to say 'yes, I'm fine' when really she wasn't and never would be again. November brought a bleak grey rain, constant and driving, making the world beyond the glass of her windows grey as well.

Izzy thought she'd never see colour again.

But they couldn't watch her forever. And when neither Dylan nor Clodagh came to the house one afternoon, when Gran was downstairs and Mum and Dad had to go back to work, she climbed out of her bedroom window and took off.

It didn't take too long to find a magpie. There had been one or two around the area the whole time. She'd watched them from the window, and they'd watched her too. Waiting for her.

She nodded her head to the magpie, who bobbed his in return. One for sorrow, two for joy. She only knew sorrow now and there was only one magpie.

'Good morning, Mister Magpie,' she said, the old rhyme sing-songing through her head. *One for sorrow, two for joy ...* not the two she knew. 'I need to talk to the Amadán.'

She thought she heard the sound of wings and twin shadows suddenly flanked hers. The Magpies stood behind her and she turned to face them.

'Amadán said we were to do whatever you asked,' said Mags. His gaze roamed over her body as if he wanted to follow suit with his grubby little hands.

'And not to *touch* her,' Pie added urgently. 'Remember? He's picky about that.'

'*Dead* picky,' Mags emphasized the first word and twisted his mouth in distaste. 'Said whatever bit of us touched you, he'd slice it off. So ...' He smiled in what he probably thought was a reassuring way. It wasn't. 'We good?'

Good. Oh, they were so far from good it wasn't funny. But yeah ...

'I need you to get me in somewhere. Somewhere they won't want us going.'

'Sounds like a bit of craic, really.' He popped his knuckles so they sounded like walnuts breaking.

'Why us though?'

Izzy smiled, although she didn't feel like it. She couldn't

show them any weakness. No matter what. 'Because everyone else will try to stop me.'

What they lacked in brains and charm, Izzy discovered, they made up for in ability and willingness. One of their greatest abilities was kicking down doors, and with a willingness to do it without any qualms or concerns about to whom those doors might belong.

The Storyteller rose, a look of outrage making her placid face ugly.

'What is the meaning of this?'

'Where's the book?' asked Izzy.

'You have no right to be here, Isabel Gregory. No right at all.'

'I'll ask one more time and then I'll tell the Magpies to start looking. They're messy when they do that. Tend to break things.'

'What do you want with it?'

'I want to read it. All of it.'

'Don't you realise what that will do?'

'Yes. Do you have a problem with that?'

Eye to eye, the two of them glared at each other. Izzy wasn't going to back down. She needed that book, and what it could show her. She felt the Blade moving inside her, sizzling in her blood and she wound her will around it, using it to force herself not to back down.

The Storyteller shivered and looked away first. Izzy was getting used to that look on those who tried to intimidate her now. And it felt good. The blade had changed her. Losing Jinx had changed her. The problem was she didn't care. It made her stronger, harder, more determined.

And if it helped her to find Jinx she'd use every ounce of it. No matter what.

'Bring the book, Grim. Don't keep the Grigori waiting.'

It didn't take long. Especially with the Magpies still circling, breaking bits of the decorations. Mags even got out a penknife and started carving a crude image into one of the fake trees.

They weren't the most imaginative, but she didn't need them for their creativity.

Izzy settled herself down to read.

'Go outside,' she told them. 'And don't let anyone in.'

They ushered the Storyteller and her attendants out and Izzy could breathe again.

No matter what it took, she had to find Jinx.

She brushed her hand down over the binding of the book, the smooth, tanned skin of a long dead prophet.

'Show me Jinx,' she whispered. 'Show me where he is now. Show me how to find him.'

She opened the book and began to read, her mind plunging into the ocean of images that spread out before her, giving up whatever it demanded in return.

Words and Phrases

Aes Sídhe: (Ay Shee) The highest caste of the Sídhe, most angelic in appearance, the ruling class.

Amadán: (Am-a-dawn) meaning Fool, also known as the Old Man and the Trickster. Member of the Council.

Bodach: (Bud-ach) Giant. A lower caste of the Sídhe.

Brí: (Bree) meaning Strength. Member of the Council.

Cuileann: (Cul-een) meaning Holly. Holly's original, angelic name.

Crom Ceann: (Krom Ken) One of the Shining Ones.

Crom Cruach: (Krom Cru-ak) One of the Shining Ones.

Crom Dubh : (Krom Dove) One of the Shining Ones.

Cú Sídhe: (Coo Shee) Shapeshifting Sídhe who sometimes take the form of a large hound. A lower caste of the Sídhe.

Donn: (Don) Lord of the Dead. Member of the Council.

Dubh Linn: (Dove Linn) The black pool, original name for Dublin.

Einechlan: (I-ne-chlan) Honour price.

Eochaid: (Yeo-hey) King of the Fear or Fir Bolg.

Geis: (gaish) A taboo or prophecy, like a vow or a spell, which dictates the fate of a member of the Aes Sídhe.

Íde: (Ee-da) meaning Thirst. Member of the Council.

Leanán Sídhe: (Lee-ann-awn Shee) Fairy lover, the muse, Sídhe who feed from the magical lifeforce of others, but can inspire unbridled creativity in return.

Míl Espáine: (Meel Es-pan) meaning Soldier from Spain. An early Grigori who entered into legend as the father of the Milesians, the group mentioned in the 11th century *Lebor Gabála Érenn*, the Book of Invasions, as the last to arrive in Ireland."

Púca: (Pooka) Shapechanging supernatural creature, king of the wandering fae, those not affiliated with any of the hollows. He often takes the shape of a wild black horse, but can take human form as well, though retaining animal features such as horse's ears and hooves. He can be helpful, or extremely dangerous.

Sídhe: (Shee) Irish supernatural race.

Seanchaí: (Shan-a-key) Storyteller. Member of the Council.

Suibhne Sídhe: (Shiv-na Shee) Sídhe with birdlike attributes. A lower caste of the Sídhe.

Touchstone: the source of a Sídhe matriarch's power.

Tuatha dé Dannan: (Too-atha Day Dan-ann) The People of the Goddess Danu, or The People of God, the Irish faeries.

Read also..

A CRACK IN
EVERYTHING

welcome to the other side

RUTH FRANCES LONG

Izzy learns the truth about the secret world of the Sídhe coexisting alongside the human one, and the angels and demons who watch over the affairs of mortals, making their own plans. She becomes a pawn in this game, and it almost costs her everything. Only by taking matters into her own hands can she save her friends and family.

European Science Fiction Society Award for Best Creator of Children's Science Fiction or Fantasy books
- 2015